THREE DOG
KNIGHT

THREE DOG KNIGHT

A JORJA KNIGHT MYSTERY

ALICE BIENIA

Issued in print and electronic formats.

ISBN 978-1-990193-03-3 (Paperback)

ISBN 978-1-990193-04-0 (EPUB)

ISBN 978-1-990193-05-7 (MOBI)

Edited by: T. Morgan Editing Services

Cover and Interior Design by: Damonza.com

Published by: Cairn Press | Calgary, Alberta, Canada

In the cold dark days of winter, northerners huddled with their sled dogs to keep from freezing at night. Used as a rudimentary temperature gauge, a night requiring three dogs for warmth, is a very cold night indeed!

CHAPTER ONE

I'VE ALWAYS BEEN fascinated by the ingenuity of humans, so I shouldn't have been surprised when I discovered that someone had found yet another way to kill people. But right now, I was trying to figure out which way to insert my passport into the automated border control system at Calgary's new arrival eGate. The woman peering over my shoulder, jostled me for a third time. I pulled out my passport and retrieved the machine printout. The washed-out image on cheap paper showed a dark-haired woman with shadows under her eyes. I looked like a crack-whore on her way to prison.

I sailed through several gates and barriers, pleased at the efficiency of the system yet perturbed that the scanners accepted the photo as a good enough likeness of me to let me pass. I handed the photo to a waiting border services officer at the last security point and smiled. He took it without so much as giving me a glance, and the last set of doors slid open with a hiss.

Shaking off the residual memory of the scanned passport

photo, I entered the concourse. I didn't bother glancing at the sleepy-eyed bystanders waiting for loved ones, I knew no one would be waiting for me.

The whole place was chillingly hushed, the shops all closed for the night. I shifted my carry-on higher on my arm, stepped past the few onlookers at the arrival gate, and headed for the escalator.

Reaching the end of the corridor, I stepped onto the escalator and rested my bag on the handrail. I glanced at my watch and groaned. I was meeting Laura Bradford in less than five hours. She hadn't told me why she needed a private investigator when she called to set up the meeting, just that she might. I was hoping she'd bring me something I could dig my teeth into. Something more complicated than tailing an errant spouse or running down a deadbeat dad refusing to send child support payments. I stepped off the escalator, turned right and entered the frigid connector between the airport terminal and the parkade.

I glanced out through the glass walls of the connector as a plane landed on the runway. I shivered and turned the corner. A jumble of rubbish lay against one wall. I shook my head to clear the brain fog that had formed from too many hours of droning engines and mindless chitchat of my unduly social seatmate. *That's not rubbish.* I could now make out muddied sneakers sticking out from underneath a ratty blanket, a newspaper lay spread over the face. I shifted the weight of the carry-on, pushed back a strand of stick-straight hair, and hurried past.

The elevator at the end of the corridor seemed to take forever. A noise made me glance over my shoulder, but there was nothing there, nothing other than the human bundle. Anxious to get into my car and start the heater I stepped into the elevator as soon as the doors hissed opened. I found myself mentally calculating what my bank balance would be after this latest job. I had no regrets in leaving my previous career as a lab analyst behind, but the uncertainty of the next pay-cheque was something I was still trying to get used to. The doors opened and I stepped into the dim light of the parkade.

The buzz of an occasional florescent light broke the eerie quiet of the parkade. My footsteps echoed on the frosty pavement. The air was colder here, biting through my jacket. A bank of lights in the next aisle flickered and went out. Just the storm, nothing more, I reminded myself. The pilot had mentioned an Alberta clipper was moving in, bringing a fresh dump of snow. I pulled up my jacket collar and tucked in my chin.

I stopped, suddenly alert, all my senses in overdrive. Were those footsteps behind me? I glanced over my shoulder at the ghostly rows of vehicles and held my breath. Nothing.

I hurried along then ducked between two cars and stopped. The footsteps continued for a stride then halted. Shivering in the cold, I took a deep breath and re-entered the aisle, my ears straining for sounds other than the empty echo of my own feet.

I veered left and, reaching the open parkade wall, peered at the lit corridor below. The human bundle was gone. I pulled back into the shadows, waiting for whoever was following me to pass. No one appeared.

Searching the aisles for some sign of a human presence and finding none I moved on.

The footsteps resumed.

I unzipped the top of my bag, my previous exhaustion gone. My fingers closed in on the cold metal of my car keys. Slinging my purse up higher on my arm, I picked up my pace.

The steps behind me quickened.

My eyes swept from side to side, searching for some sign of him. Behind me, the footsteps grew faster—louder. My feet pounded on the pavement, my breathing ragged, loud in my ears.

Section H, Section H. There it is.

I grabbed at the car door. My carry-on slid down my arm as I inserted the key, my eyes scanning the cars around me. The footsteps had stopped.

I wrenched the car door open, threw in my carry-on, and jumped in.

Locking the door behind me I whipped my head around, expecting to see a grotesque face, half man—half bird, with red eyes, curved beak, and clawed hands.

My hand shook as I turned the key in the ignition. Certain some evil apocalyptic creature lurked nearby, ready to drag me from the car, I shoved the gear shift into reverse. My eye caught a piece of paper jammed under the windshield wipers. It would have to wait.

Backing out, I laid rubber and reached the exit ramp, my sense of dread still on high. Faster, faster, my brain urged as my car entered the darkened tunnel. My eyes jumped back and forth from the rear-view mirror to the beams of light cutting the darkness in front of me.

Tires squealing, I rounded each spiralling curve down

the concrete ramp to the main level. My car shot out of the tunnel and into the frost-laden night.

Nothing appeared in the rear-view mirror. Several cars stood idling at the exit gate ahead of me. Breathing a sigh of relief, I headed to an empty payment lane.

I pulled up to the payment machine and got out of the car, inserted a credit card, and snatched the paper from under the windshield wiper. I glanced back at the ramp as another vehicle emerged. Its headlights caught the snowflakes floating silently to the ground. I slowed my breathing. *Too many late-night horror movies.* I unfolded the paper as I waited for the machine to spit out my card and do its thing.

I staggered back and cursed. Each heartbeat pulsed wildly in my neck.

The machine spit out a receipt and flashed green.

Feeling lightheaded, I grabbed the receipt, threw the paper onto the passenger seat, climbed in, and rolled forward as a truck pulled up behind me. I swallowed hard as my eyes flitted back to the paper and I let out a harsh breath. My jaw clenched and a muscle twitched under my left eye. *Why won't my past stay where it belongs.*

Staring back at me, centered in a crudely drawn black heart, was a newspaper photo of my dead parents.

CHAPTER TWO

UNBUTTONING MY COAT, I breathed in the warm coffee aroma intermingled with cinnamon and vanilla. A coffee bar on the left and the dozen or so small tables and chairs to the right made the place feel cozy. A wall of windows at the far end overlooked the lake, the snow reflecting a mesmerizing display of sparkling crystals in the morning sun.

I had dozed fitfully for a couple of hours last night, more perturbed by the note left on my windshield than I cared to admit. This year marked the twenty-year anniversary of my parents' deaths. It was only recently that I managed to separate the memory from the emotion that threatened to overwhelm whenever it came to mind. But someone didn't want me to forget. Someone had dug up the story and left a copy of a twenty-year-old newspaper photo on my car windshield for me to find.

I selected two easy chairs by the windows, overlooking the lake and the spruce-lined patio below. I pulled out my phone and checked my text messages. My finger hovered over Luis Azagora's name. Inspector Luis Azagora was my current love interest and one of two men in my life. As tempting as it was to send him a text about what happened last night, I couldn't do it. We weren't in that place yet.

A waitress brought coffee, dropped off breakfast menus and pointed out the coffee refill station. I took a few sips, the hot liquid sliding down my throat and easing the tension in my shoulders.

My eyes drank in the scenery. The warmth of the room, and happy murmurings swirling around me, displaced the unease from last night. Still revelling in the comforting surroundings, I noticed a woman at the door. Her eyes searched the room uncertainly. At her second pass of the room, I raised my hand, and she headed my way. She was near my age, late thirties or perhaps a few years older. I stood.

"Are you Laura Bradford?"

"I am. You must be Jorja Knight. Sorry to keep you waiting. My daughter has taken to dawdling in the morning, delaying her inevitable departure to school."

"Not to worry. I've been quite content to sit here and admire the view."

She slipped off her coat and stared out at the lake blankly. "I suppose it is pretty. I never seem to have time to notice."

"You live in the neighbourhood?"

"Yes, on the other side of the lake. My daughter's school is quite close to here, on Fairmount Drive."

The waitress arrived, refilled my coffee and returned a few minutes later with a cranberry scone and green tea for Laura. Laura took a few breaths. Her hand shook as she reached for her tea. "I've never talked to a private investigator."

I shrugged. "It's just a job like any other. All I do is

run around asking questions, hoping to sort out fact from fiction."

She gave me a weak smile. "I suppose I should tell you why we're here. Do you remember hearing about a murder in Calgary a few months ago? A man named Stephen Wallis?"

"Stephen Wallis. That name sounds familiar. Wasn't he found shot in his home?"

Laura's chin quivered as she reached for a napkin. "Stephen was my brother."

"I'm so sorry to hear that."

Laura took a sip of tea and dabbed at the corner of her eyes. "My brother was a brilliant man. Even when we were kids, I knew he'd go far. He was so smart…and funny. He never let his success change him. He was just the same kind, dependable Stephen he always was. And now he's gone."

"I'm so sorry. This can't be easy for you."

"No. Sorry. I get so emotional just thinking about him. Imagining that the killer might get away makes it that much worse."

"No need to apologize." Something about the case stirred in my brain. I leaned forward. "Now I remember. It was all over the news when it first happened, and for weeks afterwards. Calgary's first homicide of the year. The papers said he was shot by an invisible assailant and even though the home security cameras captured the whole thing from a bunch of angles they never provided an image of the killer."

"That's right. The press dubbed him the Houdini Killer."

A tingling sensation rippled down my spine followed by a moment of panic. *The Houdini Killer*. I forced myself to sit back. "But there hasn't been much on the news since."

"No, there hasn't. The police told me they don't have much to go on." Laura's eyes swept over the lake for a moment, and when she turned back to me, her eyes were filled with tears. "Not the best way to start. I guess I should tell you what I know."

"Take your time," I said.

Laura nodded gratefully. She set her tea down and stared vacantly at the lake.

I wondered if she noticed the ice crystals sparkling like fairy dust in the air or whether all she saw was vast cold ice.

She gave her shoulders a shake and turned back to me. "I last saw Stephen on Christmas Day. He spent the day with our family, but he left around eight o'clock that night. He had to catch a red eye to Vancouver, to meet with a potential investor the next day." She paused, choking on the last few words. "Sorry. That's the last time I saw him alive."

"That's okay. Tell me more about Stephen. What did he do?"

"He owned a company called Xcelerate. They help entre-preneurs get set up." She smiled shakily. "You know, provide them a space to work, put together business plans, help raise money, that kind of stuff."

"Oh, a business incubator," I said.

"That's right. Stephen called his entrepreneurs game changers. One of his start-ups created edible wrappers for ice cream bars. They sold the rights to Brun-cow last summer and it's going to be used for several of their products."

"That's amazing," I said. My brain was already whirling, trying to recall what I knew of Stephen's case.

Laura squared her shoulders. "Stephen planned to be

back from Vancouver on the twenty-ninth. The police confirmed he did catch a flight back that evening. The next day, he dropped by the lab. A couple of his guys were there working, they're always working. They said Stephen left mid afternoon, said he was bagged and was going to spend a quiet night at home."

I nodded. Homicide would have confirmed his movements.

"Friends of his had a New Year's party the next night, but Stephen never showed."

"Do you know their names?"

"Oh. Yes. Rob and Nancy Bailey."

"Your brother said he'd attend?"

Laura shrugged. "Stephen hadn't been dating anyone for a while. Rob said he figured he didn't want to come alone. Nobody saw him at the office or lab the next day, but it was a holiday, so no one expected him to drop by." Laura pulled down the sleeves of her sweater until only her fingertips were showing and wrapped her arms around herself. "His driver showed up at his house the following day to take him to a meeting. When Stephen didn't answer the door or his phone, he called the lab. No one had heard from Stephen. The police were called." Laura's chest rose and fell rapidly, her breathing shallow. "They found Stephen in the den. He'd been shot." Her hand shook as she reached for her tea and took a shaky sip. She put her cup down and drew in a long slow breath, expelling it through pursed lips.

"It's all coming back to me," I said. "His house was highly wired and secured."

"That's right. Stephen had one of those smart homes.

He was always showing off how he could control everything from his phone or computer."

"A break-in?"

Laura shook her head. "The police found no sign of break-in or forced entry. The deadbolts were engaged from the inside, the windows closed. Nothing was taken, none of the electronics or paintings or Stephen's coin collection."

"But someone did get in. What about the security cameras or data files on his security system? They must have shown that he unlocked the door to let someone in."

"According to the police, no one went in or out except for Stephen, early New Year's Eve. The security cameras were all on, but they only showed Stephen. Alone."

"Hence the Houdini Killer handle," I nodded slowly.

"The police called for witnesses or anyone who might have been in the neighbourhood at the time. They interviewed several people. No one saw or heard anything out of the ordinary. Stephen had security cameras inside and out. None of them show anyone entering or leaving his house. I've hardly had a full night's sleep since it happened. It's been hard on our mom. I already see the toll it's taking on her."

"So where is the investigation now?"

"Detective McGuire is in charge of the case. They're no closer to figuring out what happened than they were on the second of January," she said, shaking her head. "Now they're shifting some of their resources to more current cases."

"I'm sure they'll keep at it, but no telling if it'll get solved next month or years from now." I didn't know what she was going through, nobody could. But having dealt with my own parents' unexpected deaths, I could empathise. The finality of death was overwhelming, hopes and dreams irretrievably broken.

Laura looked at me through tear-rimmed eyes, her mascara in need of repair but her voice defiant. "My mother doesn't have years and years. My kids adored their Uncle Stephen. I can't sleep, I can't eat or focus. I figure the only way I can get my life back is to find the person who did this. I know it's only been a little over two months, but I need answers. Besides, there's one person the police haven't considered carefully enough."

"Oh? Who would that be?"

"Chloe, our darling half-sister."

CHAPTER THREE

LAURA BRADFORD HARBOURED a great deal of resentment toward her half-sister, Chloe. Perhaps justifiably so. Laura was thirteen when her dad shook off the marital chains weighing him down and ran off with a much younger woman. Ironically, he became a father for the third time, ten months later.

"At first I'd be invited for dinner or the weekend. It didn't take me long to figure out the real reason," said Laura with disgust. "They were having me over to babysit so they could go out and party. And the way he fawned and cooed over Chloe, when he couldn't give me or Stephen the time of day, made me sick."

Laura's father's relationship with his new woman lasted five years. He grew tired of her partying with his money, staying away for days, leaving their little daughter, Chloe, in his care. By the time Chloe was eight or nine, her mother was out of their lives for good. Laura's dad began to drink. He lost his job, then his apartment. He and Chloe ended up renting in a trailer park.

"Our father was killed in a fire when Chloe was about twelve or thirteen. She went to live with her mother's sister for a while, but by the time she was sixteen she had quit school and was living on her own.

"I didn't see much of Chloe for a while. She'd call me up once in a blue moon or drop by for a visit. But each time, she'd hit me up for money. I felt sorry for her. I caved. One day I caught her stealing from me. Found out she was doing drugs. We had it out. I told her I didn't want her coming around anymore."

"What about Stephen? Did he and Chloe see much of each other?"

"Stephen was only ten when our father left. Neither of us saw much of Chloe after our dad died. Then about four years ago she contacted us."

"What about?"

"She said she wanted to reconnect. She apologized for how she had behaved. She even said she was sorry her mother ruined our family, which is ridiculous since Dad cheating on Mom was entirely his own doing. Stephen and I realized Chloe likely got the short end of the stick."

I felt a twinge of something stirring. It would have been tough growing up as Chloe. "Sounds like she matured."

"We thought so too…at first."

The tone of Laura's voice made me think Chloe might still be an outsider, looking in on the Bradford's rather Rockwellesque family life. "That's not the case?"

"No. A few weeks later she contacts us to say she'd like to do something with her life, maybe become an aesthetician."

"Let me guess. She would, if only she had the funds."

"You got it. Stephen was doing well, and with no kids of his own he figured he'd do the right thing and give her a hand up. But it never stopped. We were bombarded with request after request. Her car died, and she couldn't afford a replacement. She lost everything in an apartment fire and didn't have insurance. She had to quit her job slinging beer due to carpal tunnel. You get the picture."

"I do."

"Then about two years ago, she met this guy. Conner Weston. Her dream man." Laura rolled her eyes. "Their love was real and pure. No one had a love like theirs," she added scornfully. "It was Conner said this, Conner is going to do that. They were well suited. Swindling con artists, lazy moochers, both. Suddenly, instead of just having to deal with Chloe's disastrous life, we were expected to shore up the two of them."

"Did you?"

"Not for long. I had a talk with Stephen. It was causing arguments between me and my husband, Wayne. I told Stephen we couldn't support her anymore. We have two kids, and I gave up my job to stay home with them after our youngest was born. Wayne said we were insane to hand money to two able-bodied people who were laughing their asses off at how gullible we were."

"What was Stephen's view?"

"He agreed. He said he'd let his own desire to feel good, by helping Chloe, mask the reality of the situation."

"You cut off financial support?"

"Yes. Stephen, Wayne, and I sat down with Chloe and told her we'd be happy to visit with her, but she needed to get a job, take care of her own business. I mean she's a grown-ass woman for heaven's sake."

I couldn't imagine myself drifting from job to job, looking for handouts. I needed the mental stimulation, and the ballast work provided in my life.

"How'd she take it?"

"Chloe promised she'd change her ways if we gave her one more chance. When we didn't budge, she threw a fit. The next few times we included Chloe and Conner in family events left everyone irritated. Conner's a loudmouthed jerk. He's one of these guys who gets louder and pushier when he doesn't get his way, you know, like he's going to intimidate you into agreeing with him. My husband can't tolerate him. Even Stephen had a hard time hiding his disdain for the guy."

Laura sat up and looked at me squarely. "Wayne was right. They had been taking us for complete idiots."

"Why do you think Chloe killed your brother?"

"I don't know if Chloe actually killed him, but she had a hand in it, that's for sure. She and Conner."

"What makes you so certain?" Murder takes work and planning, especially given how Stephen had been killed. From the little Laura told me, it didn't sound like Chloe and Conner had the ingenuity to pull something like that off. Their style would be more along the lines of a hit and run.

"I ran into one of Chloe's friends a few months after we cut her off and she told me Chloe and Conner had broken up. Chloe was living with a new man down in Palm Springs." She laughed. "I mean a new man for Chloe. She told me the guy was at least eighty years old but quite well-off. I figured Chloe finally found her golden ticket."

"Doesn't sound out of character, based on what you've told me about her."

"True. What threw me is that Stephen hired Conner about three months before he was murdered. To be his driver."

"You mean he was the driver who went to pick Stephen up the morning he was discovered dead? I thought Stephen couldn't stand him."

"That's exactly what I said," she exclaimed. "I couldn't believe it. I asked Stephen why, in a city full of guys hunting for work, he hired the one guy we all disliked."

"Why did he?"

"Stephen said Conner was apologetic about having been a jerk. That it was only after he and Chloe broke up that he realized how bad they had been for each other. Like matches and gasoline. Said he'd work for free for a month to prove himself."

"And Stephen believed him? Your brother certainly was more kind-hearted than most."

"That's one word for it. I called him a sucker. But Stephen defended Conner. He said Conner had some redeeming qualities. I asked him to name one. Then he said the oddest thing. Of course, I didn't think so at the time, but it struck me as odd after Stephen was killed. He said besides being punctual, Conner provided a disarming presence."

"Interesting."

"I thought so too."

"Did Stephen say anything that might hint at his need for more than chauffer services?"

"No."

"Did he seem worried or nervous?"

"Maybe a bit. I figured he was working too hard."

"Did you tell the investigating detectives about his former dealings with Conner and your sister?"

"I did. Apparently, Conner has an ironclad alibi."

"But you still believe he and your sister are involved."

"Half-sister. Yes. Besides finding the idea that Stephen would voluntarily hire Conner hard to swallow, he lied to me."

"Who? Stephen?"

"No. Conner. He came by Christmas Day to take Stephen to the airport. While Stephen said his goodbyes, I had a quick chat with Conner. I asked if he stayed in touch with Chloe. He said he hadn't seen her since they broke up. He lied. I saw him and Chloe with my own eyes two weeks before Christmas."

"Where?"

"At McIsaac's."

I knew the place. A little neighbourhood bar and grill on Tenth Avenue, not far from my office.

"You're sure it was them?"

"I'm positive. I stopped in for a drink with a few of my girlfriends and saw them slobbering all over each other in one of the booths."

"Maybe she didn't want you to know she was back in Calgary. She knew how you felt about her and Conner. Did you get a chance to ask her about it?"

"Yes. At Stephen's funeral. She told me she had flown in

the day before. To make sure, I asked her if she'd been back since she moved to Palm Springs and she said no, she had just arrived the day before."

"Couldn't she have just been trying to avoid a confrontation? Maybe she thought you'd be upset that she hadn't told you she had returned."

Laura chewed her bottom lip for a second. "I doubt it. She's never shown consideration for anyone before."

"You seem convinced she had something to do with Stephen's death There must be more."

"There is. After I got access to Stephen's house, once the police were finished, I went over to sort out his things." Laura swiped at a tear. "Sorry. It's just...his whole life... there in those few boxes. It's...it's all that's left."

I felt the familiar sting behind my eyes. All I had of my past was my mother's watch. I hadn't kept any of her other meagre but prized possessions. Without her, they were meaningless and only created a constant and inconsolable ache in my heart whenever I gazed at them. I reached into my purse and extracted a Kleenex, handing it to Laura.

Laura nodded gratefully. "Thanks." She turned her head toward the window. After a few minutes, she went on. "When I was packing up Stephen's belongings, I came across a topaz and silver bracelet. Our father gave it to Chloe for her twelfth birthday. She always wore it. I'm actually shocked she didn't pawn it off."

"Maybe she left it there, before she went to Palm Springs."

"No. See, that's the thing. When I saw her that evening, with Conner, she was wearing it."

"Did you mention this to Detective McGuire?"

"Of course. He asked her about it, but she claims I lied about it. She insists she wasn't in the bar with Conner and that her bracelet had been missing for some time. She accused Conner of taking it when they broke up. Conner of course denied it. But I know. I saw it with my own eyes. And I'm not buying whatever bullshit those two are serving up."

CHAPTER FOUR

DETECTIVE MCGUIRE WAS already seated, eating his sandwich, when I got to the Good Earth. He raised his hand as I entered, sparing me the awkwardness of having to guess which of the three lone men there was the one I was meeting. He got up as I approached, wiped his hands on a napkin and reached out to shake mine.

"Jorja—right? Name's Al. Al McGuire. Detective Sergeant."

"Thanks for seeing me. Please, go on with your lunch. I'll just grab a coffee." I took off my coat, draped it over the chair and went up to the counter to order.

I had called my good buddy, Mike Saunders, after meeting with Laura, and asked him if he knew Detective McGuire or could get me an introduction. Mike was the other man in my life. I met Mike six or so years ago, when we both found ourselves working at Global Analytix, my former place of business. As newbies to the city, we quickly bonded as friends. Retired after a long stint with the Toronto Police Service, Mike now provided consulting services to various police departments and a smattering of other clients. He knew a lot of the detectives in the Calgary Police Service, including Inspector Luis Azagora. But unlike Azagora, he had no problem with me being a private detective. Then again, Mike's and my relationship was strictly platonic. Two quick phone calls later, it was all arranged.

By the time I got back to the table, Al was devouring his last bite.

"I hear Stephen Wallis' sister hired you," he said.

"That's right. She knows you guys are doing everything you can but thought adding a little more manpower to the mix wouldn't hurt."

Al grunted. "What have you heard?"

I filled him in on what I knew.

"Damnest thing," said Al when I finished. "I've investigated over a hundred homicides in my career and this one baffles me."

"You mean because someone managed to shoot him in his own place where he was locked in from inside, yet no sign of anyone entering, invited or otherwise?"

"That and other things. But yeah, the place was locked up like a drum."

"Is there any way he could have been shot elsewhere and then brought back to his place."

"Nope. He was definitely shot where he was found."

"What about the AC or heating system? Could it have been used to get in and out of the place unseen?"

"You not get a look at the place yet? The AC vents are about a foot wide, maybe six inches high. No way anyone came through there."

"No, I'm meeting Laura there on Thursday. She told me the house is wired up the ying-yang."

"The place is like Disneyland, Fort Knox and Cheyenne Mountain rolled into one. Should have listened to my mother and become a lawyer or something."

I nodded and chuckled. "I know the feeling. Laura says her brother was an honest upstanding citizen. No enemies, no troubles in the past."

"That's what they all say, but in this case, I might buy it. Wallis' record is squeaky clean, not even a traffic violation. Guess the guy was too busy becoming a multi-millionaire to waste time messing with the law. The way everybody talks about him, I figure he's in the running for sainthood."

"What about his driver, this Conner Weston?"

"Bradford tell you he once dated Wallis' sister?"

I nodded. "She believes Chloe and Conner had a hand in Stephen's death."

"You meet Weston?" At the shake of my head, he continued. "The guy's a thug. Too bad he's got an ironclad alibi. But I can smell a rat when I see one. If he didn't kill Wallis, you can bet he's guilty of some other crime."

"What's his alibi?"

"He was visiting family down east over Christmas. Has plane ticket receipts to prove it."

"Laura mentioned Stephen had some rare coins and expensive paintings."

Detective McGuire snorted. "Did she mention they were still there when we found Wallis?"

"She did." I drank a mouthful of coffee. "What about the sister? Chloe. Laura thinks she's being overlooked as a suspect."

"That's an understatement. Laura Bradford is determined to pin this on her."

"She swears she saw Chloe a couple of weeks before Christmas, but that Chloe lied to her and said she was in Palm Springs until Stephen's funeral," I said.

"We followed up. Chloe returned to Calgary on the twenty-seventh of November. Moved in with a girlfriend who helped her pick up some work at a scuzzy joint off Macleod Trail, called Vinnie's. She's also got an alibi for the time of Stephen's death. It checks out."

"Why lie to Laura about it?"

"Who knows. She didn't lie to us when we asked her about it."

"Do you know if she saw Conner, after she got back?"

"She says no, didn't see him until the funeral. We asked Weston, he said the same thing."

"Laura swears she saw them together at a pub called McIsaac's."

"Trouble is no one recalls seeing them there. Not the waitresses, not the bartender. If they were there, they used cash. When I pushed her on it, Laura admitted it was dark, she didn't get a good look at their faces. She figures it was them because she spotted a bracelet on this woman's wrist resembling the one her father gave her sister. You know how well that would stand up in court," he guffawed.

"Yeah, I hear you. So how did Chloe's bracelet get into Stephen's house? Laura did tell you she found it there when she was packing up Stephen's things, didn't she?"

"Yeah, yeah. But when we told Chloe someone spotted her at McIsaac's, wearing her topaz bracelet, she denied it.

She claimed the bracelet's been missing for some time. She believes Weston swiped it."

"Hmmm." He was shooting down any hope of a lead. "I read the medical examiner put Stephen's death down to sometime between noon on New Year's Eve and two the next morning."

"That's right. If you read the papers, you also know that he went for a run that morning. Security cameras show him returning home shortly after ten a.m. No one sees him again. At least not alive. Nobody goes in or comes out after he gets home. Some flyers were stuck in his mailbox later that afternoon. No one else comes to the house until Tuesday morning when his driver arrives."

"You're saying this is the perfect murder?"

"I don't believe in perfect murders but this one ranks right up there. Remember Marie Ann Chardin, found murdered in her home back in 2002, no signs of forced entry? It hasn't been solved either—yet. But someone out there knows something about it. You can bet on it."

"Laura assumes the case has gone cold. No one's been named a suspect or person of interest."

"You know I can't tell you much more than what's already out there but she's wrong. We're still digging. You know, company files, emails, searching everything in the digital footprint he left behind."

"I'd love to access his data. Maybe I should have been a cop."

Al squinted then raised one eyebrow. "So, what are you going to do that you don't think we've already done?"

I shrugged. "I'll dig around in his relationships, same as

you guys did. You know, old girlfriends, bitter family members left out of the will, skeletons from the past. Maybe I'll get lucky, and someone will tell me something they didn't tell your guys."

"Good luck with that." Al leaned back and crossed his arms. "Just make sure you don't get in our way. You could end up hurting the case more than helping."

Our eyes met. Yeah, this was my life now. I didn't want to piss off the Calgary Police, but I couldn't work as a private investigator and not run into a homicide or two.

"I'll let you know if I come across anything interesting," I said without breaking eye contact.

"You do that."

I thanked Detective McGuire for his time, and we exchanged contact information before he headed back upstairs. I knew he wouldn't be able to share much in the way of information on an active homicide case. He didn't seem interested in Chloe and Conner Weston, or at least he made it sound that way. He seemed well aware that Laura was maligning both of them and couldn't let go of the idea they might be involved.

Watch what you wish for Jorjie. My mother's words floated through my head. I had finally caught a big case, but the enormity of the task ahead was already biting into my confidence. Little did I know that my confidence would be the last thing I needed to worry about.

CHAPTER FIVE

I LEFT THE café and debated whether to head to the C-Train station or hike back to the office. The wind had calmed, leaving the air feeling warmer, so I opted to walk, telling myself it would be my workout for the day. I pulled on gloves, pulled the collar of my coat up around my ears and started back.

With no sign of forced entry, the easiest explanation was that Stephen knew his assailant and let him in. But Homicide would have reviewed every second of available security camera footage. Stephen hadn't let anyone in, or if he did, it wasn't the sort of thing McGuire wanted me to know about. As hard as it might be for Laura to accept, Stephen may have simply decided to give Conner Weston a second chance. And even if Chloe had gone to see Stephen when she got back to Calgary, what did it prove?

Two blocks further on I became aware of footsteps echoing mine. I turned but saw no one. Staying alert, the feeling I was being followed hit me again a block further on.

I glanced over my shoulder.

Two women scurried along the sidewalk behind me. A man in a grey coat sat on a nearby bus bench, his chin tucked into the collar. I picked up my pace and tried using the windows in the buildings across the street to see if anyone followed, but most were too high off the ground to serve my purpose.

I was two blocks from the office before I was a hundred percent certain. A seedy, unkempt man had zig-zagged across the road several times behind me. He slowed and sped up his pace to match mine. I was jostled out of my ruminations by the arrival of a bus, disgorging its load in front of me. I stepped aside, getting out of the departing passengers' way.

My breath caught as a grizzled old man stepped off.

He paused momentarily to settle the beat-up brown felt fedora more firmly on his head, in the same way my father had. I stared after him as he walked away.

It couldn't be him. My father was dead.

I arrived at the office in a snit. Some creeper knew the make and model of car I drove and now where I worked. Or maybe whoever was following me had already known that. With one final glance over my shoulder, I opened the door and stepped inside.

I took the stairs up to the second floor. My best friend, Gab Rizzo, and I occupied space at the end of the hall. Technically, the lease belonged to Gab. Her last serious boyfriend sweet-talked her into renting the office space for him then stiffed her with the lease. Now it was home to Thyme to Dine, Gab's personal catering business, and Knight Investigations, my sole proprietorship.

The English Language School across the hall was the main reason anyone came up to the second floor. I had rented their space on two separate weekends this past winter to run my first private investigator course—my way of supplementing a somewhat unpredictable PI income. Five students enrolled, but with a little more marketing I might be able to turn it into a regular and profitable offering.

I unlocked the office door and flicked on the light, but it did little to brighten the dingy interior. I snaked past the desk in the tiny reception area, where Gab usually worked when she wasn't off prepping or making gourmet meals, and into the slightly larger interior office.

The lighting here wasn't much better. The only window in the room faced an alley, and the red brick building on the other side prevented any natural light from coming in. The musty, stale smell reminiscent of left-over Chinese takeout and cigarettes was offset by the presence of a small wall safe, an internet connection, and the ridiculously cheap rent considering its proximity to downtown.

I plunked myself down at the desk and booted up the computer. It wasn't the first time I imagined I saw my father. I knew that sometimes a facial profile, the way someone held their head, or the way they walked, could trick the mind into thinking it was someone we knew, but this seemed different. I shook off the notion. *He's dead.*

Gab was always reminding me to focus on the present and to look for the bright side. She was the most positive person I knew. Gab even found the silver lining in my being attacked by a knife wielding, half-crazed, fellow employee at my former workplace. After all, it had been the impetus for my career change and in fact, shifted my perspective on life. Surviving a near death experience, has a way of doing that.

My previous career as a forensic lab analyst had suited me well. Perhaps too well, doing little to counterbalance my inherent introversion. So, after I healed, I got my PI licence and went into business for myself. In just over a year, I had managed to establish a clientele, if not a steady one, blogged regularly, met a couple of interesting men, lost ten pounds, learned how to load and fire a gun, and developed and taught my first PI course. My life was still a far cry from fabulous, but I was out of the rut I had dug for myself.

My thoughts turned back to Laura and her brother's murder. Had Stephen really accepted Conner's apology about his past behavior or had Conner somehow pressured him into giving him the job? The comment about Conner providing a disarming presence stirred my spidey-sense. Had Stephen needed protection, or was he merely justifying his action to Laura?

With Outlook now open, I scrolled through my email. A message from Thorton and Thorton caught my eye. I had asked Laura for a copy of Stephen's will and her lawyers had complied. I opened the attachment. The parts of the will I wasn't privy to, like addresses and other personal information, were blacked out. Skipping all the legal mumbo jumbo I jumped right to the bequests.

Stephen had left Laura his house, its contents and close to one million dollars held in various investments accounts. Stephen left his mother the royalties to about a dozen patents, which generated roughly a hundred thousand dollars a year. The Calgary Homeless Foundation was listed as beneficiary to an insurance policy that would pay out two hundred thousand dollars. Several smaller insurance policies were gifted to various other charities.

Stephen also left various items and smaller amounts to other individuals. A patent for an oral camera was left to his friend Rob Bailey and several other patents listed went to his buddy, Tony D'Silva, including a pending patent for something called a Nano-skin fuel cell.

At some point, Stephen had set up two trust funds, containing a mix of stocks, bonds, and mutual funds, both trusts valued at just over two hundred thousand dollars. One of the trust funds had been set up in Chloe's name and was to be administered by his lawyer. The details around the management of the trust funds would likely be outlined in a separate document but considering that Chloe's trust fund was to be managed by Stephen's lawyer, access to the funds probably came with provisions. Perhaps Stephen had set it up this way to prevent Chloe from squandering her inheritance in mere months.

The second trust fund had been set up for someone named Henry Albern and was to be administered by an Antonia Williams. Who the hell were Henry Albern and Antonia Williams? I sent Laura a quick email asking her if she knew who Henry Albern was, then set up appointments to meet with Stephen's closest friends, Rob Bailey, and Anthony D'Silva. Laura had already told me she had no idea how to get a hold of Chloe nor where I could find Conner.

I googled Vinnie's, the place McGuire mentioned Chloe worked at when she got back from Palm Springs. My eyes scanned their website page. "Live Girls" screamed the header. *I should hope so.* I called the phone number listed. The woman who answered said she didn't know Chloe Wallis, or any Chloe for that matter. She told me to call back in the evening when Mary Lou, the manager, would be in then put me through to her voice mail. I left my name and number and said I'd try her later in the evening if I didn't hear from her before then.

I started my search for Conner Weston. He wasn't listed anywhere, not the white pages, not the usual internet sites, nor in any of the city's public files. I was going to have to use some shoe leather on this one. I laced my fingers together and stretched my arms over my head, hoping to ease the knots from my neck and shoulders.

I checked my phone. Zippo from Luis. Inspector Luis Azagora headed up Calgary's Special Crimes unit and we had recently started seeing each other. He wasn't my type, which is probably why I found him intriguing. Besides, I wasn't sure what *my type* meant anymore. He and I were still in the early stages of trying to figure out what we were doing in each other's lives.

For the hundredth time that afternoon, my mind drifted back to my stalker and the reference to my parents' deaths. *Don't go back down that rabbit hole.* Who could have known that my car would be at the airport? Only Gab and Mike knew about the short job in Albuquerque. Why was someone poking around in my past, tailing me, leaving me messages? And what message were they trying to send me?

I turned back to my email, hoping for a quick reply to the email I had sent Laura. Nothing yet. I started deleting emails, most were ads from places I had shopped at, offering me great deals on stuff I couldn't afford. I sat up, my finger already on the trash icon, ready to delete a message with Friend-Protector-Keeper of Secrets in the subject line. I opened it and read: *A haunted woman sometimes wearies of distrust and longs for friendship*. It was signed S. Wise.

What the hell? I inspected the IP address, but it had been sent through a fake account or through something like ProtonMail. I googled S. Wise. Nothing jumped out at me from the jumble of responses, everything from rabbis, high schools, to infrared survey companies. I googled the phrase. It brought up a similar array of references from modern-day movies to fan fiction.

I closed my computer and packed up. I was making too much out of some spam. As I locked up the office, the knot in my gut grew.

It's not spam.

CHAPTER SIX

Anthony D'Silva's executive assistant announced my presence and ushered me through the door. Anthony D'Silva shot out of his chair and rounded the desk, his open, blue-grey jacket flapping behind him.

"Pleasure to meet you, Ms. Knight," he said pumping my hand. He wasn't much taller than me and although slight of build, his mannerisms told me he was wound tight.

"Please, it's Jorja."

"Call me Tony. Anthony is my father." He laughed. "And grandfather."

"Thanks for seeing me. As I said on the phone, Stephen Wallis' sister asked me to help investigate his death."

"Please sit." He waved me to a small round table tucked into the corner of his office. "Can Sharon get you anything? Water? Coffee?"

His assistant waited patiently at the door. "Coffee would be wonderful."

"Make that two, Sharon. Thanks."

The bulk of Stephen's estate had been left to Laura and

her family, but several business patents were left to Stephen's friends, Rob Bailey and Anthony D'Silva. Rob owned a dental practice in a nice upper-middle-class neighbourhood on the west side of town. Anthony was President and CEO of IQtel, a private company investing in micro electrical technology and artificial intelligence.

I sat, noticing the scuff mark my boot had made on the gleaming Terrazzo floor. Shifting my glance, lest I draw attention to it, I crossed my leg over my knee, and cleared my throat.

"Thanks for fitting me in today. I'm curious. What exactly does IQtel do?"

"We're all about integrative technologies. We're working on next generation object recognition software and improving a computer's ability to understand human voice. The technology's been around for a while but there are still some challenges. Humans have different accents, use slang. They find themselves in environments with a lot of background noise. We're working on developing a system that trains the computer to recognize these differences."

"Sounds challenging."

"That's what makes it fun," he said rubbing his hands together. "It's critical as we merge advances made in computer-recognized objects with language. The evolution of artificial intelligence. AI will change how we do everything."

"You mean like self-driving cars?"

He snapped his fingers leaving the index one pointing at me. "Exactly. The Honda CRV already has a range of voice commands the driver can use. But it needs to work for everyone, regardless of accent or other speech nuances. And it needs to be able to identify unexpected objects in addition to the standard objects encountered while driving." He spoke rapidly, his eyes gleaming. "The technology will allow surgeons to direct highly sophisticated robots by voice, and with AI capability the robots will be able to verbally provide data back to the surgeon as the surgery progresses, literally becoming their ears and eyes."

Sharon returned with a tray, two cups of coffee and some cream and sugar. After she departed, and I'd made appreciative comments about the astounding technology his company was working on, I asked him to tell me about Stephen.

He met Stephen playing soccer when they were still in high school. They clicked instantly. Both were science nerds, recent victims of parental discord, loved soccer, and came from struggling lower-middle-class families. When it was time to go to university, they chose U of C, the most logical and financially accessible. They moved out of their respective homes, and into a rental property within walking distance of the university.

I put my empty coffee cup back on the table. Tony hadn't touched his coffee. He was too busy talking, his hands gesturing enthusiastically.

"What happens to Stephen's incubator company now? Xcelerate, right?"

"Everything's still up in the air. The company itself isn't worth much. It's just a shell to house start-ups. Mark Fowler is the operations manager. He takes care of the day-to-day stuff, like dealing with the landlord, ordering supplies, paying the bills, that sort of thing. There's enough investor money earmarked to support the current incubators until the end of the year. Mark approached me to see if I would be willing to take it on."

"Are you interested?"

"Not sure." Tony pulled out a small rubber ball from his jacket pocket and bounced it on the table in front of him in small quick bounces. With one final bounce, he caught up the ball, carefully placed it on the table and looked up at me.

I watched Tony's fingers tap out a steady beat on the table. The ball rolled a few millimetres. I shifted in my chair and fought a sudden urge to grab the ball and bounce it across the room to see if he'd go after it.

"I told him I'd give it some thought, but IQtel is about to get a lot bigger. I'm having a hard time seeing any benefit in taking over Xcelerate."

"You're one of their current investors?"

"I am, or at least I've put money into a couple of their business ventures. But not much changes there. I'll see where they are at the end of the year and what makes sense going forward. At that point I can stay the course, sell my interest in the few innovations I've invested in or put in more money for a bigger percentage. Being an investor in some of the projects makes sense to me but taking on the job of marketing and finding funding for these projects less so."

"Stephen left you some patents. What do patent rights give you, if you don't mind my asking?"

"It gives the patent holder the right to have someone produce or manufacture the item for them, or more importantly, prevent others from producing it. The patent holder gets a royalty in return for assigning the right to manufacture and sell the product to someone else."

"But the patent holder can manufacture and produce the product themselves, can't they?"

"Yes of course. Most don't due to the upfront costs involved. It takes a lot of money to launch a start-up. It's one thing to fund the research and develop a prototype but manufacturing, production and distribution requires funding of a whole different level."

"Did Stephen personally invest in all the start-ups he supported?"

"He invested in most but not all of them."

"What can you tell me about Stephen's personal life? What was he like?"

"He was a quiet guy, but brilliant. Hard working. Heart of gold."

"What about friends?"

Tony leaned forward, both arms now crossed on the table. I watched the ball roll a few centimetres to the right.

"Stephen knew a ton of people. Just look at his LinkedIn page. He had over two thousand connections. Stephen could pretty much go to any city anywhere and find friends to join him for breakfast, lunch or dinner and fill his daytime schedule with business meetings. But these weren't his real friends if you get what I mean."

"I get it," I replied. These weren't the people he would have poured his heart out to, shared his worries with, or asked for personal advice.

"Did he keep in touch with old high school or university friends?"

"Naw." He leaned back. "We both occasionally ran into

people we knew in the old days, but I'm not aware of him reconnecting with anyone."

"What can you tell me about his driver, Conner Weston?"

Tony grunted. "Can't help you much there. I spoke to the guy all of two or three times. He used to date Stephen's sister, not Laura, the other one." Tony leaned over and picked a piece of fluff off his pant leg, now resting casually across his knee.

"Chloe."

"Right, Chloe."

"Any idea why Stephen hired him?"

Tony shrugged. "I figured he was one of Stephen's projects."

"Projects? What do you mean?"

"Whenever Stephen experienced a jolt of social consciousness, he felt compelled to act. I used to tell him the best way to deal with it is to donate money to someone whose job it is to address the issues. But every so often, he'd take matters into his own hands. Like the time he got a homeless guy a job delivering office mail." Tony dissolved in laughter.

"What happened?"

"Last year, this poor guy took to panhandling outside Stephen's office building. He'd just stand there every morning, hat in hand, never bother or hassle anyone, politely thank those who donated. Stephen wasn't content to just drop him a buck or two. He had to engage the poor fellow in conversation."

I'd been there, done that. It's hard to turn away once you know someone's name, their story.

"Next thing you know, Stephen sends this guy off to his barber, buys him new clothes and gets him a job delivering the mail in his office building. The guy shows up three days in a row then does a no show. Takes off with the mail cart and all the mail. No one sees him for about three weeks and suddenly he's back, wearing his old clothes, panhandling in front of the building." Tony dissolved into laughter. "Guess Stephen didn't fully appreciate what's involved in rehabilitating an alcoholic and getting them to adopt an alternate lifestyle."

"Gotta give him A for effort."

"An A plus if you ask me. That project ended with Stephen's donation to the Calgary Dream Centre. He sure was something else." Tony blinked rapidly and looked away for a minute. "You know what they say. The good die young. Thank god for my callous and greedy ways."

"What do you think happened, Tony? Could someone interested in one of Stephen's innovations have killed him? Or an entrepreneur who didn't like the deal Stephen negotiated?"

Tony picked up the small red ball, gave it a few turns and put in back on the table. He leaned back. His fingers tapped out a tune on the table in time to the one in his mind. "Naw. I don't see it. Stephen would have renegotiated terms if someone wanted out of their contract—why kill him?"

"Well, this wasn't some spur of the moment crime."

Tony's face darkened. "I agree. Whoever killed Stephen had the smarts to carry out his execution without leaving clues behind."

"Do you have any inkling as to who or why?"

His brown eyes met mine steadily. "I wish I did. Sorry."

After thanking Tony, the ever-gracious Sharon escorted me downstairs, where I turned in my visitor badge before stepping outside. I took a deep breath. Why did it feel like we just had a meeting on a tilt-a whirl?

During my short time inside, it had started to snow. I dug out a snow brush and pushed the wet snow off the car. By the time I finished clearing the back window, the front windshield was covered. I gave it one last swipe and jumped in, my hands red with the cold.

Stephen's death had been well planned and meticulously carried out, leaving little evidence for police. Not something an annoyed co-worker, family member or jilted lover would do in the heat of a moment. Someone had carried out a methodical and meticulously crafted plan, undetected. Someone Stephen's death meant a lot to. Maybe someone with a personal grudge, one of his beneficiaries, or someone from his past. Or maybe something was happening at Xcelerate that needed to stay hidden. Tony's words repeated in my head as I drove away. Stephen's killer had the smarts to carry out his execution.

CHAPTER SEVEN

THE NEXT MORNING Crowchild Trail was slicker than bear scat and littered with fender benders. By the time I got downtown and found parking, I regretted my decision to go to the office instead of working from home. The weather report said a second system was heading our way and expected to bring more snow. Hard to believe we were just a few weeks away from official spring.

I shook melting droplets off my coat and stamped my feet to dislodge snow from my boots and got into the waiting elevator. The doors creaked closed, and it lurched upwards. Water dripped off the ends of my hair and down my neck. I congratulated myself on having skipped time with the hair dryer this morning.

As soon as I disembarked on the second floor the lights flickered. The wet snow was going to provide the electrical crews with some overtime today. Halfway down the dimly hit hallway I noticed someone hovering by the office door. As I got closer, a woman's voice called out.

"It's about bloody time."

"I'm sorry, did I miss a meeting?" I was positive I hadn't.

"Your office hours say you're open," she replied, clearly annoyed.

"And you are?"

She was unnaturally thin, her sunken, kohl-rimmed eyes and bright-red lips garish against a Morticia Addams-like pallor and bottle-black hair.

"Chloe. Chloe Wallis. Bet you weren't expecting me."

She had that right.

"No, but I do want to speak with you." I had finally reached her boss at Vinnie's last night and got confirmation that she still worked there. Her boss must have passed on the message that I was looking for her. I reached around her and inserted my office key into the lock. The odour of stale cigarettes and cloyingly sweet perfume filled my nose.

"I bet," she challenged.

Nudging open the door, I stepped aside, to let her squeeze by. "Come on in."

I ushered her past the front desk, and into the interior office, snapping on the overhead light as I entered. The light flickered, then emitted a harsh white light unflattering to all but the darkest of skins. I hung my damp jacket over the back of my desk chair and sat down, waving my hand at the lone wooden chair in front of the desk.

"I'd offer you something, but my secretary seems to have run out. There's water if you want."

She sat but didn't remove her pale-blue car coat. Gold threads ran through the woollen fabric, but the frayed collar and cuffs detracted from its earlier glamour. Her eyes swept over the room and she snickered. "I see my dear sister isn't sparing the expenses. She's clearly hired the best."

"My time goes to helping my clients, not to decorating. Let me start off by saying how sorry I am that you lost your brother."

My statement caught her off guard. She tilted her head away from me and stared at the far wall. She wiped her nose with the back of her hand and turned back.

"He was the only one of the bunch that gave two cents about me."

"When you say bunch, you're referring to...?"

"All of them. Laura, her mother, Laura's husband, his family, all their uppity friends. I never met a Bradford I liked."

"You and your brother were close?"

"Close enough. Stephen understood me. We both liked taking chances, trying new things."

"When did you last see Stephen?"

"In August, just before I went to California."

"Why'd you go to California?"

"I met someone. He had a place down there."

"When did you get back to Calgary?"

"The day before Stephen's funeral. Not one of them had the decency to call. I heard it on the news."

"And you were in California the whole time, from August until mid January?"

She studied me, her eyes calculating. Her face twisted into a pinched look; her lips pursed together. "You know that isn't the case." I suddenly saw a shrewd woman, a woman who read people well, one who would use whatever she could to her advantage.

"So why lie?"

She shrugged.

"Why don't you tell me your version of what happened?"

"There's nothing to tell. I left Ted in November. He's so damn borrrr...ing. He's retired, not me. I got sick and tired of doing diddly 'cept laundry and slinging hash. I told Ted he could stuff it."

"Did you look up your ex-boyfriend, Conner, when you got back?"

"We're done. He can go to hell." Her eyes stared defiantly into mine.

"Did you go see your brother?"

"No." She looked away. "I tried calling him, but never got through." Her fingers pulled at a loose thread on her sleeve.

"What did you do when you got back?"

"A friend got me a job where she works and said I could stay with her for a bit. Then one night it was on the news. Stephen was dead."

"When did you notice your bracelet was gone, the one your dad gave you?"

Her hand flew to her wrist. She stiffened and stared at me, pale-grey orbs floating in a sea of black. Something flickered in her eyes.

"In California. At first, I thought I packed it away somewhere. I went through all my stuff but couldn't find it. I figured Conner took it. He knew how much it meant to me."

"Did you call him, to ask about it?"

"No."

"Really?"

"You don't know Conner. If that jerk-ass took it, there's no way he'd give it back. He'd want something for it in return. And I'm not doing anything for that asshole."

"So, what would you like to tell me about Stephen's death?" Stephen had left Chloe close to two hundred thousand dollars in a trust fund. But something wasn't making her happy.

She slid her hands into her coat pockets and pulled them together, bunching her coat in front of her. Her thin pointy chin lifted to one side. After a moment, she turned her face toward me.

"I'm no dummy, you know. I know Laura is trying to throw me under the bus. She wants you to prove that I did it. That I killed Stephen. 'Cept I didn't."

"Why would she do that?"

"To throw suspicion off Wayne. Don't you wonder how a guy in construction and a stay-at-home mom can afford a two-million-dollar house on the lake? *And* a condo in Fairmont? She thinks she's so damn clever, hiring a PI to make it look like they're all innocent. All she cares about is paying off all them thugs hounding her precious hubby."

"What thugs would that be?"

"So, you don't know," she said smugly

"Why don't you enlighten me?"

"Hah! And do your job? Here's a big tip. Take a look at who really gains from Stephen's death. It sure isn't me."

Chloe jumped up, two red circles now visible on her cheeks. "So, you'd better look elsewhere." She pulled her hand from her coat pocket and punched the air with her forefinger. "Laura is playing you for a fool. She's expert at it. Sweet, kind Laura." Chloe delivered the last few words in an oozy, syrupy tone. Then she announced, "She's a liar. And her husband's a thief. I don't use a lot of fancy words, but at least I'm honest. What you see is what you get." With one last air poke, she turned and stomped out of the office.

What the hell was that about? How were Laura and Wayne thieves and liars? I weighed out the possibility of Laura's involvement in Stephen's death but couldn't see it. What I did see was that Chloe Wallis was one scared girl.

CHAPTER EIGHT

THE PICTURE WAS grainy, taken years ago by some fledgling photographer eager to see his name in the credit section of the Dino Gazette. I had no trouble picking out Stephen Wallis and Tony D'Silva in the photo, a snapshot of the U of C soccer team's last victory of the season. Tony still had the same thousand-watt smile. Lean and wiry, he had one hand on the trophy he and the team captain hoisted in the air, his other arm casually draped around the shoulder of a fellow teammate, which the caption below identified as G. Albero. Stephen stood in the back row, second from the end. A lanky, dark-haired young man, with serious eyes and a shy smile.

I scrolled back to the news articles about Stephen's murder. The pictures they ran with the story showed a man in his early forties, his face now fuller, the smile confident. His eyes remained serious. I sat back. This was the type of guy I should consider dating. But I always seemed to go for the Tony D'Silvas. Gregarious extroverts, talkative, full of energy. Full of bullshit.

I had already read the news articles about Stephen's death, at least the ones from reputable news sources. But as usual, Stephen's death was being capitalized on by bloggers, shady news sites, people using his death to promote their own message or just get their names out there. I settled back in my chair and took a sip of coffee, already cold. I read, scanning sites, quickly passing on those that suggested Stephen's death had been carried out by the government, or one of the many aliens who had infiltrated earth and lived among us.

An article caught my eye. A woman came forward shortly after Stephen's death, claiming to be pregnant with his child. Detectives investigated the story but found no evidence of a relationship between her and Stephen. The woman claimed she had since miscarried, but her history of setting up bogus go-fund-me pages for the many tragedies she claimed befell her told a different story. The one hundred thousand dollar reward Laura's family had posted was drawing out the crazies. I picked up my coffee, remembered it was cold, and set it back down.

I sat back and stared at the ceiling. Laura had made Chloe sound like an out-of-control, spoiled child. But the woman who came to my office yesterday was shrewd and conniving, and perhaps too clever for her own good. What if there was something behind her accusations that Laura and Wayne were liars and thieves.

I spent the next hour searching the internet for information on Wayne Bradford. The W. Bradford's on LinkedIn didn't sound like him. I kept digging and found his Facebook page. He listed his occupation as a general construction manager, specializing in residential projects. It said he'd been in business since September, nothing about what he'd been doing before that.

The phone rattled me out of my search.

"Hey Gab. What's up?"

Like Tony and Stephen, my friendship with Gab went back to university days. We had grown into women together, weathered first-day job jitters, the deaths of loved ones, relationship disappointments, career moves, and knew each other's deepest, darkest secrets. Okay, not every secret. I had kept a few back. But after twenty years, I was certain if I revealed them now, nothing would change.

"Same old, same old. Grand Mamma is driving me nuts."

Gab had grown more concerned about her eighty-six-year-old grandmother this past year. A formidable woman who the Rizzo-Worsley-Bell family referred to as Grand Mamma.

"What has she been doing this time?"

"I'm afraid she's losing it. The other night she went to a Steampunk parasol duelling championship at Lougheed House. Now she wants me to drive her all the way to Rocky Mountain House to look at some miniature horses someone has for sale. She says she's always wanted a miniature horse."

"Maybe she's working on a bucket list."

"What's she going to do with a horse? She lives in a bloody condo for Pete's sake."

"That's hilarious."

"I'm sure I'll look back fondly on these moments after she's gone. Right now, I don't have time to deal with this craziness. What about you? What dastardly crime are you trying to solve now?"

"Remember that guy who was killed back in January? Shot to death, locked in his house, no sign of entry or the killer, even though there were security cameras everywhere."

"OMG. You're looking for the Houdini Killer? That's big. Imagine the publicity you'll get if you catch the guy."

"There's a better chance I won't find him. But it would be cool if I could find something that helps the police solve the murder. Like twenty years from now, when I'm working as a grumpy lunch lady at the local junior high and pilfering stale bread to take home to my three-legged dog."

"Oh Jorja, you crack me up. I want to hear all about it. I've got catering jobs lined up right through the weekend. Drinks next week?"

After agreeing to connect next week, I sat back and rubbed my temples. Laura and her family inherited the lion's share of Stephen's estate. And yet Laura was insisting Chloe had something to do with Stephen's death. Although Laura's theory that Chloe had something to do with Stephen's death was largely unsubstantiated, it wouldn't be the first time someone's gut instinct ended up being right, however implausible it seemed at first glance.

I closed my computer and packed up to leave. What reason would Chloe have for killing Stephen? She must have known he would leave the bulk of his estate to Laura and her family. Did Laura really believe Chloe and Conner killed her brother or was Laura throwing up a smoke screen to keep me and Detective McGuire from focusing too much attention on her and Wayne?

CHAPTER NINE

Dr. Rob Bailey's dental office was unlike any I had experienced. The reception area was light and spacious with high ceilings. A floor-to-ceiling water feature burbled behind the two receptionists who sat at a long, glass table, computers ready at their fingertips. Soft music filled the air, the sound meshing harmoniously with the gurgling water. There was no one waiting in the curved white-leather chairs. I approached the counter and both receptionists flashed me wide smiles, their perfect teeth gleaming. I suddenly grew conscious of the small gap between my top front teeth.

"I'm Jorja Knight."

"Oh yes! Dr. Bailey is expecting you. Come with me please," said the taller of the two.

I followed her down a white marble-tiled floor into a small consultation room. After being offered water, choice of coffee or tea, magazines, and urged to help myself to the fruit arranged in a glass bowl in the middle of the round meeting table, she left me to my own devices, saying Dr. Bailey would be in to see me in a jiff.

I sank into one of the leather chairs and surveyed my surroundings. Chirping birds, waterfalls and the occasional far-off cry of a Howler monkey filtered into the room. I eyed the fruit and fought the urge to slip an apple or two into my purse for later. I was scanning the ceiling for hidden speakers when the door opened, and a man strode confidently into the room.

"Rob Bailey," a deep voice announced. The door closed behind him, and the rainforest sounds dropped a notch in volume.

"Nice to meet you." I stood up as he paused by my chair to shake hands.

"Would you like something to drink? Or has Andrea already asked you?"

"She did, and I'm fine, thank you." I tore my eyes away from the fruit bowl as my stomach gurgled, reminding me I hadn't had lunch.

A deep California tan made his white smile seem even whiter. Or it could have been a Florida or Mexican Riviera tan, for all I knew. The lack of wrinkles around his eyes and smooth forehead smacked of Botox. A sharp crease ran down each leg of his dark-grey dress slacks all the way to the top of black penny loafers. His blue, short sleeve shirt, showed off strong, tanned arms.

"Thanks for seeing me. As I mentioned on the phone, Stephen Wallis' sister hired me to look into his death."

"How is Laura doing? Horrible shock for her, and for all of us." Rob dropped the smile and gave his head a small shake.

"She's taking it pretty hard. Sounds like her brother was an upstanding guy."

"He was. He had so much going for him. I can't believe he's gone."

"Did you know Stephen long? How did you meet?"

"Laura didn't tell you? I met Stephen in first year university. We roomed together."

"You roomed with Stephen and Tony D'Silva?"

"We rented an old four-bedroom house near the university. Sometimes there were five or six people living there. It kept the rent reasonable."

"A party house?"

Rob laughed. "No. We were nerdy types. Kind of like the guys on the Big Bang Theory TV show."

"Right." I nodded. "I'm trying to get a sense of who Stephen was, the people in his life. What can you tell me about him?"

"He was a great guy. Successful. Personable. Kind-hearted. He had so much going for him." Rob leaned back in his chair, hand on his chest. "I'm still reeling. He wasn't just successful in business, he was big on giving back, building resilient communities. He was a big supporter of the Calgary Homeless Foundation."

"I read about that in one of the news articles. When did you last see Stephen?"

"New Year's Eve. We went for a run in the morning. Stephen kept himself fit. He used to say, fit body, fit mind."

"Oh. So, you would have likely been the last person to see him alive."

Rob shifted, folded one fisted hand into the other, placing both in front of his chest, while his elbows rested on the arms of the chair. "I had invited him to a New Year's Eve party my wife and I were hosting that night, but he said he didn't know if he was going to make it. Said he was bagged and might stay home."

I nodded. Stephen had been shot while his friends were out celebrating. "So, you weren't surprised when he didn't show."

"I should have called him later, insisted he come. I knew he'd been working through most of the holiday and figured he wanted a quiet night at home. Still…" Rob rubbed one hand with the other.

"There's nothing you could have done."

"I know, I still wish I'd called."

I nodded. "I get that. Laura sent me a copy of the will. Stephen left you one of his patents."

"He didn't have to do that." Rob smiled sadly, shaking his head.

"Did you invest in any of Stephen's start-ups?"

"A few. I invested in the intra-oral camera, one of Stephen's earliest ventures. Later Stephen negotiated a deal with an international medical equipment manufacturer. He left his ownership in the camera to me. It won't make me rich, but it'll pay for my annual trip to Vegas."

"What was Stephen like that day—the last time you saw him?"

"I could tell he was tired, but excited. He told me he had several investors keen on one of his initiatives."

"Any idea who or which initiative?"

"Sorry. It was just a passing remark. He didn't go into details."

"Did he ever mention anyone threatening or harassing him in any way?"

"Not to me." Rob leaned forward. "Well, there was that one incident last summer. Someone attacked him outside the lab one night. Stole his watch and his wallet."

"He report it?"

"Of course. The police can't do much about these types of robberies. Seems to happen daily to someone."

"Is that why he hired a driver?"

"I wouldn't blame him if it was. But no, he told me he wanted to address the one thing in life he didn't seem to have enough of: time. I ribbed him about it anyway." Rob smiled ruefully. "Asked him if we should all be calling him Sir or Mr. Wallis."

"Were you aware of his history with the driver, that he once dated Stephen's half-sister?"

"I was. Then again, if Stephen was worried about his safety, who better to hire?"

"What do you mean?"

"Weston is ex-military. Afterwards, he got into security services, overseas. Armed security, private army combat support."

"Whoa. You mean he was a mercenary?"

"In a manner of speaking, yes."

And now he was working as a glorified taxi driver. "How'd you hear that?"

"Stephen told me they were having a drink late one night at the airport and the guy tells him some general in Burundi is looking for him."

"Burundi? That's interesting. Why?"

"According to what he told Stephen, this general hired him to spy on his private army, figured they might be planning a coup. Weston can't keep it together, lets his little man do the thinking for him, if you know what I mean. Sleeps with the general's daughter. The general's mistress finds out and tells the general, who, ignoring any moral deliberations about his own infidelity, goes berserk. He's enraged that Weston has ruined his seventeen-year-old daughter's chances for a 'virginal' marriage with some fifty-eight-year-old prince. Who in all likelihood isn't a prince but uses the title anyway. He's so angered that he leaks to his army pals that Weston's a spy, thereby proving he has their backs and can be trusted to look out for their common good. Several of the general's men go after Weston, tracking him to Kenya then to Pakistan, where again, according to Weston, one of them met his demise. Weston goes into deep hiding. He then heads back to Canada and loses himself in the masses."

"That's quite the story."

Rob chuckled. "Yeah, I don't believe it either. But that's what he told Stephen."

"Can you think of any reason someone would want to harm Stephen?"

"Stephen's murder doesn't make any sense. I mean, I know it happened. The news is full of stories like Stephen's. I'll never understand what makes somebody go out and kill. I mean unless there's a mental illness."

"What about jealous or bitter ex-girlfriends?"

"Stephen had a few girlfriends along the way, nothing serious. Most ended amicably."

"What about his last relationship?"

"That was his most serious relationship. It ended a year ago."

"Who was that with?"

"Stella Seller. Maybe you've seen her real-estate commercials on TV. Stell-ar Sell-her?"

"No, can't say I have. Do you know why they broke up?"

"It ended for the same reason all his other relationships ended. I told Stephen, no woman wants to be number five on your list of things to attend to. Except maybe for someone who's only interested in your money. As far as I know, he wasn't seeing anyone else."

"What do you suppose happened, Rob? What's your theory as to who killed Stephen or why?"

Rob sat up, leaned forward, and placed clasped hands on the table. "I've asked myself the same question, more than a few times these last months. Maybe someone broke into the wrong house. I don't know." He shrugged. "It can't be anyone who knew him. I mean really knew him. Someone wanted him out of the way. Don't ask me why. Maybe it was a long-standing grudge. And the way he was killed. Whoa." Rob lifted his hands in defeat. "I'm nowhere near as tech savvy as Stephen was, but whoever got into that house undetected knew what they were doing."

"A long-standing grudge. Know anyone who might fit the bill?"

"Gee, I don't know." Rob ran a hand over his face. "Could be someone he beat out when he was just getting started. Half of these innovations get their start in someone's garage. I'm not saying that's what happened, but you never know."

I thanked Rob and left him my contact information. Now I knew why homicide was scratching their heads. Laura was convinced Chloe and Conner had something to do with

Stephen's death. Chloe was pointing her finger back at Laura and her husband. Tony hadn't a clue. Rob speculated it might be someone with a long-held grudge but that it couldn't be anyone who truly knew him. I crossed the lobby, buttoned my coat, and pushed through the revolving glass doors. *Did anyone ever truly know someone?*

Squinting against the glaringly bright sunshine, amplified by the melting snow, I paused to dig sunglasses out of my purse. I was starting to understand Detective McGuire's comment about Stephen being in the running for sainthood. But his near-perfect life had flaws. He'd been a workaholic, and his relationships suffered. Laura and Rob both mentioned he looked tired, maybe a bit anxious. And he didn't notice, or he'd ignored warning signs that someone was gunning for him, until it was too late. I knew the pattern well.

I slipped on my sunglasses, lifted my face to the sun and breathed in the crisp air. I reminded myself to be grateful. Stephen could no longer enjoy the beauty in simple moments like this. The revolving door spun behind me. I continued down the steps and crossed the drop-off lane. The snow was melting fast now that the sun was out. Skipping over a few puddles, I entered the parking area.

I quickened my steps. A piece of paper was plastered against the windshield of my Chevy. None of the other cars held similar papers. I glanced around. No one paid me any attention. As I closed in, I could tell the paper wasn't a ticket or an advertisement. Reaching my car, I hesitated. The folded sheet, thin blue lines and ragged edge told me it had been torn out of a coil notebook. Skin prickling, I snatched the paper, unlocked my car door and slid in.

My eyes scanned the parking lot then flit back to the building. Rob came rushing through the revolving doors, pulling on a camel-coloured coat. He looked frazzled. Maybe I had made him late for a meeting. I watched him run down the stairs and into a waiting taxi. My eyes swept the area one more time. Everyone moved at a normal pace, nothing unusual caught my eye.

I opened the note carefully by its corners. The pasted news headline, overtop a hand-drawn cross, shouted "Daughter claims father was abusive." I stared down at the grainy black-and-white newspaper picture of my eighteen-year-old self.

CHAPTER TEN

I TURNED OFF Eighth Avenue onto Crescent Road, which ran along the north edge of McHugh Bluff Park. Most of the original homes were in the process of being torn down and replaced with enormous modern structures sporting a lot of glass. I pulled up to the address Laura had given me. The house was a two-storey infill, square, sleek with floor-to-ceiling windows. The nineteen-forties bungalow to the right of Stephen's was tiny in comparison. A gaping hole encased by wire fencing stood to the left of Stephen's house. A yellow sign, attached to the fence, proclaimed it a construction site and warned of danger.

Climbing out of my car, I glanced at the scene behind me. The bluff rose over a hundred feet from the floor of the Bow River below and provided an unobstructed view of the downtown skyline. A mass of grey concrete, shiny steel and glass, the newer high-rises immediately identifiable, their tops angled, curved or stepped, a noticeable contrast to their older, square, flat-topped cousins. Plumes of white smoke rose from the rooftops and melted into the blue-grey canopy above.

I turned, crossed the street, and made my way up the short sidewalk. Pressing the buzzer next to a ten-foot-high, solid black door, I noted the security camera mounted in the corner. A metallic, female voice asked me to identify myself. I stated my name, and the door swung open. I had half-expected the door to be opened by a robot and shrugged off my disappointment.

"Jorja. Come on in." Laura ushered me into the towering foyer.

The white marble floor gleamed in the grey light cascading through the glass. Laura led me across the foyer and up six stairs to the living area.

"Wow, this is spectacular," I said.

A sad smile crossed Laura's face. "I suppose it is." She wrapped her arms across her body, hugging herself. "I find it stark...lonely."

It was a big place for one person. Especially for someone who lived alone and was away on business a lot. The towering ceiling made the place seem even larger and the wall of windows contributed to the spaciousness.

The main floor was open, a large living area occupying most of the space. I followed Laura past the low modern furniture, through a dining area and into a sleek kitchen. The kitchen cabinetry glistened, the light tiger wood, imported from Italy and ecologically certified, topped with white quartz. Stephen had liked the minimalistic look, or his decorator did.

The left side of the house was accessed by climbing another

set of stairs, which led to a walkway open to the living room below and separated by a wire railing. Two bedrooms opened off the walkway, the master at the front, overlooking the city, the second bedroom facing the back of the house.

The master bath contained the same Italian-made cabinets, and above the double sinks, a large mirror TV. The floors were white-and-grey marble. The glassed-in steam shower was fitted with two showerheads and a multitude of spray jets, the walls marble, the floor a pale blue-grey glass tile. A long narrow window ran floor to ceiling, the glass frosted for privacy. Skylights opened the ceiling to the sky. The minimalist style was consistent throughout.

"The house is completely wired," Laura said as she walked me through the rooms, like a real-estate agent pointing out features to a prospective buyer. "Recessed ceiling speakers in every room, controlled separately for each room of course. All the lights and appliances are controlled via Bluetooth. Stephen could use his cell phone or ask his voice-enabled digital assistant to turn up the heat, or turn on the stove, or play a certain song from his music library. He could see who was at his door even when he wasn't home. The window sensors detect rain and close automatically if they're open, or open if the humidity inside is too high. There's even an app that controls the convection oven. It adjusts oven temperature to perfectly create whatever recipe you enter. Not that he ever used it, Stephen didn't cook."

"This is impressive. I guess given what he did, I shouldn't be surprised."

Laura nodded. "He loved showing off all his fancy gadgets."

"Detective McGuire told me the place has a top-notch security system," I said.

"It does. There are several cameras mounted outside. Stephen could be at work and pull up a live feed of the outside of the house if he wanted to."

"What about inside the house?"

"There's a camera in the garage, one in the den and one in the foyer, but none upstairs," said Laura. "The inside is monitored by motion detector sensors, as well as smoke and CO_2 detectors and water detection sensors in case one of the appliances leaks."

Laura wrapped up the tour, taking me to an underground garage which held spots for two cars. A cobalt-blue Mazda Miata was parked there.

"Did Stephen have another car?"

"Yes. He had a Mercedes Benz." Her lips tightened. "It's the car Conner used to drive him around in. Stephen sold it to him for ten dollars."

"What?"

"That car's worth at least eighty thousand dollars. Why would he sell it to Conner for ten dollars?"

"A very good question. By the way, thanks for getting your lawyers to send me a copy of the will. It appears Stephen updated it last fall. Any idea why?"

"No. I mean I just assumed he kept it updated with the various patents that he acquired." We returned to the main floor.

"I've been putting off dealing with Stephen's den until last. You want to see it?"

"Yes, if you don't mind."

I knew this was where Stephen had been found. I followed Laura to an area off the living room, on the opposite side of the house from the kitchen. This part of the house jutted out from the main two-storey portion of the house. The back wall of the study was lined with custom built bookshelves, artfully arranged with books, several awards and objects d'art, the hardwood floor anchored by a white rug.

"I've taken out most of Stephen's personal things. There wasn't much. I'm going to sell the rest of the furniture with the house if someone wants it. I've lined up an auction house to sell the paintings and Stephen's coin collection."

"Speaking of, do you have any idea what his coin collection was worth."

"I'm still waiting for the appraisal. I do know Stephen had a rare coin in the collection that he always referred to as his million-dollar baby."

"Did he keep it here in the house?"

"Yes. There's a safe in his den. Laura walked to the bookcase and removed a pair of Ammonites, artfully mounted on a stand, from the shelf. She pressed the centre of a Jade medallion mounted to the back of the bookcase. The back section of the bookcase swung open to reveal a wall safe.

"This is where Stephen kept his coin collection, a copy of his will and other important papers." The safe was empty now.

"Was anything taken?"

"Not as far as I know."

Laura locked the safe while I made my way to the front of the room. A glass side table emphasized the gaping space next to it where the sofa had once stood. A white-leather armchair and a sleek black cabinet housing liquor decanters and glasses stood against the outer wall. I peered into the eyepiece of the telescope standing at the front window, the scope aimed at the city centre.

Laura's voice sounded hollow. "The movers are dropping off boxes today, so I can pack up most of the books and such."

I turned back. The room had double frosted glass doors that slid across the doorway, closing off the area from the main living space, if needed. When open, the den flowed seamlessly into the living space and kitchen beyond. Further down were a guest washroom and a small office. "The security system was engaged, wasn't it?"

"Yes. It went off like blazes when the police gained entry," said Laura. "There's a security camera there. She pointed at the top of the front window. "The motion detectors were turned off of course, since he was at home."

I peered at the camera. It was so small I wouldn't have noticed it had Laura not pointed it out. "The camera didn't capture the intruder?"

"Apparently not."

"Chloe came to see me."

"She did?" Laura's face told me her surprise was genuine.

"She showed up at my office claiming you're trying to throw her under the bus. Her words, not mine. She insists she had nothing to do with Stephen's death."

"Of course not." Laura's voice dripped with sarcasm.

"She made a comment about someone hounding your husband?"

"That's it." Laura lifted her hand in defense. "She's

always mouthing off about things that are none of her business. Nobody is hounding my husband."

"Maybe the company he works for?"

"He's self-employed."

At least the mention of Chloe broke Laura out of her melancholy. "She did come off sounding a bit theatrical. Thought I'd mention it. The will states Stephen left some money in a trust to Henry Albern. The trust is to be administered by an Antonia Williams. Do you know who they are?"

"No. They weren't present when the will was read. I assume the lawyers have been in contact with them."

I nodded. "Do you mind if I take a few pictures of the inside and the outside of the house?"

"No, go ahead," said Laura, backing out of the room. "I'll be in the kitchen if you need me."

I snapped photos from several angles. I don't know what I expected to capture, but if the house sold, this might be my one and only chance to see the crime scene. Laura had told me Stephen was found on the couch, wearing headphones, listening to music. A book lay open next to him, its cover facing up. He may have fallen asleep and wasn't aware of his assailant's presence.

None of the downstairs windows opened, the windows and skylights on the second floor did but the police found them all secured. If something had been taken from the house, it wasn't anything his friends or family expected to be there. I returned to the foyer just as Laura's moving guys arrived. I thanked her for showing me around and said I'd be in touch.

I walked around to the back of the house, which was separated from its neighbours by a gravelled lane. The wind had picked up but was less noticeable back here. I stared up at the second-floor windows. Unnoticed access would be tricky as Stephen's house was overlooked by a multi-level condo. With at least seven or eight condo units facing the back of Stephen's house, scaling the wall without being seen would be unlikely.

I took a few photos of the back of the house then walked down the alley. It was quiet, no sign of the neighbours. Presumably, they were at work, putting in long hours to pay for the privilege of living in one of Calgary's more prestigious neighbourhoods. Or at their villa in Spain.

Rounding the corner, I spotted someone by my car, back to the wind. I quickened my pace. The figure ducked down, now obscured by the car.

"Hey, you," I yelled, my heart racing. A man popped up from behind my car, glanced over his shoulder, his eyes wide. "Yeah, you," I yelled breaking into a run as I crossed the street.

The man ducked down a second time, popped back up, turned and ran. I reached the other side of the street, leapt onto the sidewalk and barrelled after him. His gait seemed unsteady, the space between us shrank. Suddenly he stopped and turned to face me, his shocked face white beneath his grey hair, a Pomeranian clutched in his arms. I followed his gaze. The wind had plastered a small bag against the wall of my back tire, a small brown lump remained next to it.

"Oh, crap," I muttered. Giving him a weak wave, I slunk around to the driver's side, got in, and pulled away from the curb.

CHAPTER ELEVEN

AFTER TOURING STEPHEN'S place, my condo felt smaller than usual. I hung up my coat, turned on the coffee maker and moseyed over to the couch. The living and dining spaces sat off the kitchen in one open room. A small bedroom and a bathroom completed the unit. The whole place could fit into Stephen's living room. But my place had a decent sized balcony, and the dark wooden floors made the place feel cozy.

I clicked on the TV, muted the sound, and opened my laptop. I opened my file on Stephen and added notes from my afternoon visit to his house. Having now seen the house for myself, I could understand Detective McGuire's comment about it being a fortress. My mind ran through possible ways someone could have entered the house undetected. Could someone have hidden in Stephen's car trunk and let themselves out later? The coffee maker beeped, and I got up and poured myself a cup.

Back on the couch, I pulled open the copy of Stephen's will. Laura and her family were the biggest beneficiaries. Surely Detective McGuire would have eliminated them as suspects by now. Unless of course they were still gathering the needed evidence to charge them. The various charities that benefited from Stephen's death weren't of interest to me. What did interest me was why Stephen updated his will a few months before he died.

Laura didn't know who Henry Albern was nor the woman who was to administer the trust. I typed Henry Albern into the search engine. Nothing came up. Nada. Zilch. Where had I seen that name? I checked the notes from my meeting with Tony and Rob. Nothing.

I typed in Antonia Williams and filtered through a few dozen names that came up on Facebook, narrowing them down to two. Both women listed Calgary as home.

The first Antonia Williams was a dark-haired twenty-something posing with a pouty pucker. Her Facebook account was an open book. I scrolled through hundreds of posts and photos of "Toni" wearing Daisy Dukes, low-cut tank tops and consuming an astonishing array of liquor. Clearly, she still hadn't settled on a signature drink. Her life-style sounded a lot like Chloe's, lots of job hopping and partying. If this was the Antonia Williams in Stephen's will it was more likely she'd have been left money, rather than named a trustee.

The second Williams I found used a photo of herself as a little girl to anchor her page. At least I assumed the photo of a child with dark curly hair, sitting atop a pony, was her, but it could easily be a daughter or granddaughter. This Antonia Williams was a nurse, married with two children. I scrolled through her timeline.

There were a bunch of photos of kids at various events

and a few of a heavier-set middle-aged woman with tight, curly hair. Many of her recent posts referred to her mother, her absence felt even stronger during Christmas. There was mention of a visit from her brother, Joey. No signs of a Henry. She worked at Vista Greens nursing home. I called Vista Greens. Antonia Williams was off work for the day, so I left a voice message.

Sitting back, I rubbed my temples. A headache had formed, and I realized I hadn't eaten since breakfast. I knew the fridge held little besides some expired condiments. I walked over to the sliding glass doors and surveyed the sky. Low grey clouds spread across my view, threatening snow. I peered through the balcony rails at the spruce trees lining the street below. Their tops swayed with childlike abandon. Forty kilometres an hour would be my guess. I debated taking the car, but if I did, I'd have to exercise when I got back.

Sighing, I walked to the closet and pulled out my coat, gloves and hat and made my way downstairs. Stepping through the lobby, I opened the door and gasped as the wind hit my face. My evergreen wind gauge hadn't prepared me for the wind chill factor. Eyes watering, I pulled up the collar of my woefully inadequate car coat, tucked my head down into the collar and embarked on my six-block jaunt to the mall.

Two blocks further on, I crossed the street. Another soul was out braving the cold. Except that fool was encased in snow pants, a heavy dark-grey coat and wore a knit scarf and Beanie. *Smart.*

I had a Down-filled jacket somewhere in the back of my

closet but hadn't worn it in a while. Most of the Down had escaped from a hole in one of the sleeves, the result of an unfortunate encounter with a .22 calibre bullet. Besides, the duct tape bush-fix didn't exactly leave potential clients with confidence in my abilities as a PI.

I entered the grocery store, my face bright red, my thighs numb. I slid a gloved hand across my nose, as it and everything else started to defrost. Grabbing a basket, I traipsed over to the interior aisles, ignoring the voice in my head telling me to stick to the outer ones.

I was reading the fine print on a yogurt container when a flash of grey at the end of the aisle caught my eye. A grey coat slid by again while I was in the cereal aisle.

Proceeding to the frozen food section I stood in wait. My brain examined every detail fed to it by my peripheral vision as I stared blindly at the frozen vegetables. The grey coat entered the aisle from my left. I turned, and it did too, disappearing back around the corner.

I rushed down the aisle and rounded the end, but no one was there. I jogged forward, peering down each aisle as I passed.

With a last glance over my shoulder, I turned down the last aisle and fell over someone crouched down by the bottled water. Stumbling forward, I regained my balance and turned, an apology ready on my lips.

"Sorry, miss. Are you all right?" snivelled a thin voice.

An internal groan sounded in my head. I knew that voice. An annoying tone with lisped s's and p's that came out sounding like th's and usually followed by fine droplets of spit. Bernie Ing. He had signed up for my private investigator course and had driven me nuts from the get-go when he introduced himself as "Bern-ing, Bern-ing ball of love." I fought the urge to keep my head down and run. Except he'd know I recognized him. I shuddered and turned.

"Bernie. Right?"

"Well, I'll be…if it isn't the inconceivably prodigious Ms. K."

"Sorry. I didn't see you there," I muttered as my eyes swept the length of the aisle. A frazzled woman with one kid in her shopping cart and a second one making loud demands at her side pulled cans of something into her cart. I looked back at Bernie.

"No worries, Ms. K." He leaned in dangerously close. "You shadowing someone?"

"No, Bernie. Just picking up some items for dinner."

"Oh, me too, me too," he said, scrunching his face into a sly smile. He licked his thick lips and winked.

"Well, I gotta run. Nice seeing you, Bernie," I said as flatly as I could muster.

"Okie dokie. Nice bumping into you too, Ms. K. Get it?" He snorted. "Bumping into you?"

"I get it, Bernie."

I watched him wobble away. Bernie wasn't going to be a good private investigator. He was in love with the idea of becoming an investigator. I felt bad about introducing the profession to him. Of course, there was still hope; maybe he'd fail the private investigator's exam.

On my way to checkout, I added a quart of ice cream and a bag of Oreos. I paid for my groceries and headed outside. Facing into the wind, I lowered my chin into my coat collar and didn't even bother to check if anyone was following me.

My mind went back to Stephen Bradford. Were the patents the reason he had updated his will, as Laura had suggested? Maybe it was just a coincidence that he died three months later. Stephen also sold Conner his eighty-thousand-dollar car. For ten dollars. Who does that?

The cold no longer registered as my mind whirled through the possibilities. The car had to be payment for something. Maybe it was payment for that ridiculously entertaining story Conner had told him about his time in Burundi. Or maybe Stephen had some reason to think he wasn't going to need it much longer.

CHAPTER TWELVE

THE NEXT MORNING, I was up at the crack of dawn. If Conner got Stephen's car, there had to be a transfer of car registration. Too bad I didn't know anyone at the Alberta Motor Vehicles Registry willing to lose their job by providing me Conner's personal information. I was tempted to call Mike. He'd know someone who'd be willing to do him a favor if asked. But I had to stop calling Mike whenever I needed something.

I poured myself a coffee, left over from last night, nuked it in the microwave and opened my laptop. I searched for Mercedes Benz dealerships near Stephen's residence in hopes that Conner would be keeping the warranty intact on his new expensive car. I knew it was a long shot. In all honesty, Conner sounded like the kind of guy who could easily hoist the car and change the oil himself. Maybe even make his own oil.

The closest dealership was just off Bow Trail on the west side of the downtown core. I phoned and asked for the service department. I told the woman who answered that my husband and I had been left a car by Stephen Wallis, upon his death. I asked her to check when Stephen last had the car in for servicing as we wanted to make sure we kept the warranty up to date. The car had been in for an oil change and winter tires in November. Next, I asked her what address she had on file for us, claiming my husband was supposed to have updated them on the change in ownership, but that he was notoriously forgetful. She asked for my address instead. I gave her a street address in Gab's neck of the woods.

"Sorry. The address I have is in Fairview."

"Oh. We have a rental property in Fairview. Now why would he have given you guys that address? Fairview Crescent?" I hoped she'd play along.

"No. The address we have is on Fairmount Drive."

"That's weird. I have no idea what my husband was thinking. I'm going to have to call back. Wait. What's the phone number he gave you. Maybe he just misspoke."

She read back a phone number which I scribbled down. "Well, the phone number is correct. What the heck? Sorry, I'll get back to you."

As soon as I hung up, I pulled up a satellite photo of Fairview. There were several apartment buildings along Fairmount Drive. Of course, Conner might be living in a house, but I pegged him as a renter. A Mercedes in that neighbourhood wouldn't be that common. I tried the phone number. It was no longer in service. I would take a drive through the neighborhood later. Of course, Conner might have sold the car by now.

I scrolled back through my notes. I hadn't asked Rob if

he knew where I could find Conner. On an off chance he would know, I gave him a call. He wasn't available so I left a message.

Next on my list was the ex-girlfriend. I found Stella Seller right away. She was the CEO of Stellar Realty. I pulled up her bio page on her company's website and stared at her photo. She was an attractive woman, mid-thirties maybe, with long blond hair and eyes so vibrant they jumped off the page. She was no slouch either, having won numerous sales awards, first as an individual and now credited to her company. I called the number listed for her on her webpage.

I introduced myself and the reason for my call, then eased into my questions.

"Rob Bailey told me you used to date Stephen. How did the two of you meet?"

"I met Stephen through Nancy and Rob. I sold Nancy's townhouse after she moved in with Rob. That was about seven, eight years ago. We became friends. One night they invited me over for dinner. Stephen was there. A total setup." She laughed. "Six months later Stephen and I were living together." Her voice was strong, confident, one of those voices that made you believe they were on the verge of having a good laugh.

"How long were you together?"

"Almost three years. We broke up last year, in June."

"Do you mind my asking what caused the breakup?"

"We both worked long hours, but when I'm not working, I want someone to share life with, go out, have fun. Stephen's idea of relaxing was hunkering down to pour through a contract or business plan. At least we parted friends."

As an introvert, I recognized the ill-fated attraction to an extrovert. At first, one hoped the extrovert would balance out the hermit-like life one was living, inject some fun, adventure. But inevitably we needed to balance that with solitude. For extroverts like Stella, downtime meant hosting an intimate dinner at home with a dozen friends. I knew of cases where extroverts and introverts were making it work, but I hadn't figured out how to make it work for me. Guess Stephen and Stella hadn't either.

"It must have been hard to hear about his death."

"It was. I thought I had moved on, but clearly I hadn't."

"You probably knew him better than anyone. What was he like?"

"Stephen was a calm, even-keeled guy. Unflappable, at least on the outside. He wasn't unemotional, just really good at keeping things inside. Maybe too good."

I knew what that was like. "I gather he didn't talk much about feelings or what might be bothering him."

"You got that right. I don't ever recall him initiating any discussion about his feelings, or dreams for his future. He didn't like talking about his past either. Our life and conversations pretty much centered on our day-to-day activities. We both liked movies and the theatre. We had a good group of friends that we talked with about all the regular stuff. You know what was happening in our lives, in the world."

"Did he talk about his business dealings?"

"Not in any detail. I wouldn't have understood half the technical jargon anyhow."

"Did you ever meet his half-sister Chloe?"

"I knew of her, but never met her. I gather she's a bit of a wild child."

"You must be familiar with Stephen's Crescent Heights place."

"I was the one who found it for him. When I met Stephen, he lived in a tiny, refurbished warehouse loft, downtown. Right around that time, I learned about the house on Crescent Heights. The guy who had it built got transferred and never even got a chance to move in. I told Stephen about it." She laughed. "I told him it was time he found a grown-up place. A month later it was his. Great property. Have you seen it?"

"Yes. Stephen's sister gave me a quick tour."

"Is she putting it on the market? I should give her a call."

"I believe she is. Hard to imagine someone got in and out undetected, given the way the house is wired and monitored."

"I had the same reaction. Stephen was religious about arming the system. He even kept the security system on when we were home, just turned off the interior motion sensors so as not to set off the alarm."

"Did he ever give out his security code to anyone? Maybe friends who stayed over, or contractors needing access to the house when he was away?"

"No, certainly not while I was with him. I knew the code of course. I'm sure he changed it after we broke up."

"What about maintenance people, cleaners?"

"No. Stephen didn't let people into the house if no one was home. He did have a cleaning lady, Marianna. She always came when one of us was home."

"Rob said he went running with Stephen the morning of New Year's Eve. Did they run together often?"

Stella laughed. "Stephen ran alone. He'd usually be up by five. He'd meditate, write out his goals for the day, then head to the gym for a workout or maybe go for a run. When he got back, he'd make one of his horrible green protein shakes, then start his workday. I'd join him for a workout on the weekend. Stephen had a membership at Frank's Fitness studio, just down the hill from where we lived. We wouldn't go until around seven. Then we'd pick up bagels and a paper on our way home and relax and read for an hour or so."

"Sounds like you had a routine going."

She laughed. "Stephen definitely had his morning routine down pat. Me, not so much."

"But he must have occasionally gone running with other people?"

"Hmm. I suppose…but I can't recall anyone in particular. He liked to listen to music while he ran."

"I know you said he didn't talk much about his feelings, but did he ever mention a disgruntled employee, or a business acquaintance who was angry or upset?"

"No, I don't recall anything like that."

"Rob told me he was mugged last fall. Did you hear about that?"

"No. That's awful. He never said anything to me. Of course, I didn't see him that often after we broke up."

"When was the last time you saw him?"

"Late November, at the homebuilder's annual awards gala. I know most of the builders and I usually go to their award shows and charity events. Stephen and I weren't dating anyone else, and well, I needed a date. I mean, it's not like we parted on bad terms."

"How did he seem that night?"

"Okay, I guess. Well…ummm, no. This is silly. I can't even believe I'm mentioning this."

I waited, hoping the part of her who wanted to share would win out.

"Something happened on the way to the gala. We were running late. That's why it stuck with me. Stephen saw this derelict waiting at a bus stop and suddenly yells for the cab driver to pull over."

"Derelict?"

"The guy looked totally whacked out. He was pacing back and forth, talking to himself. Anyway, Stephen tells the driver to stop, then jumps out of the cab to talk to him. The guy kept shaking his head and backing away. Then Stephen pulled out his wallet and this guy got furious. The way he came at Stephen, I was sure Stephen was going to get stabbed. I rolled down the window and yelled out that we were late, we had to get going."

I didn't know many down-and-out people who got angry at the sight of a wallet. "Then what happened?"

"Stephen got back into the cab. I'd never seen him that flustered. I asked him what that had all been about, maybe not in quite those words. He said he knew the guy. Someone from his past."

"Did he say anything else?"

"Not really. I was annoyed since we were already late, so I didn't press for details. I may have made some snotty comment about the quality of his friends." She laughed embarrassedly. "Not my finest moment. I do remember what he said though. He said, 'We don't all move past life's hurdles, like we want.'"

"That's all?" I tried not to sound disappointed.

"That's it. We both dropped it. But it wasn't just my annoyance at Stephen for delaying us further that stuck in my mind. I glanced back as we drove away. This guy stood there clenching his fists and flicking his fingers out, like he was ready to kill him. And his face…it was pure hatred. I forgot all about it until a few weeks after Stephen was killed. It's probably silly of me to mention it."

"Not at all. Sometimes things we think are insignificant turn out to be the most significant of all," I replied.

After disconnecting, I sat and stared at my computer screen. I didn't want to read too much into what I just heard. Maybe the guy was one of the street people Stephen knew. He could have been in the throes of a drug-induced rage or in the middle of a psychotic episode. On the other hand, I knew there were people out there hurting, hanging on by a thread, ready and capable of snapping, suddenly killing themselves or others.

My mind flashed back to my father. No. People didn't suddenly snap. There were always signs and warnings. Signs no one paid attention to. Signs captured and stored in one's brain like seeds lying ready beneath the soil until they eventually sprouted into a roaring anger and guilt that grew and grew until it entangled and smothered everything.

CHAPTER THIRTEEN

I TOOK THE long way to Laura's house, but my side trip down Fairmount Drive didn't net me much. There were several apartment buildings along the route but impossible to tell if any of them housed Conner Weston. My conversation with Stephen's ex had given me a lot to mull over. She described an emotionally reserved man who had kept his thoughts private. I wondered how well his friends and family had really known him.

I pulled up to Laura's house just as Tony D'Silva stormed out the front door. Tony crossed the street and climbed into a black Maxima. A second later the engine roared to life. It rocketed off with a throaty rumble, leaving behind a faint smell of exhaust.

I got out, made my way up the walk and climbed the steps to the front door. My hand reached for the doorbell and paused. The door wasn't completely shut.

"Tell me you're not going to do anything stupid." Laura's voice filtered through the crack.

"We should have done something about her years ago.

This is going to cost us. And I mean big time. You know what's at stake," growled a male voice.

"I'll talk to her. Promise me you won't do anything rash."

"I'm not promising anything."

I turned at the approaching footsteps, ran down the steps and turned back as a man pulled open the door. He glared at me. "Who are you and what do you want?"

"Hi. I'm Jorja Knight. I'm here to see Laura."

Laura appeared behind the man. "It's okay, Wayne, she's the private investigator I hired."

Wayne stormed down the stairs and brushed past me. "Fat lot of good it's doing us."

Laura stood in the doorway. A frown creased her face as she watched Wayne's retreating back.

"Is this a bad time? I can come back."

"No," she said as she turned. "This is as good a time as any. Want coffee? It's fresh."

"I'd love a cup. I saw Tony leaving as I pulled up. What's got him in a knot?"

"What else? Chloe. She has a way of getting into everybody's business." I followed Laura back to the kitchen.

"What's Chloe got to do with Tony?"

"She's been threatening to contest the will. I assumed she was bluffing. Tony called this morning and said she's filed with the courts. It's going to slow everything up. First, it'll go to mediation. If it doesn't get resolved there, it could go before a judge." Laura brought over two mugs of coffee and placed one on the island in front of me, waving at me to sit.

"I know wills can be challenged if one of the parties

believes the property has been unfairly distributed," I said. "But the courts don't take these things lightly. You need to have something solid to make your case, not just say you don't like how the estate is being distributed," I said.

Laura nodded, a frown between her eyes. "That's what Tony said too. He doesn't think she stands a chance, especially with her history. Whatever money she gets goes to feed her self-destructive habits."

"It was decent of Stephen to leave her money in a trust fund."

"You're right about that. He didn't have to leave her anything. I knew she'd cause trouble. Chloe had a complete meltdown when the will was read. She kept screeching that it wasn't fair, that she deserved more than some homeless bums in a shelter. The ungrateful little... Can you believe it?"

"So why is Tony so upset?"

"It's the patent assignment. I don't pretend to understand it all. But there's some Nano cell thing that Stephen left Tony. I guess you have to file somewhere to have the patent ownership registered and then transferred. Tony said his lawyer already did that. But now that Chloe's challenging the will, the patent office can't reassign the patent to Tony until the issue is resolved."

"He seemed pretty upset."

"He said Stephen had been negotiating with someone to buy it. But there's a deadline, so if Tony can't deliver, the deal will fall through."

"That puts an interesting spin on it," I said. "Do you know who the potential buyer is?"

"Tony didn't say."

"What about you and your family? Your husband seemed upset. Will Chloe challenging the will affect you guys?"

"Not really. I mean, of course we have bills like everyone else. I just can't believe she's haggling over Stephen's will while his killer runs free. Wayne's had it. He wants her out of our life. Didn't I tell you? Whenever Chloe shows up, trouble follows."

"Can you settle with her out of court?"

"That's what Tony wants us to do. But Wayne was off work most of last year. We had to take out a loan and we still have a large mortgage on the house. We don't exactly have a bunch of money lying around."

I nodded. "I hope it gets settled soon. It's a lot of added stress for everyone."

Laura hugged herself. "I give up. I hope she realizes what she's doing."

"Anything else new?"

Laura shook her head. "No. I've listed Stephen's house. Now I'm worried that the sale will be held up too."

"I hope not. By the way, when I talked with Rob Bailey, he mentioned Stephen was mugged last summer. In August, I believe. Do you know anything about that?"

"Mugged?" Her eyes grew big, her mouth remained open.

"Apparently the guy tackled him to the ground, took his watch and wallet. Luckily, nothing more."

"My god. No, he never said anything to me." She clutched her fist to her chest.

"It might be why he hired Conner. You said Stephen

told you Conner provided a disarming presence. He hired Conner only a few weeks after the attack."

"I never knew," Laura cried. "I feel so awful. I wish he would have told me."

"I'm sure he didn't want to worry you. I still haven't located Conner or talked to him. You have any ideas on how I can reach him?"

"No. I bet Chloe knows, but good luck getting her to tell you."

"Yeah. Well, I'd better get going. Thanks for the coffee."

On my way out, I noticed several pieces of mail lying on the hall table, addressed to Wayne, all marked urgent. They were from a law firm, but not the one handling Stephen's estate. Looked like the Bradfords were steeped in legalities of one form or another.

As I drove away, I couldn't help thinking there was more than money behind Chloe's move in challenging the will. I remembered her twisted face and the look in her eyes as she left my office. Chloe was shrewd and conniving, way too clever for her own good. It wouldn't surprise me if Chloe was throwing a monkey wrench into the works to retaliate for the contemptuous way she perceived the Bradford-Wallis family had treated her. I couldn't help but wonder what Laura meant by her urgent plea to Wayne, to not do anything rash.

CHAPTER FOURTEEN

TINY PELLETS OF snow bounced off my windshield as I drove. Even though I now had some food in the house, I had no desire to make dinner. I checked my rear-view mirror for the tenth time. Perhaps I was being overly paranoid. The anonymous messages about my parents' deaths had left me unsettled. Seeing someone getting off the bus who resembled my father hadn't helped either. Each time it happened it made me consider the possibility that he'd set it up to look like he died in the explosion. The police believed he committed suicide by blowing up the garage and himself after shooting my mother. But DNA wasn't routinely collected back then, and there had barely been enough of him left to cremate.

I swung into the mall, parked, and ran into a fast-food place. The driver's side window didn't roll down on the Chevy I was leasing, making stops for fast food slightly inconvenient. I returned with two burgers, fries, and a milkshake. I could hardly wait to get home, lock myself in, and crash on the couch.

My phone rang as I struggled to unlock my door. I set my purse and bag down and extracted my phone. There was no caller ID on the screen, just a number. I hesitated then tapped the accept icon.

"Jorja Knight?" snarled a man's voice.

"Yes."

"It's Conner Weston. I hear you're looking for me."

"Yes, I am. I'm looking into the death—"

"Meet me at the bar, downtown Ramada, seven-thirty," he said.

I stared at my phone. The screen was already black.

*

The lounge at the Ramada provided a welcome change from the storm raging outside. A long mahogany bar bisected the room. A dozen or more small tables were tucked along the walls on both sides of the room. The place was deserted. A lone man sat at one end of the bar. He looked like I imagined Conner would look. Big, maybe six-two, thick neck, shoulders straining his jacket as he sat hunched over, hands curled around a drink, the glass barely visible. If he needed money, he could always get a job making horseshoes with his bare hands. He turned his head as I approached.

"You Jorja?" he asked.

"Yes," I said, holding out my hand.

He slid off the barstool, hesitated a second, then wiped his hand down the front of his shirt and gripped my hand without saying a word.

Stepping back to the bar, Conner picked up his drink

and ambled over to a small table against the wall. I followed. A minute later the bartender came over.

"Can I get you anything, miss?"

"Single malt scotch, if you have it."

"Sure thing," he replied and went off to get my drink.

I slid off my car coat, the outer layer damp from the snow. Conner made no attempt to hide the fact he was ogling me. I resisted the urge to check my shirt to make sure it wasn't gaping open. "Not what you expected?" I asked.

A guttural snarl escaped his lips, but the bartender arrived with my drink, interrupting what I was sure would be a lewd comment. As soon as the bartender retreated, Conner leaned forward.

"You've been looking for me, so here I am, doll. What do you want?"

"I've been hired by the Bradford family to look into Stephen Wallis' death. I'd like to ask you some questions about your relationship with Mr. Wallis."

His fingers loosened their death grip on the drink in front of him; he moved back an inch and his shoulders dropped a smidge.

"What do you want to know?" A small smirk appeared on his lips.

"Why did Stephen hire you?"

"He needed a driver."

"Laura Bradford tells me you used to date Stephen's half-sister, Chloe. She said you and Stephen didn't exactly get along."

Conner leaned even further back in his chair. "Things change. Maybe I didn't read him right the first time. Maybe he didn't read me right. Stephen was an okay guy."

"You're the one that raised the alarm the day he was found dead."

"That's right. I went to pick him up, but he didn't answer the door. I called his cell a bunch of times. When he didn't answer, I knew something was wrong."

"You began working for him when, September?"

"That's right."

"How did you hear about the job?"

"I didn't." Conner picked up his drink, drained it, and signalled the bartender for another.

"He contacted you?"

"What if he did?" Conner sat back, smugly.

"What else did you do for him, besides drive?"

He shrugged. "Run stuff out to the lab for him, pick up food if he was running late." He gave me a lopsided grin.

"Did you ever get the sense that he was worried about anything?"

"He was always worried about something. Meetings cancelled, delayed flights, so what?"

"Maybe worried is the wrong word. Did he ever seem overly nervous or afraid?"

"If he was, he never let on."

"Did anything ever happen that struck you as odd or peculiar?"

Conner's face twisted into a smirk. "You mean did I notice the guys in black suits following him, or those midnight visits with that hot dame? The one dripping with diamonds her old man bought her?"

I switched topics. "Did Stephen know you and Chloe were seeing each other again?"

Conner's face darkened; his eyebrows furrowed together. "That's bullshit. Whoever said that is lying."

"You and Chloe didn't meet for drinks after she got back from Palm Springs?"

"Nope." He smirked. "Guess the old guy in California didn't pan out."

"Okay. Did you ever see Chloe meeting with Stephen during the time you worked for him?"

"Nope."

"Have you seen her since she got back?"

"Yeah, at the funeral."

"I hear Stephen sold you his Mercedes for ten dollars. That's a hell of a gift, wouldn't you say?"

He shrugged, a smart-alecky grin spreading across his face. "I'm a likeable guy."

"Who was he meeting with, the morning you went to pick him up and found him dead?"

He eyed me warily, his smile faded, his shoulders tensed. "What does it matter?"

"Someone went to great pains to plan and kill Stephen. It has to be someone he knew, a business partner he burnt, a competitor who wanted him out of the way."

He leaned forward, his forearms on the table, his drink glass all but invisible in his cupped hands. "Wanna know what I think?"

"Yes, I do."

"I think you're one foxy lady. I bet you've got a sexy little pistol in one of them little holsters strapped on under there." He nodded at my chest. A leer split his meaty face. "How about I show you where I keep my pistol?"

If he weren't so disgusting, I would have laughed. I could hardly wait to share his come-on line with Gab.

"From what I hear, there's not much to see." I stood up, noticing the light had gone out of his eyes, and picked up my coat. "Thanks for the drink, Mr. Weston." I turned and strode out of the bar.

CHAPTER FIFTEEN

MY MEETING WITH Conner had killed my appetite, but my growling stomach reminded me that the milkshake I drank on my way to meet him, wasn't a meal. The burgers were now cold, the buns wrinkled and soggy. I microwaved the fries and wandered over to the living room window, leaned against the frame, and ate fries while the snow swirled outside.

The wind rattled the windows and the metal railing on my small balcony, sending a small plant pot sliding across the concrete until it lodged against the railing. The temperature was dropping like a stone and the snow no longer melted but blew across the frozen ground like wisps of smoke.

I had made it home in record time from the Ramada, the streets already deserted. Conner was a disarming presence. He was also every bit the pig Laura Bradford had portrayed him to be. He had looked visibly relieved when I asked him about Stephen and not about whatever else he was trying to hide. The meeting left me certain of one thing. Stephen hadn't hired him for his charm and eagerness to please.

I turned and surveyed the room. My eyes fell on my vision board, hanging on the hallway wall. The board was covered in photos, houses with floor-to-ceiling windows, infinity pools, lush gardens, and stunning landscapes where it clearly didn't snow. A picture of a red Ferrari 599 GTB Fiorano and a fluffy grey kitten anchored the right side. Smack in the middle I had pinned a picture of a woman, cut out of some magazine. She was perched on a stool, her smooth-fitting skinny jeans ending an inch or two above tan, open-toed booties. One heel was casually hooked over the bottom rung of the stool. There was an air of strength about her. And something mysterious, sexy. Like if I knew her story I'd be blown away by her accomplishments or the hardships she'd weathered.

The picture of the large glass-fronted house pinned there, reminded me of Stephen's house. Laura was right. Without friends and family to fill it, a house like that might make one feel lonely. A familiar hollow feeling started to build inside.

I put the now empty container into the garbage, schlepped into the bedroom and changed into an old Grateful Dead T-shirt and black waffle-weave capri pyjama bottoms. I returned to the couch with the bag of Oreos and surfed the internet, keeping one eye on an episode of the Game of Thrones I'd already seen. My phone buzzed, Azagora's name on the screen.

"I hear you're working one of our files," a strong voice announced.

"Good lord! You'd think living in city with a million and a half or so inhabitants would provide me a semblance of anonymity. Suddenly I'm on everybody's radar. I can't make a move without a dozen people knowing about it." I was still puzzled as to how Conner knew I had been looking for him but pleased to have Azagora interrupt my solitude.

"You're always on my radar," he said.

My face got warm, and shivers ran down my spine. "If you were some normal, ordinary guy I knew, I'd take that as a come-on. But I suspect you're phoning to check up on me. To make sure I'm not going to cause you any grief." I knew he wouldn't be pleased about me taking the Wallis case. Both of us wanted to keep our private and work life separate, him more so than me. Which meant Azagora preferred I chase down deadbeat dads skipping out on child support and leave the murders to him. I'd prefer he become a traffic cop.

"I'm normal."

"No," I laughed. "No, you're not. Actually," my voice softened, "there's nothing normal about you."

I waited while silence filled my ear. The image of his fit, six-foot-two frame formed in my mind's eye. His smouldering dark-brown eyes, the straight nose and firm jaw. I tried to imagine what was happening on the other end. Was his head bent, a half smile on his lips. Was his hand running over his closely shorn hair, in that way it did when he was either totally frustrated or overcome with some other emotion. Was he grinning like a schoolboy and pacing, trying to come back with something profound?

"What's your schedule like? Can we set up a meeting for tomorrow?"

"A meeting? You're at work," I accused. "What's wrong? Don't you want the guys and gals in the office to know you're hot for me? Or maybe we should go back to being strictly professional."

"No."

"No what, Inspector?" I'd give up a week of coffee to see him right now, see the small crack in his usually firm, tough demeanour. I grew weak thinking about how his eyes turned black whenever we flirted.

"Would later in the day work? Say eight?"

"I can't wait." I breathed into the phone. "Is there, ummm…anything special you want me to wear?"

Someone yelled out in the background. "Let's go, Bobbie's here."

"I'll send you the details."

I hung up laughing. I did want to see him, although I was sure tomorrow's so-called meeting was going to conveniently kill two birds with one stone. We clearly had some insane chemistry between us. But before this went any further, I needed to figure out what I wanted from him. Was it only sex? *Only sex?* Who was I kidding? But if more—what? I knew I would always take second place to his job. On the other hand, being second had its merits. I had never been number one in anyone's life. It might suck. I'd have to reciprocate, act grateful or at least appreciative. Or be labelled a bitch. Sounded like a lot of pressure I didn't need.

I turned off my laptop and the TV. I was steps from the bedroom door when I heard a knock. I checked my watch. It was already after eleven. I waited, listening. Nothing. No one had rung from the lobby. Then again it could be one of my neighbours. I crept to the door and peered through the peephole. The hallway walls bowed outward, the distorted strip of blue carpet devoid of life. Leaving the safety chain in place, I unlocked the door and peeked out. Nothing. I stepped back, and something caught my eye.

A green cone stood waiting, its top folded over and stapled down along with a small card and gold and green ribbons. Maybe Azagora sent flowers and called to see if I received them. I slid the chain off its latch, opened the door and picked up the bundle. I secured the door locks, carried the package over to the kitchen and set it on the counter. Why hadn't the delivery company buzzed me from downstairs? Besides, who delivers flowers this time of night.

I dismissed the idea they were from Azagora and gingerly pulled apart the green paper sleeve. My heart skipped a beat then thundered against my chest. A half-dozen dahlias greeted me. The dahlia's normally dark-burgundy petals and distinctively recognizable globe-shaped flowers were tinted black. Carefully lifting the vase from its cardboard base, I checked for a card. Finding none, I turned, heart pounding, to the paper wrapping lying at my feet. I picked up the wrapping, found a card stapled to it and flipped it over.

"Jeez." I flicked my hand, dropping the paper to the floor. The back of the card read, Watching Over U.

"No, damn it," I hissed through clenched teeth. My initial fear now swept aside by hot anger. Racing to the balcony door, I yanked it open and ran to the railing. Clutching the rail with one hand and holding back wind-whipped hair with the other, I scanned the street below. Nothing out of the ordinary. I peered across the trafficless street to the other side. Snow swirled in every direction. It took me a minute to spot him. Dark grey coat, hood pulled well over the head, just standing, pressed up against the spruce trees.

I leapt back over the doorsill and ran to the front closet. My hand scraped along the upper shelf until my fingers touched the smooth leather case. The binoculars where already out by the time I jumped back over the door ledge to the balcony. I raised them to my eyes, fingers frantically spinning the dial to bring the lenses into focus. Suddenly, the shapeless blob below turned and disappeared through the trees, releasing a cascade of snow, which drifted from the branches to the ground like a gauzy veil.

"Freakin' bastard," I uttered as I climbed over the sill and pulled the door shut, my bare feet like ice. Still shaking, I marched over to the kitchen counter, grabbed the flowers, and stuffed the vase back in its paper-padded box. I picked up the wrapping paper, jamming it down, crushing the flowers. I unlocked the door and stomped out into the hallway and deposited the whole thing down the garbage chute.

I turned back down the hall to my condo and quickened my pace. The hair on the back of my neck bristled and goosebumps erupted on my arms. I looked back over my shoulder. The creep knew where I lived.

CHAPTER SIXTEEN

THIS MORNING I was antsy, restless. I hadn't wasted any time getting out of the condo this morning. I had slept badly, waking at every noise, last night's flower delivery from some wacko still fresh in my mind. After my parents' death, it had taken me years to give up the notion that I was helpless, weak, ineffective. I swore I'd never feel like that again. *I'm in control of my feelings. I can choose how I feel.* The rhetoric flooding my brain was delivered in my therapist's voice, a thin, birdlike woman, big on platitudes and short on empathy. I pushed her voice aside. I needed to stop wasting time focusing on why someone was doing this and start figuring out who was doing it.

I pulled into the Vista Greens nursing home parking lot and got out of my car. Antonia Williams was waiting at the entrance. She looked just like her photos on Facebook, not the one of her riding a pony, later ones. I figured she was in her late forties, but up close she looked older. Maybe it was the style of her once-dark brown hair, now tinged grey and permed into a short, unflattering cap of tight curls. She wore pale pink nurse's scrubs, which surprised me but shouldn't have. Despite the name, Vista Greens wasn't a golf resort.

"Thanks for meeting me," I said once we introduced ourselves. I followed her to a small sitting area just off the entry. Several residents lounged in the room. A flat screen TV mounted on the wall was tuned to some talk show, the volume muted so low even I couldn't hear. The whole place had the charm of a doctor's waiting room. The seating was restricted to hard, wooden-armed chairs, but they were likely more practical for getting in and out of than soft cushy ones, if one was ninety years old. Antonia and I sat at a small round table.

"You don't mind if I eat?" Antonia asked as she pulled out several Tupperware containers from her bag.

"No, not at all. Please," I said. "I appreciate you giving up precious lunch time to speak with me."

She nodded and pried open a container of stew. "Would you like a tea or coffee? I could get you one."

"Thank you, but I'm fine. Please go ahead," I said, nodding at her container. "As I mentioned on the phone, the Bradfords hired me to look into Stephen Wallis' death."

"Tragic, it was. I first read about it in the paper. Seems like every day there's another murder. I guess it's what we can expect now that we're a big city." She clucked, shaking her head.

"Did you know Stephen Wallis or the Bradford family?"

"No, not at all. I don't recall ever hearing my brother mention his name. When the estate lawyer called me up, I was completely taken aback. I had no idea anybody would be leaving Joey money."

"Joey? Your brother's name is Joey? Not Henry?"

"My parents named him Giuseppe Enrico Albero. Giuseppe is Joseph in Italian and Enrico is Henry. But he hated both, so we always called him Joey."

"Yet he changed it to Henry, not Joey? And anglicized his last name to Albern?"

"Yes," Antonia sighed.

"When did he change it? And why?"

"He changed it about two years ago. We still call him Joey though. He only uses Henry Albern professionally."

"Professionally?"

"I know. It's crazy. What professionally? He doesn't work, or even have a permanent residence." Antonia shook her head. "My mother wasn't happy about it. She passed last summer."

"I'm sorry to hear that."

Antonia glanced around the room. "I miss her. It's selfish, I know. I see how some of these poor folks linger when they'd rather be gone. My mother would have hated that. She was in good shape for her age, then had a massive stroke. She was gone in five days. Never regained consciousness. That's the only thing I regret. It would have been nice to say goodbye."

I nodded. "Why didn't Stephen leave the money directly to your brother. Is he incapacitated in some way?"

She scraped the last bite out of her container, put it in her mouth, and chewed thoughtfully.

"No," she said. "As strange as my brother might be, I believe it's a lifestyle choice not some other issue. I imagine the trust was set up because Joey's not easy to find. He lives off the grid."

"Off the grid?"

"He lives off the land."

"What land? You mean out in the wilderness somewhere?"

"Yes."

"So, he's homeless?"

"What do you know," she exclaimed, sitting back in her chair. "I suppose in a way he is homeless."

"Does he have an addiction or some reason he doesn't work?"

"We all have our little addictions. But not like you think. Joey is a bright guy. He was so smart in school. Went to university at age sixteen."

"So how did he end up homeless, living in the woods?"

"It happened slowly, you know, over time."

"After university?"

"Sort of. He dropped out in third year. I don't know why."

"You never asked?"

"I did once. He said a university degree was just a piece of paper that told people you did your time. It had nothing to do with how smart you were or how successful you could be. I suppose in one way he's right."

"What university did Joey attend?"

"The University of Calgary."

"Do you remember when?"

"I'm not sure of the dates, early nineties. Maybe ninety-two to ninety-five?"

"And his full name used to be Giuseppe Enrico Albero?"

"Yes. I don't care what he changes it to, the kids and I still call him Joey."

"What was he studying?"

"A bit of everything—computer science, math, engineering. I don't remember if he ever declared a major."

"Is that how Stephen knew him? From university?"

"The lawyer didn't say. He just said Stephen was an old friend."

"What did Joey do after leaving university?"

"He had all kinds of jobs. Most of them with small companies. Start-ups, I think he called them. You know, a couple of guys in someone's garage or a warehouse somewhere."

"Do you know what he was working on?"

"Computer stuff. He was big into computer games at one point."

"Then what happened?"

"Mom and I didn't see much of him for a while. You know how it is when you're in your twenties. Then in his early thirties, he got into this whole green movement. Joined an activist group in British Columbia. He would occasionally show up for a visit. He grew this big Grizzly Adams beard and carried all his possessions in a backpack."

"Do you remember what this group was called?"

"No. I do remember him telling us about how they chained themselves to some old trees to save them from being cut down. Or maybe it was because endangered birds lived in them."

"Is that where he is? In BC?"

"Yes. But he's no longer with the activists."

"Do you know where he is or what he's doing now?"

"Not really." She gave a little embarrassed laugh. She

pried open her second Tupperware container and held it out it me. "Date square? I made them myself."

"No thanks. I had a late breakfast." I was still feeling guilty about the dozen or so Oreos I consumed last night.

"How does your brother feel about the two hundred grand Stephen left him?"

"He doesn't know. Well, he might know by now, but I have no way of knowing."

"Sorry, I'm not following."

"Joey isn't big on possessions. He says most people believe they own their possessions, but their possessions end up owning them. Lately, it's just him and the land. No cell phone, no credit cards, no bank account, no vehicle, no address. At least, as far as I know."

"Are you saying he doesn't know Stephen left him money?"

Antonia shifted in her seat and shook her head in exasperation. "Joey showed up a couple of months after Mom died. I didn't know where he was, so I couldn't even let him know she had passed. I was so mad at him. I told him it was unfair that he traipsed around free while I had to look after Mom and everything all by myself. What if something happened to me, or my kids? I told him he'd better figure out a way for me to get a hold of him in an emergency. I've never asked him for anything, and I'm fed up with making excuses for him. First to my mother and then my kids, our relatives, my friends. If he can't be bothered to stay in touch, why should I?"

"So, you know how to reach him?"

"Sort of. He gave me a map. A sketch, really. It shows directions to an abandoned hunter's cabin, near Sparwood."

"That's where he's staying?"

"He lives out in the woods, hunting, fishing. He uses the cabin only when necessary. After the lawyer contacted me, I wrote Joey a letter. I let him know what I knew about Stephen Wallis' death and that he left him money in a trust. That I was named the executor of the trust. I imagine because no one knows where he is and, besides, he doesn't believe in banks. I also attached a newspaper article about Stephen's death. Three weeks ago, I drove down there."

"By yourself?"

"My husband refused to go. He thought I was insane. He said it could wait till Joey showed up again." Antonia reached down and whipped out a tissue from her purse and dabbed at her eyes, then continued. "This is what I mean. This is what he doesn't get. I care about him." She sniffled. "I can't just turn it off, like he can."

"You left the letter at the cabin?"

She nodded miserably. "I almost didn't. I had to leave my car on the road and walk in a long way. It's scary out there."

"Any signs of him at the cabin?"

"There was some wood chopped. There's just one room. It had a small wood-burning stove and a bed in one corner with some blankets and there were some boxes and stuff underneath. I didn't notice any footprints or anything."

"The cabin was unlocked?"

"No, the key is kept under the front steps when not in use."

"So, you left the letter and drove back?"

"Yes."

"He hasn't been in touch?"

"No. I don't know if he's even seen the letter."

"Are you aware that one of the beneficiaries has challenged the will?"

"The lawyer called and told me. He doesn't think it will come to anything, but he needed me to know as executor of Joey's trust. That's the other thing, what am I supposed to do with this money? Joey won't want it."

"You never know. Two hundred grand is a fair chunk of change. Maybe he'll be happy to settle down somewhere, rent a small apartment."

"I'm not so sure. Lately he's been talking about this David Meade guy. Do you know about him?"

"No."

"I'm not sure that's his real name. This guy has a theory about how the world is going to end. Some kind of collision between earth and an object from space."

"Really? Are you telling me your brother is a doomsayer, a world fatalist?"

Antonia nodded.

"Is that why he lives like he does? Because he believes the world is about to end?"

"That's partially it. It's easier for him to believe that our destinies are determined by someone or something greater than us. That we really can't change the course of events in our lives."

Bells went off in my head. "That's a pretty dramatic turnaround for him isn't it? I mean he's bright, smart, he's working in the computer industry and now…seems like he's given up."

"I guess in a way he has. But like I said, its been a long slow progression." Antonia stared down at her hands.

I waited, hoping for more. Finally, she looked up. "I don't know what happened to Joey, but something must have. I've tried asking him a few times, but he just gets mad. Tells, me I should stop trying to find reasons for why he's living his life the way he is and just accept it."

"I appreciate you sharing that with me." I was having a hard time myself, understanding the change. "Well, if he shows up one of these days, I'd like to talk to him."

I thanked Antonia, left her my business card, and walked back to my car, mulling over what I heard. I found the whole situation odd but appreciated hearing her take on things. Despite Antonia's claims that Joey's lifestyle was simply a choice, I suspected there might be more of a reason.

Could Stephen and Joey have a shared history? Like from one of the start-ups Antonia mentioned? Why hadn't Tony or Rob mentioned him? On the other hand, if they hadn't been in contact with him for some time, they may have simply accepted the fact that he was no longer part of their life.

Antonia said Joey had always hated his name. Why wait decades to change it? Why at all if he was convinced the world's about to end. An idea popped into my head. Could Joey be the guy Stella saw Stephen with on the way to the builders' gala last fall? Stella said the guy was angry. Angry enough to attack Stephen. Maybe the money Stephen left Joey wasn't an act of kindness.

CHAPTER SEVENTEEN

SOMETHING HAD BEEN niggling at me since my conversation with Antonia and now it came to me in a flash. I pulled up the U of C soccer team photo I had found a few days earlier. There he was, on the left, Tony's arm slung casually over his shoulder. G. Albero, or Joey, as he was called. Joey and Tony were identical in height, but Antonia mentioned Joey had gone to university at age sixteen, so he might have added a few inches to his height since the picture was taken. He wasn't quite as wiry as Tony, but lean, with dark-brown hair and eyes. The two could have been brothers. Now that I knew the connection, I was anxious to talk to Tony. Stephen must have been in contact with Joey fairly recently. Recently enough to know he had changed his name to Henry Albern. I called Tony's number. His assistant said Tony was in a meeting, he'd call when he was out.

I dug deeper. I found Joey's and Tony's names on an old under-eighteen soccer league roster but little else. I was packing up for the day when my phone rang.

"Jorja. Tony D'Silva, here. Sharon said you left a message to call."

"Thanks for calling back. I'm trying to track down Henry Albern, but you might know him as Giuseppe or Joey Albero."

"Whoa. There's a blast from the past. What do you want with him?"

"Stephen left him some money in his will."

"He did? Aww damn," he yelped.

"Are you okay?"

"Damn. Sorry. I'm fine. This shirt is going to have to go to the cleaner's though. Damn, that coffee's hot."

"You and Stephen knew Joey. Played soccer together, right?"

"That's right."

"What else can you tell me about him? What about his relationship with Stephen?"

"Not much to tell. He was a good soccer player but a bit off the wall. Eccentric, or that's what they'd call him if he were rich. Then again, most brilliant people are."

"Eccentric? How so?"

"He wore a bow tie to school, wouldn't eat anything that was white, and insisted on speaking the Queen's English. Sometimes with a fake British accent. He didn't much care what other people thought. If you could get him to talk, usually after a few beers, he'd try to engage you in these mind-numbing discussions about consciousness or declare nothing and nowhere were meaningless spatial concepts because everything was right here."

"His sister said he dropped out of university. Do you know why?"

"He was just marking time there. He knew more than most of the profs. I figured he was eager to get on with life."

"What happened to him?"

"I'm not sure. I got the impression he and a couple of guys were building some sort of computer-based member community. Keep in mind this was before the internet became mainstream. After that I heard he got into games. Online gaming was the up-and-coming big thing, back then."

"Did Stephen ever work with him, or back one of his enterprises?"

"I don't believe so. He never mentioned it."

"What about you? You stay in touch?"

"Naw. I last saw him about five or six years ago. Ran into him on Stephen Avenue Mall. I walked right past him before realizing it was him. He looked like son of sasquatch. We chatted a bit. Said he had been in BC when I asked him what he was up to. Saving tree owls or some damn thing."

"What about Stephen? Did he stay in touch with him?"

"Hard to stay in touch with someone who opts out of society."

"He must have run into him at some point. I mean, he knew he had changed his name to Henry Albern. His sister says he only did that recently."

"Wait a minute. That's right. Stephen did run into him a while back. Said he seemed more put together with his beard trimmed and hair pulled back."

"When was that?"

"Maybe a year and a half or two years ago."

"Here in Calgary?"

"Yeah. I got the impression Joey was just walking by or something. I don't recall Stephen saying anything about him changing his name, or if he did, I forgot."

"Did Stephen say what he was up to?"

"He said Joey was vague. Sounded like he broke with the activists and was living off the grid, for some damn reason."

"Any idea why Stephen left him money?"

"Maybe he felt sorry for the guy. I don't know."

"Do you think Joey would ever restart tinkering with technology?"

Tony laughed. "I doubt it. Pretty hard to do that living off the grid. You haven't talked to Joey yet?"

"No. His sister hasn't been able to contact him. He might not even know Stephen left him some money."

I was met with silence on the other end.

"Makes me curious as to what happened to get him to change course like he did. You wouldn't know, would you?"

"Your guess is as good as mine."

"Laura mentioned Chloe is challenging the will. Is that going to impact you much?"

"I hope not."

"What about the patent reassignment, mentioned in the will? The Nano-skin fuel cell."

Wariness crept into his voice. "I already hold a ten-percent interest in it. It's just a matter of getting Stephen's sixty percent interest reassigned to me. Chloe doesn't stand a chance. Two hundred grand is nothing to sneeze at, especially for someone who wasn't in his life all that much. It's not like she's Stephen's daughter, or wife."

"What's this Nano-skin fuel cell do?"

"It's going to solve the main issue we have with all the new technology being developed—fuelling it. Companies have been trying to improve battery life in smart phones, electrical cars, everything, really, for years. Now there's even smaller and more powerful technology being developed. Like medical equipment, robots, miniature cameras. Companies are researching how to use nanotechnology to improve fuel cells, make them smaller, more powerful, not to mention green, safe, economical."

"Wow. And what's that worth if you don't mind my asking."

"It's hard to tell."

"Let's assume it's successful. What's your guess?"

"Let's just say there's a lot of zeros in that number."

"More than six?" I asked.

"Possibly," he replied. "Anything else I can help you with today?"

"One last question. What were Stephen's vices? I refuse to believe he was a saint. After all, he was human."

Tony laughed. "No, he wasn't a saint. Darn close though. Vices? He didn't gamble or womanize if that's what you mean," he said, laughing.

"But everybody's got a thing. The one behaviour that shows up in everything they do. The guiding force in their life that's both a blessing and a curse."

Tony took a moment before answering. "If I had to pick something, I'd say Stephen felt like he had to fix everything. Could be a control thing, or the need to feel needed. I don't know what the motivator was. Maybe it's why he was always helping people out, taking in stray dogs, or trying to reha-bilitate addicts."

After we hung up, I sat back and rehashed the conversation in my mind. Tony made it sound like he wasn't that concerned about patent transfer delays resulting from Chloe challenging the will. That didn't mesh with the level of frustration he exhibited when leaving Laura's place. Unless that was about something else.

His comment about Stephen wanting to fix things or feel needed made sense. It may have even stemmed from his parents' divorce. We often don't realize what family trauma does until years later. Maybe it's why he kept giving Chloe a chance or why he hired Conner.

Maybe I was making too much of this and Stephen left Joey some money because he knew he could use it. But what if it was something else? I couldn't let go of the idea that Joey might be the derelict Stella saw Stephen arguing with. What if it had something to do with one of the earlier start-ups? What if he was trying to fix or set something straight with Joey?

CHAPTER EIGHTEEN

ESCOBA'S WASN'T BUSY when I got there. Luis had made reservations, but I arrived first. The waitress led me to a small table by the window, overlooking Eighth Avenue. I slipped my coat off and shivered, the cold from the window immediately cutting through my thin sweater. It wasn't much of a sweater. A loose, black crocheted top, draped over a silver gauzy fabric underneath, sliding off one shoulder. Shorter in front, longer in back, I knew it looked good with my skinny jeans, which were tucked into knee-high black boots.

It was dark outside, and the street was quiet, most people opting to stay indoors. The snow had stopped, at least temporarily, but a cold front had moved in right behind it. Rubbing my arms, I suddenly felt exposed, sitting in the backlight of the restaurant, made more obvious by the blackness outside. I stood and reached up to pull a set of wooden shutters across the window. The waitress rushed over to give me a hand.

"A little cold, isn't it? Would you prefer a different table?" she asked.

"I'm sure this will be fine, with the shutters closed."

We just finished sliding shut the last shutter when Luis walked in. His coat already unbuttoned, he reached over, pulled me to him and kissed my cheek. The contrast of his warm body to the cold layer of air around me made me want to snuggle deeper into the folds of his coat. He moved his hand from my back and over to my side, slipping his hand under my top. I felt his cold fingers on my skin, moving upward, until he discovered I wasn't wearing a bra.

"Jorja. You make me crazy," he said, stepping back, his eyes dark pools. He hung his coat on the hooks anchored along the wall and sat down.

"Why, what ever do you mean, Inspector," I said, batting my long, thick lashes at him. I don't know why nature had blessed me with such awesome eyelashes, maybe to make up for the small space between my top front teeth.

He sat down, reached under the table and squeezed my knee.

The waitress came by and we ordered our food and wine. After she left, he reached over and took my hand in both of his. "I've had you on my mind all day."

"Didn't that mess with your concentration?"

"Maybe I should arrest you for interfering with police business." His dark eyes met mine. The cop eyes were gone. I groaned internally.

"Hmmm. Did you bring your handcuffs?" I really did need to figure out where we were going with this before things took a course of their own. Like they usually did. Which never worked out. Which is why I really needed to figure out what I wanted from this relationship.

Our appetizers and wine came, and we chatted away. By the time our entrees arrived, Luis was onto me. "What's going on?"

"Nothing."

"I'm not buying. Tell me. Is it the Wallis case?"

My gaze met his. The cop eyes were back, steady, steely, watching my face, giving away nothing.

"You know," I snapped, "you're killing me. Can't a girl have some secrets?" I had been planning to tell him someone was stalking me, but now I was annoyed.

"I'd prefer my girl not to."

My stomach lurched at *my girl*. Could I really become a well-known and respected private investigator with a cop at my side? A high-profile cop. Who interrogated me at every turn? He would always be trying to run my agenda from the sidelines.

"See, this is what I mean," I said.

He sat back, his hand shooting back over his dark, razor-short hair. It was an unconscious habit, one that gave away he was thinking, maybe reconsidering. One that made me go weak in the knees. His face remained unflinching, then he sighed, and his eyes softened. "You're right. Not the most sensitive way of asking. I can see you're worried about something. I should trust you'll share with me when you're ready. Badgering won't help."

"Thank you."

After a minute of eating silently, he asked, "So are going to tell me?"

"You really are something else." I laughed. "Okay, okay. No big deal. Someone's stalking me." I told him about the times I noticed someone following me, starting the night at the airport and up to the delivery of the black dahlias. I didn't mention the newspaper articles. I hadn't told Azagora about that part of my life. I suspected he knew anyway; I'd be shocked if he hadn't had me checked out before our first date. But I wasn't ready to talk about it.

Two vertical lines formed between his eyebrows. "I don't like this, Jorja. Black Dahlia is the nickname they gave to Elizabeth Short. You know about her, don't you?"

"Wasn't there a book or a movie named the Black Dahlia?"

"There are various books and movies based on Elizabeth Short's murder. It's one of the longest running unsolved murder cases in North America. She was sliced in half, her mutilated body found by a woman and her daughter in a Los Angeles neighbourhood. The name Black Dahlia was given to her by newspaper reporters sensationalizing the story."

"Why Black Dahlia?" I shook my head, puzzled.

"Some said she was known to tuck a Dahlia in her hair when going out. She was last seen wearing a black suit. That got translated into a tight skirt and sheer blouse, and all that it implied, back in the 1940s." He shrugged. "You know how newspapers are."

My hand flew to the neckline of the sheer blouse lining my black crocheted sweater. "What about suspects?"

"Over the years there've been many theories. Crime writers speculated her death might be related to a serial killer working the east coast a decade earlier. There have been over sixty people, most of them men, who have confessed to her murder."

"That's insane," I said.

"The detectives on the case ruled them out one by one. Every few years, someone contacts the newspapers or writes a book, claiming they've figured it out."

"Thanks. Now I'm totally freaked out."

"I want you to be. You need to stay alert. What cases are you working on? Maybe it's related."

"Just the Wallis case." I don't know why, but I still didn't want to reveal the stalker's reference to my parents' deaths.

"McGuire mentioned some sexy PI contacted him."

I rolled my eyes and shook my head. "I don't see how the Wallis case and this Short woman, and me getting black flowers have anything to do with each other. Everything's different. Manner of death, gender of victim, how and where they were found."

A thought that had been trying to weasel its way out of my brain flashed then disappeared again.

"There is one similarity," said Luis.

"What's that?"

"There's a killer involved. Certain aspects of both cases point to the probability of a personal connection between the killer and victim."

I nodded as my chest tightened. "Too well planned and executed to be a random act," I said. And whoever was stalking me was making it personal as well. I looked up and saw the concern in Luis' eyes.

"Be careful."

CHAPTER NINETEEN

THE GOLDEN STUBBLE of fields harvested long ago glistened under bright blue skies. Snow lay in every dip in the landscape, and the intricate frost pattern forming on the side window of my car reminded me true spring was still many weeks away. I had stopped in the town of Cayley to refresh my coffee, and turned onto Highway 540, a secondary highway, one lane each way. I encountered two vehicles on that stretch of road and had been glad to reach Highway 22, a much busier thoroughfare. I now turned onto Highway 3, the last stretch to Sparwood.

Something gnawed at me. Stephen had been one of those people who found good in everyone. He apparently took in stray dogs and helped the homeless, even his breakups had been amicable. After a few miles, I realized I felt let down. Was it insane to miss someone you never met? I could have learned a lot from someone like Stephen, maybe taught him something in return. Tony's comment was interesting. He said Stephen needed to help, maybe even more than those that needed it. So, who killed him?

It was still morning when I rolled into Sparwood and made a pit stop at the Husky station. The gigantic thermometer hanging next to the restroom doors said it was minus ten degrees Celsius. The breeze felt like ice on my cheeks. If the wind picked up any more it would get nasty.

The mountains in the distance stood dark against the pale sky, each fold and dip in the rock layers highlighted by a light skiff of snow. Perhaps I was crazy to come, but I needed to talk to Joey. No guarantee I would, of course, so my three-hour trip from Calgary might be all for naught.

The map Joey had drawn for his sister was crude and not drawn to scale. But Antonia had found the cabin, just northeast of Grave Lake, leaving me confident that I would too.

Sparwood and its neighbour to the north, Elkford, were booming coalmining towns in the sixties and seventies—less so these days. After filling my car with gas, I took the Elk Valley highway north and, twenty kilometres in, turned onto Line Creek Mine Road. I noted the miles on my odometer and continued north-eastward on the gravel road. Popular in summer, the area was devoid of signs of humanity this time of year. I glanced up. The earlier pale-blue sky was now a distinctly dark-grey hue.

My car bounced along the rutted and pocked surface as I continued past the turnoff to Grave Lake. The crusted snow pushed along the side of the road and lack of tire tracks told me it had been days since it was last ploughed. I slowed and kept to the middle, watching for any sign of oncoming traffic. I encountered none by the time I reached the fourth forestry road, little more than a cut line on my left.

I pulled the car as far off the road as I could, my passenger door scraping on the built-up, crusty snow shoulder. Pulling out my cell phone, I checked signal strength. Now I knew why Joey didn't bother with a cell phone. Maybe I'd get a signal from a higher elevation.

I folded up the copy of Joey's map that Antonia had sent me and tucked it into the inside pocket of my coat along with my phone. I hated guns, which was why my Walther Compact BB pistol was safely tucked away in my dresser back home. Not exactly a great defense weapon but now I wish I had brought it.

Locking my purse in the trunk, I pulled on my gloves and toque, crossed the road, and climbed over the mounded snow at the side of the road. Once on the cut line, walking became more difficult. The snow was deeper here. Deep enough that each step took effort.

The cut line was bordered by a mix of spruce and bare deciduous trees which blocked out everything except the path in front of me. I stopped at every crackle and snap, my eyes scanning the tree line to my right and left, my neck sore from constantly rubbernecking. The cutline was well travelled, but all the animal tracks, footsteps and snowmobile tracks looked weeks old.

The voice in my head, the one that usually argues loudest, screamed at me to turn back. I checked my watch. According to Antonia's map the cabin should be close now. *Forget it! Go back.* I forged on.

It was all uphill now. The air was uncannily still. My breath sounded loud and ragged in my ears. I stopped and looked back. It wasn't much of a hill, and nothing stirred on the path behind me. Six hundred and fifty-eight steps later

I reached the crest. Off to my right stood a small cabin, a wooden shack. No signs of smoke from the pipe poking out of the roof. I leaned forward, resting my hands on my knees, and slowed my breathing, my heart hammering against my chest. Straightening, I stepped off the cutline into knee-deep snow and picked my way around half-buried vegetation to the front door. Several footprints were visible, all days old, just caved hollows in the snow.

It wasn't much of a cabin, barely twice my arm span. The front was made of unpeeled logs, sawn into one-inch planks, weathered grey. One small window, less than a foot wide and high, sat near the top of the front wall. Two rough-hewn planks set on cinder blocks served as steps to the door, which was fastened with a rusted padlock. The place felt evil. *Stop it, that's ridiculous.*

"Hello," I called out. "Anyone here?" My voice sounded weak, unsure. I unbuttoned the top buttons on my coat and reached for the inside pocket. My fingers touched the cover of my phone. I pulled it out. No coverage. I swore under my breath and tucked it back inside. My shirt was damp, and I shivered as the cold air made its way beneath my warm outer layer.

Climbing the wooden steps, I knocked on the door. "Hello? Joey?" I knocked again.

Peeling off a glove, I stepped back down and ran my hand under the top step until my fingers located a small metal box. I yanked it out, pried open the lid and lifted out the key.

I fumbled with the lock, finally getting the rusted arm to release. Visions of Elizabeth Short's mutilated body flashed across my mind. "Thanks, Azagora," I muttered as I pushed the door open and peered inside.

The room was dark, made only slightly lighter by the open door. I stepped into a small room, maybe all of twelve feet deep. A small black stove stood near the far wall, the stovepipe running up and through the roof to the outside. An old, dented, galvanized bucket stood next to it, filled with wood split into pieces. Two open shelves on the wall next to the stove held a few pots, bowls and tinned supplies.

"Joey? Are you here?" I took one last glance over my shoulder and moved further in. As my eyes adjusted to dimness, I could make out a bed against the far wall, a metal frame with a thin dirty mattress lying on top. The floor of the cabin was made of odd, salvaged bits of wood nailed to whatever was underneath. It gave a little under my feet. Maybe there was a tunnel or storage room underneath. Images of a woman bound and gagged in a dark earthen cellar, from some old movie I had watched, flashed through my mind. Intrusive and unwanted images followed. The Pickton serial killer case came to mind and chills ran through my body like electricity. I stepped back and turned. A small wooden table stood behind the door, its top scarred, two wooden chairs anchoring each end.

I stepped forward. "Oh shit." A long bone-handled hunting knife skewered the pale-blue sheet to the table, below it a newspaper clipping. I leaned forward just far enough to read *Love, Antonia* at the bottom.

I rushed through the open door, my eyes scanning the trees around the cabin. My hands shook as I slid the padlock through the latch and pressed it shut. Replacing the key in its little magnetic box, my hand searched frantically for the metal plate it had been secured to underneath the step.

A branch cracked and I dropped the box. My head snapped back. An elk stood in the trees, watching me, eyes unblinking.

Leaving the box where it had fallen, I plunged through the snow back onto the path. The uneasiness filling me earlier exploded into full-blown panic.

I ran, slid, and stumbled down the cut line, certain I'd be grabbed from behind any second.

Each breath I expelled came with a whimper, a sob or an expletive. I begged my mother in heaven to watch over me. I cursed myself for not bringing my gun. Sweat trickled down my forehead and down my back. Finally, I saw a gap ahead.

The road.

I slowed to a more normal pace and gulped in huge mouthfuls of air. With one last glance behind me I scrambled up the snow embankment ridging the road.

Blood rushed from my head. My heart pounded a staccato in my chest.

A man stood by my car.

CHAPTER TWENTY

"HEY THERE! THIS your car?" the man called out as I clambered over the ridge and stopped.

"Yes." The guy was clad in a dark-green jacket, brown Watch Cap, and khakis. A white pickup with some sort of green logo on the door was parked, running, behind my vehicle.

"You've got a flat," he announced.

I examined the car from where I stood. The tires on this side were fine. I contemplated my next move. There weren't many options. I slowed my breathing.

Keeping my voice even, I called out. "I do?"

He seemed normal enough, clean shaven, neat. But that's how they got you. Murderers don't look evil and crazy, they look normal...until their eyes go dead and their lips curl back in an evil grimace.

"Yeah, back right. I noticed it as I drove up. My name's Ted. Ted North. I'm with BC Forestry, RST Branch."

I steeled myself for a confrontation, my legs already weak at the possibility. It was entirely too early to go all

Elektra on him—besides, I had nothing in the way of ninja moves. I moved nonchalantly toward my car but stayed on my side of the road.

"RS what?"

He laughed. "Sorry. RST, Recreation Sites and Trails."

Taking a few steps, I bent low and peered at the back of my car. The tire was sitting on the rim. I could now see the BC Forestry Lands and Natural resources logo on the door of his truck. I straightened and walked across the road.

"I can't believe I have a flat. I have a spare though, so I'll be fine." I was still spooked by the whole last hour and didn't like this one bit. My gut was telling me this was going to end badly. My brain confirmed. I was miles from civilization, alone with some guy who said he was with Forestry, while my car was incapacitated, and my cell phone was out of range.

"That's great. Come on, I'll give you a hand. We'll have it on in a jiffy and I'll still have plenty of time to finish my rounds and get home to my wife and kids for supper."

I knew the reference to wife and kids was an attempt to make me more comfortable, but I'd rather be cautious than dead. I nodded and pulled out my car keys and popped the trunk. He immediately reached in and a second later pulled out the small spare tire and the jack. Dropping the tire and jack on the ground he closed the trunk lid and turned to me.

"Maybe I can get you to pull the car out from the snow bank a couple of feet, so we can get at that tire. I'm going to put a few cones out on the road just in case someone else is out here."

"Thanks. My name's Jorja."

"Glad to help, Jorja. I'll be back in a sec."

I waited until he was back in his truck, then climbed into my car and started the engine. The interior was like an icebox, but it wasn't why I was shaking. I put the car in gear, checked the rear-view mirror and pulled out into the road. Ted, if that really was his name, was setting out a bright orange cone in the middle of the road about twenty feet behind his truck. I pulled out my cell phone. Still no service. I tapped on text messages, selected Gab's name, and typed in his name and truck description, and hit send. Hopefully, she'd get the message at some point or the cops would notice the last message on my phone when they found it and my dead body in the bottom of a ravine.

Ted walked past my car, carrying a second orange cone. He placed the cone in the middle of the road and turned back. Would a killer really put out orange cones before killing his victim? More likely, he was just a nice guy out doing his job, helping a stranded woman. But my car tire was fine when I left it parked. Maybe the cold air had shrunk the seal around the air intake valve and the air leaked out. The rational part of my brain scoffed at the idea. I turned off the engine and got out.

"I appreciate your help, but really, I can change the tire."

"No problem. You wouldn't believe how many times I do this. Half the time people get stranded on one of these trails and discover they don't have a spare."

I watched as he loosened the lug nuts with the small wrench he separated from the jack, then slipped the jack under the car and began cranking.

"What brings you out here today? You a photographer?"

I suddenly realized his job put him into situations or face-to-face with potential crazies as well. He had to be a people person, trusting that everybody was just like him until they proved different. That's why people like me didn't take jobs like his. I preferred to have people prove they were just ordinary people first. I decided to come clean.

"I'm a private investigator. I'm looking for a guy named Joey Albero, although recently he's been using the name Henry Albern."

Ted glanced up, his face concerned. "What's this guy up to?"

"Nothing, as far as I know. It's a legal matter. He was named as a beneficiary in an estate and his sister wants me to find him. He apparently lives off the grid. She figured he might be holed up at a hunter's cabin back there." I waved in the direction of the cut line.

Ted pulled off the flat tire, fitted the small spare on the axle and started screwing on the lug nuts. He grunted. "Beneficiary, eh? I'm sure he'll be happy to hear that."

The hunting knife through Antonia's letter didn't indicate the level of happiness Ted imagined.

"You don't know who's using the hunter's cabin up there, do you?"

"The locals use it during hunting season. I was there in the fall. The place was locked up tight, but I could tell it had been used recently. Might be several people have keys to the place or know where one is stashed."

"You haven't run into this Joey Albero or Henry Albern? His sister says he's a recluse, looks like the proverbial mountain man, long brown hair, long beard?"

Ted loaded the flat and my jack into the trunk, straightened, and shook his head. "No, can't say that I have. You might try Merle's Trading Post. It's the first right after you cross the railway tracks on your way back to town. If this guy's living up there," he said, nodding toward the mountains, "he may be getting what supplies he needs there instead of going all the way into Sparwood or Elkford. Merle's carries everything from canned goods and bug spray to ammunition and spark plugs."

Five minutes later I was back on the road. Ted was retrieving the last of his orange cones as I drove by and gave him a final wave. I drove slower than normal, the small hard spare made the car pull to the right, at least in my imagination. I took a huge breath and blew it out. That had been downright stupid. Now I understood why Antonia's husband freaked when she told him she was coming out here. The whole knife through the letter had left me undone.

The car interior was barely warming up by the time I got to Merle's. The sprawling building had a hip roof, the exterior clad in horizontal planks sporting remnants of badly peeling red paint. I parked near a long wall made entirely of old tires, noticing mine was the only vehicle here. My boots squeaked on the snow as I walked to the door. The sign in the window announced Merle's was open but before I could turn the handle, a small, bearded man rounded the corner of the building.

"Hi there, missy. Go on in, I'll be there in a jiff," he called out, eyes twinkling.

I opened the door and stepped over the sill. A small bell over the door merrily tinkled my arrival. The place was packed to the rafters. Shelf after shelf, crammed with cans, air mattresses, sleeping bags, kitchen supplies. I walked past the aisles, peering down each one. I was gawking down an aisle filled with mouse traps, propane canisters, jerry cans, ropes, and various tie downs when he returned.

"I see you got yourself a flat there," he announced as he came in. "I can fix that for you if you want. My shop's just back there." He tilted his head toward the dark interior door he had materialized from.

"How long will it take?"

"Depends on what's wrong with it. I could have a boo and let you know."

"Okay," I said. He followed me outside to the car. I turned. "Are you Merle?"

He laughed. "No. Name's Dale. Don't know who Merle was. My old man bought this place in the fifties. Maybe time I replaced the sign, eh?"

"I'm Jorja. I was up near Grave Lake when I got my flat. A guy working with the forestry department named Ted North stopped to help me."

"I know Ted. Good guy."

For some reason, the fact that a stranger named Dale knew another stranger named Ted lessened my nervousness. I'd give some serious consideration as to why later.

I popped the car trunk and stood back while he heaved the flat tire out, his short jacket riding up his back and exposing a band of flesh above baggy jeans about to slide off his hips.

"You go on in inside. It's colder than a witch's tit out here. There's some coffee behind the front counter. Help yourself. I'll be back in a jiff."

I went back inside and questioned why I continually put myself in these situations. I should have driven back to the Husky station in Sparwood. Now I was dealing with some guy who apparently knew how cold a witch's tit got.

I made my way behind the wooden counter and found the coffee pot among the dismantled radios, boxes and giant spools of wire lying on top of a workbench. The glass carafe stood on a heating plate. I leaned forward. The interior was coated in brown gunk. A strong, burnt odour hit me. A chipped dirty coffee mug stood next to it. I had been contemplating asking about a washroom, but one look at the coffee station changed my mind. I was reading a ten-month-old People magazine when Dale returned.

"Might take some doin'," he said without preamble. I got an old Chevy on the back forty, rim might be the same size. Yur goin' to need a new one."

"You can't just repair the tire?"

His blue eyes met mine, his jovial demeanour gone. "The sidewall's been sliced, through to the fabric. If the damage was on the tread, I could fix it. A damaged sidewall means a new tire. Lucky you didn't have a blowout on the highway."

"A slice," I repeated like an idiot. Fear radiated down my spine, tightening every muscle and joint on its way down.

"Might have hit a piece of sharp metal somewhere, or a pothole. Potholes can do a lot of damage, 'specially in winter. Unless you got someone mad at you?" he said, his eyes on mine.

"No. I mean, maybe. No. I don't know anyone who would do this." I couldn't imagine some random person doing this, especially on a side road, miles from anywhere.

Unless it was whoever was stalking me. But I hadn't seen anyone. I probably ran over something sharp on the road.

Dale was watching me, his eyes sharp, calculating. I owed him an explanation. I told him the same story I had given Ted North.

"You don't know anyone named Joey Albero or Henry Albern, do you?"

He stroked his short reddish beard with one hand, his head cocked to one side. "'Fraid I can't help you there."

"Well, thanks for all your help, Dale. It's getting late. I'll just head into Sparwood, get the tire fixed there."

"Suit yourself. I'll go 'round and put your old tire back in the trunk for you."

I went outside and got in the car. The car swayed as Dale dropped my tire back into the trunk and shut the lid. I rolled down my window to call out my thanks.

"You take care, missy. Don't go wandering down any more deserted roads by yourself."

Twenty minutes later, I re-entered Sparwood, my shoulders and neck sore and tense. I had expected each vehicle that came up behind me to try and run me off the road. I reached my arm back to try and work out some of the tension in my neck.

Despite what Ted had told me, I knew someone had been at the cabin in the last three weeks. And judging by the way Antonia's letter had been skewered, my guess would be Joey. Had he watched me approaching today? Did he double back, while I was in the cabin, and slash my tire? What if Ted hadn't arrived on the scene? A shudder racked my entire body and my teeth chattered even though the car interior was now comfortably warm.

Why would inheriting money be so unwelcomed? Or was it just unwelcomed coming from Stephen?

CHAPTER TWENTY-ONE

I was back on the road before sunrise. The forecast called for more snow, and I hoped my early start would keep me ahead of the storm. Highway traffic was sparse until I reached Fort Macleod. Now that other vehicles shared the road with me, I breathed a sigh of relief.

The whole time in Sparwood, I had felt watched, but now thought it highly unlikely. While waiting for my tire to be replaced I had called BC Forestry's Recreation Sites and Trails Branch and asked for Ted North. The woman who answered said he was out doing trail inspections and asked if I cared to leave a message. I said I was phoning to thank him again for his assistance with my flat.

Joey's sister thought her baby brother was just a smart, eccentric loner. Tony seemed to agree. And maybe that's all he had been, back then. The knife through the letter and the possibility he slashed my car tire screamed instability. Or anger management issues. Why was he so angry?

It wasn't even noon by the time I pulled into my parking spot in the underground garage. My phone had been steadily pinging for the last thirty minutes. I turned off the engine and sat back. It felt like I'd driven all day instead of a few short hours. I checked my messages. There were seven from Gab asking if I was okay. *Oops.* I had forgotten about the text I had sent her. I replied in the affirmative and apologized for causing her any concern by sending her Ted North's name and truck description. We firmed up plans to get together the next night.

Joey's sister Antonia was in denial, chalking up her brother's strange behaviour to self-chosen eccentricity. I just hoped someone else didn't get killed before she came to terms with his illness. And maybe I was in denial about Laura and Wayne. Just because Laura was my client didn't mean she was lily pure. I called Stella Seller and left her a message asking her to call.

An hour later, I finished Jillian Richard's Shred workout. Jillian and her two fitness models urged me from the television screen to hold the plank position just twenty seconds more, cheerfully telling me I could do it. Good thing they couldn't see I was already on my back patting out the knot in my stomach, which looked nothing like the six pack all three of them sported. My phone buzzed on the floor beside me. I rolled over and picked it up.

"Jorja, it's Stella. Returning your call."

"Stella. Thanks for calling me back." I sat up and tucked a strand of hair behind my ear. "Can I ask you how well you know Laura and Wayne Bradford?"

"We're not close if that's what you mean. Why?"

"It's somewhat awkward. I'm trying to find out a bit more about Wayne, or rather Wayne's friends or acquaintances. It's staggering, how many times someone the victim's family or friends knew ends up being the perpetrator."

"I can see how awkward that would be for you. What can I tell you?"

"Laura said something about Wayne having been out of work for a while. Do you know where he was working or what he did for a living before he became a construction manager on residential projects?"

"I believe he's a civil engineer. He's overseen some big projects in the Middle East, Bolivia, Mexico. You know, dams, interstate highways and bridges, shipping docks, that sort of thing."

"Do you know who he worked for, or has he always worked for himself?"

"I believe he owned his own company."

"Did the work dry up or something? Sounds a lot more lucrative than what he's doing now."

"I should know this. Give me sec. I'll be right back."

Maybe Wayne switched jobs because Laura and the kids got tired of him being away from home all the time. Maybe he now blamed Laura for their financial situation.

I waited for several minutes.

"Yes, here it is. I knew there was some sort of big scandal. He was working for a company called Ultrafina. They're headquartered in Spain. Mexico bridge disaster 2015. Five people were killed, twenty-seven injured."

"Whoa. Was Wayne involved?"

"I believe so. I remember Stephen saying something about it being a tough break for Laura and her husband. I don't pretend to know the details."

"Was Wayne an employee at Ultrafina?"

"I got the impression he was one of their subcontractors. All I know is there were multiple companies involved and a lot of finger pointing. Some said it was a design flaw, but others speculated that the materials weren't up to code, that the job was rushed, mistakes were made."

"What was Wayne's roll in all of that?"

"I'm not sure, but Stephen said he wouldn't want to be in Wayne's shoes."

"What a nightmare," I said.

"The investigation went on for a long time. I can't imagine it doing Wayne's reputation any good."

"That must be why Wayne's LinkedIn page makes no mention of previous employment."

"Must have been tough on Laura too."

"I can only imagine. Stella, while I have you on the phone. Did Stephen ever mention or talk about Joey Albero, a former pal from university? Or maybe someone named Henry Albern?"

"No, those names don't sound familiar. Stephen didn't talk much about his past, though."

After thanking Stella, I googled the bridge collapse in Mexico. Several companies were found to be at fault. Ultrafina was one of them. Several of their employees were named immediately after the incident: the design expert, the chief architect, and the construction engineer. Assets of three material companies were frozen. A few weeks later, Wayne's company, Bradley Compliance Corporation, was named in the ensuing lawsuit for signing off on project materials and failing to notice any deficiencies.

The investigation went on for close to two years. There was political fallout. Several government officials were fired. A committee was set up to address issues in the construction sector, including state and municipal supervision of the construction. I couldn't find much about what happened to the companies that were investigated. I found an obscure reference in a related case that a man was fined for signature forgery on documents related to several construction projects dating back to 2014. No other information was disclosed.

I sat back and rubbed my temples. No wonder Laura was stressed to the max. The info on Wayne gave me pause but didn't link directly to Stephen. Unless they were hurting so badly financially that Wayne killed his brother-in-law.

I had to assume the police knew all this. Maybe they hadn't eliminated Wayne as a suspect. Detective McGuire did say they were digging into Stephen's files, data, and his digital footprint. Perhaps that included Wayne and Laura's digital footprint too. Either way, it didn't give me much to go on. It did confirm one thing. Chloe may come off as a wild child, but she was astute. It made me curious about what other bits of information she was holding onto. Unless what happened to Wayne was just a red herring she dangled in front of me to throw me off her trail.

CHAPTER TWENTY-TWO

CHLOE CAME FLYING out of the apartment building, coat over her arm, hair in disarray. She skidded to a stop and hopped on one foot, while fitting the remaining shoe she was carrying on the other. Holding her purse straps in her mouth she fit one arm through the sleeve of her coat then the other, purse flapping against her chest like a wattle. Once in her coat, she gripped her purse with her left hand and flicked her hair from under her coat collar with the other.

She slid and slipped down the sidewalk until she reached a beat-up red-and-white Mini Cooper. As soon as she folded herself into the passenger seat, it roared off, leaving a trail of blue exhaust. The apartment she was staying at belonged to her new boyfriend, a bartender who worked at Vinnie's. I had followed them back from Vinnie's a few days earlier.

Following Chloe was a cakewalk, the exhaust leaving an excellent trail aided by the sound of a missing muffler. The Mini Cooper double parked momentarily outside an office tower, and Chloe jumped out. She now had her hair pulled back into a messy-looking knot. The Mini Cooper roared off and Chloe ran into the building, the revolving doors spinning behind her. The building she entered housed the law firm handling Stephen's will.

I continued up the street and found parking on the side street. I made my way up to the second-floor skywalk connecting the CORE and TD Square malls which stretched over several downtown blocks. A fresh Starbucks in hand, I sat at a counter in front of floor-to-ceiling windows facing Eighth Avenue. I had an excellent view of the building Chloe had entered.

The last few years had been tough for Laura's family. I shuddered. Even if Wayne wasn't directly responsible for the bridge collapse in Mexico, just having his name dragged through the investigation would be hellish enough. Then Stephen was killed. Murdered. Now Chloe was dragging them through mediation and maybe the courts, fighting over Stephen's spoils.

I watched a hat blow off a woman's head on the street below. A teenage girl ran after it. After several attempts she caught it and returned it to its owner. I sat back and sipped coffee. Chloe said Laura and Wayne were somehow to blame for Stephen's death and that Laura was playing me. If Laura was involved or suspected Wayne of doing something stupid, would she have hired me to poke into Stephen's death? On the other hand, the Bradford's might be bleeding red ink. It wouldn't be the first time a devoted family member killed one of their own for financial gain much to the shocked testimonies afterwards from loved ones declaring it impossible.

I sat up as Laura came out through the revolving doors her face set in a grimace. She held the arm of an older woman, who I assumed was her mother. I watched their tiny-stepped progress to a white SUV parked several cars east of the building.

Chloe came out next and stood expectantly, scanning the street in both directions. A minute later Tony flew out of the building, tan overcoat flapping behind him. He stopped, looked left and right, and marched over to where Chloe waited. Words were exchanged, Tony's face red, his right arm jabbing the air above him. Chloe smugly stood her ground, her head occasionally shaking a negative response. Tony continued to rant.

Rob came out and joined them, laid a hand on Tony's arm. Looked like he might be trying to get Tony to back off. The Mini Cooper whipped around the corner and screeched to a stop. A yellow cab behind the Mini Cooper swerved at the last second to avoid a collision. Chloe ran out into the street and climbed in, flipping Tony the bird as she did so. Rob and Tony spoke for a few minutes, then shook hands. Rob turned left, and Tony rushed off in the opposite direction, cell phone already to his ear.

Must have been one heck of a meeting. I hopped off my stool, used the washroom and took the escalator down to the main level. I headed west and turned at the corner to where my car was parked. I saw it immediately.

Moisture popped out on the back of my neck. I plucked the paper from under the wiper blade and scanned the street. Nothing seemed out of the ordinary.

The paper was cheap, unlined, its one edge obviously torn from a coil bound notebook. I took a shaky breath and unfolded it. A huge red heart was drawn in the middle of the page, a black dagger drawn through it, the handle protruding to the right and the tip visible on the opposite side. The centre of the heart contained a photo. A black-and-white photo printed on ordinary stock paper.

"Son of a bee-otch," I exclaimed. The picture was of me, sitting by the window of Escoba's the night I met Luis for dinner.

The first few notes had made me think that the stalker might be trying to tell me something about my parents' death. That maybe my father hadn't died after killing my mother. It wouldn't be the first time the notion crossed my mind. But the notes and old newspaper photos revealed nothing new. The police were quite certain it was an open-and-shut case, my parents' deaths a murder-suicide.

This picture was about the here and now. My photo pasted on a heart creeped me out enough, but the black dagger made it something more. This wasn't about my parents' death. This was about me.

I scanned the street and shivered involuntarily. He could be watching me from any of the hundreds of windows above. I slid into the car and pulled out into traffic. The feeling I was being watched wouldn't go away.

I pointed the car back toward Chloe's apartment. The Mini Cooper was parked down the street. For some reason, I felt safer here than at my condo. But I couldn't stay here forever. The car interior became frigid minutes after I turned off the engine. I was already wearing everything I had with me, coat, toque, mitts. My toes were like ice in my leather boots and my legs cold even though they were wrapped in a blanket I always carried in the back seat. I tucked my chin into the collar of my coat and tried to direct the warm air my lungs expelled down the front of my shirt.

Keeping one eye on the front of the apartment, I racked my brain as to who knew about my past. It's not as if the story came up when you googled my name. Of course, anyone could find the newspaper articles from twenty years ago, if they dug hard enough. The news hadn't been widespread; the few articles written were restricted to the Timmins News and several local papers in the area. A murder-suicide of two low-income, low-key citizens wasn't exactly national news, no matter how devastating it had been to me. My stalker knew me.

CHAPTER TWENTY-THREE

I TOOK A sip of bourbon and swirled it around my tongue. The warmth of the fire washed over me, the tension in my shoulders eased. I turned at the sound of footsteps. Several sets of eyes followed Gab as she wove confidently through the tables toward me.

She leaned over and gave me a hug.

"What a day! Have you seen the traffic out there?" Shedding her coat, Gab sank into the leather wingback chair across from mine. The fire caught the golden highlights in her dark-red hair. She glanced down at her green silk blouse and patted her chest. "Still locked and loaded." Her laugh cut through the air and made me smile.

Gab always made me smile. She was rarely in a bad mood and something about her laugh was infectious. Gab perused the drink menu and ordered the featured drink of the day, a Mar-Tea-nie.

"So why were you in BC?" Gab leaned forward; lips parted in an easy smile.

"Yeah, sorry about that text. I should have told you

before going out there, but the plan was to go up and back the same day. Then I got a flat. There was no cell reception and when this guy stopped to help me, I guess I panicked."

"Well glad you're okay. So, you're on the Houdini Killer's trail. I know you don't always believe me, but I get this sense that you're going to find him. You're going to become famous."

"Yeah, you know how much becoming famous means to me." I lifted an eyebrow and laughed. "So, what's new with you?"

Gab's bright-green eyes sparkled, a dimple formed in her left cheek as her smile grew wider. "I might have found the one."

Gab had found the one before. Several times. The last one left her with an ironclad lease on the dump we were renting for an office and a pile of credit card debt. The one before that left in the middle of the night, a week before their wedding. He left a note saying he wasn't ready to settle down. Three months later he married a woman with four kids.

"Okay, tell me."

"He's a composer," Gab squealed.

"A composer. Like music?"

"Of course, silly. What other kind of composer is there? And he plays piano."

"Is it David Foster?" I asked hopefully.

"You're too funny. No, his name is Sebastian Bell."

I caught myself in time and shook my head instead. "Never heard of him."

"He's working on the music score for a new computer game, glass bubble, or was it blue bubble?"

"Does he get to do this from home, wearing pyjamas?"

"I suppose he could, but he does a lot of his work at a studio, up in the northwest."

"What makes him the one?"

"He's smart and really funny. Whenever we're together we just laugh our asses off. I've never felt this comfortable with any other man. We can talk about anything and I don't feel like I'm being judged, you know? What about you? How's it going with that hot inspector of yours?"

"Azagora? We're still in the exploration stage. I'm not sure I need a man in my life, especially one who's got his eye on being chief of police. And I'm quite sure he's happy keeping me at a safe distance from his untarnished and rather public image." He hadn't exactly been thrilled to hear I was poking around in the Wallis case.

"He's definitely going places," said Gab.

"Oh, I have no doubt." That was one of my sticking points. I was never going to be the smiling woman on Azagora's arm attending local charity events or organizing a support group for wives of injured police officers.

"I get it." Gab giggled. "It's the sex, isn't it?"

"You know I think he's damn hot; the physical attraction is insane." I squirmed. "I'm not sure if that's all I want from him."

Gab's eyes widened.

"I mean, is that all I want? Then maybe. I don't know. It always starts out that way. Then one person goes beyond the just-sex rule and feelings develop and it becomes awkward and eventually untenable. So why go there?"

I didn't mention it was usually me that threw my emotions into the mix and got hurt. It was something I had worked on with my therapist for years. Relationships would work out or not. Avoiding them was not a good option. The idea of being single didn't worry me, the idea of being celibate did. The truth is, I couldn't afford to get into something with Azagora right now that had the potential of leaving me hurt or him totally pissed off.

"You don't believe that. You need to find a guy that's kind, attractive, funny, maybe a nerdy science geek, but geeky in a good way. Someone who's so involved in his own thing he won't even notice you're off doing your own thing, or better yet encourages you to chase your own dream."

"Sounds like the guy who got murdered in January." I was surprised she didn't bring up Mike's name. Gab was always telling me how well-suited Mike and I were, but I was determined to keep Mike as a friend. Maybe she had finally accepted it.

Gab and I spent the few hours savouring the fire's warmth, helped by drinks and a plate of calamari. Even though we shared office space, we rarely ended up there at the same time. Gab was usually off meeting clients at some venue or roaring around town sourcing organic products. Her private chef catering company was gaining attention after a somewhat rocky start and Gab happily recounted some of her latest successes.

"What about you? Still happy with the way your PI business is going?"

"Of course. Especially now that I'm getting bigger cases."

Gab lifted her glass and gazed at me over the rim, raising one eyebrow. "So, what's got you worried?"

About to declare nothing, I reminded myself that I had

vowed to connect with the people in my life in more profound ways. If I couldn't be totally honest with Gab, I might
as well throw in the towel.

"Someone's been leaving me notes."

"Love notes?" Gab joked, but her eyes grew serious, as
she set her glass down.

"No. They're weird. Copies of newspaper articles about
my parents' deaths, left on my car windshield."

"Oh gawd, Jorja. That's creepy. What do they say?"

I told her how one had been centered in a black,
hand-drawn heart, the other newspaper article taped to a
hand-drawn cross. Both times, I felt someone watching me.

"Holy Hanna. You should report this, Jorja. I hope
you've at least told your hottie cop friend."

"I told Luis someone's stalking me, but I didn't mention
the clippings about my parents. I'm sure he's already questioning his sanity in getting involved with me and now I'm
going to bring up my parents' deaths?"

"Why not? It's not like you had anything to do with it."

I had spent a lot of hours debating that statement in my
head. I used to see a woman shrink about it. She tried to get
me to see I had nothing to do with my father's decision to
kill my mother and then himself, tried to get me to believe
I wasn't somehow flawed because I shared genetic material
with a murderer. Recently, I started to believe it. But someone had scratched the scab and it was starting to bleed again.

The police had told me they found my mother on the
bathroom floor, two bullets in her chest. There were five
bullet holes in the bathroom door, a sixth one in the wall
next to it. My father was found in the garage, or at least what

was left of him. The propane tank that turned the garage into an incinerator was found on the lawn, along with other charred items from the explosion, including bits of a rifle. I blinked back tears blurring my vision.

I had been living in Vancouver at the time but had gone off for the weekend with several friends and didn't find out until three days later. By the time I made my way back to Timmins, Ontario, my childhood home, the reporters were waiting for me at the airport. They wanted to know if my parents' relationship had been volatile. I didn't see any point in lying, but my comments infuriated my brother. He accused me of betraying the family. The seven-year age difference between us grew wider. I tried to keep in touch at first, but it soon became crystal clear that he no longer wanted me in his life. I hadn't spoken to him in years.

Gab leaned over and patted my arm. "You really should tell him."

"I know. Unfortunately, I've discovered that revealing this tidbit of family history does little to kindle the flames of a burgeoning romance. It's just some sicko who's trying to mess with my mind."

"Jorja, please be careful. Of course, it's a sicko. Normal people don't do this. I don't want you to go missing and then have them find you chopped up in pieces in a freezer."

"Thanks Gab, nice visual."

But she had a point. This wasn't an irate customer or someone dealing with road rage. At minimum, someone was getting a kick from scaring me, at worst someone was out to settle a score.

CHAPTER TWENTY-FOUR

GAB'S LAUGHTER AND the bourbon had warmed my soul and the fire had thawed out my frozen toes, a welcome break in what ended up being a long night. After leaving the restaurant I had prowled the apartment buildings along Fairmount Drive. By early morning I had the address of Conner's apartment, the licence plate of the sedan, and knew the underground stall number it was parked in. Best of all, the GPS tracker I left under Conner's car provided real-time location updates to my smart phone or laptop.

My laptop pinged, and I watched the red dot on the screen turn west off Macleod Trail onto Tenth Avenue. I turned my car in the same direction. A few minutes later I pulled into a parking lot and watched the red dot on my laptop pause briefly on Thirteenth Avenue, then continue west. It turned at the corner, looped around the block, and turned back onto Thirteenth. I expanded the map. The dot crept across Sixth Street and stopped. My guess is someone had been let out at The Ranchmen's Club and now Conner was waiting for the pickup.

I moved the car west and pulled into a spot in front of a fire hydrant. I could make out the back of the sedan just in front of The Ranchmen's, a posh private club offering members a place to meet, dine, and host personal or business events. My phone vibrated. Laura's number appeared on the screen.

"Hi, Jorja. Just a sec."

I heard her muffled voice telling someone that they had to do homework now.

"Sorry," she said coming back on the line. "Kids. I love them, but I swear they're going to drive me to an early grave. I won't keep you, I just wanted to tell you I got a call from the realtor. He's seen a couple of guys hanging around Stephen's house. One of them seems to be taking photos."

"Probably just looky-loos with a macabre fascination for the house. If you give me his name, I'll call him. How are things otherwise?"

"We had a meeting with the lawyer yesterday. I told you Chloe's contesting the will, didn't I?"

"You did."

"She's throwing around the most insane accusations. She claims Stephen had money stashed away that isn't accounted for in the will. She even implied...no not implied, she accused me of hiding some of Stephen's assets."

"Why would she think that?"

"Some asinine idea that he should have had more money than he did. The lawyer recommends we stay out of court. After all the legal costs, it often turns out a lot worse than if the parties just sort it out themselves. He recommended a mediator as the best way to settle this."

"Is that what you're going to do?"

"Tony called me afterward. He wants to know if Wayne and I'd be willing to negotiate with her. But I have no confidence she'd be open to settling reasonably. Wayne's livid. He just wants this settled and Chloe out of our lives for good. Have you come up with anything?"

"I'm following up on some interesting bits but nothing definite yet." I glanced up. Conner's car hadn't moved. "I'll give the realtor a call. Hopefully, they're just curiosity seekers, but you never know."

A minute later I had the realtor on the phone. He'd noticed a guy at the construction site next door when he brought a couple around to see the place in the evening. He found it odd, since the construction company had an order to cease activity at six o'clock. The next day he popped by the house mid-morning. He couldn't find his iPad and figured he'd left it at the house. He noticed the same guy, this time across the street, pacing.

"When he saw that I spotted him, he hurried off. There's been a second guy as well. He's been sitting in a green Toyota Corolla across from the house, taking pictures. Then yesterday, the guy in the Toyota was parked across the street from my realty office."

I sat up. "You sure it was the same guy?"

"I'm ninety-nine percent sure."

"Can you give me a description?"

"Caucasian, brown hair, rounder face. He was wearing a grey coat, and a navy beanie."

"Any idea as to age?"

"If I had to guess, I'd say mid thirties to early forties."

"What about the other guy, the one at the construction site?"

"Hard to tell, his clothes maybe added bulk. I'd say six feet tall, brown beard, longish hair. He was wearing a brown work parka, hood pulled up, brown coveralls. That's what caught my eye, the way he was dressed seemed out of place for the neighbourhood."

"You haven't seen him on the property, have you?"

"No. Should I call the police?"

"If you see either of them again, I'd call it in. I'd hate to hear someone had their house broken into while we sat on this."

"That's exactly what's been going through my mind."

After I hung up, I pictured the guy he had described sitting in front of his office in my minds eye. Why would my stalker be interested in Laura's realtor?

CHAPTER TWENTY-FIVE

THE COLD SEEPED into the car and I shivered. I was letting this stalker get to me. It was cold, the city was full of guys wearing grey coats and navy hats. I shook my head. The man spotted at Stephen's house must be someone else.

A movement ahead caught my eye. I looked up in time to see Conner's sedan roll up the curved driveway to The Ranchmen's and double park by the front doors. Conner jumped out and hustled over to the passenger side. He opened the back door as a distinguished-looking man came out from the club, pulling on leather gloves. The wind caught his silver hair and tossed a wisp over his forehead. I watched as he smoothed it back, ran down the steps and slid into the back seat. He looked strangely familiar, but I had no idea why. Perhaps it was the silver hair, not common among Asian businessmen.

Conner ran around to the driver's side, got in, and the sedan rolled away. I was about to follow when the front doors opened. Tony came out, buttoning his coat against the wind, his face contorted in anger. He ran down the steps and stormed off down the street. Tony and Conner at the same location, seen within minutes of each other? This couldn't be a coincidence.

Tony reached his car and a minute later pulled out into traffic. I cranked up the heater and followed him until I was certain he was going back to his office. I watched the red dot on my laptop screen turn south on Elbow Drive. I turned the car around and headed toward it.

Other than the fact that Conner was a creep, I had nothing concrete to suggest he had anything to do with Stephen's death. I was grasping at any straw the wind blew my way. I had no clue as to how anything I had learned so far would help me find who killed Stephen.

Conner's sedan stopped momentarily at an address in the ritzy part of Mount Royal then it continued south. I followed the dot until it returned to Conner's apartment. I parked across the street and waited.

The flakes of snow falling earlier turned into miniature pellets, now steadily bouncing off the hood of the car. I don't know what I was waiting for, I could just as easily track him on my app from home. I kept the car running and checked my watch. I pulled open my file on Stephen and read through the notes.

I knew it was a long shot, but I had nothing to lose. I called Rob Bailey's office and left a message. He called back twenty minutes later.

"Rob, thanks for calling back."

"Sorry. I've been meaning to call you. You left me a message that you're trying to find Stephen's former driver?"

"I did, but I managed to locate him. I'm trying to find

out more about one of Stephen's other beneficiaries. A guy named Henry Albern. He used to go by the name Joey Albero. Do you know him?"

"Joey? Yeah. I know him. Joey roomed with us for a while, back in university."

"You mean you, Stephen and Tony?"

"Yes. Not for long though, less than a year. He dropped out of university right after that."

"Did you guys meet him at university?"

"I did, but Tony knew him from before. They played soccer together in high school."

"Do you know why Joey dropped out or what he's doing now?"

"I understand he's pretty much a recluse. Lives in the mountains, somewhere in BC."

"Did you or Stephen keep in touch with him?"

"Me? No. I don't know about Stephen. He never mentioned him, not recently anyway."

"Joey's sister told me he changed in university. That something might have happened to him. You wouldn't know anything about that would you?"

Rob stayed silent for so long, I checked to see if we were still connected.

"Hmmm. I seem to recall hearing a friend of his disappeared right around then. Makes you wonder, doesn't it. I mean, people react differently, you know. To losing someone."

"Someone disappeared?"

"A kid from Joey's old neighbourhood. I didn't know him, but he and Joey used to pal around."

"What happened to him?"

"The guy just disappeared, left his friends and family without a word, and vanished."

"Was he reported missing?"

"I don't know. He would have already been what, nineteen, twenty, at the time. His folks might have reported him missing."

As strange as it sounded, I understood. Sometimes people just got up and left their past behind. Unless there was foul play, or some reason to suspect they were in harm's way, loved ones didn't always go to the police.

"You think this affected Joey? His life choices?"

"Maybe. He was bummed about it at the time. I don't recall anything else out of the ordinary."

"Did you know the family? This kid's name?"

"The family was from India. They lived in Forest Lawn. Now what the heck was his name? If I heard it, I'd recognise it."

"Joey told you about this?"

"No. Tony told me."

"Tony?"

"Yeah. I'm sure I heard it from Tony. We were having a few beers one night, griping about life in general, and talking about Joey quitting university and he told me the story. Said it was a guy he knew from his old neighborhood."

Rob couldn't remember any other details. I sat back, puzzled. Why didn't Tony mention that Joey was an old roommate? Had Tony lied to me? I shook my head. Maybe not. My last boyfriend had been gregarious, loud, talked constantly. There had been more than one occasion when

I brought up something he said, which he in turn denied. I used to think he was lying, but later I came to realize that he simply couldn't keep track of everything that spouted from his mouth, a jumble of truth, lies and partial fabrications. His denial or confirmation of what he said, was also made on the spur of the moment, chosen as to what suited him best.

My app beeped. The sedan was on the move. I watched it emerge from underground parking. I kept a few blocks behind him and followed him to Macleod Trail. "What do you know," I muttered as the dot turned right at Forty-Second Avenue. I pulled into the parking lot of a Vietnamese restaurant. The red dot continued east and stopped. The street he was on dead ended in Vinnie's parking lot. Now what were the chances he was just dropping by Vinnie's for a drink?

CHAPTER TWENTY-SIX

My CELL PHONE vibrated as I slid into my vehicle. I pulled it out of my coat pocket and glanced at the screen. No caller ID. I hesitated then swiped *accept*.

"Jorja Knight, here."

"I want to find the asshole who's been harassing me. I'm going to sue them."

"Hi Chloe. What can I do for you?"

"You can catch the asshole that's harassing us. Someone keyed Trace's car," she said, her voice rising. "Etched in a filthy word. I want him caught and arrested."

My tongue stuck to the roof of my mouth. "When did this happen, and where?"

"Last night. They let the air out of Trace's tires and scratched the word 'bitch' into the hood of his car. While we were at work."

"Okay, that's ugly. Any idea who or why someone would be doing this?"

"Who do you think? I just want my fair share. Why does everyone hate me?" Her voice rose to an ear-splitting whine.

I knew the answer to her question. She was obnoxious and childish. I had little sympathy for her. She was given her own life to live and as best I could tell she wasn't making the most of it. Or even a tenth of the most of it. Now she coveted the spoils from her brother's efforts.

"You sure it's because you're contesting Stephen's will? Any chance it could be an ex-boyfriend or someone sending your new boyfriend a message?"

"Trace noticed someone's following us."

"Does he have a description or a plate number?"

Chloe clammed up.

Conner's sedan had stopped at Vinnie's but etching a vulgar word into a car didn't seem his style. Even though Conner's car had been in the vicinity, it proved nothing. I could relate to how she must be feeling. Being followed or harassed was unnerving and creepy, no matter what the reason.

I swallowed. "Look, if you really want to hire a PI, the standard fee is a hundred and twenty dollars per hour, plus expenses. But I can't help you. Your sister hired me; it would be a conflict of interest."

I lied about the fee, praying it would dissuade her. It was the least I could do for the members of my profession. She'd be one of those clients who held back bits of the truth yet demanded answers. Not to mention the possibility that she had a hand in killing her brother.

"Forget it," she mumbled.

"Chloe, while I have you on the phone, I want to ask you about Wayne. I did follow up on your comment about people hounding him. I gather his company is or was being sued for a project disaster in Mexico. Do you know if that's been settled yet?"

"Oh, it's settled. Didn't Laura tell you Stephen lent him money to pay his lawyer bills? Money, that's never going to have to be paid back."

"No, she didn't. Is that why you're challenging the will?"

"I want everyone to see who Laura and Wayne are. I'm sick of them making me out to be the bad one. Now she's claiming the coin collection Stephen left her isn't worth much. Stephen had a million-dollar coin. Now it's missing. You figure it out."

"The cops are certain no one broke into Stephen's place. Maybe, he sold the coin."

"Stephen, promised he'd leave the coin to me."

This was getting too wild. The obvious answer as to who flattened the tires and etched vulgarities on her boyfriend's car was someone angry about her challenging Stephen's will. On the other hand, I imagined it could be any number of people who knew her.

"Well Chloe, I hope you have something concrete to back up your allegations."

I waited, holding my breath. Then in an instant the defiant, angry Chloe was back.

"You'll all be sorry when I end up dead. And you'll have no one to blame but yourselves."

I was about to ask her why she supposed the current level of harassment would escalate to death, but she had already disconnected. Every time I got a tiny lead into who or why Stephen may have been killed, I got dragged back to Chloe, or Chloe, Laura, and Wayne.

I checked the tracker app on my phone. Conner's car was still parked at his apartment. I started my car and headed to the office, picking up a coffee on the way. The caffeine did little to chase away my forming headache. Mulling over the last few conversations I'd had, I suddenly found myself at my office door, with little recall of getting there.

I glanced over my shoulder, down the dim corridor. As intriguing as the Wallis case was, my creepy stalker warranted my vigilance, if I didn't want to end up dead myself.

I settled down at my desk, logged on and glanced at the time. I pulled open the file I had set up on Stephen Wallis and made a note to ask Laura about this supposed million-dollar coin Chloe mentioned. If such a thing existed and he did sell it, it might explain why he changed his will in the fall. Hard to bequeath an item one no longer possessed.

Tapping a pencil against my teeth, I sat back and pondered my next move. Tony and Antonia believed Joey was just an eccentric loner. A loner who wasn't pleased to learn he'd been left some money. Why? Was it because it clashed with his live off the land philosophy or was there something else? Maybe I was following dead ends and making connections between events and people where there were none. Unless Joey showed up, I was sort of at a dead end.

I didn't know what to make of the story Rob told me about Joey's missing friend. I'd have to ask Antonia and Tony what they knew about him. A name would be nice. Tony hadn't made mention of anyone disappearing but then again, we all placed different importance on events in our lives or those of others.

I shouldn't get too distracted by someone who might or

might not have disappeared and find Joey instead. It's what I should have been doing from the start, but I let the deserted cabin, the bone-handled knife and stories of an angry derelict get in my head. Before I could come up with a plan, my phone rang. I stared at the screen.

"Tony. How are you?"

"Great, just great. Thanks for asking. I might have something for you."

"Awesome." I could use something right about now, anything actually. "What've you got?"

"Don't know how much help it'll be. Your questions the other day brought back memories of when Stephen, Joey, and I all played soccer together. The more I thought about it, I realized something did happened the year Joey dropped out of uni. I have a vague recollection that a friend of his died or disappeared that summer. I don't even remember the guy's name. I'm seriously lousy with names."

I let Tony keep talking. Then again, he didn't leave much room for me to break in.

"There was a guy on our U-18 soccer team though, who knew everybody. His name's Greg Kowalski. Great guy, great guy. If anyone remembers Joey's pal, Greg will."

"That is helpful. Any idea where I can find Greg Kowalski?"

"He still lives in the Lawn. Owns the Kielbasa King on Seventeenth Avenue."

I sat up, excited to have a lead that might go somewhere. "Thanks for the info Tony. I owe you one."

"Hey, don't thank me. Just find the pond scum that killed Stephen."

CHAPTER TWENTY-SEVEN

I DROVE PAST the International Avenue arch, turned off onto the service road, and kept one eye on traffic while the other searched for the sausage shop. I found Tony's sudden recall of Joey's missing friend suspicious. Especially as Rob had told me Tony was the one who had told him about the guy's disappearance. And as lousy as Tony claimed to be with names, he didn't have any problem recalling Greg Kowalski's name.

Two blocks on, I spotted a seven-foot-high sausage rotating on the roof of a one-storey strip mall. The sausage likely once stood vertically over the store, but now wobbled in a semi-horizontal position, one end protruding over the front of the building. The sausage had red ketchup-dot eyes, a mustard grin, and bright green letters along one side that might have at one time represented relish. It rotated in a strangely obscene way. I made out, *ielba...Kin*. This was it.

I pulled into an angled parking spot in front of the strip mall. Forest Lawn had originated as its own separate town just east of Calgary. Annexed in the sixties, it became Calgary's easternmost community and housed many of the city's new immigrants. Now it was an inner-city neighbourhood. The European immigrants from the fifties and sixties were, over the years, joined by the Chinese, Pakistanis, Vietnamese, Filipinos, Hispanics, Sudanese, and lately Syrians. Many set up small shops and businesses and earned their livelihoods by providing products or services to the rest of the community.

International Avenue had a lot to offer. Tattoo parlours to restaurants, laundromats, funeral homes, specialty food stores and money marts, all advertised proudly and loudly with neon signs, twirling figures, brightly coloured banners and those inflatable, arm-flailing tube guys. If your shop was successful, you replaced the four-foot bowling pin on the roof of your bowling alley with an eight-foot bowling pin that spun. One could immediately see who was doing well— or was just plain cheap.

I took the two concrete stairs in one bound and pulled open the glass door. A smiling cardboard sausage stood immediately to the right, with today's specials printed on its chalkboard front. Sauerkraut stew with pork topped the list. One whiff of the warm air greeting me confirmed it.

A small glass counter ran along the left side of the shop. A kid wearing a green bib apron and a brown cap, which on closer inspection resembled a soggy sausage, was scraping something from one metal bin into another. Behind the counter, metal tray after metal tray stood ready, with the dozens of offerings listed on a board. Black sausage, liver sausage, bologna sausage, barbeque sausage along with pierogi, cabbage rolls, barley and potato soup, potato pancakes, and the usual sides, cucumbers in brine, marinated mushrooms, pickled herring, and a variety of salatka or salads. Everything was handwritten in Polish, complete with celeriac swirls and dots and the English translation next to it.

I noted the two rows of empty tables. Maybe they did a booming lunch or dinner run. A guy wearing a green bib apron, minus the sausage hat, sat at one of the dozen or so tables that lined the back and opposite side of the shop. I made my way back, and as I got closer, he looked up from the newspaper he was reading.

"Hi. I'm looking for a Greg Kowalski?"

"You found 'im," he replied.

I held out my hand. "Hi, I'm Jorja Knight. I called you earlier. I'm trying to locate Joey Albero. I heard you might know him."

He stood, wiped his hand on his bib and shook mine. He was shorter than me by an inch or two, well padded but not fat. The olive skin on his face stretched over full cheeks, his brown eyes round and lively. His grandma must have loved pinching those cheeks when he was a boy.

"Albero. Giuseppe Enrico Albero. Now there's a wander through memory lane."

"I was hoping you'd remember him."

"You kidding? Joey and I go way back. We met in junior high. Wanna coffee? Hey, Aayush," he called to the boy behind the counter before I had a chance to reply. "Bring us two coffee." He pulled out a chair for me. "Please, sit."

I told him there was an estate being settled and Joey had some money coming to him. That I found Joey's name on the U-18 Calgary soccer website, his name listed in an archived soccer team photo. I was hoping some of his high school or university buddies, had stayed in touch.

"Man, that guy was brilliant. He had a real mind for math, and anything mechanical. Didn't matter what you gave him, he could take it apart, fix it and put it back together. Anything. Radios, car engines, washing machines." Greg laughed, leaning back to make room for Aayush to put down the coffee cups he brought to the table. "He loved soccer. Man, could he move."

"When is the last time you saw him?"

"Oh, 'bout five…no, maybe six or seven years ago now. You know we both went to U of C, don't you? Not bad 'ey, for a couple of boys from the Lawn?"

"I hear he got into computers."

"He loved that stuff. I took one computer science course and barely passed. Wouldn't have if Joey hadn't helped me." He looked around his shop, picked up his coffee cup and slurped back a mouthful. "He sure got into the right field, didn't he? Everything is computerized these days. Even the damn cash register." He laughed. "I can barely work it. That's why I hire these young kids." He nodded in Aayush's direction, now back behind the counter washing up something at the back sink.

"Yet he didn't finish his degree. Do you know why?"

Greg put his coffee mug back on the table, his eyes and voice now serious. "Neither of us finished. I dropped out after my second year. My old man died of a heart attack. He used to run this place," he said, his eyes sweeping the place nostalgically. "My mother worked here too, as well as taking care of my dad and six kids. You get the picture."

I nodded.

"Anyway, Joey dropped out the next year, near the end of

first semester. I couldn't believe it. At least finish the semester, write the exams, I told him. Why waste the last few months? But he didn't. He could have aced those finals without even studying."

"Why did he quit?"

Greg leaned back, crossed his arms, and sat for a minute. "I'm not sure. He said he didn't need a piece of paper to prove anything. He'd be hired on his own merits, you know." He shook his head slightly, staring down at the table. "He went to work right after that. Got together with a bunch of guys building computer programs, and all kinds of stuff I still don't understand. That guy could have been the next freakin' Steve Jobs."

His voice revealed his admiration.

"So, what happened?"

"Not sure," he said, shrugging. "I ran into him a few years later. He wasn't doing so well. He seemed kinda…I don't know, down on himself, you know?"

"You mean down on himself, like depressed?"

Greg shrugged. "Don't know. But he was different. He lost some of that zip, that spunk he had. I know he and his buddies worked long and hard, and they didn't have much to show for it. I mean, how could they? It's real competitive out there, and there's all them big companies spending millions—no, billions—on all this technology. A small business can't compete."

"Is that the last time you saw him?"

"No. I ran into him again a couple of years later. I was paying my property taxes. Ran into him right outside city hall. I'd have walked right past him if he hadn't stopped me. He looked rough."

"You mean ill?"

"Truthfully? He looked like a bum. Clothes all dirty and ratty. He had long hair and a big beard. Said he was an environmentalist. When I asked him what he did, he told me he and a couple of others chained themselves up in a tree to keep it from being cut down. Can you imagine? He stayed up there for twenty-seven days." Greg shook his head. "That's crazy. At least it explained why he looked like crap."

"Did he seem okay?"

"Other than looking like crap, yeah. Once we got talking, some of the old Joey came back. He yakked about some damn tree owl they were protecting. I remember thinking whoa, this guy could do anything and he's spending his life protecting a tree owl." Greg shook his head.

"And there was nothing that happened to make him quit university, like in your case? No one died, got sick? He just left and over time ended up on a somewhat eccentric and reclusive path?"

Greg fished out a toothpick from the shot glass of toothpicks standing on the table next to the salt and pepper, peeled off the cellophane wrapper and stuck it in his mouth. I waited while he used his lips to manoeuvre the toothpick into the corner of his mouth. Finally, he spoke. "I wondered the same thing. Life can really hit you hard sometimes." I watched Greg chew on his toothpick, the end bobbing and swaying as if conducting some unheard miniature orchestra.

"Joey's sister said the same thing. One of Joey's university roommates said a friend of Joey's disappeared right around the time he dropped out. He thinks Joey took it harder than anyone imagined."

Greg nodded. "Oh yeah, yeah. Now I remember. Indian kid. Smart, younger than us, but in the same grade. He loved soccer too, but his parents wouldn't let him play. At least not outside of school. He ended up going to university same time we did. Joey hung out with him more than the rest of us. Then the year Joey quit, he didn't show up."

"You mean at university?"

"I mean anywhere."

"Could he have moved, or changed schools?"

"It didn't sound like it. I remember talking to Joey about it. He said he had gone and talked to Ajeet's mother. That was his name, Ajeet Jayaraman."

"What did his mother say?"

He shrugged. "She didn't know where he was. He just left."

"Did she report him missing?"

"I'm not sure."

"Do you know the Jayaramans? Ajeet's parents or the family?"

"No. They lived somewhere north of Seventeenth Avenue, near the swimming pool. I was only there once. Ajeet's folks kept to themselves."

"Did his disappearance strike you as odd?"

"It is odd. My parents lived through the war in Poland. Families got split apart, people disappeared. My own mother lost touch with her two brothers. They never returned home after the war. A few years later, rumours surfaced that one of them was living in a distant town. A friend of the family tracked him down. Found out he was secretly married to two women. Never found the other one."

"Ahh, rumours. People stay hidden for a reason. You've heard rumours? Does someone know what happened to him?"

He nodded again. "I reckon Joey knows."

"Tell me why you think so."

"He'd get angry whenever anyone brought up Ajeet's name. There was this one time a few months after Ajeet disappeared we were all out for beers at Dinny's Den. Someone said he hoped Ajeet had run off with some hot white chick and that the next time we saw him he'd be getting out of a limo in front of Microsoft's head office."

"That made Joey angry?"

"See what I mean? It's not like the guy slagged him. Joey jumped up and yelled that we were all idiots and stormed off. He knocked his chair over on the way out and pushed a guy out of his way. The guy he pushed fell into a waitress carrying a tray of beer. Glass and beer everywhere. That's why I remember."

"It does seem like a strange reaction. What were the rumours floating around?"

Greg fiddled with his coffee cup. He shifted in his chair, his foot tapping on the floor a mile a minute.

"Nice to see Joey might be coming into some money. His folks were poor like the rest of us. Not sure bringing up the past is going to help you find him," he said.

"Maybe...maybe not. His sister sees him from time to time but doesn't know how to get hold of him. I was hoping he stayed in touch with someone from his past. Or that someone would know where I might find him. Besides, from what I've learned, here was this bright guy with his future ahead of him and now he's some sort of recluse living in obscurity. My experience is people don't change that dramatically. Not unless it's a mental illness. Or something major throws them off course."

"Okay." He leaned forward. "But I've never told anyone this before, no one. I don't know why, just that it's weird and kind of pointless. It's probably nothing. Just remember, you didn't hear it from me."

Twenty minutes later, I knew it was something.

CHAPTER TWENTY-EIGHT

GREG TOLD ME Ajeet was the guy in their group of friends they most "joked around" with. I knew what that meant. Just friendly ribbing from your best buddies, better known as relentless harassment, if you were on the receiving end. As Greg told me the story, I tried hearing it from Ajeet's point of view.

Ajeet was a slight, soft-spoken kid who wanted to fit in, like all kids do. He had the extra challenge of trying to fit in with skin colour that didn't match his friends, an accent that made his speech stand out. He ate food his friends were unfamiliar with and his family seemed overly strict and controlling. At least by North American standards.

They had all met up at Pearce Estate Park for a Labour Day party. A time to say farewell to four months of freedom from books, and hello to labs, last-minute papers to write, and nights of cramming for exams. It was a common ritual, maybe even becoming a tradition. Even though Greg was no longer at university, he still hung out with some of the old crowd, whenever he got the chance. That night, about twenty young men and women convened. Ajeet was there as well as a few other guys from their U-18 soccer days. Joey had been there as well as Tony and another roommate of theirs, a guy named Stephen.

The evening started out ordinarily enough, someone brought out a soccer ball to kick around, a few people played Frisbee. Drinking in the park wasn't allowed, which is why everyone had liquor in their water bottles or soft drinks. The group ate a potluck dinner and as the night wore on a few people left to join parties elsewhere. The remaining group wandered down the river pathway, pushing one another in at the edge and egging each other on to jump in, swim across or any number of ridiculous stunts.

The dares escalated. Copious amounts of liquor made everything seem hilarious, fun, less risky. Ajeet didn't drink and as everyone got drunker, they taunted him, saying he was no fun sober. Ajeet resisted. Someone suggested if he wasn't going to drink, then he'd better take a dare. They dared him to drink four litres of water. Ajeet drank about one and a half litres, then threw up. The dare changed. They laid bets on how much water he could drink and keep down in two hours.

Greg vaguely recalled someone daring Joey to kiss one of the guys, full on the mouth. Joey picked Ajeet. Ajeet tried to run away, but a couple of the guys ran him down and dragged him back. Greg's recall was fuzzy, just disconnected bits and pieces. Ajeet had been crying and yelling at Joey, something about promising not to tell. Greg couldn't remember a whole lot after that. All he knew was that at some point he crawled into an unlocked car and fell asleep in the passenger seat.

"It's kind of weird, because I don't know if it was real, or I just dreamt part of it. I guess that's why I've never told anyone."

"I know what you mean," I said, hoping to dispel his unease about recalling something that might be inaccurate. "Don't worry, it's not like I'm going to hold you to anything you say, I'm just trying to find out what happened that night. Why Joey is the way he is."

"Okay. I remember that at one point I had to take a leak. I got out of the car to, well, you know. Stephen and Joey were stumbling toward the car, holding up Ajeet. He could barely walk, he seemed totally out of it."

"Ajeet?"

"Yeah. I staggered back to the car. Joey and this guy Stephen were getting Ajeet into the passenger seat. I tried getting into the back seat, but someone was passed out back there." Greg laughed. "I was so hammered. I didn't even realize I was trying to get into someone else's car."

"Where was this car?"

"Parked at the far side of the parking lot. There were only three or four cars left there by then. My car was parked way over, on the other side. I knew I'd never make it to my car. I sat down on the grass. Everything was spinning."

"What happened after that?"

"Like I said, I was pretty wasted. I must have passed out. Next thing I know, it's light outside. The car was gone."

"Did you see Stephen get into the car, the one with Ajeet slumped over in the passenger seat? Did you see it leave?"

"I believe I did."

"Did Joey go with them?"

"No. I woke up at one point. It was still dark. Joey was crying and wandering around the parking lot."

"What about Tony?"

"I'm sure it was Tony lying in the back seat. He was dead to the wind. That's all I remember. Weird, huh?"

"Every bit helps," I said. I wasn't sure this did. It might be a fragment of a dream. Or maybe the sequence of events that night were jumbled in his mind. One minute he's saying he passed out until dawn, the next minute he tells me he saw Joey wandering around in the dark.

"Did you ever ask Joey or Stephen or Tony about what happened?"

"Tony said he didn't remember being passed out in the back seat of the car. I met up with Joey a few weeks later. That's when he told me Ajeet had dropped out of school, no one knew where he'd gone."

"Did Joey see him after the party?"

"I don't know. I do know he felt godawful about what happened to Ajeet that night. I tried to lighten things up by making some comment about how scared Ajeet got when Joey kissed him, but he got mad, told me to lay off."

"So, did anyone say anything about what happened that night?"

"Bits and pieces came out over the years. Stephen supposedly drove Ajeet home that night. Dropped him off at his parents' house. Ajeet was in a bad way. He seemed disoriented, nauseated, like he was drunk except he'd only been drinking water."

"Do you know how dangerous drinking large volumes of

water can be? Water intoxication is a real thing. Symptoms can include nausea, vomiting and mental confusion."

"I don't think anyone knew it at the time. A few years later I read about a guy who died in California, during frosh week, from drinking too much water."

"There's been more than one person who's died drinking a lot of water over a short timespan. Runners know the risk. Too much water depletes salt in the body, overwhelms the kidneys. It literally leaves the blood waterlogged."

"I didn't how dangerous it was until years later. I'm sure the other guys didn't either."

"So, Stephen just dropped off Ajeet at his parents' place that night. Did anyone else talk to his parents, besides Joey?"

"Joey is the only one that I know of. Like I said, the parents claimed he never came home that night."

"Nobody found that odd?"

"A lot of us thought it was weird. But rumour had it that Ajeet had a big argument with his mother the night of the party. The general scuttlebutt was that she told him if he went to the party he wasn't to come back."

"That's rough."

"Still odd though. You'd think someone would have heard from him by now."

"What do you think happened to him?"

Greg looked at me sombrely. "I've thought back to that night off and on over the years. It's so weird. I wish I remembered more, or more clearly." Greg shrugged. "I suppose he might have split after Stephen dropped him off." Greg's eyes met mine. "But I'm betting he died that night."

CHAPTER TWENTY-NINE

GREG'S RECALL OF what happened twenty years ago was sketchy to say the least. But a couple of things intrigued me. Joey had been a hard-working, keen young man, who suddenly changed course. He dropped out of university, moved from job to job, and eventually ended up living off the grid, convinced the world was about to end. Something must have happened to make him change his life. Around the same time, his friend, Ajeet, disappears after a big drunken party that Joey, Tony, and Stephen all attended. A night that included taunting, bullying, and dangerous dares. Emotions ran high. Joey had been distraught. Maybe. According to Greg, Stephen had taken Ajeet home. He may have been the last person to see Ajeet alive.

On the other hand, Ajeet may have taken his mother's words to heart and severed ties with his family. My own heart grew heavy at the thought. I knew the destructive power of severed relationships and how unanswered questions could morph into unhealthy obsession.

Maybe I was over-thinking the situation or making

connections where there were none, projecting my personal history onto the current situation. But I couldn't shake the idea that Ajeet and Joey held the key to each other's situation in life and maybe even to Stephen's death. Like Greg, I found it hard to believe that Ajeet would not have made some effort to reconnect with family or friends, if he were still alive. Then again it had been ten years since I last contacted my brother.

Tony was in a meeting when I arrived for my appointment. I could see glimpses of him through the partially closed venetian blinds in the conference room across from his executive assistant's office. He was working the room.

Four dark-suited men of varying age, height, and girth, along with an Asian woman with coppery-coloured ends to her pitch-black, shoulder-length hair watched his theatrics at the front of the room. He paced from left to right, then back again, his one hand jiggling in the pocket of his navy-blue pants, the other gesturing in small quick movements at something on the wall, not visible to me.

The meeting was breaking up, everyone was standing. Tony shook hands with the woman and slapped one of the guys on the back. They came out of the meeting room, Tony's voice loud, boisterous, the smile on his face brittle, strained. Tony walked with them to the end of the corridor while continuing his one-sided banter.

I leaned toward Sharon. "Oh, my gosh," I gushed in a loud whisper. "Was that Alice Kim, the actress from Down Fall?"

Sharon looked up. "What?" She peered down the hall. "Miss Olivia Li? You think she looks like Alice Kim?"

I stole a glance at the little group saying their goodbyes. "Yeah, but I only caught a glimpse of her. You sure it's not her?"

Sharon chuckled. "No such luck."

"Oh," I said, faking disappointment. "Too bad for me." I pulled out my phone, muted it, and snapped a few photos while pretending to check email. Tony turned and sailed back down the hall. I quicky dropped my phone into my tote.

"Jorja," he said, reaching out an outstretched hand as he approached. "How's the PI biz? Sharon, sweetheart, be a doll and get us a coffee." He turned to me. "Black, right?"

The *Sharon, sweetheart* thing was getting under my skin, but Sharon slid her hips from behind her desk and smiled impishly at Tony.

"Yes, black. Thank you."

"Come in, come in." Tony waved me into his office, peeled off his navy jacket and hung it on the back of the door. "Making any progress?" he asked as Sharon delivered our coffees and sashayed back out.

Tony's wide smile was tight, his voice and movements taut, mechanical.

"I believe I am," I replied. "I met with Greg Kowalski yesterday."

"Oh yeah? Was he any help?"

"He told me about the last time he saw Joey's friend Ajeet. Apparently, the last night anyone saw Ajeet. At a summer's end party in Pearce Estate."

"Told you. The guy's memory is better than an elephant."

"You don't remember the night? Labor Day, 1998?"

"Pffff. I worked hard at university, but I played hard too. Frankly, I don't remember a lot of details from back then if you get my drift." He smiled beguilingly.

"Ajeet was in a bad way that night. Nauseated, disoriented from a stupid water-drinking dare. Stephen was supposed to have taken him home. His parents said he never turned up. Greg seems to recall you were in the back seat of Stephen's car that night."

Tony lifted his hands up and shook his head. "What can I say. The way I drank back then. Let's just say I'm amazed I didn't end up an alcoholic."

"Stephen must have said something about that night. I mean, a guy went missing and he was one of the last people to see him."

Tony leaned forward, elbows on the table, hands clasped in front of his mouth. Tiny, almost imperceptible shakes of his head told me he was deep in thought. After a minute he looked up. "You can't believe that had anything to do with Stephen's death. That happened twenty years ago."

"There's no statute of limitations on anger and revenge."

"So…you think what? That Stephen was somehow responsible for this fellow's disappearance?"

"Stephen never said anything to you?"

"About what?"

"The night Ajeet went missing."

"Stephen must have dropped the guy off at his parents' place, like Greg said."

"You don't remember telling Rob about this one night, over beers?"

Tony shook his head. "No. He must be mistaken. Why?

You think someone killed Stephen over what happened that night?"

"I don't know. I mean why wait all these years. Then again, the way Stephen was killed, someone must have known how to circumvent his security system. Everyone says Joey is brilliant at that kind of stuff."

"I guess if Stephen knew…or had something to do with Ajeet's disappearance, it might explain things. He could have left Joey money because…well, out of guilt."

Tony grew still. We studied each other for a moment.

"Naw." Tony waved his hand across himself and sat back. "Joey's had a run of bad luck. More than likely there's a mental issue there that's not being addressed. Stephen likely wanted to help him out; just another one of his charity cases."

"His sister doesn't believe there is anything wrong with him."

Tony leaned forward. "She talk to him lately?"

"Not since Stephen was murdered."

"So, what's next?"

"I guess I'll just have to keep digging. Try to find Joey. See what he has to say."

"Good luck with that."

"Well, thanks again for putting me in touch with Greg. By the way, did you know Stephen's driver has found himself some new clients?"

"Good for him." Tony smile froze on his face.

"I wondered if maybe you had put in a good word for him."

"Why would I give Stephen's driver a reference? I don't even know him."

"You've never had any dealings with Conner Weston on your own?"

"No. I don't understand where you're going with this." He was no longer smiling.

"Just trying to tie some loose bits and pieces together. You know what they say, the devil's in the details. Laura and Chloe believe Conner knows more about what happened to Stephen than he's saying. It's a small world, not many private chauffeurs working in the city. Thought you might have run into him."

I thanked Tony for his time and left. He hadn't admitted to seeing Conner picking someone up at The Ranchmen's Club. It's possible he hadn't noticed him there. But I was getting tired of making excuses for Tony's lack of attention to details, faulty memory and lies of omission.

Now I was keener than ever to find Joey.

CHAPTER THIRTY

Traffic crawled and I, along with thousands of others, inched along in near whiteout conditions. I pulled over twice to scrape off the snow which first melted on the windshield then froze into an opaque film of ice. My mind swirled in all directions, mirroring the storm outside.

It was close to noon by the time I arrived at the office. The whole city had slowed to a crawl. The few graders and gravel trucks the city sent out barely made any difference to road conditions. I was starving, but decided I'd wait until the lunch crowd finished before grabbing a bite to eat.

After settling in, I checked my tracker app again. The sedan was parked at Conner's apartment. It hadn't moved since yesterday. I pulled up the browser and googled Olivia Li. With thousands of hits coming back I refined my search for recent press releases. I came across one announcing her appointment as Chief Operating Officer at StarTu, a technology company founded in 2008.

After some digging, I discovered Miss Li was born in China to a Canadian mother and Chinese father. She obtained a law degree at Harvard and then returned to China where she joined the government's New Territories Administrative Service. By 2002, she had risen to become the Deputy of Trade and Industry and by 2006 she was no longer in China. Now she was the COO for StarTu.

StarTu's website described them as a private company, focused on technologies with transnational appeal. I read about a competition they hosted annually. Ten teams vied for a prize of twenty thousand dollars and a six-month mentorship at StarTu. In return, StarTu acquired a five-percent equity stake in all ten of the teams' inventions, twenty percent in the winner's entry. Hundreds applied but only ten teams made it to the finals. The competition ended with a huge pitch event for venture capitalists and other investors for all the participants.

Several businessmen and women stood next to Olivia Li in a photo from the last pitch event, including the silver-haired man that climbed into Conner's limo at The Ranchmen's Club. The photo caption identified the man as Jack Tián, president and owner of Tián Technologies, better known as T&T. Now I knew why he seemed familiar when I first saw him at The Ranchmen's Club. His smiling face had been on the TV numerous times last year after his company acquired two competitors in quick succession.

The Tián family history made for fascinating reading. My eyes skimmed the Wikipedia page which in turn led me to other articles. Jack's grandfather, a dishwasher from San Francisco, staked six gold claims in the Yukon and struck it rich. Unfortunately, he died shortly after returning from the Yukon, having little time to revel in his new-found wealth.

He left behind a son, Charles, the only child from his marriage with a Tagish First Nations woman.

Charles was a bit of a wild man and die-hard adventurer. But the war dampened his plans and in 1941 he headed north, to the Canadian Shield, an area rich with nickel, copper, lead and silver. Fast forward five years and his small nickel mine blossomed like algae on a lake. The Canadian and US defence industry were buying up every ounce of nickel they could get their hands on, nickel being a critical element in weapons production.

Charles' son Jack, having inherited the Tiáns' missing fear gene, moved west to join the wildcatters searching for oil. Continuing in the tradition of his ancestors and with the proverbial Tián horseshoe nailed to his ass, Jack cashed in his oil and gas holdings at their peak in 2010 and entered the high-tech industry. In six short years, his revenue tripled, profits doubled and when he took the company public two years ago, stock prices rose thirty percent. T&T was the Tián family's flagship venture into the brave new world of artificial intelligence.

These were serious players. Maybe Tián and StarTu were the companies Stephen had been negotiating with for the Nano-skin fuel cell. Or perhaps they were interested in something else Tony was working on, or his whole company. Either way, I had seen Tony with or at the same location with top executives from both companies and Tony seemed strained, stressed. Maybe negotiations weren't going well. The image of Tony, his nervous chatter and polite, empty smile told me there was more on the line than a business deal.

Maybe Chloe knew there was a big windfall in the works for Tony and her stall tactics were a deliberate way to get Tony to pay her off so he could move forward. But how would she have known? Conner could have told her. Especially if he was now working for one of the players interested in acquiring Stephen's patent. Chloe might be playing with fire.

Noticing the building had grown quiet, I glanced at my watch. It was just after two. With a full-blown blizzard threatening, most people had gone home early. I decided I would too.

I packed up, went downstairs, and stepped outside. The wind immediately pushed me in every direction. I tucked my head down and fought my way against the wind to the car.

I slid into the front seat and sat for a second to catch my breath. I turned the key in the ignition. A rapid clicking, told me this wasn't good. I tried several more times. I laid my head on the steering wheel. *Seriously?*

Maybe just as well it didn't start. The car no longer served my need for anonymity. I called JumpIn Jalopies' road-side service and was told it would be several hours before they could get to me. I rented all my cars from JumpIn Jalopies. They offered great rates and had an entire fleet of roadworthy older vehicles with some annoying features needing repair which, given the age of the vehicles, were too costly to undertake. The windows in the Chevy couldn't be rolled down. Not a big deal, if I didn't go through a restaurant drive-thru or pull in too close to a ticket-dispensing machine.

Jamming my toque low on my forehead, I cursed and

gathered up my stuff. I'd be frozen long before help arrived. I left the keys in the coffee holder, got out and headed toward Macleod Trail.

I arrived at Nicky's Bar and Grill chilled to the bone. I peeled off my gloves and blew on my fingers while following the hostess to a table in the lounge. The lounge wasn't overly busy, most of the patrons, lingering after lunch, on the restaurant side. I slid my coat off, letting it drape over the back of my chair, called Gab, and left her a message. The bartender came around from the counter and over to my table.

"How's your day going?" he said.

"Better now that I'm here. How's yours?"

"Better now that you're here," he replied, winking. "What can I get you?"

"How about a Manhattan?"

"You got it," he said and slid away.

I looked the place over. I hadn't been in here for years, but it hadn't changed a bit. Buffalo wings, high top tables and flatscreen TV's on the left, booths, wooden tables, and better lighting to the right.

The bartender returned and placed my Manhattan in front of me. "Tell me if you like it."

I picked up my drink, gave the liquid a quick swirl with the short green straw and sipped.

"Oh, that's good. What's in here? Vanilla?"

"Yeah. I soak a whole vanilla bean in the bourbon for an entire month. You should try it at home. It's easy to do."

"But I'd have to keep an opened bottle of bourbon around for a whole month."

He laughed and held out his hand. "I'm Kurt."

I took his hand. "I'm Jorja."

"Jorja. That's a beautiful name. Don't hear that name very often."

I examined him in earnest. Average height, muscular. Reddish-blond hair cut in a short Mohawk, pale-blue eyes. His arms were covered in tattoos. Not really my type. Too talkative. Besides, I already had two men in my life, and truthfully, it might be one too many.

A waitress came by with water and a menu and Kurt slid back to the bar. I ordered a fish taco and salad and, once the waitress departed, called JumpIn Jalopies and told them where to find the car keys.

The waitress returned with my order and set it down in front of me. "Enjoy. Let me know if there's anything else you need."

Gab sent me a text saying she was with a potential client and wouldn't be able to pick me up until after five. I texted back and said I'd take the train home. I cleared old messages from my phone while I ate. I declined a second Manhattan, slipped thirty dollars under my glass, and slid off my barstool.

"Jorja," the bartender called out after me.

I turned.

"Don't be a stranger."

I lifted my hand in reply, turned, and ran smack into Bernie.

"Ms. K. Fancy meeting you here. Must be fate." He snickered, head bouncing up and down, quick breaths snorted in, nothing coming out.

"What are you doing here?" I blurted out, staring at

his face, which scrunched and twitched under my gaze. He giggled nervously; his eyes looked hurt. "Just celebrating a co-worker's ten-year work anniversary." He waved his arm in the direction of a group of seven or eight people seated in the dining room. They had two tables pulled together and were engrossed in lively banter. I looked back at Bernie. I felt like an ass. This case was getting to me, every tiny lead going nowhere.

"Of course, sorry if I sounded angry."

"No worries, Ms. K, no worries."

I finished pulling on my hat and gloves and went outside. Bernie was one odd duck. Was he odd enough to leave me black dahlias and photos of my dead parents? Why would he?

Pulling my coat collar up, I jammed my hands into my coat pockets and headed to the C-Train station. Why would anyone be stalking me? The voice in my head remined me that stalkers didn't need a reason. At least no reason any sane person would have.

CHAPTER THIRTY-ONE

I ARRIVED HOME physically and mentally exhausted. My nerves were jangled, and I had a massive headache. I slipped my key into the door, pulled off my boots, hung my damp coat on the doorknob and headed for the shower.

The hot water slid down my back and loosened the knot in my neck. I stood there until the water lost its heat. After drying off I pulled on black Lululemon yoga pants, fuzzy pink socks and an old stretched-out grey sweater. I poured myself a scotch and flicked on the TV. The evening news was on, and the top story was the storm hammering southern Alberta.

Still feeling restless, I retrieved my envelope of stalker notes from the TV stand and carefully spread them out on the coffee table. I regretted throwing out the card that came with the black dahlias, the only one written by hand. Of course, it might have been the florist's handwriting dictated by someone over the phone. The florist shop listed on the card insisted the flowers had not come from them. I had checked each note for fingerprints and came up empty.

I stared at the most recent one. The dagger through the heart was a classic symbol, often used in tattoo design. I pulled up my laptop and googled. I discovered that in Christian-themed ink, the dagger through the heart represented the grieving Mother of Christ, often referred to as the Lady of Sorrows. More commonly, the combination of the heart and the dagger was used to represent the heart in great pain. A heart mortally wounded, a love betrayed, or some great sacrifice made.

According to the internet, and aside from the obvious religious symbolism, crosses were used to pay tribute to a person's ancestry or represent the link between the physical and spiritual world. I picked up my scotch and sank back against the cushions.

Now I understood why the notes contained crudely hand-drawn crosses and hearts along with newspaper headlines and pictures of me and my family. The notes weren't about my parents, they were about me. My stalker was telling me he knew my pain.

Taking a sip, I swirled my tongue against the scotch, noticing its full weighty feel as it slid down my throat. I tipped back the glass and downed the rest in three quick swallows. Wiping my mouth with the back of my hand, I stood up and made my way to the kitchen and shakily poured myself a generous second. My eyes roamed over my sterile living space. Nights were when I really felt my isolation. Tonight's storm threw up yet another barrier between me and the rest of humanity. I considered texting Azagora. The problem was I wasn't sure if I wanted to be with him, or just be with someone. I picked up my glass with one hand and the bottle with the other and traipsed back to the couch.

My eyes flew open, darting to the patio doors. I must have dozed off, the half-full glass of scotch safely resting on my chest, cradled in both hands. Sitting up, I strained to hear. The wind howled outside. Feeling exposed now with the living room brightly lit against the darkness outside, I crossed over to the window, cupped my hand around my eyes and peered out.

A ghostly round face stared back at me.

"Jezus mother of mercy," I yelled, jumping back. Scotch sloshed across my hand. The lights flickered, went off and came back on.

In the brief second of darkness, I realized the face was nothing more than a white drip tray off someone's planter, now firmly plastered up against my balcony railing. Wiping up dribbles of scotch off the floor with my fuzzy sock, I checked the patio door to make sure it was locked and drew the blinds across the glass, shutting out the storm and eliminating the reflections from behind me. The lights flickered again and went out.

Guided by the faint glow from my smart phone lying on the coffee table, I made my way back to the couch. Trading my drink for the phone, my shaking fingers swiped the screen and found the flashlight icon. Pointing the phone ahead of me, I made my way to the front door, checked the lock, and engaged the deadbolt.

"Candles, candles, come on, where are you," I muttered as I poked through the hall closet and then the kitchen cupboards. The phone vibrated in my hand, making me jump and yelp at the same time. I must have turned off the ringer. I peered at the screen and sighed in relief.

"Hey Gab, how are you doing?"

"I'm good. At my cousin Connie's place. Are you home?"

"I am. I just lost power. How about you?"

"Not yet," she reported cheerfully. "But the lights have been flickering like crazy. Connie's been dragging out her candles and flashlights. We have a pizza baking in the oven. If the lights go out, we're going to turn our movie night into ghost story night and see who does the best job of scaring the pants off the other."

I could hear Connie's boys laughing and chattering excitedly in the background. I also heard a faint but familiar double-beep in my ear. I glanced at the phone screen. My battery was nearly dead.

"I'm glad you're safe at home," continued Gab. "If it wasn't so godawful out there, I'd suggest you come over."

"Thanks for thinking of me. I still haven't found candles or my flashlight, but the scotch is poured, the doors and windows are locked and I'm ready to settle in for the night." I barely finished the last word when my phone went dead plunging me into darkness.

"Screw the candles," I mumbled. I groped my way out of the kitchen and into the bedroom. I pulled the quilt off the foot of the bed and made my way back to the couch.

Crawling onto the couch, I tucked the quilt around me and reached for my scotch. The apartment was eerily quiet, my heart rate now at the pace it reached when I jogged. I jumped at a loud metallic bang somewhere in the building, my brain scrambling to identify it. Probably the garbage chute. I could turn on my laptop but decided it best to save the battery. I glanced at my watch. It was only nine o'clock, but it felt like midnight.

Footsteps pounded down the hallway. Someone shouted and hammered on my door.

I stopped breathing.

Then six more sharp raps. A voice yelled something, muffled by the door.

Where the hell was my gun? I pushed back the quilt as someone yelled again and pounded on the door. A voice floated faintly from down the hall.

What the hell was going on?

I made my way around the coffee table and slid sideways across the room until my hand touched the far wall. I followed it around the corner to the bathroom door and stood stock still, heart pounding. The inside of the bathroom was like a tomb. Wiggly specks floated across my retina, my hands now damp with sweat, my feet unbearably hot in the fuzzy socks.

I reached forward, my hand grazing the coolness of the porcelain sink. I jumped as my hand touched something soft, knocking it to the floor. *My purse.* I froze. No more pounding at the door. Faint laughter came from down the hall.

Crouching, my fingers scrambled across the floor for my purse. I pulled it toward me, spilling contents along the way. Reaching in, my fingers closed around a wadded tissue. My gun must still be in the bedroom. Standing up I turned back toward the living room.

Someone rattled the door handle.

I stood paralyzed, my back pressed into the hallway wall for what seemed like hours. The voices in the hall quieted and a door slammed somewhere.

Probably just a disoriented condo-dweller who ended up at the wrong door.

I abandoned the idea of trying to load my gun properly in the dark and retrieved a knife from the kitchen. I hated knives even more than guns. Knives were messy and I had the scar to prove it. But if push came to shove, I wasn't going down without a fight.

CHAPTER THIRTY-TWO

I awoke to the sound of voices, and after a moment of panic, realized I must have left the TV on. A sense of relief flooded over me—the power was back.

I had slept fitfully and each time I woke the air had been frigid, the apartment devoid of the usual buzz of the fridge or the sound of the heating system. The TV screen a gaping black hole across the room.

I plugged in my laptop and dead phone, and listened to the TV news reports, the comforter still wrapped around me. An emergency had been issued for all southern Alberta. A massive cold front hit the city yesterday and had stalled overhead. It was being touted as the worst storm recorded for this time of year since 1924. The temperature had dropped to minus twenty-three degrees Celsius overnight, minus thirty-five with the wind chill. Not to mention the snow which forecasters were predicting could reach forty to sixty centimetres before the storm moved off.

Many businesses and all schools were closed, but everyone was working frantically to get things back to normal.

Police were advising people to stay off the highways, the wait time for a tow truck still days. I hoped JumpIn Jalopies had gotten around to fixing my car.

I picked up my phone and listened to the one voicemail in my inbox. The Chevy had been towed to JumpIn Jalopies' shop. They would contact me when it was repaired. With conditions being what they were, it might take a while.

I checked my email and text messages. There was one from Mike, telling me to stay inside and watch old movies or something. I smiled. *Good old Mike.* He was in Vancouver, delivering a training course, but must have heard about the storm on the news. I sent him a reply then texted Gab asking her if they managed to get the pizza baked before the power went out.

I scrolled through the remaining messages. Nothing from Azagora. Why hadn't he reached out? My fingers paused over the keyboard. I reminded myself that I hadn't reached out to him either. The little critic that lives in my head jumped in. *Yeah, but no one is sending him black flowers and pictures of dead loved ones.* The more rational voice in my head reminded the critic that I hadn't told him about my dead loved ones.

I glanced at the window. Blowing snow obscured any sign of life outside. The rant in my head continued. Sure, I managed on my own. I always had. And my pals Gab and Mike were always there for me. But having two connections with the external world was disturbingly depressing. The kinder voice in my head argued it wasn't true. I had other contacts. I mentally ticked off the names of all the people whom I could call if I needed help. I came up with seven. Azagora was one of them, but I was quite sure he'd be annoyed if I called him for help. I reminded myself that I could hardly expect him to act like we were in a relationship when I was still questioning if I wanted a relationship with him.

I told myself I was being ridiculous. There were people all around me. If I needed help any number of them would come to my aid. Except I didn't want the help of strangers. I picked up my phone and scrolled through contacts until my finger reached Luis Azagora. I paused, then threw my phone down and pulled over my computer.

"Hi, Cortana. How many friends does the average person have?" This was stupid. Why couldn't I let this go?

Cortana answered, "The average person has forty friends."

I swore under my breath. *Must be the stat for extroverts.* I googled to see if I could get a better number. The articles I read said humans weren't meant to be solitary animals. They needed to belong to a herd. Only old or injured animals who couldn't keep up wandered alone. If I were a gazelle, I'd be dead.

I got up, wearing the quilt like a cape, and made my way to the window. Snow lay drifted a foot high on my balcony, the frost halfway up the glass. What about old Mrs. Wilson and her three cats down the hall from me? I hadn't checked up on her. What kind of person was I?

Walking into the bedroom felt like I'd crawled into a freezer. I shivered as I dropped the comforter and pulled off my sweater. *Could a witch's tit be any colder?* I donned fresh jeans and a black cashmere sweater, then brushed, fluffed and sprayed my hair until I was satisfied with how the messily arranged strands framed my face. I pulled on an extra sweater, grabbed my comforter, made coffee, and settled back on the couch.

Minutes later I marvelled at how something simple like coffee could restore a sense of wellbeing. Maybe it would help get rid of the heavy ball occupying my midsection. Or perhaps it was hunger and would go away after a proper meal. But I knew that wasn't the case.

An hour later my insides still ached like a Damien Rice song but at least I was warmer. My laptop pinged and I picked it up. *What's this?*

Another email from S. Wise. I opened it and read. *The end lies ahead. I have much to do.*

What the hell?

CHAPTER THIRTY-THREE

THE TRIP TO the bus stop, usually a ten-minute jaunt, took half an hour. Most of the sidewalks and roads were still waiting to be ploughed. Understandably, the bus had been late. The only difference between being inside the bus rather than outside was the lack of wind. I had arrived at JumpIn Jalopies half frozen, my scarf frozen stiff with icy breath. It took two hours to get home, but that included a quick stop to pick up some groceries. I was still chilled, but at least I had wheels again. And being outside, however unpleasant, lifted my spirits.

The last two days in my condo felt like an eternity. With no heat, power or water for most of that time, the building had quickly reached the brink of being uninhabitable. The condo board had posted a notice downstairs advising us that Southland Leisure Centre was providing emergency services for anyone who had no place else to go. I hadn't ventured out at all, but one more day might have pushed me beyond my limits.

After my hands thawed, I made two phone calls. The first

was to Joey's sister Antonia. She still hadn't heard from Joey. She didn't recall a childhood friend named Ajeet Jayaraman.

The second call went to Laura.

"Just calling to give you a quick update. I'm trying to track down an old school friend of Stephen's, a guy by the name of Ajeet Jayaraman. Is that name familiar?"

"No. Doesn't ring a bell."

"Looks like Tony might be proceeding with finding a buyer for one of the patents Stephen left him. It occurred to me that maybe Chloe knows this and it's the real reason she's holding things up, hoping Tony will pay her off so he can move on."

"Wouldn't surprise me in the least."

"How's it going with Chloe? Will you and Tony be settling with her?"

"No. We're calling her bluff. Wayne is furious but if she wants to take this through the courts she can. I don't know how she plans on paying the legal costs though. Her inheritance from Stephen will be held up as well."

"She called me a few days ago. Someone vandalized her boyfriend's car."

"Wouldn't surprise me if was an annoyed customer. She needs to stop running that mouth of hers."

"She claimed Stephen promised her some million-dollar coin, that apparently is missing."

Laura laughed bitterly. "I bet she accused me of taking it didn't she? That woman is delusional."

"I did tell her she should be careful about levelling accusations without concrete proof."

"I don't know what coins were in Stephen's collection but

the whole of them were appraised at three hundred thousand dollars. The million-dollar coin was just a phrase Stephen used to refer to a coin that might grow in value over time."

"Makes sense. Anything, new on your front?"

"We got another call on our tip line, the day the storm hit."

"Really? Anything of interest."

"No. The guy just wanted to know if we were still offering the reward. Then he called back a second time to confirm that providing information that led to the arrest of Stephen's killer was all that was required."

"He didn't say what he had?"

"No. He didn't give a name either. Tony was over meeting with Wayne and I when the call came in. He took down the guy's phone number. He said he would try a reverse call and see if he could get more information from him."

"Did you give the number to Detective McGuire?"

"No. Our previous efforts to pass on phone calls with no real information led nowhere. Detective McGuire said unless someone was willing to leave a name and a number to call, they weren't interested in wasting time chasing down calls from curiosity seekers."

"Have you had many of those?"

"When we first put up the reward, we got hundreds of calls, some showing a phone number, some with caller ID blocked. But none of the calls came with any information. Most callers wanted information from us, like wanting to know if the reward money would be split if several people brought forward information, that sort of thing."

"I see. Do you mind sharing the number from the last caller, with me?"

"Just a sec, I'll get it for you."

After I hung up, I did a reverse lookup for the phone number Laura gave me. It wasn't registered, leading me to believe it came from a burner phone. I had told Laura that if she got a second call from the same number, she should pass it along to Detective McGuire. They'd have the resources needed to find the owner or at least determine the location of the call.

I made a pot of coffee and jotted down my next steps. My two days of isolation had given me a lot of time to mull things over. Detective McGuire had told me they were digging into Stephen's data files, his business dealings, that sort of thing. I imagined they would have also looked into Laura and Wayne's affairs seeing as they were Stephen's largest beneficiaries.

I didn't have the resources to dig very far in either of those directions. Which left me Chloe, Conner, and Joey Albern. Although Chloe and Conner had alibis for the time of Stephen's death, I was convinced they knew something that would lead me to Stephen's killer.

Conner knew Stephen, his sister, and her family. He had met or at least knew who Stephen's close friends were. And despite his rather loathsome reputation, he ended up working for Stephen. I wasn't convinced that the ten-dollar price tag on Stephen's Mercedes Benz meant it had been a gift. More than likely it was a payoff. Even if Conner didn't have a direct hand in Stephen's death, I, like Detective McGuire, figured he had played a role in it.

206 | ALICE BIENIA

The fact that I had seen Conner picking up Jack Tián at The Ranchmen's made my spidey senses tingle. If Jack Tián showed up somewhere, you knew it wasn't for a casual chat. Tony had also been at The Ranchmen's at the same time. Something big was cooking. And the level of anger Tony was displaying around a possible delay in assignment of patent rights to the Nano-skin fuel cell Stephen left him, made me think the patent was on the table in whatever deal they were crafting.

I had also decided I would keep delving into a missing kid from Forest Lawn named Ajeet and step-up efforts to find Joey. Stephen, Joey, and Tony had all known each other and Ajeet, Joey better than the other two. All three had been at a summer's end party with Ajeet and, according to Greg, were the last few people to see Ajeet before he dropped out of sight. Perhaps Rob had been right when he suggested someone may have killed Stephen as an act of retribution for a past wrong.

Tony's offer to look up the recent caller to the Bradford's tip line was odd. Which brought up an interesting idea. Could Chloe and Conner still be working together? Maybe one or both were trying to ferret out enough information to qualify for the reward money. For that matter, any of Stephen's friends or acquaintances could be doing the same.

Getting information out of Conner wasn't going to be easy. His sedan had sat stationary at his apartment since the day the storm hit. If it didn't move by morning, I'd go check it out.

I put away my laptop and threw a frozen pizza into the oven. Once it was ready, I ate pizza and binge watched four episodes of Blacklist. Feeling the effects of several restless nights, I turned in early.

I woke during the night to a loud bang. I lay still, holding my breath, afraid some scumbag was breaking in to kill me. I told myself it was just the pipes in the building, heating up. The second time I woke, I heard scratching sounds at the door. I laid awake until a faint grey light grew around my window blinds.

As dawn broke, I fell asleep and dreamt Joey was ringmaster at a circus and I was running around with my narcissistic ex-boyfriend looking for several circus chimps who had escaped, all wielding crosses or daggers.

CHAPTER THIRTY-FOUR

THIS MORNING, THE sun shone weakly in a bright-blue sky, the temperature already a balmy minus five. The city was nearly back to normal. I considered calling Detective McGuire, to share my theory that Joey might have had it in for Stephen, maybe blamed him for his friend Ajeet's disappearance. Then what? He waited twenty years and bypassing the latest and greatest home security system available, entered Stephen's house, and killed him. The inclination passed.

I checked the tracker app several times, but Conner's car hadn't moved. By mid-morning, curiosity got the better of me.

I drove past Conner's apartment building, did a U-turn, and drove back, parking a block from the apartment. I opened my laptop on the seat beside me and settled in to eat the bagel I had picked up on my way. A few people went in and out of the building. Three hours later, the dot hadn't budged.

I climbed out of the car, locked up and sauntered down the street. A young man approached from the opposite direction. I stopped and fiddled with my purse. I continued to rummage in my purse as the man passed me and turned toward to the apartment doors. I glanced up. He was waiting, holding the door open for me. I hustled up the sidewalk, flashed him a smile, and stepped into the lobby. I stopped at the elevator and pressed the up button. The young man walked past the elevators and disappeared around the corner.

I followed a young couple down to the parkade level and waited until they were in their car, before turning down the aisle I was interested in. I reached Conner's parking stall and stopped. *WTF.* I scanned the surrounding aisles.

Why was the GPS tracker showing the car here when it clearly wasn't? My eyes swept the aisles. There were about a dozen vehicles parked, but the sedan wasn't one of them. I turned. Conner stood blocking my way.

"You looking for this?" he said, holding out the GPS.

I tried stepping past him, but he sidestepped with me.

"What are you doing here?" he demanded.

"Why didn't you tell my you were driving for Jack Tián?"

"Says who?"

"You picked him up at The Ranchmen's Club. Was he the one who Stephen was supposed to be meeting with, after New Year's Day?"

"You see me at The Ranchmen's? Or did this piece of crap say I was there?" He dropped the tracker button, crushing it into the concrete with his boot. "You should get a new one, that one's defective."

"What's your connection with Tony D'Silva?" I countered. The couple I followed into the garage were exiting, their Honda taillights disappearing up the exit ramp.

"What the fuck are you talking about?"

"I find it odd that you're still involved in Stephen's business, even if it is at arms length."

I stepped to the left. He moved right, looming over me, cords of muscle stood out in his neck. My breathing became shallow, then non-existent.

"Or are you helping your ex-girlfriend, Chloe, extract money from Stephen's beneficiaries by holding up probate?"

"You'll never know." He laughed, an ugly, cold, forced laugh.

"I did mention to Detective McGuire that I spotted you in the vicinity of Chloe's place of work last week."

"You're crazy. I have no desire to go near that bitch."

"That's what you say, but the evidence says otherwise." My stomach clenched. The logical part of my brain told me to stop goading him, but an old childhood urge kicked in, searching for soft spots I could poke. Out of the blue, I heard myself say, "The police are onto you. Phone records don't lie."

He reached out, grabbed my hair, and spun me around. The arm clamped around my neck tightened. He grabbed and twisted my other arm behind me. Too late, I remembered he wasn't just some disgruntled boyfriend, or limo driver. He was an ex-mercenary. The pressure on my neck grew, until I could no longer breathe.

Panic rose up from my feet, reaching higher, closing in, tightening my chest, threatening to consume all of me.

Each second ticked by slowly. My strength ebbed away. My vision dimmed. A surge of adrenaline exploded in my brain.

I lowered my head and bit the exposed skin on his hairy wrist. I felt a loosening flicker in his grip. I lurched forward then threw my head back.

The sickening crunch made my stomach roil.

He let go just as the automated garage door rattled and began opening. I turned and ran up the exit ramp. I flew under the half-open door, past the waiting car outside and ran full tilt toward my car.

Suddenly, I was in the front seat, my hand searching frantically across my chest, clawing through purse pockets until they closed in on the keys, my eyes glued to the street in front of me. My breath came out in heaves. I revved up the engine, and without a glance, pulled into the street. Only then did I notice the Altima. The man behind the wheel gestured rudely, his mouth working furiously.

Tires squealing, I roared out onto Macleod Trail, still shaking.

After putting some distance between me and Conner, I pulled over into a parking lot. I leaned my head against the headrest but couldn't bring myself to close my eyes. I pulled down the sun visor and flipped up the mirror. My eyes, large and fearful, stared back. My hand shook as I pulled down the collar of my jacket and shirt. The red mark stretching across my neck already showed a purple hue. *Eff you, Conner Weston.*

CHAPTER THIRTY-FIVE

AFTER MY SECOND scotch last night, I texted Luis, asking him if he'd like to hang out on Saturday. Maybe I'd make him dinner. I was counting on the bruises on my neck fading by then. He hadn't yet replied. *Suck it up, Jorja.* I reminded myself that guys went through this all the time. As the morning wore on, my mood worsened.

I tried convincing myself it was because Azagora was being rude, not replying. But who was I kidding? My little run-in with Conner had unnerved me. I knew I wouldn't mention this to Luis. He'd go all cop on me, order me to back off, maybe insist that I press charges. Besides, Azagora's silence confirmed a niggling suspicion I'd been carrying around in my head. Maybe I wasn't the only one who had been making a mental list of the pros and cons of taking the relationship to the next level. Maybe a committed relationship wasn't the inevitable next step. Maybe his cons outweighed my pros. And now, of course, I was growing certain my investigation into Stephen Wallis' death was the reason he'd put me on hold.

I understood Luis' need for caution. Calgary's Police Chief was on a witch hunt. Someone in CPS was leaking confidential information to the media. This was probably why I knew Stephen Wallis had been shot multiple times at close range with a small-calibre gun. Of course, the news media could have gotten the information legitimately as several reporters did have strong, respectful relationships with members of the police force.

Whatever the case, the Police Chief had announced that he was setting up an internal unit to investigate the leaks. Not specifically about the Wallis murder. There had been several instances where information had been released inappropriately, the latest involving the fatal shooting of an officer. Luis Azagora wasn't going to allow a woman to mar anyone's perception of him as the tough, squeaky-clean, morally upright, and righteous law enforcer he made himself out to be. And he sure as hell wouldn't want to be seen with a woman who had handprint bruises on her neck. *Screw him.*

I opened my email and noticed a reply to the one I had sent last week to Nancy Mayer, Ted Mayer's sister. Chloe had been living with Ted Mayer in Palm Springs before all this happened. I had tracked Nancy down through the friend who told Laura that Chloe had moved down to Palm Springs with her new eighty-year-old man-friend last fall. She in turn let me know that Ted had suffered a stroke shortly after Christmas but was now out of hospital and recuperating under her watchful eye. I opened the email and read.

Dear Ms. Knight.

I am writing in response to the email you sent inquiring about a topaz and silver bracelet belonging to a Chloe Wallis. My brother confirms that such bracelet never left that woman's wretched hand. I certainly hope that she is not trying to accuse my brother of stealing her precious bauble, for I assure you that is not the case. Neither my brother nor I have had any contact with Chloe since my brother drove her ninety-two miles to the Los Angeles airport, on November 27.

Thank you for inquiring after Ted's health. He is doing remarkably well, and his speech is improving daily. I have enclosed my current contact information, should you wish to discuss the matter further.

Warmest Regards – Nancy.

Chloe had lied. Laura may have been mistaken about seeing Chloe in the restaurant, but she wasn't mistaken about finding a silver and topaz bracelet, just like Chloe's, in Stephen's house. A bracelet that had been in California until November 27.

I needed to talk to Chloe, but she wouldn't likely be up this early. Maybe she and Conner had connected for one last fling right before Christmas and Conner had swiped her bracelet. How it ended up in Stephen's house though was a mystery. Unless Laura was right and the two of them were working together. Conner's car had been in the vicinity of Vinnie's. Maybe he went there to meet Chloe, not to let the air out of her boyfriend's tires or scratch the finish on his car. I told myself to slow down. I'd have to tread carefully with Chloe and Conner as neither were prone to offering up the truth.

Realizing a lot of dots still needed to be connected, I pulled up my tracking app. Conner may have removed the tracking device, but the historical data, right up until the tracker was removed, would still be cached in the GPS data log.

The data record showed that Conner's vehicle had sat at his apartment until the day after the storm, the day I had retrieved my car from JumpIn Jalopies. On that day, the car had moved to a location on the west edge of the city and sat there for close to fourteen hours. I double checked the location; it was for a private airstrip.

Two charter companies operated out of the airstrip, along with a few privately-owned planes and jets. A minute later I had the numbers for both charter companies, Buffalo Wings and Conayre, and called them in that order.

I told the woman at Buffalo Wings that I was trying to contact Conner Weston regarding a family emergency. I told her that I had been informed that he may have flown out with them two days earlier and asked if she could confirm that information. The woman was extremely helpful. All their flights had been grounded until yesterday afternoon. She told me only two flights had gotten off the ground the day before, one was a private plane owned by a friend of her son's, and the other was a Conayre jet. A minute later, I repeated my story to a guy at Conayre.

216 | ALICE BIENIA

"Yes ma'am. One of our private jets departed just after nine that morning to the Sparwood Elk Valley airstrip."

"Can you confirm that Mr. Weston was on that flight?"

"There were two passengers on that flight, miss. Mr. Weston was one of them. But both passengers returned to Calgary the same evening."

"Oh. I didn't realize he was back. He's not answering at his residence. Hmmm, that's concerning. Well, thank you so much for all your help."

What the hell was Conner doing in Sparwood? Maybe he had accompanied someone who had rented a vehicle on the other end and needed a driver.

I pulled up a map of the area and sat stunned. The Sparwood Elk Valley airstrip was just four nautical miles north of Sparwood and pretty much in Joey's backyard.

CHAPTER THIRTY-SIX

GAB GAVE ME a hug as I offered up the plastic bag. "I brought wine and a blood orange, feta and fennel salad, all store bought, of course."

"That's my girl," she said, taking the bag and wine from me. She stepped back as I slid my coat off and gave me a thumbs up. "You look awesome."

"Thanks. You look your usual fabulous self." I meant it. Gab's auburn hair was loose, soft waves cascading past her shoulders. Her strikingly green eyes, made even more noticeable with carefully applied liner and eye shadow. She wore sparkly gladiator sandals, white Capri pants and a cropped cobalt-blue top. I wore jeans, a black shirt with gold threads woven through it, and a scarf to hide the fading bruises on my neck.

Gab had thrown her first Spring Equinox party in second year university and each year since. The attendees and location changed over the years depending on what Gab was doing or where she was living but it was the one constant in her life, no matter what else was happening. This year I, along with most, was ready to celebrate any indication that winter was on its way out.

"Here, I better shut off the TV," said Gab.

Something on the news caught my eye. "Wait, wait." I picked up the remote and increased the volume. A man walking his dog had come across a body near the Centre Street Bridge. A newswoman was interviewing the man, his black lab at his side. He pointed toward a stand of barren trees while explaining that his dog had alerted him to something buried in the snow at their base. It was still too early to say whether the victim had suffered a natural death, fallen prey to the storm or foul play. Had anyone reported him missing? I shuddered. That could be me.

"Poor bastard," I said and clicked off the TV. A telltale ping told me I had a new message. I pulled out my phone.

"Great, now he texts me."

I hadn't heard from Azagora since the storm hit. Well until now. During the intervening silence, I had convinced myself that he wasn't keen on progressing our "interested" status to something more. I told myself that it was just as well. I was still trying to let go of past hurts and had my hands full with a new career.

I read the text. *Meet me tonight?*

Tonight? So much for my offer to make him dinner Saturday night. *Well too bad for him.* I typed back. *Sorry, out with the girls tonight.*

Pretty much everyone living north of the 49th parallel knew how significant Spring Equinox was and I wasn't about to miss Gab's party for a guy. Besides, did he really expect me to just be hanging around waiting for him to call?

"Here's to us," Gab announced, handing me a glass of white wine.

I put my phone away, along with the self-pity plaguing me since the storm hit. Soon the other gals arrived, in ones or twos, until there were fifteen of us.

True to her part-Italian heritage, no gathering at Gab's went without food and wine. The dining table groaned under a staggering array of dishes prepared by Gab or brought by guests. I noted the smiling faces around me and pushed aside thoughts of Luis, my stalker, Conner, and Stephen Wallis.

The party broke up before midnight, most of the women wise enough to value sleep and cognizant of the fact that morning came with early exercise classes, children, jobs or other responsibilities. Gab and I weren't among them. After the other ladies left, we spent half an hour cleaning up, declared good enough, and opened another bottle of wine.

I told Gab about my encounter with Conner. She gasped when I showed her the bruises on my neck. Gab asked me if I was going to have him charged with assault. I told her that when you climb into the lion's den and get mauled you really can't insist that the animal be put down.

Then Gab hit me with her news. She had applied to the Grande Diplôme program at Le Cordon Blue Paris. The program taught classic French culinary techniques in pastry and cuisine.

I had given Gab my brightest smile and hugged her. She assured me that the nine months would fly by—assuming she got in. We talked about our plans for the future, and the men in our lives, until the wee hours of the morning, which explained why I felt like crap this morning.

"Hey Gab, I'm heading out," I called out. Gab emerged from the kitchen, cradling a mug of coffee to her chest. Hair gently tousled, she still managed to look spectacular in a green tank top and black silk pyjama pants.

"You sure you have to go?"

I checked my watch. "I'd better. Thanks for letting me stay over, and the loan of PJs."

"All right, go." She brushed my cheek with pursed lips. "Go do your thing and don't get killed."

I laughed. "I won't," I said as I slid on my coat and stepped outside.

The air was noticeably warmer this morning. Maybe we'd have spring after all. The sun was already shining, and I lifted my face upwards. I imagined I could feel the faint warmth of its rays on my skin. But the dull heaviness occupying my midsection wouldn't go away. Nine months or so without Gab was going to hurt.

I was steps from my car, which I'd left parked across the street from Gab's townhouse, when she called my name. I turned.

Gab was in the doorway, holding up her phone, gesturing at me to come back. Worried that I forgot something or that she got a phone call about some family issue, I turned back.

"What's wrong, Gab?"

"Jorja!"

I felt a huge push from behind before I even heard the explosion. I rolled several times and reached up to cover my head as a fender hit the ground.

CHAPTER THIRTY-SEVEN

I WAS LYING in the flower bed, flattened up against the wall of the building. I got to my knees and glanced back. The front of the Chevy was engulfed in flames, black smoke billowing above.

"Gab?" The word reverberated in my skull as I pushed myself up, struggling to stand. Gab was sitting in her doorway, her arms covering her head.

I held my hand against the wall of the building. My legs wobbled and the world around me seemed distant, muffled. Gab lowered her arms.

"Are you okay?" My voice sounded garbled, and my mind flashed back to when my brother and I were kids and would try talking underwater at the neighbourhood pool. I shook my head and rubbed at my ears, but it didn't help.

Gab stood, grabbed my arm and pulled me inside, locking the door behind her. I stood in the entryway and watched Gab stagger to her fridge, take out a half-full bottle of wine, tip her head and guzzle. She turned and stared at me.

"What the efff?" I saw her lips form the words.

She walked back unsteadily and held out the bottle. I shook my head, not really understanding how it would help.

Gab stumbled into the living room and stared out the window for a minute, then sank into her couch. Her lips moved but I couldn't make out what she was saying.

I pressed two fingers against my right ear, jiggled them and yawned. "I can't hear a thing. My ears are ringing." It was weird how low my voice sounded.

"You lost your ring?" Gab replied. I looked at Gab and shrugged.

I stepped over to the window and peered out. A small group of people stood near the remnants of my car, which continued to billow black smoke. I turned around. Gab stared vacantly into space, resting the wine bottle on her thigh.

"Gab, are you okay?"

She slowly raised her eyes to mine, gave me a thumbs up and took another slug of wine.

Bright flashing lights reflected in the window. Peering to my right, I watched the cavalry arrive. I shrugged my shoulders back, gave my ears one last rub, pointed at myself and then out the window. Why was I pantomiming? I was the one having trouble hearing.

I stepped outside, the acrid smell of burning plastic and rubber now prevalent. The fire truck dispatched two firefighters in full gear, who soon sprayed foam at the car from a safe distance. Two other firefighters moved the onlookers back to a safer distance. I scurried over to join them, aware that a second explosion might be possible. The police arrived.

I watched as one of the officers walked over to talk with

the firefighters. After some head nodding and pointing, the officer returned to his partner, still sitting in the vehicle. I stepped off the curb and took several steps in his direction but was waved back. Smoke was now replaced with clouds of steam as the firefighters continued to cool down what remained of the car.

I gently massaged the area in front of my ears until the pressure eased, the sound of faint voices, comforting. One of the police officers approached. He looked young. Real young, like maybe this was his first year on the job. If so, a burning vehicle would be a welcome deviation from having to attend to fender benders or a puking drunk.

A woman wearing a parka over pink flamingo pyjama pants, and work boots sizes too big, stood next to me. Next to her, a middle-aged woman wearing a hard hat, gestured wildly while speaking into a cell phone. An older, white-haired couple stood on my other side along with a young man with a backpack. The officer reached our group.

"Anybody know whose vehicle that is?"

Amid murmurs of no, I raised my hand. "It's mine." My voice sounded far away, muffled and weak, but for all I knew I might be shouting. All eyes turned toward me.

"Want to tell me what happened?"

"I was visiting my friend there." I waved in the direction of Gab's townhouse. "I just left her place to head to work when she called me back. I turned around, and the next thing I knew I was on the ground next to her building. Am I shouting?" I asked, tipping my head from one side to the other. Except water did not drain out and the ringing noise continued.

The officer stepped closer. "I'm going to need some information from you."

I followed him back to the police car. I could see Gab staring out her window. He opened the back door and I climbed in. Leaving the door open, he handed me a clipboard and pointed at the attached form. "Fill this in if you can. Take your time."

I watched him walk away to chat with the firefighters again. The older couple shot me a look of disdain and made their way up the sidewalk of the townhouse next to Gab's. I could hear the officer behind the wheel of the car talking on the radio but couldn't make out much of anything. I picked up the clipboard and filled in my name and address. My legs no longer felt like rubber, but I was nauseated.

I just answered the last question on the form when I detected a siren making its way up the street. An ambulance arrived and parked in front of the police car. A woman in uniform got out, made her way over and leaned in.

"Hi there. What's your name? Can you tell me what's happened here?"

I was tempted to hand her the clipboard and let her read for herself, but I figured there might be more behind her questions than just curiosity. I repeated my story.

Her colleague arrived, carrying a small bag. "This here is my partner. I'm just going to ask you some questions. Can you hear me okay?"

I nodded, now totally exhausted. They had more questions for me. Was I in pain, did anything hurt, could I tell them my address, was I on any medications, what was today's date, had I been drinking? The woman checked my heart rate, blood pressure, pupils, and pressed a point behind my ear until I flinched.

"You want to tell me about those," the woman nodded at the bruises around my neck.

"No. I've already dealt with that." I had. I told Gab all about it. The woman stared at me for a minute but let it go.

Glancing past her, I noticed they had stopped spraying foam and now one of the firefighters was prying open the trunk. The hood still lay in the street. The paramedics just finished up when the young police officer returned, his lips set in a straight line. Gab was right behind him. She had changed into jeans, lace-up brown ankle boots and a white ski jacket.

"Is she okay?" Gab's eyebrows puckered together. "Jorja, are you okay?"

I nodded. The woman paramedic turned toward me. "No sign of concussion. A bit of hearing loss and ear pain from the shock wave of the explosion. We'd like to take you to the hospital to get checked out."

"I can decline, can't I?"

"Yes, but it's a slow day so we'd be happy to take you to the hospital," the guy with her joked.

"If you feel fine and don't want further assistance, we'll need you to sign a refusal of medical assistance form," added the woman.

I filled out yet another form. As soon as EMS departed, I got out of the patrol car. A tow truck pulled up to my smouldering vehicle. I realized that I'd need to let JumpIn Jalopies know about the Chevy. For once I was glad that my gun was still back at the condo. Although my gun didn't need to be registered as the pellets it shot were delivered at under five hundred feet per second, it always raised more questions than it answered in situations like this. It's why I rarely took it with me. That and the fact that it still scared the bejezuss out of me.

The police officer returned. He glared at me for at least a full minute.

"What?"

"We'd like you to come down to the station with us."

"Why?"

"It appears someone planted a detonation device in your car."

"A detonation device," I repeated like an idiot. "You mean a bomb?" I stopped and chided myself. Of course, it was a bomb. Cars didn't usually blow up by themselves. Even JumpIn Jalopies' cars. I realized how close I had come to dying. If Gab hadn't called me back, I might not be standing. I turned to Gab.

"Why did you call me back?"

"Here," she said, pressing a phone into my hand. "You picked up my phone by mistake." I glanced down. Yup, my phone. I dug through my purse, found Gab's phone, and returned it to her before climbing back into the police car. Azagora wasn't going to be happy.

CHAPTER THIRTY-EIGHT

IT WAS NOON by the time I left the District 2 police station. They now knew I was a private investigator, that I was working on the Stephen Wallis case, and was being stalked by someone. When they asked if I had any idea who might have tried to kill me, I didn't tell them that I suspected Conner Weston. It would have forced me to get deeper into the whole Wallis case and I didn't want to go there. Mentioning the Wallis case had already netted me a comment about interfering PI's. I laughed off the question instead, suggesting that perhaps my stalker was tired of leaving me black flowers and juvenile artwork.

I checked my phone. I had several missed calls from an unknown number, a voice message from a Detective Keating and a text message from Azagora. I read Azagora's text first. *Need to talk to you.* Not exactly the love note I was expecting. I typed back, *Okay.*

I listened to my voice message next. Detective Keating asked me to give him a call and left a number. He didn't say why he was calling. I phoned a cab company and called Detective Keating while I waited for my ride.

Detective Keating was out; his phone went to voice mail. I left a message telling him I was returning his call. I had two more terse text messages from Luis by the time I hung up, each saying nothing more than to call him. He couldn't possibly have heard about the car bomb this quickly, or should I say, *alleged* car bomb?

I called Luis' number. Whoever tried to kill me failed. But they were seriously jeopardizing my love life. I thought back to the photo my stalker had taken of me at Escoba's, the night I met Luis for dinner. *Love life?* Who was I kidding? Azagora was a cop first and Luis second. More than likely, he was checking up to make sure I wasn't doing something illegal.

"Inspector Azagora here," sounded a deep voice in my ear.

"Inspector," I said. He must be within earshot of one of his team, or other staff. "Ms. Knight here."

"Are you all right?"

This wasn't what I was expecting. "Yeah, still a little deaf and the ringing in my ears hasn't completely stopped, but otherwise okay."

Silence. Or I had gone deaf again? "Hello?"

"One second please," he said.

I held and waited, checking the phone screen several times, convinced we had been disconnected. Finally, he came back on the line.

"Jorja. What are you talking about?"

"Luis. What are you talking about?"

"Did Detective Keating get a hold of you?"

"He's been trying, but due to circumstances beyond my control, I haven't been able to connect with him. Why?"

"You heard about the guy who was found dead near the Centre Street Bridge?"

"What about him?" I asked. I was peeved. The call wasn't personal, it was business. It was always business. Then I remembered the way his lips felt on mine, and his hand sliding up my bare back. *Not always business.*

"Look. Jorja. You need to get a hold of Detective Keating."

"Listen. Luis. I've been trying. We've been playing telephone tag. And we might have to continue to play phone tag until tomorrow, as I have pressing business to take care of this afternoon."

I did have pressing business. I needed to let JumpIn Jalopies know their Chevy had been incinerated, and I needed a replacement.

I heard him expel a loud sigh, a good sign my hearing was returning to normal.

"You're the most exasperating woman I've ever met. This is what I get for trying to keep you in the loop. Forget it."

"No, no, no, not so fast. Forget what? Sorry, I'm not my usual self. A little off kilter after nearly being killed this morning. What loop? What's going on?"

"Killed? What are you talking about?"

"Someone blew up my car."

"What do mean blew up your car?"

"You know. Kaboom, kapow, flames, hood flying through the air, blackened shell remains."

"Christ." I could see him pacing, running his hand over his shaven hair, eyes calculating, mind evaluating. "Where was this?"

"I just finished reporting it at District 2. They have the whole sad story. Your turn."

"We may have found the guy stalking you."

"You did? That's great. Who the hell is he?"

"Was he."

"Wait a minute, you mean he's dead?"

"Just call Keating."

"Was he the body they found down by the Centre Street Bridge?"

"Call him. I'll deal with you later."

The phone went dead just as the cab arrived. I climbed in and tried Detective Keating again. I left a second message saying I was en route to my car-leasing company, but he could try me on my cell any time.

My mind tried to sort out what was happening. They must have found something linking this guy to me. I hadn't told Azagora about the notes on the windshield, but they obviously found something that made them believe this guy was stalking me.

A muscle twitched below my left eye. Azagora hadn't told me much of anything, which totally pissed me off. But not as much as his parting remark.

CHAPTER THIRTY-NINE

DETECTIVE KEATING CALLED as I was leaving JumpIn Jalopies. He would come by the condo at seven o'clock. I was glad I'd get a chance to talk to him tonight, I knew I wouldn't sleep until I knew what was going on. Not that I expected to get a lot of answers from the police, but he might offer up a hint or two that would prove useful. Besides, my trip to JumpIn Jalopies merely added to my darkening mood. Neil, my favourite leasing agent, wasn't in today. I had to play nice with his evil boss, a hideous little man filled with self-importance and high on the corporate Kool-Aid. Mr. 'by the book' refused to cancel the lease for the Chevy, informing me it would be terminated when I either returned the car or produced a police certificate stating it had been destroyed.

So now I was paying for two vehicles, when one was clearly no longer roadworthy. At least I had wheels again, this time a silver 2001 Toyota Rav4 complete with red-and-black Flames hockey flags flying from both back windows. It was the best they could do since the storm had eaten up their usual inventory. After I signed the lease, he mentioned the car had a couple of problems. The car stereo system was jammed and all it played was AC/DC's Shot Down in Flames. He failed to mention the music came on in ear-splitting decibels at random intervals and turned off just as suddenly.

Once parked back at my condo, I used the arm of my nail clippers to unscrew the front piece of the stereo unit. The song had come on three times in the short drive, just about putting me through the roof each time. I pulled it out from the housing and unplugged the wires from the harness connector at the back of the stereo. Satisfied, I placed the unit back into its slot and re-secured it. Problem one gone.

The second problem with the vehicle was that the passenger side airbag in this make and model of vehicle was known to occasionally deploy…for no reason. Ironically, they couldn't rent it out without an airbag, but having a defective airbag was okay. The guy at JumpIn Jalopies claimed the manufacturer was sending replacement parts and I'd be contacted as soon as they arrived, but they made me sign a waiver anyway, saying I'd been told about the problem.

Once upstairs, I noted I had plenty of time left before my meeting with Detective Keating. I hadn't exercised in days. Unless of course I counted the multiple trips up and down eight flights of stairs when the power was out and the two-kilometre roundtrip I had made through knee-deep snow to the leisure centre for coffee. Shockingly, the scale hadn't budged. Then again, I had finished off an entire bag of cookies during my internment, the equivalent of three days of calories needed for a moderately active woman, which everyone knows are denser and harder to get rid of than, say, carrot calories. I changed into workout gear and took the stairs down to the gym on the main floor.

Pulling open the gym doors, I stepped inside and shivered, goosebumps erupting on my arms as a blast of cold air hit me. The far wall, a bank of floor-to-ceiling windows, still had a small ridge of frost along the inside bottom edge. I climbed onto the elliptical. Two women ran on the treadmills nearby, each intensely focused, earbuds securely planted in their ears. I glanced enviously at blond ponytails bobbing, my hair too short for a ponytail that bobbed.

A tiny woman climbed onto the elliptical next to me, her arms and throat crêpe and covered in brown spots. Mrs. Wilson from 8C, just down the hall from me. The guilt returned. I should have checked in on her during the storm to see if she and her three cats were all right, but she wasn't the friendliest of neighbours.

Ten minutes later I was ready to call it quits, but my ego wouldn't let me. All the stair climbing this past week had taken its toll. I tried not to groan audibly as my thigh muscles screamed. Mrs. Wilson's little arms whipped back and forth, her legs churning furiously. Risking a glance from behind sweaty hair falling across my face, I noticed the step angle of the pedals on her elliptical and cursed under my breath. She wasn't even sweating.

I tried distracting myself from the pain in my thighs by focusing on the TV monitors suspended overhead. The last of the storm system had cleared out and temperatures were expected to return to seasonal. The screen flicked to a shot of the news reporter standing in the snow in front of the Centre Street Bridge. The news ticker at the bottom of the

screen said the person found in a snowbank two days earlier had been identified. The victim was a local man named
Bernard Ing.

I stopped mid-stride, cursed, and looked over at Mrs.
Wilson. She shot me a victory grin, her lips pulled back
tightly over a mouth full of small worn-down teeth. Swiping
at the perspiration on my face I got off the elliptical and
waited while the TV ticker messages cycled through a second
time. No mistake. Bernie Ing. Police were treating his death
as suspicious.

I didn't like Bernie, but not enough to wish him dead. I
knew Bernie was an accountant and his clientele mostly small
businesses and sole proprietorships, but little else. Who would
want to kill him? Not that mild-mannered, quiet accountants
were exempt from murder, but Bernie clearly wasn't your typical accountant. He was creepier than most.

Azagora said they had found my stalker. It couldn't be
Bernie. But why else would Detective Keating be wanting
to talk to me? I threw my towel into the used-towel bin and
headed back upstairs. I had to admit, at one point I had
considered the possibility that Bernie could be my stalker,
but unanswered questions threw in doubt. He wouldn't have
known I had flown to Albuquerque. I was certain I hadn't
mentioned the upcoming trip in class. Now I realized he
could have followed me to the airport. I couldn't believe I
wouldn't have noticed. Then again, I hadn't expected anyone
to be following me. I had written Bernie off as a wannabe PI,
someone more thrilled with the idea of becoming a PI than
being one. And now he was dead.

Had Bernie been stalking me? Had he been planning to

kill me? Or was I about to be accused of something? Well, I certainly didn't kill him. I left the gym on edge, convinced the other shoe was about to drop.

Detective Keating arrived right on time.

"Please, come in," I said, standing aside so he could enter. He was a burly man, his steel-grey hair buzzed short, making it look white against light-brown skin. His demeanour was friendly, his eyes kind. I waved him over to the kitchen table and we sat.

"Would you like some coffee or water or anything?"

"Water would be great," he replied, his eyes taking in the place. "You been here long?"

I laughed, positive his question was spurred by the sparse furnishings, lack of photos, knick-knacks, or pictures on the walls. "Going on two years. I'm still working on making the place feel homey. It's a process, you know."

With water in front of us, he got down to business. He asked how I knew Bernie Ing, what I knew of him, when I last saw him. I answered his questions as completely and succinctly as I could, anxious to get to the end. I knew from the news clip that Bernie's body had been found along the river, by a man and his dog. The dog got interested in something in the snow, dug, and uncovered a gloved hand. Detective Keating didn't reveal the cause of death, but the medical examiner deemed it to be suspicious. Detective Keating caught the case, having just returned from a fifteen-day vacation in Mexico.

"We found photos pinned to the walls at his place, or what's left of them. Unfortunately, there was a fire and the heat and water ruined most of what was there."

"So, you're saying Bernie's found dead and his place caught fire."

"Some people don't have any luck," he replied.

I swallowed and tried to push away the visual of Bernie leering at the photos on his wall. "What kind of photos?"

"A mixed bag—people, buildings, street shots. I can't be more specific than that. We're sorting through them now. A significant number of the photos were of you. One of our guys recognized you right off the bat."

I wondered which of the half-dozen officers I knew had ID me or if he could be referring to Azagora.

"Roughly how many photos are we talking about?"

"I'd say at least a couple of dozen."

I sat back, stunned. How could I not have noticed someone taking my picture that often? Then again, cell phone cameras made it all so easy.

"Where were these photos taken?"

"Like I said, we're still combing through them."

I nodded. I had told Detective Keating about the times I had run into Bernie over the last few weeks. But I hadn't mentioned the anonymous messages left on my windshield, or the black flowers delivered to my door. I don't know why. Maybe in someway, I was playing tit for tat. Besides, I had no idea if Bernie had left me those or why, but if Bernie had been behind them, it might explain why I hadn't received any since the snowstorm. But it's a cinch he didn't blow up my car this morning since he was already dead. Which was problematic.

"Once our guys are finished cataloguing everything, I'd like you to come down and look through the photos. Maybe you'll recognize the other people in the photos, or when and where they were taken. We'd also like the names of the other attendees at the course Bernie attended."

"Sure, I can give you the names right now."

I knew he wouldn't be able to tell me the particulars of how Bernie died. But now that I knew he'd been photographing people unbeknownst to them, I knew Detective Keating would be thinking he snapped a photo of someone or something that he wasn't supposed to see. It was certainly running through my mind.

I rattled off the names of Bernie's four course mates and their contact information. "Let me know when you want me to come by and look at those photos. I'm happy to help any way I can."

After Detective Keating left, I surfed the internet for information on the other course attendees, hoping to spot something in common with Bernie, something that might connect them.

Could he have been stalking them as well? But what about the newspaper clippings of my parents? Why dredge up my past? And the black dahlias? What were they for? If my stalker didn't contact me in the next few days, I'd be convinced Bernie Ing had been the one leaving me reminders of my sad past.

So, who blew up my car?

CHAPTER FORTY

I ARRIVED AT the Ramsay Station a few minutes before my appointed time and announced my presence at the front desk. Detective Keating came down the hall to greet me.

"Ms. Knight. Thanks for coming down."

"Please, it's Jorja, and I'm more than happy to see if I can help."

I followed him down a series of hallways, up a flight of stairs, down a corridor and into a small meeting room. A police officer sat at a table, a laptop in front of her, a second laptop next to it. She stood as we entered.

"Corporal Wood, this is Jorja Knight."

She reached over and shook my hand. "Almost done," she said. "I'll have you set up in a second."

Clearly, she knew who I was and why I was here. Detective Keating left, and I waited while she found the file she needed. She stood aside as I sat down in front of the laptop while she opened and logged into the second computer. She opened a file folder labelled J. Knight.

Corporal Wood had scanned, labelled, and categorized

the photos retrieved from Bernie's house. Many were severely water or heat damaged. Some were merely blackened bits. I was morbidly curious about the photos Bernie had of me.

"Take your time," she said. "I have the same file open on my laptop. We will go through them one by one. If you can identify anything about the photo, other people in it, where it was taken, let me know and I'll make note of it on my laptop."

There were one hundred and seventeen photos of me, some taken at a distance, some relatively close up. I studied each one. Some street shots had several people in the frame, others one or two. Many were badly damaged. I scanned faces and places for anything familiar. I recognized one from one of the field excursions held in my course. We had discussed dumpster diving, how to get in and out without getting hurt, what to wear and bring with you. I shivered involuntarily. The little creep had been photographing me even back then. But why? Had he just randomly selected me, or had he taken my course as a ploy to get closer to me?

"These photos, can they be enlarged?"

"We don't have the originals. These are scanned copies of the photos we salvaged from his place."

Did that mean Bernie's phone or camera hadn't been found? I knew it would be pointless to ask.

I easily recognized the location of most of the photos Bernie had of me, many taken downtown as I walked to meetings, the C-Train station, or the office. A good number of them were from the days I had "bumped" into the little weasel. I scrolled through the photos and Corporal Wood captured details about each photo, where I had been, who I had been seeing, who, if anyone, had been with or around me. I didn't like what I saw.

Besides the photos taken during my PI course, there were a half-dozen of me taken the day I met with Detective McGuire. Some photos were taken at a distance, others relatively close. He had been following me as I investigated the Stephen Wallis case. One incredibly good shot showed me arriving at Laura's house. I was crossing the street, Laura was standing in her doorway and in the left corner, Tony could be seen, his face frozen in anger. There were several more of me arriving at or leaving Stephen's house. Perhaps I had underestimated Bernie Ing's ability to carry out surveillance.

I cursed just as Detective Keating returned.

"How's it going?" he called out. "Anything interesting?"

I decided I had nothing to lose by being forthright.

"Maybe. Bernie Ing, knowingly or inadvertently, embedded himself into a case I'm investigating."

"What case is that?"

"The Stephen Wallis murder."

Detective Keating let out a short whistle. "That is interesting. You're positive?"

"Yeah. Here, I'll show you. Of course, he may not have known what I was working on." I felt stupid saying it. Of course, he figured it out.

Detective Keating pulled up a chair next to me. I ran through the photos of me at Laura's house and the ones smack dab in front of Stephen's executor's offices.

"Here's the clincher," I said, scrolling down the file. "These three are of me entering Stephen Wallis' house. That's where Wallis was killed. Detective McGuire might be interested in these." The photos only showed a portion of the house, but I had no trouble recognizing it.

"You know Detective McGuire?"

"I met him a few weeks ago, after Stephen Wallis' sister, Laura Bradley, hired me to look into his death. She told me Detective McGuire was handling the case, so I called him up as a professional courtesy."

"You think Ing's death might be related to your investigation?"

"No way to know for certain, but it makes me wonder if he saw or came across something that the killer didn't want anyone to know."

The fact Keating asked me the question told me he thought so too. If that were the case it meant the killer knew I was looking into the murder.

"Okay, good work. I'm going to see if Detective McGuire is in."

I sat up and stretched.

"Mind if I take a break?"

"Not at all. I should have asked. Would you like a water or coffee?"

"No thanks, but a bio break would be appreciated."

I followed Corporal Wood out of the room, down several hallways and to the women's washroom. I needed a moment to think. One of the photo's showed a bearded guy in a brown canvas work parka behind me. His face was hidden. I didn't know who it was, but I had seen this guy myself. And he vaguely matched the description of one of the guys Laura's realtor had noticed lurking near Stephen's house. But Bernie had been the one following me. Maybe the guy in the parka was just an innocent passerby whom Bernie shot a picture of the same time he was photographing me. Or could there be two people following me? Unfortunately, most of his face was obscured by his parka hood.

Back in the meeting room, I flicked back a few photos noting the guy in the brown parka was Caucasian.

"Recognize someone?" Corporal Wood asked, watching me like a hawk.

There was a possibility that it could be Joey. With nothing to back up it up though, it would be foolish to start throwing names around.

I shook my head. "No. Could be just about anybody."

I turned back to the remainder of the photos. Several were of Tony's office building. I flipped back to the photos taken at Stephen's residence and ran through them again. Something bothered me but I couldn't put my finger on it. It flicked at the edge of my mind and disappeared, leaving me with an agonizing sense that I was missing something important.

"Notice anything interesting?"

"No, just checking these photos from Stephen Wallis' neighbourhood again, I don't know why. I thought I saw something in them, but I don't see anything out of the ordinary."

We were finished half an hour later. I stretched my arms out in front of me, tired from being hunched over the computer.

Detective Keating walked into the room. "How'd it go?"

"I'm so ready to pack it in," I said. "I recognized a few of the locations."

"Good work. You didn't recognize Bernie Ing when you first met him during the course you gave?"

"No. I'm not that great with names, but I am good with faces. He didn't even look remotely familiar."

"We appreciate you coming down to look at these photos. I'll walk you out if you're ready," he said.

I followed Detective Keating downstairs and to the main entrance. Once outside I stood for a second, trying to get my bearings. What were the chances that the guy in the brown parka was Joey? And what were the chances if it were Joey that he'd made his way to an industrial park, where it just happened an old school friend had his business headquartered? A school friend whose best buddy was murdered a few short months earlier. The same man who was the last one to see his own best buddy the night he disappeared.

CHAPTER FORTY-ONE

I PULLED UP to a rundown, stucco bungalow in Bridgeland, or what was left of it. There had only been a handful of significant house fires in Calgary during the past two weeks and it didn't take me long to track down Bernie's.

The bungalow was wedged in between a four-storey apartment building and a narrow two-storey glass and concrete infill. Several pieces of bright-yellow crime scene tape fluttered around the bungalow. With the owner having been found dead under suspicious circumstances, a fire in the victim's home would no doubt be investigated for arson.

The tape had been partially torn away, and with no officer stationed outside, I convinced myself the forensics had already been completed. The other voice in my head—the louder, more critical one—reminded me that I could be arrested for interfering with an investigation by crossing a police line.

"Ready to do this?" I muttered as I approached the house. Thick icicles hung from the roof and globs of ice drooped like snot from the windows. The overhanging roof of the front porch was charred, the window to the left of the door a black gaping hole.

Glass and ice crunched underfoot as I climbed three steps up to the porch. Bits of waterlogged carpet, scorched drywall and tarry shingles were strewed everywhere. The blackened wooden door was closed but the window next to it was an empty gaping hole.

I pulled a pair of latex gloves out of my back pocket and slipped them on. With one last gander over my shoulder, I stepped through the frame and into the living room.

The acrid scorched smell was much stronger now, the room dim. The gaping window hole barely letting in the rapidly fading light outside. A soggy green rolled-arm sofa stood near one wall. Across the room a burnt-out television rested on top of what appeared to be a counter-height fridge. *Handy.*

A few pictures remained on the walls, the glass broken and yellowed, the landscapes behind the glass curled and cracked. I crept through the curved doorway into a dining room, the floor under my feet spongy, the floorboards creaking loudly.

The dining room held a large round table, no chairs. Piles of books, some singed, others partially burnt, lay in stacks on the table and in ruin on the floor beneath it. I stepped closer and examined the spine on several books at the bottom of the heaps, still faintly readable. Books on black holes, quantum physics, birds, handguns, poisonous plants, true crime. I bent down and picked up one that had at least a dozen Post-it tabs sticking out. Lord of the Rings.

I gazed around me. This sucked. It was sad. The paltry remains of a life once lived.

A shelf on the opposite wall held a lone mug. Above the shelf a collection of crosses of various styles. I walked over and picked up the mug. A picture of Samwise Gamgee on the side. The only mug to have survived. I bent down and picked up a broken fragment from the floor. The face of Frodo Baggins remained on the stained porcelain. An image of the sweatshirt Bernie had worn to every class flashed through my mind. The Tree of Gondor. Bernie had been a big Tolkien fan.

I peered into what must have been the kitchen, now demolished to blackened studs. The fire must have started here. I crossed the hall to the two remaining rooms. Holes had been punched through the walls, likely by the firefighters checking for hot spots. Water-laden wall plaster was ground into black soggy carpet. The whole place was like an icebox. I entered what I expected had been Bernie's bedroom.

It was darker back here, the rapidly fading light outside barely registering through the lone, half-open, soot-covered window. Several holes had been punched through the ceiling. A dark green-and-brown plaid bedspread covered a double bed, its sagging middle clearly noticeable even in the dim light. At the foot of the bed stood an old, dark maple chest. I pulled out my cell phone and turned on the flashlight feature.

I lifted the lid of the chest with my toe. An odd odour emerged—melted rubber or plastic, burnt newsprint and musty wet wood all rolled into one. A lumpy sodden blanket covered what lay beneath. I lifted a corner and pulled out several hair pieces and a beard, now stuck together in a disgustingly frightful mass. I held it up and compared it to the images in my mind of the homeless person I had seen from time to time the last several weeks. The long brown-and-grey straggly hair pieces could have come from anywhere.

Midway down, I came across a bluish-green taffeta dress and, below it, a second copy of the Lord of the Rings, this one leather bound. Near the bottom of the chest, I found a canvas tan overcoat, grubby, worn. Maybe he belonged to a theatre group or kept artifacts from a high school play. I checked the coat pockets then stuffed everything back into the chest. I crossed over to the closet. Several wire hangers hung from the closet bar, remnants of what must have been clothing, now charred fragments on the closet floor.

My ears burned in effort to keep alert, my throat already raw from the thick grungy air. I turned, anxious to leave. Noticing the chest's curved base left a space between it and the floor, I walked back. Squatting, I ran my fingers underneath, until they touched something cool. Shifting the chest back a few inches, I reached underneath, and pulled out a flat metal box.

Laying the box on top of the chest, I worked open the stiff metal lid.

"Holy shit!"

My face stared back at me. I recognized the photo as one from my university yearbook, this one enlarged several times. I set it on the floor next to me and continued to empty the box, cringing inwardly as I lifted each item out. I confirmed the unavoidable reality. I was looking through a Jorja Knight memorabilia box. In addition to copies of several newspaper stories about my parents' murder-suicide, there was a photo of me in my lab from a story CTV had run on Global Analytix, my former employer.

I lifted out a flattened lipstick-smeared Starbuck's cup, which I assumed was one of my discards and an obviously used serviette. *Yuck.* Rattling on the bottom were a pencil from the English Language School where I had held my PI course, a small coil bound notebook, and my missing five-year-anniversary pen from Global Analytix. Bernie Ing had formed an unhealthy obsession with me at some point.

I pocketed the notebook and pen and put everything else back into the box and slid it under the chest. The cops already knew Bernie had been taking photos of me, and the box clearly had nothing to do with the fire. I stood up, my feet freezing from standing on the damp half-frozen carpet. Now the only question that remained was who killed Bernie and why?

CHAPTER FORTY-TWO

COMPLETELY EXHAUSTED, I arrived home feeling odd, maybe early signs of a cold coming on. I stripped off my damp and dank clothing, threw my jeans and shirt in the washer and headed for the shower. Standing in the steamy shower cubicle, I let the hot water cascade down my back. On the one hand, I was relieved that my stalker was gone, but Bernie's death left me feeling empty.

I spelled out Azagora's name on the glass. A minute later his name was all but obliterated by the steam. I stared at the faint outline of the letters that remained. They too would soon be gone, just like my relationship with him. I stepped back to let the water hit my legs, still cold from my prowl through Bernie Ing's cold and damp house.

I hadn't seen anything in the photos the police showed me that would get someone killed. But someone had killed Bernie. No way to say if it was related to me, the Stephen Wallis case or something else entirely. Bernie had formed his obsession with me before Stephen was murdered. Now I wondered when he'd taken all the photos of Stephen's house.

Could Bernie have been Stephen's accountant? Or provided his services to one of Stephen's entrepreneurs? My mind shot off in that direction.

The water cooled, and I cranked the hot water tap fully to the left but soon the last spurt of hot water gave out too. I shook my head. Bernie couldn't be the Houdini Killer. More likely he had inadvertently seen something while following me around. So why hadn't I seen it? Maybe I had but didn't realize its importance. After all, someone had incinerated my car. It couldn't have been Bernie, but it could have been done by the same person who killed Bernie.

I turned off the tap, reached out and pulled a towel off the hook, wrapping myself in its softness. I stepped out of the shower, the room steamy yet cool against my moist warm skin. Rubbing a circle of condensation off the mirror I stared at the woman who stared back. She gazed back unflinchingly, face devoid of emotion, the bruises on her neck turning yellow in colour.

Sticking my tongue out at my reflection, I turned and marched into the bedroom. I rummaged through my closet, found my UBC sweatpants and pulled them on, congratulating myself on the fact that they still fit. Then I reminded myself that they had been miles too loose, back in the day. *Enough already.* I really needed to let up on myself. I pulled on a tank top, yanked my old grey cashmere sweater from the floor of the closet, gave it a shake and pulled it on.

After towel drying my hair, I poured myself a scotch, curled up on the couch, pulling a blanket over my legs, and opened my laptop. Before I could even open my mail, the phone rang.

"Hello." I half expected a telemarketer or, worse yet, a recorded telemarketer.

"Jorja?"

"Yes?"

"It's Antonia. We spoke the other day about my brother Joey."

"Yes. Antonia, hi. What's up?"

"You asked me to let you know when I next saw Joey. I talked to him today."

"You did. Where?"

"He came by work."

"So, he was here?"

"Yes. He was furious. Said I need to leave him alone," her voice broke. "I'm sorry. I've been trying to hang on to the idea that I have a brother. He clearly doesn't care to have me in his life. I guess that's it. I have to stop pretending. I had a brother, but he left a long time ago," she choked out. She was crying now.

"I'm sorry to hear that," I said, hearing my own voice waiver in response. The abyss opened, beckoning me in. I once had a brother too. He was living his life nicely without me. I shook my head and swallowed hard. After a long pause, I asked, "Was he mad that you went up to the hunter's cabin?"

"Oh, I don't know. He was mad about that and a lot of other stuff. He doesn't want the money Stephen left him. Told me I could do whatever I want with it. Then he accused me of sending people to spy on him, to suck him back in. He said they wouldn't leave him alone, that this is what happens when people stick their noses in where they don't belong."

"Who was he referring to?" I asked. A twinge of guilt passed though me, for having intruded into his life, but it sounded like he was referring to more than just me.

"Me, of course. I don't know who these people are who supposedly want to suck him into something or somewhere. I don't know. He wasn't making much sense. He was so upset I had to take him outside, he was alarming our residents."

"So, he doesn't want the money, and he believes you've sent people to spy on him or force him to do something."

"Oh, Jorja. There is something wrong with him. I've been ignoring it for years. Now what am I supposed to do?"

She was the health care worker, not me. Of course, I had a lot of coaching from psychologists, so I should know the answer to this one.

"If he's not harming other people or becoming an imme-diate danger to himself, there isn't much you can do. He may be angry, and he may believe in some strange conspiracy theories and such, but it doesn't mean he's mentally ill."

"So why is he this way?"

That was the burning question, as well as why he seemed upset by Stephen's bequest.

Despite what I was telling Antonia, I couldn't believe he was innocent. Who knew how long he'd been in town? Maybe he killed Bernie, set fire to his place. Blew up my car. But why? And how would he have even known about Bernie? But Bernie may have known about him.

"Did he say where he's staying or what he planned to do next?"

"No. I was upset and crying, and he just glared at me. His eyes were real cold. Then he stormed off."

"What time was this?"

"Around four. I was so upset after he left that I went home early. I just spent the last couple of hours crying and upsetting my family. This is what I mean. He leaves, and I end up ruining my family's evening. No more. I'm done."

"Did he say who was harassing him?"

"Probably no one, Jorja. That's what made me realize he's delusional. Paranoid. I want to help him, but I can't."

I didn't have any words that would make her heartache go away. If I did, I would have used them on myself years ago.

"Never say never. You don't know what the next year or the next thirty hold. He may come around, but it's up to him." That was the best I could offer her. I was in year ten myself. "Antonia, before you go, can I ask what he was wearing when you saw him?"

"Ahh…sure…khakis, brown work boots and his parka. A brown parka. Why?"

Several thoughts whorled and collided in my brain, forcing me into a thirty-second re-evaluation before letting them go.

"Just curious. You know—in case I see him." I thanked Antonia for calling and disconnected.

Antonia's brother had been seen in town more than a few times in the last few months. I'd bet dollars to donuts the guy in Bernie's photos, whom I saw myself, was Joey. Interestingly, his off-grid lifestyle didn't seem to interfere with his ability to get around. Maybe he kept a car in Sparwood or Elkford or one of the other small hamlets out that way. It would explain how he could make an appearance

254 | ALICE BIENIA

in Calgary one day and theoretically be out in the woods the next. Maybe he even had a place out there somewhere, and the whole mountain man thing was an act, an image he portrayed to keep nosy, interfering people away. Thinking about Sparwood brought up another thought. Could Conner's trip to Sparwood somehow factor into Joey's visit with his sister?

I opened my file and added annotations next to the names. Could Ajeet's disappearance be what triggered Joey's journey into his hermit-like life? According to Greg, Stephen and Tony had supposedly driven Ajeet home. What happened next was unknown. Perhaps Ajeet wandered off or called a cab or another friend. The other alternative was that Stephen had somehow been involved in Ajeet's disappearance.

Maybe Joey killed Stephen, revenge for his involvement in Ajeet's disappearance. What was I saying? That Stephen killed Ajeet? Perhaps Ajeet died on the way home and Stephen panicked and disposed of the body.

I rubbed my eyes with the palm of my hands. My mother had always accused me of having fits of fantasy. As a child I loved taking some mundane occurrence or event and spinning it into a fabulous story. Was I doing that now?

After further consideration I realized most of what I had found would fit into this latest fabrication. No one seemed to know where Joey was at any given moment in time. His sister saw him in Calgary a week prior to Stephen's death. Maybe a coincidence, maybe not. Could Joey have figured out how to get into Stephen's house? He worked with computers at one time, and everyone commented on how brilliant he was. What if he managed to override Stephen's security system? Surely Detective McGuire's team had already checked into that. Would a breached system look different from one turned off momentarily by someone and then turned back on? Could Joey have contacted or threatened Stephen earlier, making him believe he was at risk? Is that why he hired Conner?

I got up, poured myself a refill and rearranged the blanket back around my legs. My limbs grew warmer, perhaps from the scotch more so than the shower and blanket. Something nagged at me.

I took a sip, feeling the warmth sliding down my throat, and closed my eyes. A large amorphous blob of concrete, punctuated by two narrow windows, came into view. Tony's office building. Setting my drink on the coffee table I googled IQtel and pulled up street view.

"Damn, the same building," I muttered.

If the man in the parka in Bernie's photos was Joey, he had been ten feet from the door to Tony's office building. Tony told me he hadn't seen Joey in years.

CHAPTER FORTY-THREE

IT HAD BEEN days since I had been to the office, and it would be a nice change of scenery, such as it was. I found myself humming as I drove down Crowchild Trail. The main arteries were still wet from melting snow, the promise of spring lay just around the corner.

I pulled open the front entrance to our building and paused to remind myself where I had parked. One of these days my lack of attention to the present was going to get me killed. I veered past a few people waiting for the elevator and entered the stairwell. I was halfway down the hall before I noticed it. A package lay on the carpet in front of our office door.

I stopped. Murmured voices filtered out into the hallway from the English as a Second Language school. I fought the urge to turn and run and took several cautious steps forward. It was a small parcel, no bigger really than a hardcover book. But I hadn't ordered any books. Given the recent incident with my car, I should pull the fire alarm and evacuate the building. I texted Gab, asking if she was expecting a small parcel.

While waiting for a response, I mentally debated my choices, weighing in the safety of others with my personal embarrassment if the package turned out to be nothing. I checked my phone—no response from Gab.

I crept closer.

Whatever was inside was wrapped in wrinkled, previously used, brown paper. I could see writing but couldn't make anything out. Bells went off in my head telling me this was stupid. Why was I risking my and everyone else's life?

My heart fluttered against my ribcage. Holding my breath, I leaned forward. My name was printed on the parcel in block letters. No office address and no return address.

I turned, ran down the hall to the stairwell and stopped. I checked my phone. Still no response from Gab.

Taking a deep breath, I looked back at the package and pulled the fire alarm. The light on the wall above the alarm burst into life, flashing alternately blue and white, the ringing noise deafening. I ran down the stairs and out onto the sidewalk and called 911. I informed the operator that I had just initiated a fire alarm due to a suspicious package and gave her the address of the building.

People poured out of the building, most chatting and laughing. Within minutes, the sound of fire trucks could be heard. Now that most people were out of the building, I found myself wishing for a small explosion. Nothing terribly destructive.

A patrol car and a fire truck arrived simultaneously. I walked over to the police officers getting out of their vehicle and identified myself as the person calling in a suspicious package. One of them conferred with the firemen, the other one ordered people across the street and away from the building.

Barricades were placed on the road, detouring traffic away from the lanes adjacent to the building and funnelling it to the farthest lane. A second police car arrived, and an officer complete with flak jacket got out with a sleek German Shepherd. They entered the building with two of the firemen right behind them. After what seemed like an eternity, they all traipsed out to confer with the emergency personnel who remained outside.

The officer whom I had given my name to walked over, the one wearing a flak jacket, and his dog followed. They asked if there was any reason for me to be suspicious of the package, other than general caution. I told him someone blew up my car a few days earlier. That got their attention.

Ten minutes later, a hazmat truck arrived. Traffic now stretched back for blocks. One of the officers was dispatched to hurry the gawkers through the intersection when the lights turned green. I watched in fascination as two people donned hazmat suits and respiratory equipment then, armed with what looked like a white toolbox and something resembling a five-gallon pail, went inside. I spent the next ten minutes answering questions. What did I do for a living? Had I touched the package? When and where had my car been incinerated?

It didn't take long for the hazmat suits to return. They all chatted for a bit and then the police officer with the dog came over to talk to me.

"It's not bomb. There's no scent of explosives, nor did we detect protruding wires, metal, or any sounds. It's not radioactive. We've tested the package surface and it came up clean for unknown substances. We're going to take it down to the lab to give it one final going over, but we're all clear here."

"I kind of feel stupid calling this in," I replied.

"You did the right thing. It had your name on it but no return address or anything. Lots of tape on the packaging and no postage, and more importantly you weren't expecting a package."

"Any idea what's in it?"

"At first glance, I'd say maybe a book or a packet of paper. Given your car incident, we're going to have the lab check for biochemicals or anything nasty, but we don't expect they'll find anything."

"Will I get the package back, when they're done?"

"Someone will let you know when you can come pick it up. It'll take a few days, there's usually a backlog."

I nodded. The firefighters were taking away the barricades and people were pouring back into the building. I had a massive headache and just wanted to go home. But my day was far from done.

CHAPTER FORTY-FOUR

As soon as I got upstairs, I called Laura. She wasn't in so I left a message. After the phone call I sat back and weighed up what I knew. Okay, so Chloe lied. What else was new? Sometime between late November, when Chloe returned to Calgary, and January 2, when Stephen was found, Chloe's bracelet made its way into Stephen's house. If someone had stolen the bracelet and planted it in the house to throw suspicion her way, why hadn't she reported it missing? According to several reliable witnesses, she was never without it.

Knowing what I knew of Chloe, if it had gone missing, she would've accused everyone from her co-workers to the local priest. And loudly. Which left the other option. She left it in Stephen's house herself or knew who had, sometime between when she arrived in Calgary and when he was found dead.

I checked the time and reached for my phone. If Chloe was working a split shift today, she might be in. I called Vinnie's. A woman picked up after about twenty rings. I could barely hear her over the background laughter and music. I asked to talk to Chloe.

"Chloe doesn't work here anymore," said the woman.

"She quit?"

"Don't know. Boss called me yesterday to cover her shift. I see she's not on the work schedule."

After disconnecting, I called the number that showed up on my screen when Chloe had called to tell me someone had vandalized her boyfriend's car, but no one answered. The voice mail box was full. I knew where she was staying, but I really didn't want to venture over there. I'd end up freezing my ass off staring at an empty house for hours while she and her boyfriend were out having a good time. Sighing, I packed up and pulled on my coat. Several people were just now returning to their offices. I bypassed the elevator and took the stairs.

I was almost at my car when I spotted him. Well, a guy in a brown parka. Heavy duty, like the kind construction workers wear. Head down, he was heading east on Twelfth Avenue. I debated my options. I could follow him and see where he went, or I could call out Joey's name. Even if he heard me, he might choose to ignore me.

I didn't have a whole lot to convince me that this was Joey, except both wore a brown parka and had a beard. This time of year, parkas were popular—for that matter, so were beards. I pulled the collar of my coat up against the wind that had kicked up, stuffed my gloved hands in my pockets and headed after him.

Staying well back wasn't a problem. Parka-man took long strides, not unusual for someone at least six feet in height, and fit. Probably from chopping his own firewood and eating a lean diet, like berries and squirrel.

I followed him to Macleod Trail, where he turned south and entered a game store on the main floor of a crumbling three-storey red-brick building. Other than the game store, the main level stood empty. The upper floors contained apartments, some shuttered permanently, a few still occupied by those in desperate straits. I crossed the street and entered a bus shelter. The plexiglass walls cut the wind and provided an unobstructed view. I stamped my feet to get more blood circulating.

I watched the store, called Stumpy's Game Emporium, and waited for parka-man to come out. I googled Stumpy's and learned that the store sold everything from board and computer games to movie toys, collectibles, and gaming systems. The place was known for its huge inventory of remote-controlled model cars, boats, drones, and airplanes. I just finished asking myself how long I would stand there waiting for him, when he stepped outside. Whipping out my phone, I snapped a photo before he turned back in the direction we came from.

He glanced across the street. I hoped he hadn't noticed me standing on a street corner, ten blocks west of here, just an hour ago. I watched him head into the downtown core. I remained where I was and boarded the next bus that came by. Parka-man checked over his shoulder as the bus passed, maybe to see if I remained at the bus shelter.

I got off at city hall, along with a dozen or so passengers. Making my way across the street, alongside a mass of huddled pedestrians, I veered left and entered a small coffee shop. Thankful to be inside, I ordered a coffee to go and waited.

Parka-man strode by a few minutes later and turned west down Stephen Avenue. I pulled on my gloves and stepped outside. It was easier to follow him here, with office workers dashing out of one building and scurrying across the out-door mall to enter the next. I stayed a block behind and had no trouble following, his hooded head often the tallest around.

At the corner of Fourth Street, I pitched my half-drunk coffee into a garbage receptacle and entered a Starbucks. I stood near the door, watching out the window. Parka-man slowed and came to a stop beside an older, pale-blue Ford Taurus. I managed to capture more images of him in the ten seconds or so that he surveyed the sidewalk around him. Then he dashed around to the driver's side and clambered in.

As the Taurus pulled away, I turned and entered the coffee shop proper. I was thoroughly chilled but satisfied. Now if Antonia could confirm the photos of parka-man were of her brother, Joey, I'd be one step closer to catching Stephen's killer.

CHAPTER FORTY-FIVE

BACK AT THE office, I sent Antonia an email and two of the photos I managed to snap of parka-man, asking her if they were of Joey. After thawing somewhat, I set off again. I detoured into the café on the main floor and bought a coffee, a bag of pretzels and a slice of banana bread.

On the way to Chloe's boyfriend's place, I practiced staying alert to my surroundings until I realized I was hyper-tuned to my phone. I pulled in two doors down from the boyfriend's place, cut the engine, and checked my phone for messages. There were none. What was I even doing here?

I reached into the back seat and pulled out the sleeping bag I had thrown there after the blizzard ended and tucked it in around me. I only raised my chin from inside the collar of my coat to take a bite of banana bread or sip on my rapidly cooling coffee.

Laura claimed she saw Chloe with Conner a few days before Christmas. Both denied it. Detective McGuire found no one who could confirm it. If they had met up, and Conner did take her bracelet, how and why had it ended up in Stephen's house? Clearly there wasn't any love lost between them now. Maybe they had been concocting a plan of some sort. A plan Chloe no longer wanted to be a part of.

Chloe and Trace came out of the apartment building an hour later. I slid down in my seat and, as their Mini Cooper roared by, pushed aside the sleeping bag, started the engine, and pulled out after them. They made several stops before Trace dropped Chloe off at a No-Frills grocery store and roared off. I waited ten minutes and went inside.

Picking up a grocery basket, I made my way past several aisles to the soft drinks, chips and cracker aisle. No sign of Chloe in any of the aisles I passed. I picked up a bottle of Perrier and threw in a bag of liquorice twists. I stomped to the end of the aisle and continued down to the vegetables and fruit section. No sign of Chloe. Maybe she was working here as a cashier, or bagger. I added several apples, a bunch of carrots and a bag of kale salad to my basket and headed to the cash registers.

I was already past Chloe before I realized it was her. She was wearing a fuzzy and somewhat ratty bunny costume, handing out small, tinfoil-covered chocolate Easter eggs. I turned back.

"Chloe?"

The bunny looked up at me. Its face was half hidden by a giant rubber bunny nose which, due to its size and where it sat on her cheeks, did twitch when she talked.

"Great. What are you doing here?" she replied somewhat nasally.

"Just stopped in for a few groceries," I said, holding up my basket. "What happened to your job at Vinnie's?"

"I quit. And as soon as I get my money, I'm quitting this stupid job too," she said. She flung a bright, tinfoil wrapped egg at a small boy who was bouncing up and down a few feet away, mimicking a hopping rabbit, hitting him squarely in the eye. "Oops," she said, turning to let two little girls pick their own eggs out of the basket she had looped over her arm.

"You reached resolution on the will then?"

"I'm not happy, but I'm willing to move on."

A woman roared up to us, pulling a small wailing boy by the arm. "Did you just throw an egg in my son's eye?" she demanded of Chloe. I moved away, leaving Chloe explaining that she gently tossed him an egg, expecting him to catch it. Good thing she wasn't counting on keeping this job for long, either.

Back in my car, I ripped open the bag of twizzlers, then drove to the gas station and filled up. By the time I returned home, the twizzlers were half gone. I grabbed my bags and made my way upstairs, feeling slightly sick. I told myself it was the liquorice, but it was the second day in a row I was dragging ass. Upstairs, I checked my cell phone for messages, popped open my laptop and ran a quick eye down the dozen or so emails that downloaded. Nothing from Azagora. No messages from anyone I knew.

I had two theories. Either Joey killed Stephen in some sort of twisted act of revenge or Chloe, or she and Conner, had orchestrated Stephen's death, hoping to cash in on an inheritance.

Chloe must have gone to see Stephen after she returned from Los Angeles. It wouldn't surprise me to learn she once again threw herself at Stephen's feet, begging for mercy and a handout, once her relationship with her well-to-do eighty-year-old boyfriend ended. But it didn't mean she killed him.

Chloe mentioned a settlement but there hadn't been enough time to ask her how her it had been settled. I was curious to know if everyone had chipped in or if Laura and Tony had paid her off. I made a note to ask Laura, but I was betting on the latter.

At least Chloe would be out of Laura's hair...for now. Tony could move on with having the Nano-skin fuel cell rights reassigned to him. Everything was settled except for finding Stephen's killer. And Bernie's. I wouldn't mind knowing who blew up my car either.

Why had someone killed Bernie? The obvious explanation is that it was related to something or someone he had seen while following me as I investigated Stephen's death. He had taken a photo of a guy in a brown parka, who I assumed was Joey, at Tony's office building. Tony claimed he hadn't seen Joey in years. Either Tony lied, or the man in the parka wasn't Joey, or it was Joey, but he never went into the building to see Tony.

Suddenly I remembered the coil bound notebook I had found in Bernie's burnt-out house. I retrieved it, switched on the TV, and plunked myself back on the couch. I flipped open the notebook and thumbed through the pages. They were all blank. *Great.* I laid my head back against the couch and closed my eyes.

My phone dinged, my laptop chirped, and someone pounded on my door. I jumped; my eyes flashed to my cell phone lying on the couch next to me. I startled at the second rap. Phone in hand, I got up and cautiously made my way to the door. I jumped back as three more quick raps rang out. *What the hell?* I peered through the keyhole. Azagora stood on the other side. I unlatched the chain with shaking fingers, expecting bad news.

"My god, you scared me half to death."

"Christ. You are here."

"Yes, I am. It's where I live. You know they've invented email, voice messages, that sort of thing, right?"

"A little testy, are we?" His hand shot over his closely shorn hair, a sheepish grin crossing his face. He pulled me to him and kissed me hard. "I've got to go. I just needed to make sure you were all right."

I stepped back, confused. "Why wouldn't I be all right?"

"Let's see, your car was bombed, one of your students got himself killed following you while you poke into Stephen Wallis' murder and someone left you a suspicious package this morning. Need I say more? One of my guys is waiting downstairs, so I gotta go. I just needed to see for myself that you're okay." He turned and walked away.

"Luis," I called out after him, but he was already at the elevator. He turned and pointed at me. "Be careful. Lock up," he called out and slipped into the elevator. I closed the door and bolted it. I hadn't been overly worried until just now.

Luis Azagora came to check on me. He kissed me.

"You're a freaking idiot, Jorja," I admonished out loud, a sure sign I wasn't normal. I poured myself a glass of wine and opened the bag of pretzels, taking both with me back to the couch. I was feeling antsy and clearly trying to eat my frustration.

I checked my email. Antonia still hadn't replied, but now there was a text from Gab, asking what was up. She hadn't been expecting any deliveries at the office today. I sent her a quick reply telling her about the suspicious package now being tested in some lab, my kneejerk reaction and that the whole incident would probably be on the evening news. After the fourth text that went back and forth between us Gab called me. We had a good laugh about how we had gotten so used to texting each other that we often forgot we could actually talk.

As soon as we hung up, my phone pinged again, then a second time. I had two new voice messages. I entered my password and listened.

"Jorja, it's Laura Bradford. Something terrible has happened. Chloe's been shot."

I sat up, spilling my wine. I had just left Chloe a couple of hours ago. She had settled her dispute with Stephen's beneficiaries. Who the hell would want to shoot her? An image of an angry mother filled my head, but I dismissed it. No way would a mother kill a woman in a bunny suit for throwing a chocolate egg in her son's eye. Would she?

I played the second message.

"Jorja, I'm on my way to the hospital. Let's meet in the morning. Same place we met the first time. Ten o'clock."

Laura's second voice message sounded less frazzled. I tried calling to let her know ten o'clock was fine, but she didn't answer, her voice message box was full. Chloe did have a way of rubbing people the wrong way, but I couldn't imagine someone shooting her. I unmuted the TV and lowered the volume. Perhaps it would be on the news later, otherwise, I'd have to wait until morning.

Chloe's angry face floated into view. She had yelled that we'd all be sorry when she was dead, but I had written off her words as more theatrics. I didn't know what Chloe's role was in Stephen's death, but I was convinced that Laura Bradford's gut feeling was right all along.

CHAPTER FORTY-SIX

No matter how much you dislike someone, when something horrific happens it trivializes any issues that may have plagued the relationship. All the petty arguments, the misunderstandings, the slights and perceived injustices drop away like so many flies after a hard frost. The anger, frustration and bitterness quickly replaced by guilt, sorrow and regret. Laura now faced the possibility she would forever lose the opportunity to get to know the real Chloe and celebrate the quirks and curiosities that made Chloe unique.

"I feel so awful," Laura was now saying. "I can't believe it. She's in intensive care, in an induced coma. She looked so fragile. And she has no one."

"Sometimes things look worse than they really are," I said. "Let's hope that's the case." I felt a pang of guilt myself—there's no joy in maligning the injured or the dead. Sure, Chloe was a pain in the ass, but a forty-year-old Chloe might be quite different from the thirty-year-old woman she was today. If she got the chance. "What happened?"

"Her boyfriend called me and told me she'd been shot.

I thought it was a hoax or some mistake. I didn't realize it was so bad." Tears glistened in her eyes. Hand on her heart, she continued. "I cursed her all the way to the hospital, mad as hell that she was inconveniencing me once again. What kind of horrible person does that?" Laura stared out at the lake then back at me, oblivious to the tears sliding down her cheeks.

"You're not a horrible person. Chloe didn't deserve this, but let's face it, most of her relationships are short lived for a reason." My internal voice spoke up, reminding me of my own similar relationship history. I shuddered mentally.

"Thank you, Jorja. I can't believe I accused her of having a hand in Stephen's death."

I cleared my throat.

"What?" She looked up. "Don't tell me," she said, her voice hardening a notch.

"I don't have any evidence indicating she had anything to do with Stephen's death," I added quickly. "But she did lie to you…and the police. I tracked down her ex in Palm Springs. He is still recovering from a stroke, but his sister says Chloe was wearing her bracelet the day he drove her to the airport, on November 27."

Laura nodded her head slowly. "She must have gone to see Stephen. That's how her bracelet ended up there. I bet she went there to hit him up for money."

"Given her past behaviour, it's a likely scenario."

Laura sighed. "I've got to hand it to her, she's been showing her true colours all along, maybe right to her bitter end."

"Did you get to talk to her when you got to the hospital?" I asked gently.

Laura shook her head. "No. They had her in surgery when I got there. By the time they let me see her, she was already in the coma, tubes coming out all over."

"What about her boyfriend, was he there?"

Laura nodded. "He told me he had gone to pick her up from work at this grocery store. I never even knew she worked at a grocery store. He said she just came out of the store when a dark-brown car drove by. Then he saw Chloe on the ground. He figured she slipped and fell. But when she didn't get up, he got out of his car and ran over. That's when he saw the blood. A lot of blood."

"How awful."

"Someone must have called an ambulance; it came a few minutes later. They took her right into surgery. That's when he called me. He didn't get a chance to talk to her either. The bullet hit her in the neck."

"I hope she makes it."

Laura nodded, her eyebrows furrowed, her eyes clear. "What the hell is going on? What are the chances someone shoots both of my siblings?"

About one in a billion. "Hard to believe, for sure. If Stephen's murder wasn't homicide's top priority, it will be now. This can't be an unlucky coincidence."

"Who do you think did this?"

"I really don't know, Laura." Conner and Joey were still good suspects in my mind but if Chloe and Conner were working together something had just gone horribly wrong. I couldn't rule anyone out at this point. I knew McGuire's team had moved on to Stephen's business dealings. There might be good reason to do so. The possibility that someone killed Stephen to get rid of him as a competitor or get their hands on the Nano-skin fuel cell was plausible. Tony said it would likely be worth a lot.

I'd seen Tony meeting with Olivia Li from StarTu, and there was a good chance he'd met with Tián Technologies the day I saw him at The Ranchmen's. Both were heavy hitters. I could see why Tony would have been antsy when Chloe challenged the will. Especially if StarTu and Tián were the two companies Stephen had been negotiating with. They couldn't possibly be involved in something like this, could they? I shook my head.

"I hear a settlement has been reached with Chloe regarding Stephen's will."

Laura nodded. "I got a call from the lawyer yesterday. Chloe is no longer contesting the will."

"How did it get resolved?"

"I don't know. Wayne and I certainly didn't give in to her demands. We all tried reasoning with her, but she didn't get it."

"What do you mean?"

"She wanted the money upfront. We told her, none of us have that kind of money just lying around. We told her she needed to drop her appeal, let the estate finalize all the disbursements and if, and I repeat *if*, we were to come to some settlement, her share would come out of those disbursements later."

"I wonder what made her change her mind. I talked to her yesterday, just briefly mind you. She made a point of telling me the dispute had been settled."

"Well, thank god it has been. Wayne was ready to wring

her neck." Laura winced. "I—I didn't mean—not like that. He was frustrated, that's all."

"Why is that? He seemed pretty stressed when I saw him."

"We've got a lot of legal bills to pay. Wayne's company was involved in a lawsuit a few years back. He's innocent, he did nothing wrong, but it took every bit of our savings to prove it. We were on the verge of losing the house, everything."

"I'm sure the police will be asking everyone questions about their relationship with Chloe, where they were when she was shot. I'm assuming you and Wayne won't have any trouble explaining where you were."

"No. I mean, I was at my daughter's volleyball game, along with several of the other moms. I was there when I got the call from Chloe's boyfriend."

"What about Wayne?"

She looked startled. "At home, I guess."

"With your son?"

"No, our son is on a school trip. Christ. Here we go again. Not that I imagine Wayne shot Chloe. That's ridiculous. It's just that we barely get out from one issue when we're thrown one more."

"Don't worry. I'm sure the police will eliminate your husband from potential suspects once they talk to him."

I left Laura sitting at the coffee shop. I had never told this many lies in my life. At least in that short a timespan. Laura had just confirmed that she and Wayne had a big motive for Stephen's death. If anything, the cops would be looking at their financial situation carefully. I wondered who inherited from Chloe if she died.

I needed to talk to Tony. He or Rob or Antonia, or all three of them, had settled with Chloe and it had to be for a pretty big reason. My money was on Tony.

CHAPTER FORTY-SEVEN

TODAY I HAD a message from Calgary Police Services, telling me I could pick up my package at their Westwind station. Following the various signs greeting me, I moved to the appropriate waiting area and took a ticket. Several people were ahead of me. I used the time to catch up on email and delete stale messages.

When my number was called, I went up to the counter and a young woman, with the word *intern* stitched on her sleeve, retrieved my package. I signed the form she pushed at me and picked up the package, rewrapped loosely in its original wrinkled brown Kraft paper, now with a CPS barcode sticker on the back. Reaching my car, I got in, turned on the engine and took a closer look. My name was spelled Georgia and written with a thick black marker. Knight was spelled correctly. The word *personel* was written above my name, by someone not familiar with its proper spelling and usage.

I peeled back the brown wrapper and lifted out a small flat Christmas card box. Lifting the box cover I discovered an inch-thick stack of black-and-white photos. Pulling them out, I flipped through the top few photos. They were of Stephen Wallis's house. Why the hell would someone leave me a bunch of photos of Stephen's house? Anonymously? I flipped through a few more and then checked a few in the middle. Most were street shots. My heart beat faster. I put the photos back in the box, dropped them on the seat next to me and backed out of the parking stall. Someone had delivered the photos right to my office door. They must contain something of interest.

*

I had the photos laid out like a game of solitaire on my office desk. I had examined the brown wrapping paper more closely. The box once held Hallmark Christmas cards, the front showed two children sledding down a snow-covered hill, a dog romping by their side. At the base of the hill, a few skaters twirled on an ice-covered pond, the surrounding snow-covered evergreens sparkling under a pale winter sun. Idyllic. Peaceful.

After determining there was nothing of interest about the box or the wrapper, I went through the photos, one by one. Fifty-two black-and-white photos, all remarkably similar in appearance, many taken at odd angles. Bernie must have taken these. But they had been delivered to me days after Bernie's death. By whom?

Rummaging through my desk drawer, I found my magnifying glass. It had been a gag gift from Gab's cousin Connie when I got my private investigator licence. That and a fedora and a fake moustache. I picked up each photo and examined it through the magnifying glass.

Most of the photos of Stephen's house were of the upper floor windows. There were also a few birds-eye shots that must have been taken from the adjacent condo building. The windows in some of the photos appeared to be covered by sleek, black, mesh blinds. Images from my tour of the house formed in my mind's eye. The photo I held in my hand was of the main window in the master bath.

I picked up the magnifying glass and peered through it, hoping to see through the window and into the inside. I looked for reflections or anything else that might be of interest. Nothing. I picked up the few photos of the skylights.

There were two skylights, both about a quarter of the width of the main window and at least four or five feet in length. As I recalled, they were set into the angled part of the bathroom ceiling and let in massive amounts of light. Laura had told me the skylights could be opened and closed remotely, when needed. I re-examined the windows with the magnifying glass. I detected no reflections, and nothing odd or visible inside the bathroom. I had a hard time imagining anyone entering the house through the skylights. Inside, they would be faced with a fourteen-foot drop to the tile floor below. And how would they have gotten out? The front and back doors were locked from the inside.

I picked up the bird's-eye-view photos. There was nothing of interest on Stephen's roof or any of the neighbouring roofs. Just the usual chimneys and air vents. I sat up and rubbed my neck. My fingers were cramped, my shoulders ached from sitting hunched over the photos.

I pushed back my chair and stood up and paced back and forth. What the hell did Bernie or whoever sent me these photos want me to see? They were all black and white, like the photos police had found in Bernie's house. Most of the shots were taken from crazy angles. It made no sense. Perhaps the crazy angles were an attempt to get artsy.

Unfortunately, our office building didn't have security cameras, or I might have been able to see who dropped off the photos. There was something in these pictures, something I should be paying attention to, if only I could put my finger on what.

My phone beeped, and I jumped. I had a reply from Antonia. Parka-man was indeed her brother Joey. It appeared Joey frequented Calgary way more than one might expect of a recluse. Was he lying to his sister because he didn't want to see her or was there some other reason?

I picked up the batch of street shots. Most showed several pedestrians walking to or away from the camera. There must be something in the photos I was meant to see. Or were they just Bernie messing with me? Like the notes on my windshield and the black flowers?

It was after I left the office and was making my way back to the SUV, when it hit me. I had assumed Tony lied to me about seeing Joey, when I saw the photo of Joey in front of Tony's office building down at the police station. Now I considered the idea that maybe Tony hadn't lied. Maybe he didn't know Joey was skulking around, casing his building. Maybe Tony's life was in danger.

CHAPTER FORTY-EIGHT

THE FRONT WINDOWS of Stumpy's were heavily covered in caricatures, logos, arrows and various other symbols aimed at drawing in customers. I pushed open the door and a small bell tinkled overhead. I stood, letting my eyes adjust.

A wooden counter ran the length of the store immediately to the left, and behind it stood a man, his bald, egg-shaped head barely visible over the counter. Behind him, shelves reaching the ceiling stood crammed with every conceivable game and gaming system ever invented. The man straightened as I approached. His eyes were oval shaped like his head, his nose wide and flat and below that, thick puffy lips.

"Can I help you?" he asked, his lips barely moving.

"I hope so. I'm trying to locate someone, regarding an estate settlement." I pulled out a copy of one of the photos I had taken of Joey. "This man. A friend told me he comes in here. Do you know him or know where I can find him?"

He took the photo, glanced at it, and handed it back.

His whole body was egg-shaped, and a bit wobbly and pale like he hadn't seen daylight in years.

"You a cop?" he asked.

"No. Private investigator. He was named a beneficiary in a will and I'm trying to locate him, so the estate can be settled."

"I know Joey. Known him for years. You're going to have a hard time tracking him down. He doesn't live here."

"His sister says he lives off the grid somewhere, but he comes into town occasionally. You wouldn't happen to have a file on your customers?"

"Most certainly not."

"How does he pay you?"

"Cash. Always cash."

"Seems like a guy living off the grid wouldn't have much use for gaming systems or electronic gadgets."

"I wouldn't know about that."

"What do you know about him?"

"I know he's a real whiz. He could've easily invented everything in here. He likes to build his own stuff."

"What kind of stuff?"

"Robots, drones, custom gaming keyboards, mini power bots. He doesn't like the kits. He designs and builds everything himself."

"Do you have any idea where he stays when he's in town or how to get in touch with him?"

"It's not my business to know where he stays or what he does. He's been coming in here on and off for years. Always pays with cash. What more could I want?"

I nodded. "Okay, thanks."

Back outside, I pulled on my gloves and turned in the direction of my vehicle. Interesting that Joey paid with cash or even had cash. Maybe he sold the items he built. I couldn't imagine someone who lived in the woods wanting to be tied down by a bunch of stuff. Maybe it's how he paid for gas for the car he was driving and other necessities. He'd need a way to advertise when he had something to sell, or maybe he sold to a distributor. I needed to go back out to Sparwood, spend more time asking folks around town if they knew him. He must have a place in or around there where he kept his car. I checked my phone. There was no reply from Tony on the message I'd left earlier.

The wind howled from the north making the walk back to the car a lot nastier. I reached the mall and went inside, bought a coffee. I told myself it wouldn't hurt to browse a little, warm up, let the rush-hour traffic clear.

I checked messages but there was no update on Chloe. I just hoped her death wouldn't be the top story on the evening news. Laura said Chloe's boyfriend saw a brown car driving by right when Chloe was shot. Not exactly useful information, but perhaps the police had managed to get more detailed eyewitness accounts.

I was feeling guilty and a little worried about Chloe, especially as I may have thrown her into Conner's path by claiming that they were in cahoots. But Conner had no reason to shoot Chloe unless he had done something illegal, and Chloe knew about it. Something he didn't want anyone else finding out.

Part of me wanted to tell Detective McGuire or Detective Keating everything I knew, every tiny detail, then walk away.

If any of it helped them find Stephen's killer, then hallelujah. After deliberating it further I decided against it. I didn't have anything concrete. Although Conayre could verify Conner's flight to Sparwood, the reason for the trip could be explained away in the blink of an eye.

Did Detective McGuire even know about Joey or that Stephen reportedly was one of the last people to see Ajeet Jayaraman before he disappeared? If Joey suspected Stephen of killing Ajeet or burying him after he died, it might explain why he didn't want anything to do with Stephen's bequest. But why kill him now, twenty years later? Then again, he wouldn't be the first person who lived with hurt or pain for years before deciding he'd had enough.

I was frustrated and on edge at the same time. I distracted myself by trying on shoes. Then I hit the food court and inhaled a plate of Chinese food. The same thoughts and theories I'd been fighting with for days ran relentless circles in my head, but I couldn't spit out anything logical.

Someone blew up my car and left me photos of Stephen Wallis' house days after Bernie was already in the morgue. What was with that? The car incident might be courtesy of Conner, but not the photos. Had Bernie given someone the photos to deliver to me? Bernie had been stalking me, the memorabilia box found at his place confirmed it. Why the newspaper articles about my parents and the black flowers? Was he hoping to frighten me, make me sad or point out that I was every bit as flawed as he?

What was I saying here? First, Bernie is stalking me and trying to scare me to death and next he's trying to help me solve Stephen Wallis' murder? How did the photos help? I already knew Stephen had been killed in his own house.

Now there were two murders to solve, and if Chloe died it would be three. Maybe Bernie had been blackmailing someone, or had been messing around with several people's minds, not just mine. People who weren't as nice as me. My mind was going in circles and I had to stop. If I didn't get out of the mall soon, I'd end up owning a dress to go with the one hundred and eighty-dollar dark-teal booties sitting in a bag on the chair next to me.

I was on my way back to my car when my phone rang. Juggling purse, shoe bag and a large frozen yogurt, I fumbled for my phone. A number I didn't recognize was on my screen.

"Is that Jorja Knight?" a voice asked.

"Yes. This is Jorja."

"It's Rob Bailey. You still looking into Stephen Wallis' death?"

"I am. Do you have something for me?"

"Maybe, maybe not. But something's come up and it's driving me crazy. Do you have a minute?"

An hour later, another piece fell into place. A big piece.

CHAPTER FORTY-NINE

"Thanks for coming, Jorja."

We were in a different meeting room this time, smaller than the last one, no Howler monkey or rain forest sounds.

"Can I get you a coffee or anything? The coffee is rather good, I have it shipped in from Costa Rica."

"No thank you, I'm all coffeed out. You said you had something to tell me?"

"I had to call someone. I believe Tony's in danger."

I sat up. "What's going on?"

"A few days ago, Tony and I met up for drinks. I think we're both suffering from cabin fever."

"I know the feeling."

"We met at the Playbill in the northwest. We were sitting at the bar, having a drink, watching the game on TV, when Tony gets this call. He listens for a few minutes then goes all pale. I heard him say, 'I'm not doing this' and 'no way'."

"Do you know who he was talking to?"

"Not at that point. I could see he was agitated. He got

up and went outside, still on the phone with whoever was on the other end. He comes back about ten minutes later, totally flustered. He throws back his drink and orders a double. As soon as it's set down in front of him, he throws that back as well. I didn't want to pry but clearly something had unnerved him."

"I can see how you'd be concerned."

"I asked him if everything was all right. He tried to wave it off. You've met Tony. Everything's fine, he says, but I can clearly see it's not."

I nodded. Tony came off as Mr. Amiable, always cheerful, treated every business problem as an opportunity. Like Tony Robbins, but shorter.

"After a couple more drinks, I asked him again if everything was all right. I told him I could tell he was upset. That I'd listen if he wanted to talk—no advice, no judgement."

"He said no, it wasn't like that. The call was from some nutjob, threatening to kill him."

"What?"

"Exactly. I almost fell off my stool."

"Does he know who called him?"

Rob nodded. "Took a while to get a name out of him but he says it was one of our old roommates from university. The guy I told you about. Joey."

Maybe one of my theories was about to play out. "Why is he threatening to kill Tony?"

"Tony said Joey wants to even up the score. I asked Tony if he had any inkling as to what the guy was talking about."

"Did he?"

"He said the guy's delusional. Tony is convinced Joey has

some sort of medical reason for why he is the way he is. Even back in university, the guy was slightly off the wall."

"Even more reason to be worried about a death threat."

"I know. I told Tony I'd just listen, but I urged him to tell the police. Tony said one threatening phone call would hardly spur them into action."

"Under normal circumstance he might be right. In this case, a mutual friend was murdered. The police will be very interested."

"What really shook me is Tony said Joey had called Stephen a few months before he was murdered."

"What? Let me get this right. You're saying Joey called Stephen and threatened him?"

"Maybe not that specifically, but I would have taken it as a threat."

"Do you know what was said?"

"Tony told me that Stephen had run into Joey a few months earlier. Stephen thought Joey was on drugs or was maybe psychotic. When Tony asked what happened, Stephen told Tony that Joey had been furious. He started in on him, saying he knew what Stephen had done. Stephen asked him to explain. Joey yelled that no one could be trusted. That Stephen's time had come. Bizarre proclamations about justice being served where justice was needed."

"Whoa. That's disconcerting."

"Tony said Stephen got a bunch of hang-up calls after that. Late at night, weekends."

"When was this?"

"Shortly after he was mugged."

"That's when he hired his chauffeur," I murmured out loud.

"Then Stephen got the most disturbing call. A man said something like, 'I know what you did and you're going to burn in hell'."

"Was it Joey?"

"Stephen wasn't a hundred percent certain but who else could it be?"

"Is Tony going to talk to the detective handling Stephen's case? Tell them about all this?"

"One minute he says yes, next minute, no. He posed an interesting question to me. He asked me if I ran into a university friend, who might be struggling with a mental illness, then weeks later got a few hang-up calls, would I connect the two."

"What did you say?"

"I wouldn't have."

"No, of course not. But seeing as Stephen's dead and hindsight is twenty-twenty?"

"I know. I don't want to circumvent what Tony wants to do. I didn't feel right not reporting it either. I figured you'd know what to do."

"The police will have gone through Stephen's phone records by now." Would a few calls from an unknown caller months before he died trigger any suspicions? Not likely. Especially if they didn't come from the same number. "Theoretically, Joey doesn't own a phone. If he was the one behind the calls, he likely used a public phone. Or several different phones. But the police might be able to tie the calls to a particular location. Now that Tony's received a similar call, they might be able to connect the two. I'd definitely call Detective McGuire."

"So, you do think it's important?"

"Definitely. The police chase down clues like this all the time. Most not nearly as good. Let them eliminate Joey as a suspect if he's innocent. Joey's sister finally admitted to me she's worried about his mental health. What's the worst that can happen?" A few scenarios came to mind, but they didn't support the point I was trying to make.

"You're right. I'm glad I talked to you."

"So, you'll call?"

"I'll call Tony tonight. Tell him he needs to talk to the police. If he doesn't, I will. I'll let Tony know how worried I am for him. I know I told him I'd stay out of it, but I don't need another dead friend."

CHAPTER FIFTY

Traffic ground to a halt south of cemetery hill. I turned on the radio and tuned to the road report. A three-car accident at the bottom of the hill had traffic snarled for miles. My location on Macleod Trail didn't leave me or my fellow commuters much in the way of options to bypass the accident.

The radio announcer warned that we should brace for one more blast of winter. A rapidly moving cold front was making its way north from Idaho and Montana and was expected to hit Calgary early evening. The weather forecasters were promising that it would clear out by morning. The meteorologists always promised warmer, milder weather two or three days out. Probably a coordinated effort by them and psychiatrists to curtail winter depression and lower the suicide rates.

I parked on a residential street, blocks from the office. By the time I got there, I was sweating under my layers and dying for a coffee. I pulled open the entrance doors and stepped inside, dismayed at the line snaking out of the small café off the lobby. I debated whether to run two blocks to the next nearest coffee shop or just head upstairs. My phone vibrated in the pocket of my coat. I pulled it out. The number wasn't familiar.

"Hello?" I answered tentatively, ready to disconnect if it was a telemarketer.

"May I please speak to Jorja Knight?"

"This is her."

"Jorja. It's Tony D'Silva."

"Tony. I was meaning to call you."

"We need to talk. There's something you should know. It's about Stephen. And Joey Albero."

Each heartbeat pulsed against the side of my neck.

"Okay. What do you want to tell me?"

"Not now. I have a meeting in about two minutes. Can we meet this afternoon?"

"Sure. Your offices?"

"No. It's best we meet off site. Hang on a sec."

I waited until he came back on the line. "I have a meeting from one o'clock until two near the airport. Is there any way you could meet me at Air Espresso at two-fifteen? There's always a seat, the coffee is great, and they make the best banana bread in the world. I can send you the address."

"Sure, that works for me," I replied. "See you this afternoon." Maybe I wouldn't need to warn Tony to keep clear of Joey. Maybe Tony already knew he was in danger.

Joey knew something about the night Ajeet went missing. I had one witness who claimed Stephen left the party with Ajeet and Tony in his car that night. Ajeet's family said he never made it home. It wasn't a far stretch to think Ajeet died that night. Perhaps Stephen panicked, hid his body, covered up the truth all these years. Did Joey believe that with the world soon coming to an end, it was time to make him account for what he did? It might explain why he didn't want Stephen's money. He might believe Tony knew what happened and had kept quiet about it to protect Stephen.

I checked the time. I had a couple of hours before I'd need to leave for my meeting. I entered the stairwell and hustled up the stairs. I breathed a sigh of relief, the office door was closed, and no strange parcels lay outside.

Unlocking the door, I let it creak shut behind me, and was already at the computer with my coat off by the time it clicked shut. Tony made good on his word, sending me both the address and a link to the coffee shop. I clicked on the link to get a sense of where it was. Google maps showed a dot at the far end of a large industrial mall. I selected street view and checked it out.

The café was at the end of a long, low warehouse-type building. The industrial park was located near the airport and built to keep up with Calgary's booming economy, which had stopped booming months ago. Fifty minutes should give me enough time to retrieve the Rav4, make my way out of the downtown area and over to Air Espresso.

After meeting with Rob, I spent most of the night rehashing everything I knew. Yesterday, I convinced myself the photos of Stephen's skylights and upstairs windows had come from Bernie. He may have left them with a friend or co-worker with instructions to deliver them to me if anything happened to him. That would fit in with his image of himself as a cloak-and-dagger persona, working alongside a private eye on a fascinating murder case. But why would he have thought anything was going to happened to him?

Now a weird idea as to how Stephen may have been killed popped into my head. My fingers flew over the computer keys. An hour later, I sat back. Today's skylights weren't like those in the nineties. Sure, some were still constructed to open to a forty-five-degree angle, but many allowed for full entry to rooftop gardens or expanded into Juliette balconies. Some, like Stephen's, were wired to sense moisture and open and close accordingly. Some models could be fitted with fans to circulate fresh air or deter insects from entering.

I glanced at my watch, my excitement growing by the minute. I knew technology was being embedded everywhere, even in mundane household items. Our use of technology was only limited by our own imaginations. That's why Stephen and now Tony's nano cell technology was so important. Everything needed extended battery life or energy to work properly.

My fingers flew over the keyboard. When I left Global Analytix, drones were just coming into the mainstream, although the military had them for years. Today drones were being built to fly longer distances before needing to recharge. Not only were they small and light they could carry weights up to eight pounds. They even had drones the size of an insect. Joey wouldn't have needed an insect drone, just one small enough to fly through an open skylight.

My phone dinged, reminding me of the time. I logged off, shoved my laptop into the desk, grabbed my coat and bag, and locked up behind me.

I ran down the stairs, my mind evaluating the possibilities.

Maybe Joey had found a way to override Stephen's security system or open a window. Maybe the skylight had been the point of entry. Could a drone be jury-rigged and made to shoot a gun remotely? Maybe I was letting my imagination get away on me. Or maybe, with Bernie Ing's unwanted and unappreciated, creepily delivered help, I had just figured out how Stephen Wallis had been killed.

CHAPTER FIFTY-ONE

DEERFOOT TRAIL CRAWLED for about a kilometre north of Memorial Drive and suddenly I was free of the bottleneck. My eyes darted to the clock on my dash, and I grit my teeth. I hated being late and it would be a miracle if I got there on time. I talked myself back off the ledge, reminding myself that usually I was the one who arrived early or on time and sat fuming while the person I was expecting sauntered in late without even noticing. This wasn't exactly a life-or-death situation and Tony would hardly run out of the café if I wasn't there at two-fifteen on the nose. Even so, I didn't loosen my hands on the wheel or let up pressure on the gas pedal. I got there with two minutes to spare.

I had never been to this part of Calgary, somewhere slightly south and east of the airport. Construction near Barlow Trail had forced me into a detour, rerouting me through a series of side streets that left me disoriented.

Keeping my eyes peeled, I found Freight Avenue and turned. I drove past a warehouse containing a mattress wholesaler, a hot tub dealer and little else. The second block

I entered remained eerily underpopulated. The recent downturn in the economy wasn't doing anyone a favour. If Google maps was right, I'd find Air Espresso in the end unit on my left.

A barricade blocked the far entry into the parking lot. A hand-drawn sign taped to the barricade read "parking" and pointed me to the right. I continued to the end of the street. The pavement ended at a second barricade. A handwritten sign read, "parking at back" and an arrow pointed down a hard-packed dirt track to the side of the building. I was at the right place, I just needed to park. I could see the tail end of a vehicle already parked there.

I slowed as I drove over the curb and down the rutted lane. Air Espresso looked deserted, but a sign in their window declared they were open. I bet they regretted opening before other tenants moved in. I rounded the building and the dashboard exploded.

Cursing, I jammed on the brakes and sat dazed. *WTF.* The space next to me was filled with a white mass. The adrenaline hit me, and my legs went rubbery. I tried pushing down the deployed airbag with little success. Putting the Rav4 in gear, I rolled forward and pulled in next to the lone car in back. It would appear I had beat Tony after all.

I turned off the engine, glanced at the airbag and laughed. I'd have to find some way to deflate it before I left, as it obscured my view out the front and side window. Gathering up my purse and keys, I pulled open the door and stepped out. A second explosion hit me.

*

The room tumbled over and over. My eyes wouldn't open. A peaceful calmness washed over me. I wasn't afraid. My mother would be waiting.

*

I tried opening my eyes but couldn't. Panicking, I forced one open. Grey walls spun dizzyingly fast. I fought back the nausea and closed my eyes until the room slowed, then pried open my right eye. I tried opening my other one, but it wouldn't budge. I turned my head and the room burst into motion. Clamping my eyes shut I put my hands out to my sides and waited for equilibrium. *I'm alive.*

I swallowed, but the saliva built up again and again. I knew I was going to be sick. Pushing myself up on one elbow I leaned forward, and the room tumbled. I crawled to the edge of the matting and threw up. I gripped the edge of the mat and remained kneeling. A while later the nausea lessened. I moved my head an inch to my right. I was still off balance, but the room stayed put.

My heart raced, hammering against my side. Why couldn't I see? I reached up and touched my left eyelid. I pulled up on it. It stuck for a minute then freed itself. A sharp pain stabbed my eye and it watered. I closed my right eye. The room blurred but I had some vision. I opened my right eye. Where the hell was I?

I inched my way into a sitting position, stopping when the room spun. After a while, I pushed myself up and carefully turned my head from side to side. I was on a mattress, on the floor. My heart hammered against my chest. I opened my mouth, but I couldn't feel air going in or out. I held my hand up to my mouth, my breath non-existent. My hand fell to my chest, my eyes widened in fear.

I couldn't breathe. My heart pounded in my ears, the room swam in red. Then nothing.

CHAPTER FIFTY-TWO

MY TEETH CHATTERED, and I couldn't stop. I was lying down. My eyes searched up and around. Scared to lift my head and set the room whirling I took a deep breath. I could breathe. My heart raced a thousand beats a minute.

I pulled my hands out from between my knees and straightened my legs. My body shook, the tremors more violent now. I pushed myself up on my arm and then carefully into a sitting position. I turned my head ever so slowly. The room was small. Slivers of light cut through the darkness. The cracks of light meant there was an outside.

I lifted my wrist to my face. My watch was gone. I looked down. I was still wearing my coat, but my boots were gone. My hands searched over the mattress, but there was nothing there. I flashed back to an explosion and something big and white hitting me. Had I been in an accident? No, that wasn't quite right.

I crawled to the edge of the mattress and onto the floor. The rough wood planks were covered with frost. My hands and knees slid on the boards like ice. I sat back on my legs and patted my pockets. My gloves were gone. I made my way on hands and knees to the biggest sliver of light, near the floor. I lay down and plastered my cheek on the icy wood. All I could see was white ground and then trees. I was in a shed out in the middle of nowhere.

Sitting up, my hands scrambled over the rough wood in front of me. A door. My fingers frantically searched along the edge. My heart sank. The hinges must be on the outside. I crawled back to the mattress, sat down, crossing my legs and tucking as much of my feet as I could under me. I tucked my chin into the collar of my coat and jammed my hands into my pockets. The shaking became more violent.

I was locked in a shed, in the woods somewhere. A cut road covered in snow flashed through my mind. The hunter's cabin. A knife. I shook my head. No, not the hunter's cabin. Slowly my memory came back, in bits and jumbles. I couldn't stop shaking and found myself rocking back and forth.

Stand up, do jumping jacks, stomp your feet.

I was too cold to move.

I startled at a whistling sound, then realized it came from me. I must have fallen asleep. I was cold, but I wasn't shivering as badly now. How long could a person live without food or water? Three days? Five? What day was this? I had somehow managed to fold the thin mattress over on itself. I lay between its griminess. *Like a fish taco.* My mouth watered, and I couldn't get the fish taco image out of my mind. The nausea returned. I needed to get outside. I'd try when it got dark.

Why am I waiting for dark?

What if whoever locked me up came back to kill me? Maybe they were long gone and had left me here in the woods, with no shoes, no hat or gloves or phone or water or food, to die. The sooner I made a move the better.

I unfurled the mattress and pushed it toward the door. Sitting on the mattress I reached for the crack, trying to wedge my fingers under the bottom board. I couldn't quite get my fingers in far enough to get a grip. I gave the bottom board a kick. If the hinges were outside, the boards would be nailed from the outside as well. I groped the edge of the door and peered at its construction. A simple door with an outer frame and one cross piece through the middle. I kicked at the bottom board with both feet, feeling the sharp pain running up both shins.

My eyes searched the walls frantically for anything. My throat was parched. I licked my lips and tasted blood. I ran my hands over the mattress. It felt dense, a wad of fibre encased in a grubby covering. The edge of the mattress was rimmed. Maybe there was a wire inside. My hands fumbled over the grimy mattress cover until they found a thin spot near the middle. I sat, exhausted, my head heavy.

I unfurled my fingers and stabbed and tore at the fabric, tearing a bit with my teeth, then ripped it apart. The inside was made of wadded, felt-like material. I tore at it and it slowly came apart in chunks. I ripped off more mattress fabric. I tried tearing open the rolled rim on the mattress. "Please don't come back, please don't come back," I pleaded silently. I chewed one end, feeling for wire. There was none.

I froze. Someone or something was outside.

My ears strained for sound. My eyes glued in horror at

the crack by the floor. The light was fading. I waited, barely daring to breathe. I stood up. My feet were now padded with felt, wrapped in strips of material torn from the cover tied together and bound with mattress edging for extra measure. Maybe I could surprise him when he opened the door. Crash into him hard and run. *I have to pee.* I held out a hand to steady myself.

I knelt again, afraid to look through the crack, expecting to see a pair of boots. Whose boots? Must be Joey. What happened to Tony? Maybe Tony was dead. My mind flashed back to the Air Espresso Café. Tony hadn't been there. A shudder ran though me, and my neck prickled. I lowered my head to the floor, not daring to breathe. I peered through the crack near the floor. Nothing but dark shadows.

I stuck my hands in under my coat. My chest was warmer than my hands—my arms and legs were colder than ice. My tongue was thick, dry, it stuck to the roof of my mouth. I couldn't swallow.

I had to get out. Tonight. I sat on the mattress and kicked at the bottom board. My feet made a thumping sound, and the door shook and banged against the shed. I stopped and listened. A dog howled in the distance. More likely wolves. I'd be found torn to shreds. I resumed kicking.

Each kick sent a sharp pain up my shin, but not as bad as before. I lay down. I was so tired. Suddenly I woke, sweat rolled between my breasts, the rest of me like ice. Why was my chest so warm? I inched my way to the door and kicked. I paused and kicked again. My foot shot out, scraping on the rough board above it. I pulled it back, knelt and peered out.

A dark wall, black. I peered through the darkness and

made out a faint outline of trees. I kicked frantically at the board above the missing one and it fell off. Another kick separated the third board from its frame. I ducked and slid headfirst through the opening.

Fresh, cold air bit at my face, the snow barely registering on my numb hands. I searched the ground in front of me. Forest dead ahead, more trees to the right. I stood up and turned to my left and froze. A giant gnome stared back.

I staggered over to the gnome. It was smiling. *Am I hallucinating?* I tilted my face up to the sky. Was I somewhere magical? I teetered backwards and fell.

Reaching out, I touched the gnome. Plastic. Next to the feet lay a pile of logs, sawed into two-foot lengths, stacked messily. I pulled myself to my feet. The shed was barely visible in the dark.

I peered at the thin layer of snow covering the ground, my ears straining for sound, my brain screaming for me to run. There were footprints, boot prints. I walked away from the giant gnome. More footprints. I found a track, leading into the woods and turned down it. It was darker here in the trees. *Where the hell am I?*

I stumbled and slid, my hands out in front of me, trying to protect my face from the branches blocking my way. It was all downhill, yet I was huffing hard. I stopped to catch my breath, which sounded loud, ragged in the stillness. The cold seeped under my coat and tremors vibrated in my chin. I glanced back. The clearing was no longer visible. Pushing on, I slipped and slid forward, refusing to break into a run. The path veered to the left. Twenty steps further, I stopped. *What's that?*

A faint glow of lights flickered through the trees. A surge of joy, then a gut-wrenching jab. I was stumbling my way into my captor's backyard.

I took a step to my right and then one more. The going was tougher now. The snow no deeper but snarled branches caught at my clothing and scratched at my face. I stopped every few steps. *There must be a road somewhere.* I reached down, my fingers scraping up snow from the roots and leaves. My hands shook violently as I lifted the snow up to my mouth and bit off a piece, letting it disappear on my tongue. I ran my tongue over my cracked lips and ate more snow.

Muffled stabs of music broke the silence. Something dark loomed up in front of me, cutting off the faint light from below. I inched forward until my hand touched a solid cold mass, the faint smell of rubber now prevalent. I knew that smell. A wall made of tires flashed through my mind. I closed my eyes. Was I at Merle's Trading Post outside of Sparwood? Why was I here?

I moved left and yelped as a sudden pain tore through my knee. I reached down and my fingers came away wet. My hands made out a block of metal, the surface pitted and rough. I reached out a hand to the tire wall but five steps further I tripped over something and fell. This side of the wall hid what must be Dale's junkyard. I rested for a minute and got to my feet. The faint murmur of voices and an occasional laugh punctured the stillness.

I backtracked up the hill and continued heading right until I could once again see lights. The road must be just to my left. I headed that way.

I heard voices and stopped, hopelessly tangled in a patch of dense brush filling the ditch. The road was just ahead. I struggled to move. Suddenly, the air exploded with noise.

Someone shouted. A door banged open. I heard frenzied barking.

The snarling grew louder, and twigs snapped as the dogs pushed through the dense underbrush. Their barking grew furious, louder, obscuring the sound of men's voices yelling. I pushed against the brush with all my strength and crashed forward, falling.

The dogs arrived, two dark beasts, snarling, teeth bared. I covered my head with my arms and tucked my knees up to my chest.

Game over.

CHAPTER FIFTY-THREE

Sobs rose up my throat and my body shook, but I no longer cared. I scrunched my shoulders up to my ears and waited for the pain. The men's voices got louder. The dogs alternately snarled and whined.

"Pepsi. Cola. What have you got there?"

"There's somebody there," said a second voice.

"Pepsi. Come. Cola, come here, girl. Hey. Who's there? Are you all right?"

I sensed the dogs had moved back. *Am I all right?* I lifted my head. Beams of light danced in front of me, two dark figures stood several feet away.

"It's a girl," said a voice.

I sat up, my arm shielding my eyes from the light. I heard twigs snapping as they pushed forward.

"It's okay, we've got you. Are you hurt?"

Was I hurt?

"I don't know," I whispered. I tried to stand and fell back. Arms reached out and pulled me up. I put one foot in front of the other as they pulled me forward. We were now in the trampled-down spot they had been in earlier. The dogs' noses poked at my legs, my crotch.

"Pepsi. Cola. Back off."

The shorter one stepped next to me, lifted my arm up around his neck and with his other arm around me, lifted and dragged me forward. The taller of the two led the way, the dogs at his heels. As soon as we were out of the thicket, the light from the single light pole in the middle of the gravelled parking lot confirmed we were at Merle's. The man next to me, Dale.

"You're okay. Here, let's get you inside," he said.

The taller of the two men turned. I dug my feet into the gravel and pulled back, fighting off his arm and sinking to the ground.

"Hey, it's okay. Joey, give me a hand."

"No. Let me go," I croaked, kicking out with one swaddled foot.

"Hey, hey, it's okay. No one's going to hurt you. Hey, I know you," said Dale. "You're that detective who came lookin' for Joey the other day."

I stopped struggling. Maybe he and Joey weren't working together. Maybe Dale could help me. *No. Dale lied. He said he didn't know Joey.*

They half carried, half dragged me across the parking lot and into the store. Joey yanked a wooden chair from behind the counter and Dale lowered me into it. I shook uncontrollably. Something heavy landed on my lap, and I looked down. Dale tucked the ends of a grey army blanket around my legs. He called over his shoulder. "Joey, ring the camp for a medivac." He turned back to me.

"How'd you get here? What happened to your shoes?"

When I didn't answer he continued.

"Smart, wrappin' your feet like that." He pulled at one of my hands, and I flinched back. "Okay, okay. I'm not going to hurt you. Just checkin' for frostbite."

Joey walked over. "The medics from the Wolverine camp are on their way. Should be here in ten or fifteen minutes."

I bit my bottom lip, trying desperately to stop my teeth from chattering. Medics were good. Cops would be better. I realized I couldn't move my legs under the blanket. I couldn't feel my feet at all. I tried wiggling my toes but felt nothing. My hands were clutched in a death grip against my chest. They were a mess. I loosened my grip ever so slightly, and a pain shot through my shoulder and neck. Dale held out a bottle of water, but I was too exhausted to take it.

My eyes darted to the door as it swung open and a man and a woman in uniform stepped inside. Not cops, medics. I hadn't heard them drive up. Arms lifted me onto a narrow cot. The room rolled over and over, and I closed my eyes.

*

A woman's voice sang out, "Good morning. Are you awake?"

I tried to open my eyes and after a minute of struggle the right one opened. The left one was stuck again.

"There you are. You are awake. It's about time. It's already four in the afternoon."

I licked my dry and cracked lips and tried out my voice. All that came out was a huffing noise.

A friendly face, several large sunspots under calm brown

eyes, gazed down at me. "You're at the Sparwood HHCC, the hospital health care centre. Do you know your name?"

She might have just as well slapped me. Of course, I knew my name. Then I realized they might not know who I was. I said my name, but it came out as two low growls.

The woman cranked up the head of the bed and held a straw to my lips. *Why was drinking from a straw so bloody difficult?* I could see out the window now. It was cloudy outside. My hand hurt and I raised it slightly. It was wrapped in gauze, an IV line sticking out through the bandages. I tried again. "Jorja Knight." The woman leaned over me. I could smell her hairspray. "Jorja. Knight," I repeated more audibly.

*

I woke several times during the night, each time trying to assess the shape I was in. I could wiggle my toes, but they hurt like hell. Both hands were wrapped in gauze but the fingers on my left hand were sticking out. My teeth were all intact. I was still having trouble opening my left eye. After a long while I pried it open, the searing pain felt as if the lid had been ripped off my eyeball.

The next time I woke light was streaming in through the window. I was stiff and sore and tired of lying on my back. I struggled into a sitting position and tried to prop myself up with the pillow. I wanted out of here. What the hell happened?

I recall arriving at the café to meet Tony. My passenger airbag had deployed. I didn't see anyone when I got out of the car, but someone must have knocked me out. Next thing I knew I was locked in the shed behind Merle's. It's a four-hour drive to Sparwood. Maybe I was drugged, which might explain the nausea and the hazy feeling. Or maybe I had a concussion.

Something didn't make sense. I had gone to warn Tony about Joey. Joey must have abducted me. He must have been planning to kill me or leave me to freeze to death in the woods. But how did he know I'd be at the café? Tony had called me to set up the meeting only a few hours earlier. I suppose he could have followed me there, or Tony. But why did he seem unperturbed when he and Dale found me? Or was it a part of the act?

I couldn't assume Dale had nothing to do with my having been locked up in a shed behind his store. Dale had lied to me. He denied knowing anyone named Joey Albero or Henry Albern when I asked weeks ago. I laid my head back down and slept.

CHAPTER FIFTY-FOUR

A NURSE RUSHED in, not the friendly one from the day before. A thin, no-nonsense older woman. No doubt brought out of retirement to deal with beat-up women wearing smelly clothes and sporting a poor attitude.

"There's someone here to see you." She cranked up the head of the bed and handed me a water glass with its little bent straw. This time I had no trouble taking a drink. I set the glass down on the table next to the bed and turned as two police officers came through the door.

"Morning, ma'am. I'm Sergeant Starling and this is Constable Miller." She nodded behind her at the other woman. Both wore the RCMP logo on their hat and uniform. "Hope you're feeling better today. Are you're up to answering some questions?"

"I am, if you stop referring to me as ma'am," I answered peevishly.

The police officers were part of the Elk Valley Regional RCMP detachment. I answered their questions as best I could, anxious to ask questions of my own. I didn't go into any of my theories or any of the details around Stephen Wallis' murder. I did tell them that I was investigating his death, that I had been knocked unconscious at the Air Espresso Café, where I'd gone to meet Stephen's friend, Tony D'Silva. I suggested they might want to check to make sure Tony was all right.

They asked if I had any idea who might have abducted me. I was about to give them Joey's name, but held back, knowing if I did it would force me into blithering unsupported accusations and fanciful theories about Stephen Wallis' death and Ajeet Jayaraman's disappearance.

I didn't have a whole lot to tell them other than seeing the end of an older-model, dark-brown car parked behind the café. They ran through the usual questions. Had I been raped? Did I recall any details of the attack, my attacker, being transported to where I was found? What had I been driving? What was taken? Where did I live? I gave them details about myself, my contact information, Gab's name, and contact information as my emergency contact. After what seemed like hours, they left. They asked me to let them know when I was leaving Sparwood and heading back to Calgary. I hoped it would be this afternoon.

A young girl arrived, set a tray of food down on the side table and swung it in front of me.

"You must be hungry," she said. "You slept through dinner last night and breakfast this morning."

I was famished. The aroma of vegetable soup barely reached my nostrils before the soup was gone. I downed the carefully poured four ounces of orange juice, wolfed down a small plastic container of some mixture of pasta and vegetables and slurped up a small cup of green Jello. I had barely finished when a middle-aged man arrived. His neatly trimmed beard balanced his turban and together with the white jacket and stethoscope gave him a dignified appearance. Dr. Sharma ran through my list of injuries, which were remarkably small and relatively insignificant considering I felt like I'd been run over by a D7.

My left eye was bruised and swollen, a cut above it had been closed with three stitches, the eye itself appeared undamaged, but several blood vessels in the eye were broken. I had a cracked collar bone and two cracked ribs. Three toes on my left foot were frostbitten, but he didn't think I'd lose them. Which was great, because I was dying to wear the new kick-ass open-toed boots I had just bought. I was dehydrated when I arrived and suffering from hypothermia, both of which contributed to my dizziness and general confusion.

"When can I go," I asked when he finished.

"Possibly tomorrow. I will come see you in the morning. If everything is okay then you're free," he said, showing me his perfectly even white teeth.

By mid afternoon, I was planning my breakout. Why hadn't Gab shown up yet? How was I going to get home? Should I call Azagora? How could I call anyone? I had no phone, no ID, no clothes, no car. I got out of bed and shuffled unsteadily to the washroom, my feet still bandaged, my toes weirdly purple.

I peered into the small mirror and gasped. Okay, worse than I expected. Now I could see why I had trouble opening my left eye. The eyelid was purplish in colour and swollen shut. The colour continued down and around under my eye to mid-cheek. The stitches paled by comparison. I might have to lie low for a few days when I got home, if only not to scare the neighbourhood children.

I was back in bed when the friendly nurse from yesterday breezed in.

"I see you're doing much better today," she announced. "Which is good, because I've brought you a visitor," she said as she plumped up the pillows and re-stuffed them behind my back. "Now, don't wear her out," she said as a man entered the room.

Not Gab, not Azagora, not Mike. Not even an RCMP officer. Dale walked in, taking off his navy-blue ball cap. I fought back the urge to cry.

"Hello, young lady. Just came by to see how you're doin'. That's one hell of a shiner," he said nodding his head in my direction.

"Hi, Dale. I just caught a glimpse of it myself. Awe-inspiring, isn't it? In case you've forgotten, my name's Jorja. Jorja Knight."

"That's right," he said, slapping himself on the forehead. "My mind's like a sieve these days."

"I can't thank you enough," I said, trying to control the tremble in my voice, "for helping me the other night."

"Seems to me you mostly helped yourself," he said.

I asked him if the shed I found myself in was his.

Dale told me he had subdivided his quarter section years earlier but kept a twenty-acre parcel for himself around the main buildings. The back of the property contained a shed and an old cabin not too far off the road. He confirmed the shed I had been locked in was on his property. There was a small trail behind the shed down to the cabin, opposite from the direction I had taken. The shed was originally used to store fertilizer and seed but hadn't been used in years.

The RCMP had been out to look at it. Someone had recently been up there with a ski-doo, which might explain how my assailant had managed to get me up there. Dale said he and Joey had been away attending an equipment auction in Fernie and returned the day I broke free. I flinched at the mention of Joey.

"Joey's a good guy, you know. You don't have to be 'fraid of him."

"Why did you lie to me when I was up here a few weeks ago?"

Dale looked sheepish. "Joey made me promise I wouldn't tell people his whereabouts, 'specially people not from around here."

"What's he hiding from?"

"He's not hidin', darlin'. He's living life the way he wants to, the way the good lord intended him to. He's happy out here. He has a simple life, no stress, no worries. No one's hounding him for anything or expecting him to meet some trumped-up deadline."

"But what about his family? Why is he avoiding them?"

"You got family?"

I nodded, tears now blurring my good eye. "A brother," I whispered.

"Do you see him often?"

"I haven't seen him in more than ten years," I choked out.

"I can see you still love him, don't you? Not seeing a person doesn't change how you feel about them."

Swiping at the tears became pointless, my left eye stung like the dickens. "Sorry," I said, wiping the tears away with the corner of the bed sheet.

"Aw, I didn't mean to bring up old memories."

Dale stood silently, twirling his ball cap in his hands.

"Joey came down here with me. We could both see how scared you were of him. He wants to talk to you, if you'll let him. He wants to tell you something about his friend. The one who got himself killed a few months back."

I examined Dale's face and considered the offer. I had a gazillion questions for Joey Albero. But I had already fallen once for the *I have something to tell you* line and look where that got me. My heart raced.

Joey had been buying drone parts. Joey was smart, crafty. Maybe he was mentally unstable, showing Dale the nice Joey, showing Tony and Stephen the grim avenger. Or maybe I had the whole thing wrong. I caught the sound of laughter outside in the hallway and glanced over at the help button, the friendly nurse had taped to the side rail of my bed. I squared my shoulders.

"Okay. Tell him yes."

CHAPTER FIFTY-FIVE

JOEY ALBERO ARRIVED a few minutes later.

"I'll skedaddle, let you two talk," Dale announced.

I tried to send Dale a message with my eyes to stay. I stared at his back as he walked out of the room, willing him to turn around. I wanted to call out his name, but it would just make me appear weak and pathetic.

"Hi. I'm Joey Albero although people know me as Henry Albern. How are you feeling?"

I turned my head toward his voice. My good eye took in a lean face, muddy brown eyes. He waited in the doorway, a brown parka looped over his arm.

"I hear you've been looking for me."

It took me a second to find my voice. "The guy I'm looking for has long hair and a beard."

"That would be my going-to-town getup."

I must have looked puzzled.

"Fake," he added, shifting nervously. "Sorry about what happened to you."

"Dale said you have something to say to me."

He cleared his throat. "I swear I don't know how you got into the shed on the back of Dale's property. I've told the police everything I know. I'd like you to know as well."

A nurse walked by the door and voices filtered into the room from the corridor. I pulled in a deep breath and winced as the pain shot through my chest and shoulder. I nodded to the chair set next to the wall. Joey nodded in return, threw his coat over the chair arm, pulled the chair forward a foot and sat.

"I hear you're looking into Stephen's death." His gaze steadily met mine. "Tony D'Silva killed Stephen."

It wasn't the opening I expected. "Tony? Really?" *So, this is how it was going to go.* "What makes you think that?" I wiggled myself up higher on the pillow and studied his face. He squirmed under my gaze and looked away.

"It's complicated. I never imagined it turning out like this. I hardly know where to start."

"Why don't you start by telling me about Ajeet."

"Ajeet? Joey sat back and shook his head. That's a name I haven't heard in a long time. Why do you want to know about Ajeet?"

"I think I deserve some answers, don't you? Ajeet is one of the reasons I've been trying to find you. Tell me about Ajeet. Tell me about the last time you saw him."

Joey's face sagged and he swallowed. He cleared his throat and stared at the far wall. He shook his head and shrugged. "No more lies. I should have said something years ago. The last time I saw Ajeet was at a party, a little over twenty years ago."

"Tell me what happened that night."

"There was this party at Pearce Estate Park. We were so young and stupid. Everybody was drinking, well except Ajeet. He didn't drink alcohol. People were daring each other to do stupid things. Stupider things. Things got out of control. Somebody challenged Ajeet to see how much water he could drink. Everybody was egging him on, laying bets."

"Somebody challenged him?"

"I don't recall who, but we all went along with it. Ajeet too." He shook his head.

"Go on."

"Ajeet was slurring his words and staggering. I got mad at Tony. I was sure Tony spiked his water."

"Why Tony?"

"He was always doing stuff like that. Tony is a fire-ready-aim kind of guy."

I had already come to that conclusion myself. What he was telling me meshed with what Kielbasa King Greg had told me.

"Sounds like water poisoning."

Joey nodded. "It wasn't until years later that I found out you can actually die from drinking too much water. Then, the way Ajeet was acting that night made sense."

"What happened next?"

"It was around three in the morning. The party was breaking up. Ajeet was in a bad way. Most people were drunk, not really paying attention or passed out. I found Stephen. He'd been drinking too, but not as much as some. I begged him to drive Ajeet to the hospital. He finally agreed to drive Ajeet home."

"Why didn't he take him to the hospital?"

"I don't know. He didn't say. Or maybe he did. I was relieved that Ajeet wouldn't be left there."

"How did Ajeet get to the party?"

"I don't know. He didn't have a car. Probably the bus."

"Stephen left with Ajeet. By himself?"

"Tony was passed out cold in the back seat. I helped Stephen get Ajeet into the front. Ajeet was crying. Said he couldn't go home."

Joey ran his hands over his face. He met my gaze and shook his head. "I should have done something. I can't get the look on his face as they drove off out of my mind."

"What could you have done?"

"I don't know. Drag Tony out of the back seat and go with them? Call an ambulance."

I waited. I knew there was something else he still wasn't telling me.

"I went to his place the next day, but his mother said he wasn't there. She was angry. She had told him that if he went to the party, he wasn't to come back. I thought I'd eventually hear from him, or from somebody, as to where he'd gone, but I didn't."

"There's something else, isn't there?"

Joey wiped a hand down his face and turned his head away. After a minute, he nodded his head.

"I loved Ajeet. Really loved him. And he loved me." The pain in his eyes told me it was still raw. "It was a horrible time in my life. I knew I was gay, but I really didn't know how to deal with it. It wasn't like today. Some people had the guts to come out, but I kept it hidden for a long time."

"Ajeet was gay."

"Yes, but no one knew. Not about him, not about me. Not until that night. Tony saw Ajeet and I kissing. He went totally ape shit, laughing and mocking us. Ran around telling everyone, called us fags. I knew at that moment that my life had just changed forever."

"What about Stephen?"

"I don't know. People were laughing. Everyone was drunk. It was a lifetime ago." Joey leaned over, shielding his eyes from me with his hand.

"Is that why you quit university?"

"That's part of it. That and I needed to figure out who I was. I was pretty messed up. I also lost my best friend, the one person who knew me. Life at the house became awkward. Tony pretty much avoided me."

"What did Stephen and Tony say about that night? What happened to Ajeet?"

"Stephen said he drove Ajeet back to his place. The last time he saw him, he was going up the walk to his parents' house. Tony backed him up."

"You believed them?"

"I didn't at first, but they both insisted it was true."

"And now?"

"I don't know what to believe, but I know they lied."

My head swam. I wasn't sure what I was hearing.

"Lied about what?"

"About four or five years ago I ran into Tony. Just a chance meeting. We got to talking. He apologized, said he felt awful about how he had treated me. Blamed it on the ignorance of youth."

"You believe he was sincere?"

"I did then, but I don't now." His brow furrowed, he crossed his arms, stiffening.

I waited. I didn't know what to think.

"I ran into Tony a couple of times after that. We didn't become best friends, but we would occasionally go for a drink, get something to eat. One night, he told me the guilt was eating him alive. He wanted to make it right between us. Felt he owed it to me."

I held my breath. Was I ready to hear this?

"Tony told me his memory of the night Ajeet went missing was fuzzy, weird bits jumbled together. He said he woke up at one point during the trip to Ajeet's place. He was in the backseat of the car, confused as to what was going on. Ajeet was shaking violently and then lost consciousness. Stephen yelled that Ajeet wasn't breathing. Tony figures he passed out again. Next thing he remembers is Stephen climbing out of this big hole. Alone."

The room went silent. I became aware of a clock on the wall across from me. The second hand ticked loudly as I stared at Joey, barely breathing.

"There was a house down the street from Ajeet's that was still under construction. Tony thinks Stephen buried him there."

"Stephen?"

Joey looked up; his eyes anguished. "We were so young, so eager to start our lives, so ignorant about what really matters. Tony cried when he told me. He and Stephen made a pact not to tell anyone. There was nothing they could do, Ajeet died before they could get him home. I was mad when I heard, but I'd never seen Tony that upset."

"So, you kept quiet."

"I should have said something then. Tony said even though they were scared, it was wrong to stay quiet. None of us knew that drinking too much water could kill a person. Tony begged me not to say anything. Stephen was dealing with his own guilt by supporting a lot of charities. No one could bring Ajeet back. He said he was sorry he didn't tell me sooner. Or Ajeet's parents. He begged for my forgiveness, begged me not to say anything. It would only ruin more lives."

I eyed Joey. His head rested on his chest.

No more lies. I scanned the room, wishing I had some way to record what was coming next. Joey killed Stephen, revenge for killing his first love. I was about to hear his confession.

"You agreed?"

"At first I was angry. I went back to BC, where I was working with a group of activists, to save the old-growth forests. But it all felt so pointless. Ajeet was gone, had been for years. I didn't want to ruin more lives by telling anyone what Tony told me. Besides, they could both deny it. I had no proof. Everybody's in a race for themselves at the expense of everything and everyone around them. It's going to be what brings an end to the human species." He shook his head.

"So how did you end up here?"

"I left the activists, hitched around for a year or so, and eventually ended up in Sparwood. I was out of money, out of food, and depressed. Honestly," his eyes met mine. "I seriously considered killing myself. Then I met Dale. He would occasionally need a hand with something. I was good with engines, electronics, anything electrical. It felt like maybe I could live a while longer."

"Why did you change your name?"

"After I left the activists some of them pressured me to come back. Said I was a traitor, that I had rolled over for the man." Joey shook his head. "It was high-school all over again. I realized I'd been trying to fit in with them, but I really didn't belong with them."

I got it. I had tried to fit in at Global Analytix, but I'd never be invited to the corporate ball.

"So, once I got to Sparwood I changed my name. Dale let me stay in the old cabin at the back of his property in return for helping him."

"You stay in touch with Tony all this time?" I watched his face. *No lies.*

"I'd occasionally take one of Dale's old beaters into Calgary. Every once in a while, Tony would throw me some work. It was nice to have some extra money occasionally, although I can live pretty cheaply. And truthfully, I liked it. Tony would give me some problem to solve, some little glitch in something they were working on. It kept my mind busy, and I could work on most of it out here."

I sensed a big 'but' coming. The sins of the past were about to collide with the sins of the present. I waited, barely daring to breathe.

"But I just couldn't let it go. The more I saw Tony, the angrier I got. Then a few months ago I realized I was working for the devil."

CHAPTER FIFTY-SIX

I watched the second hand jerk its way around the clock face. Joey had just told me Stephen was guilty of disposing of Ajeet's body and Tony had known about it. He had just referred to Tony as the devil and had accused him of killing Stephen. I held my breath, my eyes fixated on Joey who seemed oblivious to my growing fear and unease.

"I ran into Stephen five or six months ago. I'd seen him around a few times before when I came into Calgary. Tony told me Stephen had changed. He was swimming with the sharks now. I got to see it for myself. I was walking down the street minding my business when this guy jumps out of a car and starts yakking about how great it is to see me and all that. I didn't even recognize him at first. He was in a tux, all groomed and slicked down. Then I realize he's got his wallet out and is trying to hand me money. Like I'm some bum or something. All I could think of was Ajeet lying in the cold ground and here was this holier-than-thou hot shot showing me what? Pity? Handing me hush money? I came close to decking him that day."

I realized this is who Stella had seen, the derelict she thought was going to knife Stephen.

"I mentioned it to Tony the next time I saw him, and he just laughed. Said that I had seen the new Stephen, the one who alleviated pangs of guilt or his own delusions of social consciousness by throwing money at the issue."

I was confused. Hadn't he just referred to Tony as the devil? "Was that the last time you saw Stephen?" I asked cautiously.

"Yes."

"But something changed between you and Tony, didn't it?"

"Yes." Joey leaned forward and rubbed his face with both hands. He lifted his head, his face grim. "Last October, Tony said he had a special project for me. He asked me to build him a small drone. It had to have a mechanical arm that could be controlled remotely and be able to lift 3 kilograms. The postal and parcel delivery companies are already using drones to deliver small packages. It's not exactly rocket science."

"Did he say why?" I could hardly get my question out.

"He was planning to use it to deliver his girlfriend's Christmas present to her on Christmas morning."

"Sweet." I had to play along, but my fingertips were pulsating with each heartbeat.

"But that wasn't its real purpose."

"What do you mean?" I held my breath. I knew what was coming next.

"I delivered the drone to him mid December. Then Stephen was killed. I didn't connect the two at first. When

I heard a private eye was looking for me, and asking about Ajeet, it got me thinking. No one had brought up Ajeet's name in years, now some PI looking into Stephen's death was asking about him?" He shook his head.

I knew how I got there. I thought Joey killed Stephen to avenge Ajeet's death. I waited, hoping my face didn't give me away. Everything he just told me pointed to the same conclusion.

"I rehashed everything in my mind. I had bought in to what Tony told me about the night Ajeet died. But some of it didn't make sense. Stephen was nice to me. I didn't sense even a shred of guilt or regret. The Stephen I knew, even back then, was always helping somebody out. Raising money for drought-stricken Ethiopia, that sort of thing. Tony was, well, Tony. He was always number one, and he'd steamroll over anyone who got in his way."

Joey shifted in his chair, his eyes turned away from mine, his lips tight, his jaw set. He laughed nervously and shook his head, staring at the floor.

"I should have learned by now." He took a deep breath then turned back to me, but his eyes refused to meet mine. "Remember the thing I said, about how Tony had me working on ironing out some glitches, in the stuff they were building?"

I nodded. "Yeah?"

"There's this annual competition. The entering teams have seventy-two hours to invent something new, innovative. At the close of the conference a winner is selected. The winner gets twenty thousand dollars from the sponsor, StarTu. The rest of the teams get a lesser amount. It's exciting. You can watch the teams from an observation gallery. The teams are secluded in rooms below, with no contact to the outside world. Tony got me tickets to the conference the last two years running. I looked up what the winners of that competition are doing now."

I had no idea where he was going with this, but my mind raced ahead of what I was hearing. I tried to quell the anticipated options swirling around my brain and told myself to just listen.

"There were lots of cool ideas that came out of those competitions. When I researched the list of entrants and what they produced, I realized some of the puzzling bits Tony gave me to work on, could actually be components of the runner-up's ideas."

"Whoa. You're telling me he was stealing ideas from these contests?"

"Yes. It happens. Ideas are free, whoever acts on them first wins. Except most people wouldn't just blatantly rip off someone else's idea."

"Are any of those contestants working for Tony?"

"No. But a runner-up from a few years earlier was working for Stephen. They already filed for a patent for their idea, a regenerative fuel cell that provides a better way to use hydrogen as fuel."

"The Nano-skin fuel cell." I sat up straighter. "Tony invested in that idea—as did Stephen."

"I don't know about that, but I do know that Tony's company was building pretty much the same thing. He was having trouble though. He asked me to examine the work they had done on designing the membrane that allows hydrogen ions to pass through the cell but not other atoms or ions such as oxygen. These days everyone is messing around using nano-technology to create more efficient membranes which can decrease the weight and yet increase the life of a fuel cell."

"So, he and Stephen were in a race of sorts," I said.

"Looks like it. Tony was having trouble ironing out the kinks in his product when Stephen's entrepreneur filed for a patent for their Nano-skin fuel cell."

"But Tony invested in that innovation."

"Maybe he was hedging his bets, or maybe he realized he was beat."

"Then Stephen is murdered, and Tony inherits Stephen's sixty percent as well," I said.

"Convenient, isn't it?"

I looked long and hard at Joey. This guy was a chameleon, a conspiracy theorist, world fatalist, self-declared hermit, possibly struggling with mental illness. It was quite the story. His face was flushed, he seemed twitchy now.

"Let me guess." Joey's eyes met mine. "You believe I killed Stephen because of Ajeet and I'm trying to throw Tony under the bus." Joey delivered this statement calmly.

The thought had just raced through my mind. "What do you have besides pure conjecture?"

"Honestly? I don't know what happened to Ajeet. I only heard Tony's side of the story and Stephen's not around to contradict it. I do know Tony had me work on something that was damn close to the same thing being built by one of Stephen's entrepreneurs and that Stephen was murdered and now Tony owns a bigger chunk of it. More importantly, I know where the murder weapon is that killed Stephen."

"The murder weapon?"

"Yes, the drone."

I heard laughter in the corridor and glanced around the room. Was this some sort of weird dream? I pinched myself under the covers. Was he telling me he unwittingly built Tony's murder weapon? If so, why did he have it or know where it was? If he didn't kill Stephen, how did he know that the drone was used to kill Stephen and where it was hidden now?

"So how is this drone supposed to have killed Stephen?"

"You know the arm I mentioned? In addition to the arms needed to hold a package, Tony wanted an additional articulated arm. Once I realized how he must have killed Stephen, I built a replica and tried it out. The four arms can easily hold a small pistol in a horizontal position, the fifth arm controls the trigger. The camera shows what the drone sees and the whole works is controlled remotely with a modified game controller."

If what he just told me could be accomplished, I feared for the world. "Why haven't you gone to the police with this?"

"I have a small problem."

No shit. "And what would that be?"

"Proving that Tony was behind the drone controls and not me."

"Yeah. I can see how that would be a problem. So where is this drone now?"

"I'd rather not say right now. What I need is some way to prove Tony did this. That Tony killed Stephen, for the Nano-skin fuel cell."

"Right." I nodded. Except I was still holding on to the idea that Joey killed Stephen to avenge Ajeet and was laying blame at Tony's feet. "How are you going to do that?"

Joey stared at his hands, now clasped in front of him. He looked up. "I haven't figured that part out yet."

CHAPTER FIFTY-SEVEN

GAB HAD ARRIVED shortly before they released me last night. I hurt all over, so when Gab suggested we overnight it, I didn't argue. We had ordered in pizza and afterwards spent a few hours contacting various credit card companies to tell them my wallet had been stolen, my cards missing. This morning I was anxious to see Sparwood in the rear-view mirror.

After Joey left, I had churned through bits of information, and fragments of conversations, which left me feeling like I'd been riding a roller coaster for days. I now had two stories; one from Rob telling me Tony and Stephen had gotten threatening phone calls from Joey and one from Joey making Tony out to be the bad guy.

There was remarkable consistency in the stories I'd heard from Rob, Greg, and Joey about Ajeet's disappearance some twenty years ago. What bothered me most was Joey telling me that Tony had cried when he told him his version of what happened that night, but Tony told me he had little or no recall of the night. One of them was lying.

First thing this morning I contacted Sergeant Starling to let her know I'd be leaving town later in the day. The RCMP were working with the Calgary Police and checking various street cameras, both in Calgary near Air Espresso and Sparwood, the day I was abducted. Sergeant Starling told me they picked up some video of a brown refurbished Grand Torino leaving the industrial park and entering Sparwood later that same day. Unfortunately, the plates were stolen from a vehicle parked in long-term parking at the Calgary airport.

I wandered down to Dixie's where I planned to meet Dale and Joey. It was a cozy little place, lots of wood and curtains at the window. Gab was checking us out of the motel and would meet me here after she filled the car with gas.

I chose a table in the far corner, trying to ignore the glances being sent my way. I briefly considered pointing at my face and announcing, *I was abducted, beat up and left to die in a shack just north of here, but thank you, I'm fine.* Instead, I murmured *car accident* when the waitress came by with coffee, gasped and lifted a hand to cover her mouth.

I still didn't know who or what to believe as each side had a story that fit with what I knew, at least logically. I could see why Joey would be angry to discover Stephen left money to him in a trust. Convinced that Tony used him to unknowingly build the murder weapon, he had been horrified and repulsed by the idea that he would somehow benefit from Stephen's death.

I recalled how Tony reacted when I brought up the idea that Ajeet's disappearance may have led to Joey's current

lifestyle and strange behaviour. Tony had taken every opportunity to paint Joey as a strange and disturbed man. I had
found him to be shockingly normal.

Then there was the story Rob told me about Joey threatening Tony, and possibly Stephen too. I didn't doubt that
Tony had told Rob about the threatening calls, but I questioned why Tony only revealed the information this late in
the game. Of course, it made sense if Tony received threats
himself, only days earlier. Maybe he hadn't said anything
about Joey threatening Stephen earlier, because it led to the
whole question of Ajeet's disappearance and his own role
that night.

Detective McGuire's team should be able to at least partially confirm what Tony told Rob by examining Stephen's
phone records from around the time he supposedly received
the threatening calls. Even if the calls came from an unknown
caller ID, they might be able to pinpoint the location of the
caller, but that in of itself would prove nothing. It did, however, raise a ton of questions.

The waitress returned and asked me if I wanted to order.
I silently thanked the universe for Gab. Without her in my
life, I'd be in the same situation Joey had been in when he
arrived in Sparwood a few years earlier—tired, emotionally
depleted, and out of money. I ordered coffee and told her I
was waiting for friends to arrive.

I looked up as the front door opened and a gust of cool
air blew in.

"Hi, darlin'," said Dale sliding into the chair next to me.
"You're lookin' more chipper, ain't she, Joey?" Joey sat opposite us and nodded, giving me a faint smile.

"Thanks for saying so but I feel like I just came off a three-day bender and am still wearing my Halloween costume."

Dale cackled. "Naw. You're goin' to be just fine."

The waitress poured more coffees and I got down to the issue at hand. Joey had told me he knew where the murder weapon was hidden, or at least a part of it. Depending on what homicide had found at the crime scene, they might be able to prove that it was indeed the murder weapon. Joey figured they'd likely find striations on the gun or the drone arms that could prove a gun had been attached. Depending on how close the drone had been to Stephen when it fired, there might even be specks of blood spatter. Joey postulated that if Tony were setting him up, he wouldn't have bothered cleaning any blood off the drone.

Joey had purchased the drone components from Stumpy's but had no idea where the gun was or whose gun was used. He was worried that Tony would come up with a way to link him to it too. Clever of him to say so. Of course, as Joey said, none of this proved who was behind the controls.

I was still grappling with the idea that Joey was artfully reeling me in by casting suspicion off him and onto Tony. At one point during the night, I even considered the idea that Tony and Joey were in this together.

"Joey, can anyone vouch for where you were when Stephen was killed? That would be between December 31 and New Year's Day?"

"I can," said Dale. "We had a bonfire, roasted smokies and had us a few beers on New Year's Eve."

Joey stared at his coffee cup, which he rotated in front of him.

"When did you say you last saw Tony?" I asked.

"About three weeks ago. I went to his office and accused him of killing Stephen. I told him I had figured out how he did it. Stupid, I know." Joey kept staring at his coffee cup.

That would explain the photo Bernie had taken of him in front of Tony's building. "Anyone see you?"

"Yeah." He grimaced. "Tony called security."

More evidence that Tony had been threatened by Joey. He wasn't exactly helping himself. "Did you call Tony? Even if it were to hang up before or when he answered?"

"Nope, I did not."

"Do you or have you ever owned a gun?"

"Nope."

"Do you own a car?"

"Dale lets me use an old car of his, whenever I need to."

"How does that work? Do you go down to Dale's place and ask to borrow it?"

Joey sighed, shaking his head. "I used to at first. Then Dale said I could keep it at the cabin if I paid for the gas and kept it running."

"Used to? But not now."

They exchanged glances. "I've moved in with Dale now."

I nodded. I could tell by the ensuing silence and the glances between them that we could all see this wasn't stacking up in Joey's favour.

"Did you ever visit Stephen at his place?"

"No."

"You've never been to his place?"

"Not while he was alive. Once I got the idea that the

drone had been used to kill Stephen, I went by his house a few times."

I asked him to tell me the dates and times. I'd have to check but they seemed to coincide with the time the realtor had seen someone watching Stephen's house. The police might even be able to confirm the dates by the date of Bernie's photos, assuming they ever located his cell phone or digital camera.

"How do you figure this all went down?"

"The news clippings my sister left for me at the hunter's cabin said the police found no indication that anyone entered the house. The security cameras didn't capture anyone either. I figured a drone flying up above wouldn't be caught by the security cameras, which would be angled to capture someone's entry through the usual means.

"I read the house was high tech. When I saw the house for myself, I thought why have this super-wired house and put in standard old-fashioned windows? I checked the windows and sky lights and noticed they weren't set into a box frame like most of the older models. When I got back here, I researched the latest innovation in windows. I found a good match. The ones in Stephen's house have a different opening mechanism, not the hinged type one would expect. This skylight slides open rather than lifts open the standard five or six inches."

"I've been to Stephen's house. Pretty hard to see anything up that high."

He grinned sheepishly. "Remember that replica drone I built? I flew it in for a closer look."

"Are you telling me Tony somehow overrode the wireless

controls and opened the window? Surely he wouldn't have spent days hanging around Stephen's place waiting for Stephen to open it."

"No, that's the beauty of it. The window opens and closes automatically when it senses a certain level of moisture in the room. Not sure where the skylights are relative to the bathroom, but if they're nearby then a shower might activate the system."

"Have you mentioned this to anyone?"

"No, you're the first."

"You say you know where the drone is, the one used to kill Stephen. That it's been placed somewhere it would point to you. When did you come across it?"

"Last week."

"What did you do?"

"You mean besides panic? It didn't take me long to convince myself that Tony was going to try and hang this on me. I figured someone must be getting close to linking Stephen's death to Tony."

"Why did you lie to your sister? Why not tell her where you are living? What's with the goose chase to the hunter's cabin?"

"I never imagined she'd ever go there. I have used it when I've gone hunting. When I told her about the cabin it seemed to satisfy her need to get a hold of me. She's always going to be my sister, but she's hard to be around. I drop in to see her and her kids a couple of times a year, but she just can't accept who I am, or that I prefer not to hold down a regular job and that I really don't want to contribute to society's pointless, laughable efforts to control things. After all, our destiny has already been written."

"What destiny is that?"

Joey gave me a half-smile. "The end of all humanity."

I sighed. And it had all been going so well.

CHAPTER FIFTY-EIGHT

THEY FOUND THE Rav4 at the Calgary airport, my purse and phone gone. I was now driving a Durango with a distinctly prevalent fish odour and no back seats. I had also contacted Tony D'Silva. He sounded genuinely happy to hear from me, or maybe I misread the gratitude for my safety in his voice. He told me his meeting had run so long he got to Air Espresso late. When he didn't see me or my car, he figured I had given up on him and left. He left me a voice message, apologizing, and asked me to call back to reschedule. He had no idea I was missing and had been flabbergasted when the police contacted him two days after I made my escape in Sparwood.

I told Tony I had been anxious to meet with him that day, as I was worried Joey might have killed Stephen, believing he was avenging Ajeet's death. I told Tony that I had been planning to tell him that his life might also be in danger. Tony's voice quickened as he admitted he had also grown convinced Joey was the Houdini Killer. He said that he'd been worried that Joey might pose a danger to himself and others. I asked him to tell me what information he had been planning to share about Joey and Stephen the day we planned to meet.

He told me the same story he had told Rob Bailey, that Joey had phoned and threatened him, and that Stephen had also received threatening calls, but he hadn't put it together until he got his own call from Joey. I, in turn, asked him if that was the reason he had Conner fly to Sparwood on March 18—to confront Joey.

The pause dragged on so long, I had to bite my lip to keep from filling the silence. When he came back on the line Tony said he didn't know what I was talking about. Then he apologized, saying Sharon had just entered his office and handed him an urgent note. He rang off saying he'd have to call me back.

After the call, I logged into my voice mail and listened to my messages. Tony had left me a message at three-twenty the day I was abducted, just like he said. There was no evidence whatsoever to tie Tony or Stephen to Ajeet's disappearance, let alone any shred of proof that Ajeet was dead.

It wasn't illegal to change one's name and cut off communication with people you knew. Tony telling Joey his version of what happened the night Ajeet disappeared could be his way of manipulating Joey into believing Stephen was a bad guy. It had kept Joey from wanting anything to do with Stephen and armed Tony with evidence that Joey had it in for Stephen. A convenient way to plant the seed in someone's mind that Joey may have, at long last, avenged Ajeet's death.

Too bad there was no evidence Tony commissioned a

drone from Joey, except Joey's word. Then again, why would Joey bring this up if he were the guilty party? I had no evidence a gun-wielding drone had entered the house and been used to shoot Stephen. Neither did Joey. I did have a stack of photos of the side of Stephen's house, the skylight and the windows, but so what. The guy who took the pictures was dead, and he had a ton of similarly unexplainable photos of buildings, stairs, and sidewalks taken at weird angles. What did it all mean? Nothing.

Tony and Joey both had an alibi for the time Stephen was murdered, but in each case a close friend was the alibi. Both denied killing him. Tony and Joey were both clever, adept at spinning stories, theories, weaving in facts, innuendos. I was convinced one or both of them tried to kill me. I needed to catch one of them in a lie, a lie that could be verified.

On the drive back from Sparwood, a theory formed, but I would have to confirm a few things before I shared it with Detective McGuire. I still didn't know where Conner fit in. Or why Chloe had been shot.

I called Laura. Chloe was still in the hospital in a medically induced coma. They hoped to bring her out of it in the next day or two. I decided to pay her boyfriend a visit.

Trace didn't answer when I buzzed the apartment, but the Mini Cooper was sitting at the curb, so I buzzed a few other apartment units until one let me in. Trace answered the door after the third time I knocked. He looked like he had been on a week-long bender, or still was.

"Trace?"

"Yeah?" he grunted.

"My name is Jorja Knight. I'm a private investigator. I talked with Laura Bradford this morning. She told me Chloe, is still in a coma. Would you mind if I asked you some questions?"

He scrunched up his thin pock-marked face and squinted at me but didn't comment on my rather battered appearance. He stepped aside. "Now her sister's concerned?" he croaked. "Where was she before this?"

I realized he assumed Laura had hired me to dig into who shot Chloe, but I didn't correct him. I stepped past him into the small entry. He waved the near-empty mickey of rye in his hand at me to follow. I climbed the stairs behind his baggy stained sweatpants up to the living room.

My first thought was the place had been ransacked. Clothes lay piled everywhere. The coffee table was littered with takeout containers and plastic cups.

"Want something to drink?" he slurred, waving the bottle in my direction, as he pushed some clothes off a worn faux-leather recliner.

"No thanks, I'm good." I lowered myself gingerly onto the edge of the recliner cushion.

Trace walked over to the couch and pulled off the blanket spread out over the cushions. I was certain he had spent the night there. His reality hit me like a ton of bricks. Some part of me wanted to give his thin stooping shoulders a hug.

He sank into the couch, the cushions folding up around him up. I suddenly saw my brother in him, when he was about fifteen. Our dog had just passed away. I say our dog, but it had really been my brother's dog, a black-and-white mutt that might have been part Sheltie. I had been sad about our dog, but my heart bled for my brother. It was the first and only time I saw my older brother cry. I shook myself out of my past.

"Trace, do you have any idea who might have done this to Chloe?"

He shook his head. "No. She's a good person, man. She doesn't have much, but she'd give you whatever you needed…if she had it."

"Was anyone threatening her or harassing her? I heard someone let the air out of your car tires one night and vandalized it."

"We figured it was some asswipe at Vinnie's who didn't like his bar bill."

This didn't jive with the phone call Chloe had made to me. "Maybe it was her ex. Maybe Conner's jealous of your relationship with Chloe."

He laughed and took a pull on the bottle. "I doubt it. Theirs was more of a business arrangement."

"Really? What business?"

"I ain't saying anything bad about Chloe but that Conner dude, he's one mean fuck. Chloe's afraid of him. That's why she went to California after she broke up with him. She wanted to get far, far away from that dude."

"I know the type. He gets his kicks by browbeating and controlling women," I said, hoping to keep him talking. "I bet when Chloe came back to Calgary, he expected to pick up with her right where he left off."

"You know what he wanted?"

I held my breath and shook my head.

"He wanted Chloe to help him get into her brother's place."

"What for?"

"To bug the place."

"Bug the place? You mean spy on him?"

"Yup."

"Spy on her own brother? What a scumbag."

"Got that right."

"Do you know what happened?"

"I promised Chloe I wouldn't tell."

I held my breath, hoping against all hope he'd say something useful.

His head lolled forward on his chest, his arm hung over the arm of the chair, the bottle still gripped in his hand. His head jerked. He rubbed a hand across his eyes and slowly refocused.

"Guess it don't matter now. She's in a real bad way, she might not make it."

"I'm sure the doctors are doing everything they can. You know, she came to see me. She wants her brother's killer found."

Trace set the bottle on the floor and rubbed his face with his hands. "Conner gave Chloe some little microphones to hide at her brother's place. He paid her to go there."

"When was this?"

"Right before I met her. Before Christmas."

"So, she went to see her brother. What happened?"

He grimaced. "They got into an argument. Next thing she knows her brother's dead. She totally freaked out. She figured Conner broke into the place and something went wrong."

"Did she plant the bugs? The microphones."

"No. Whatever happened, scared her real bad, She didn't want to talk about it."

"Why didn't she go to the police? Was she afraid Conner would come after her?"

"He claimed he didn't do it. He was out of town when her brother was killed. He said if she'd done what she was told, he'd still be alive."

"Wait. Let me get this. Chloe did go to see Stephen but didn't plant the bugs. Instead, she got into an argument with Stephen and left. This was before Christmas."

"Yeah."

"Did Chloe believe Conner? That he had nothing to do with Stephen's death."

"She wanted to."

I nodded. Of course, she'd want to believe Conner. Otherwise, she might have to accept that she had a hand in Stephen's death. Conner could be telling the truth. Detective McGuire already confirmed Conner had been out of town when Stephen was killed.

"She lost her bracelet there, didn't she?"

"Yeah. Her sister found it. Threw it in her face. She accused Chloe of killing her own brother."

"Did you tell the cops any of this when Chloe was shot?"

"I promised Chloe. If you say anything, I'll swear you're lying."

"Are you saying you don't believe Conner is the one who shot Chloe?"

"All I know, is I pull up just as this brown car's going by. I didn't hear no shots or nothing, but I see Chloe on the ground. The driver was Asian. That's what I told the cops and that's what I'm telling you."

I stood up. "Thanks, Trace. I'll do what I can to help the police find who did this. I wish I could say something that would make it all okay, but I know I can't. I'm sorry this happened to you and Chloe." I had to leave before I ended up doing something stupid like hug him. "No don't get up, I'll let myself out."

I was already at his front door when footsteps thundered across the floor, then came the awful retching from someone sick to their stomach with worry or too much rye whiskey. I don't know if I was ready to accept Trace's story that Chloe was some sort of innocent victim in this whole thing, browbeaten, threatened and coerced into helping Conner, deadly afraid of what he would do to her if she didn't cooperate. I reached up and touched my neck, recalling Conner's hands around my own throat. Chloe may or may not have voluntarily gone along with Conner's plan, but it didn't change the fact that Conner was a walking ball of coiled testosterone.

Trace saw a brown car, but maybe it was just a car driving by. Perhaps the shot came from elsewhere. Conner had been spying on Stephen or intended to. He intended to listen in on Stephen's conversations. In the end Chloe hadn't planted the microphones. Yet, she seemed to be okay with trying to milk Stephen's family and friends for more money. That didn't jive with my idea of someone who was now feeling remorse.

Maybe Conner arranged to have Stephen killed while he was out of town. After all, he'd have contacts in the hire-to-kill-or-protect business. Had Chloe been threatening to tell the police about her visit to Stephen, about what Conner wanted her to do? Is that why she'd been shot?

Conner had weaseled his way into Stephen's life and cooked up a plan to spy on him. Why and for whom? There was one obvious answer. Proving it was going to be a whole different matter.

CHAPTER FIFTY-NINE

I stopped at the information desk and was told Chloe was in room 42C on the fourth floor. I made my way upstairs, exited the elevator and paused to figure out how the rooms were laid out. Turning down the left corridor, I found Chloe's name on the door, along with a second patient's name. I tiptoed in. Chloe was lying in the bed furthest from the door, her roommate snoring loudly.

"Hi Chloe. Glad to see you out of ICU. How are you doing?"

She glanced up from whatever she was playing with on her cell phone. Her eyes were sunken and dark ringed. A gauze bandage covered the left side of her neck, partially visible under the cervical collar. A nasal cannula and an IV were still in place.

"Holy shit, what happened to you?" she croaked.

I grinned. "I had a little scuffle with the grim reaper. I see you managed to evade him too."

"They took out the feeding tube this morning. I'm able to have clear liquids."

"Do you have any idea what happened, who shot you?"

"I don't remember anything. I came out of the store and next thing I'm in here."

"Well, I'm glad you're on the mend. I see you got your bracelet back."

She nodded lifting her left wrist and studying the bracelet. "Laura came to visit me the other day. She brought it." She watched me warily. "As soon as I get out of here, Trace and I are moving to Vancouver."

"I heard you withdrew your challenge of the will. Did you find a way to settle your differences?" I figured someone must have paid her off, and I was betting it was Tony.

"I just changed my mind."

"Why is that?"

"Isn't it obvious? Someone's pissed off enough to want me dead."

"But you withdrew your request before you got shot."

Chloe's fingers twisted the corner of the sheet. "I'm tired," she wheezed, turning her head.

"Chloe, I know you visited Stephen when you got back from Palm Springs. Your ex confirmed you had your bracelet the whole time you were down there. I also know you went to see Stephen when you got back. That Conner coerced you into going there to plant some listening devices."

Chloe stared straight ahead.

"I don't know what Conner had on you to make you go, but in the end, you didn't do what he asked you to do. That says something Chloe, it says a lot about you."

"I...I shouldn't have gone."

"What happened?"

"I called Conner when I got back. I mean, compared to Ted, Conner was fun. It's not like I didn't want to be with him."

"Why did you break up?"

"He was always trying to get me to get more money from my family. After Stephen and Laura cut me off, Conner said Stephen had money and he'd pay if he had to."

"What did he mean?"

"Like if my nephew or niece were kidnapped."

"Whoa."

"I told him I wanted no part of that. I was scared he'd do it. I told him if anything happened to them, I'd tell the police. We had this big argument and I split. When nothing happened, I figured it was all talk, you know?"

I nodded, but not because I agreed with what she said.

"We met for drinks. He told me he was driving for Stephen and that he knew Stephen was about to make some serious money. That his company had something that was worth millions."

"So that was his new plan." My mind raced ahead. "He knew Stephen was in negotiations, and he figured the details might be worth something to one of the competitors."

"He said we wouldn't be hurting Stephen, that we would be helping him."

"How so?"

"If another company knew what Stephen was being offered, they would offer him more."

"And Conner would of course, make a little on the side. Except you didn't follow through with the plan."

"At first I thought why not. Conner said he was going

to make millions off this deal." Her fingers were completely twisted in the bed sheet. "I hadn't seen Stephen in months, yet he starts in on me right away. He says he doesn't have money and if he did, he still wouldn't be giving me any. I…I guess I lost it. I told him it's not why I came to see him. That I came to warn him…that…he could go to hell." Chloe started crying. "He grabbed…my arm when I was leaving."

"And that's when your bracelet came off."

"Stephen shouldn't have died." Chloe's tears now accompanied by loud, jagged, uncontrolled sobs. "I want my brother back."

A nurse entered the room and said Chloe needed to rest and remain calm. I didn't need further encouragement and left.

CHAPTER SIXTY

I RETURNED HOME from the hospital physically tired and mentally exhausted. Corporate espionage didn't just happen between top international players. People would be amazed to find that even in Calgary, oil companies were occasionally caught listening in with some powerful technology to what was happening in their competitors' offices across the street.

Conner was a lying, thieving Scumbag, but if he had been selling illegally obtained information about Stephen's business dealings, why kill him?

Tony seemed to have a lot more to gain from Stephen's death than Joey although revenge came with its own price tag. I was convinced one of them had killed Stephen, not Conner.

Tony's company was heavily in debt and according to Joey, his latest invention was in trouble. I thought back to what Joey had told me about StarTu and the technology competitions they sponsored. StarTu's COO, Olivia Li, had met with Tony at his office. Maybe IQtel was doing more than working on the same technology as last year's runner-up, now housed in Stephen's incubator.

Then there was Joey. Odd that he would have waited twenty years to seek his revenge. No, not twenty years, I reminded myself, Joey claimed Tony only told him about Ajeet's death two years ago. Joey seemed disgusted by the idea that he would benefit from Stephen's death, and claimed he felt guilty about his dubious role in it. But he admitted to building a small gun-toting drone, knew how it could be flown into Stephen's house, and claimed he knew where it was and that there was a good probability it would be identified as being part of the murder weapon.

I turned on the TV, poured myself a glass of wine and curled up on the end of the couch. Narrowing it down to two suspects didn't cut it. Maybe I should just toss a coin.

A knock startled me. I jumped, sloshing wine on my hand, every fibre of my body tense, my ears alert to every sound. A second knock, this one louder than the first, sent my heart into fourth gear. *Now what?* I set my wine down and tip toed to the door. I stared at the peephole and jumped back when a fist pounded the other side. I sucked in some air, squinted one eye shut and peered out. Mrs. Wilson stood on the other side. She was holding something. I slipped off the chain and opened the door a crack.

She leered at me, her lips pulled back tight in what I had come to recognize as her way of appearing sociable.

"Mrs. Wilson. Good evening."

"These are for you," she said thrusting a flower arrangement into my hands.

"Oh…ah…thank you." My heart started racing.

"Don't be stupid, they're not from me." Her smile made her seem creepy, her rough staccato voice made her sound mean. I must have looked confused.

"You weren't home, so the florist left them with me. Can't trust anyone these days to do what they're paid to do. That's some shiner, kid."

My hand went to my eye. "Oh, yeah. It's getting better, still looks horrible though. Car accident."

She harrumphed my explanation, turned to walk away and then turned back.

"You get your phone okay?"

"Sorry?"

"Your phone. I found it by your door. I figured you dropped it."

"When was this?"

"The night the storm hit. I knocked," she added defensively. "You didn't answer so I gave it to the super."

"Oh. No. Uh...I'll go check." I hadn't dropped my phone. Maybe she was losing her marbles. "Thanks for taking care of these for me." I nodded at the flower arrangement, still swaddled in layers of purple tissue and clear cellophane.

"Whatever. Let's not make it a habit."

I closed the door on the little troll's retreating back. Now I knew how she managed to live so long. It wasn't the exercise; she was preserved in pure vinegar.

I carried the flowers to the kitchen counter and set them down. My hands shook as I carefully removed the wrapping. If they had anything to do with my parents' death, I'd go berserk.

Pushing back the last of the wrapping, I pulled out a

beautiful arrangement of pale-green spider mums, peach-coloured roses and white Chrysanthemums. A small card was tucked in amongst the leaves. I pulled it out and flipped it over.

Hope you're feeling better. Up to ass in alligators—forgive me? Luis.

Okay, maybe he hadn't dropped me like a hot potato. I carried the flowers over to the coffee table and set them down. They were pretty. *A text would have been nice.* I cringed. Why hadn't I sent him one? I pulled out my phone and sent him a message thanking him for the flowers.

What was that Mrs. Wilson said about a phone? My phone had been in my possession right up until I had been abducted. Could that have been her pounding on my door the night I thought I was going to die? Why not—she wasn't subtle about anything else, how else would she knock. I picked up my keys, locked up and took the stairs down to the building manager's unit on the second floor.

Mr. Garriarty opened the door to my first knock. I could tell I'd disturbed his dinner because he was chewing food and still held his plate in one hand. Ten minutes later I was back upstairs, a Samsung smart phone in my sweaty little hands. It was locked, password protected.

Sighing, I sat back, picked up my wine and contemplated my next move. I had no idea whose phone this was but couldn't risk giving up the chance it was dropped here inadvertently by my stalker. If this was Bernie's phone, it would put any residual doubt, however small, away for good. It might even contain the original photos that were left for me or be the source of photos the police found at his house.

Bernie's password would likely be something meaningful to him, his favourite pet growing up, his birthday, his mother's name. Trouble was I didn't know anything about Bernie. I keyed in several unsuccessful guesses, then put the phone away. I'd call an IT guy I knew in the morning and ask him if there was any way to get the information directly off the memory card.

*

I bolted upright and glanced at my phone on the bedside table. Four-ten. Pushing back the covers, I turned on the light, got up and rushed into the living room.

Shivering with excitement, I grabbed the Samsung phone. *S. Wise, Tolkien, Samwise Gamgee.* Bernie had been a big fan of the Lord of the Rings. I held my breath and punched in Samwise. I yelped in glee when the navigation screen opened with all its lovely colourful little icons. I tapped the mail icon and grinned. I had Bernie Ing's phone in my hands. I needed to turn this over to Detective Keating, but first I'd take a little tour through Bernie's email, photos and text messages, and his recent call log.

I pulled up the photo file, scrolling through the photos he had taken in the last four months. There were several I hadn't seen. I stopped at the few of Joey in front of Tony's office. He hadn't lied about the date he'd gone there to confront Tony. Now that I had digital files, I could expand the photos.

A photo caught my eye. International Avenue. I was sure of it. Several people were strolling down the sidewalk, several more drank coffee at a nearby outdoor café. I expanded the photo until it grew grainy. *No way.* I peered closer at the photo. My excitement grew.

I pulled up Bernie's phone log and scrolled through the numbers. *Holy shit.* I knew this number. I pulled open my own phone and double checked. Words, images, fragments of conversation raced through my brain. I couldn't believe it. Tony had called Bernie. Five times. The first two calls lasted several minutes each, the last three had gone unanswered.

"Bernie, what the hell." I breathed out loud and sat back. And suddenly I knew. I reached over and grabbed Bernie's phone and scrolled further. There it was. Laura Bradford's hotline reward number. I had enough to take my theory to Detective McGuire. I knew who killed Stephen.

CHAPTER SIXTY-ONE

Rob and I were sitting in the Tim Hortons a few doors down from his office. He had declined coffee or anything to eat.

"So, what's this all about?"

"Let's call it a courtesy call."

Rob shifted in his chair. "Can we make it quick. I've got a patient coming in shortly."

"Sure. I want to give you a heads up. You're about to be charged with accessory to murder."

"What? No, no, no." Rob shook his head. "I didn't do anything."

"That's not exactly true. You helped Tony kill Stephen."

Rob paled under his tan. His eyes surveyed the café, either searching for cops or a way to escape. He leaned forward. "I had nothing to do with Stephen's murder," he hissed.

"You knew Tony killed Stephen and you helped Tony divert attention from himself."

"No. That's not true."

"You were the one who brought up Ajeet Jayaraman's disappearance. You threw out the idea that Stephen's death may have been committed by someone with a grudge. Then you threw out the idea that Joey might have had a reason to kill Stephen. The bit about Tony and Stephen getting threatening phone calls from Joey was a nice touch."

Rob was still shaking his head.

"Then Tony calls me saying he miraculously remembers someone who can corroborate your story. I talked to Greg Kowalski yesterday. He rolled over pretty quickly. He told me you paid him to tell me that whole story, about how poor Joey began to unravel when his good friend, Ajeet, disappeared. How he also figured that Ajeet died that night, and that Stephen was the last one to see him. By the way, I have photos of you and Greg meeting a few blocks down from the Kielbasa King the day before Tony called and gave me his name."

"I don't know anything about who killed Stephen. I don't see how any of this makes me an accessory to murder."

"You were the one who told me that Tony admitted Ajeet died on the way home that night. That Stephen buried him at some construction site."

"That's what he told me."

"I'm sure he did. He also told Joey the same story, quite recently, almost word for word. He built Stephen up to be an uncaring, money and status seeking narcissist. But that's not who Stephen was."

"Still doesn't prove I helped Tony kill him."

"Did you know that Tony planted the murder weapon, somewhere where it implicated Joey?"

Rob's eyes widened and a muscle in his jaw twitched. "Who's to say Joey didn't build the drone and shoot Stephen himself."

Rob realized his mistake as soon as he mentioned the drone. "I mean…that's what Tony said…thinks…must have happened."

"The police have the drone now. They picked it up yesterday. I'm fairly sure they're going to find one or more of your fingerprints." I was hoping Rob wouldn't call my bluff.

Rob was rocking back and forth slightly, his eyes staring at something to the left of my ear.

"It's why you went running with Stephen the morning of your party isn't it. You had to make sure he went running that day. Tony knew he'd have a shower afterwards. So, he had you take the drone over and leave it on the roof of the condo building behind Stephen's house before your run. He waited and watched and after the skylight opened to let the steam out of the master bath, he flew the drone in, found Stephen listening to music in his den, and killed him."

"That's pure speculation. You don't have anything on me."

"Tony's very clever. The fingerprints will say otherwise. That's why he got you to take the drone over and leave it for him. Oh, and did you know that the condo building camera's captured you entering the building at seven forty that morning? Was it your gun too?"

"I don't know anything about a gun. I had no idea what Tony planned to do with that drone."

"Yeah, well it might come down to your word versus Tony's. You think he's just going to roll over and take the blame? Who knows what other incriminating evidence he's planted. What I don't get is why you helped Tony."

"You don't understand. They were going to kill Nancy."

"Who was going to kill Nancy?"

Rob glanced around furtively. "I got in over my head, gambling. I borrowed from the wrong guys. The bastards were charging me ten percent interest on what I owed. Monthly. They were going to hurt Nancy if I didn't pay them back. I asked Stephen if he could lend me some money. He said he didn't have that kind of cash lying around. He gave me a coin he had from his coin collection; said I could sell it. But I only got eighty thousand for it. It wasn't enough."

"So, Stephen gives you money and this is how you repaid him?"

"You don't understand. They killed our dog. A couple of guys started following Nancy. I'd never forgive myself if something happened to her. So, I went to Tony."

"And Tony said he'd loan you the money if you did him a favor or two."

"I thought Tony was going to use the drone to spy on Stephen, you know, find out who and what he was negotiating for the fuel cell. When I saw the gun…"

"You saw the gun and parked in on the roof anyway."

"I'm not the one who fired it. I just had to park it where he said. I swear. I didn't kill Stephen. Tony did. He planned the whole thing. He killed Stephen."

"The police might see it differently."

Detective McGuire entered the coffee shop. Rob's head swivelled back and forth between me and McGuire. As he reached our table, I pulled the watch off my wrist and held it out to him. "The latest voice triggered audio recorder. I'm sure you'll find our conversation interesting."

CHAPTER SIXTY-TWO

IT WAS A splendid day, unusually warm for early June. This time Laura and I were sitting on the patio, where we had our first meeting, cupping mugs of coffee in our hands, staring out at the geese floating serenely on the lake.

"It is pretty here," said Laura, gazing out over the water.

I nodded my agreement and swallowed a sip of coffee.

"I still can't believe it was Tony. He and Stephen had been friends for so long. How could he have gotten so desperate?" said Laura, turning her eyes back to me.

"Apparently he was close to going bankrupt and the banks and creditors were breathing down his neck," I said.

"But to kill someone! And throw his own life away too, all because of money? Even if his company went under, why couldn't he start over? Thousands do. Wayne did."

"It wasn't just the money. Tony was jealous of Stephen, what he had, the way he lived. And when he realized one of Stephen's entrepreneurs was getting close to cracking the key to the next generation fuel cell that was going to blow the socks off anyone wanting a cheap, lightweight source of energy, all he could see was his own demise."

"But he owned a percentage too. Wasn't that enough?"

"Apparently not. Sure, it might have been enough to pay off some of the creditors, but it wasn't happening fast enough. The banks were asking for their money, not to mention the loan sharks banging on his door."

"I still don't understand. If he needed money, I'm sure Stephen would have loaned him some to tide him over."

"Stephen didn't have a lot of liquidity in his asset base. He had already given his rarest coin to Rob, to help him get out from under his gambling debt. It wasn't just a case of tiding him over. Tony bankrolled a failing idea. He had nothing to fall back on. He, in turn, had been bankrolled by a company called StarTu, who had been stealing beta technology designs from young entrepreneurs and feeding them to Tony. He was into them for over a million dollars. Besides, Tony's ego wouldn't let him just walk away."

"Ego. It's the reason behind half the bloody wars out there."

"Ego can be a strength and a weakness. As gregarious and charismatic as Tony seems, he couldn't handle facing failure. Even when he ran into his and Stephen's old roommate, Joey, who by all appearances wasn't doing well, he realized it wasn't the case. Joey may not be materially wealthy, but he had something Tony missed in his own life. Peace, self-acceptance and the ability to live life by his own standards, not someone else's yardstick."

I still didn't know all the details, but everything moved quickly once I handed over my taped conversation with Rob, and Bernie's cell phone, to Detective McGuire. The clincher for me had been when I found a call placed by Bernie to Laura Bradford's reward hotline below the calls that came from Tony. Laura had gotten a call from someone asking if the reward money for information about Stephen's death was still in play. The caller hadn't given her his name. When Laura mentioned it to Tony, he had asked her for the caller's number, which she gave to him from her phone call log. Tony or someone using his personal cell phone called that number the next day.

Tony figured out who Bernie was and once he realized that Bernie might have information that could lead police to him, he threatened him. Bernie stopped answering other calls from Tony, the last three made the day of the storm. Bernie must have panicked and showed up at my place, pounding on the door. The power had gone out, leaving me freaking out inside, and I hadn't answered. He must have dropped his phone by my door.

Bernie may not have known Tony was Stephen's killer, but once Tony started calling him, he must have realized he was on the right track. He got scared and left the bundle of photos with a barista he knew at a coffee shop he frequented. He asked him to hold the package for me, that I would be by to pick it up.

Of course, no one knew the storm would be that severe. Once the storm hit, the coffee shop was closed for days, but when everything got back to normal the barista remembered the package. Since I hadn't come by to pick it up and learning that Bernie had died, he decided to deliver the photos to me. He wrapped and addressed the package himself. Bernie had only told him that my last name was Knight with a K and that I was a PI. He found my office location on the internet.

"I feel awful about that poor man being killed. I shouldn't have given Tony his number," said Laura.

"You can't blame yourself. You had no idea what, if any, information he had, and certainly no idea Tony would go after him."

One of the more incriminating photos Bernie had on his phone was of Rob meeting with Greg Kowalski. Tony cleverly found a way to point me in Joey's direction and away from him and Conner.

Greg admitted to police that Rob paid him to tell me the story. Months earlier, Tony had already spun the tale to Joey about Stephen having buried Ajeet's body the night he disappeared. He then had Rob feed the same story to Greg, hoping that Greg's story would cement the lie. Thinking back on it, I realized they even used the same words to describe what happened.

Bernie was better at ferreting things out than I ever imagined him capable of. He had been figuring out the skylight entry the same time he noticed Joey ogling Stephen's house. I had to hand it to Bernie. He'd been in lockstep with me most of the way. The only mistake he made was calling Laura from his cell phone, rather than using a cheap burner. The one mistake which eventually cost him his life but helped break the case wide open. I guess I'll never really know why he became infatuated with me. Or how he imagined things would end. I had thought Bernie creepy, but he was just a sad lonely little man.

"I still can't believe the lengths Tony went to. Involving all these people, framing his friend Joey. You think you know someone."

"Well, it didn't start that way. Tony knew he and Stephen were working on a similar innovation. I don't believe Stephen knew. After all, Tony had been leveraging ideas stolen from a tech competition, by someone from the company that sponsored the competition, StarTu. Most of the design ideas still had lots of issues to work out though. He had success with a few, but hit a dead end with a lot of them. By then he was in deep financial trouble. He knew Stephen's Nano-skin fuel cell was working, they applied for a patent."

"You mean Stephen shared all this with him?"

"Not all the details. But remember, Tony was one of the investors. He would have at least known about the patent being filed. Tony may not have known it was Tián that was interested at that point, but StarTu had been loaning Tony money all these years and were demanding he bring them something worthy of their investment. That's why he engaged Conner."

"I knew that man had something to do with Stephen's death. Didn't I tell you?"

"You did. Tony went to Conner, offered him a deal. Spy on Stephen. He'd give him a hundred grand once he had the information he was looking for."

"He wanted to know which tech company was going to buy this Nano cell thing, right?"

"Right."

"What good would that do?"

"I expect he was planning to give StarTu whatever information Conner could get him, to get them off his back."

"It must worth a lot of money."

"Could bring in millions in royalties. Over its lifetime of course."

"But Stephen didn't like Conner. How did he end up getting Stephen to hire him?"

"After Tony offered Conner the deal, Conner hired a lowlife he knew who ran with one of the local drug gangs to mug Stephen. He also made some threatening calls, painted gang graffiti on the lab, just enough to worry Stephen. Stephen had mentioned to Rob and Tony that his biggest issue was time. Voila! Conner appears, offering to drive Stephen. The answer to both his problems."

"What a pig."

"Conner could hear conversations Stephen was having in his car, while on the phone or in person. But he couldn't tell what might be said from his house."

"So Conner goes to Chloe and asks her to bug Stephen's house for him. I told you she was guilty as sin. She was going to sell out her brother for what? Money?"

"Well, you've got to give her credit for not following through."

"Yeah? I don't know about that." Laura scowled, holding her coffee cup closer to her chest. "But why did Stephen have to die?"

"Stephen was favouring Tián technologies. StarTu is a bit of a wild card, and rumours are circulating that they might have connections to dirty money. Using the info Tony provided, StarTu offered Stephen more money than was being discussed with Tián but Stephen turned them down."

"Good for him."

"The issue was, Tián is a publicly traded company. They already had a budget for the year. To provide the kind of capital Stephen and his entrepreneurs needed to take the Nano-skin fuel cell into testing, then production, needed board approval. He couldn't get it until after the third quarter."

"Which would be too late for Tony—he needed the money right away." Laura nodded. "I get it. So, what was the plan? Kill Stephen, get a bigger share and do a deal with StarTu?"

"That was the plan."

"But it didn't go that way. What went wrong?"

"Conner double crossed him. Instead of feeding all the information he collected to Tony, he took it directly to StarTu."

"You mean sold it to them?"

"That's right. StarTu found out that the real reason Stephen was going with Tián was because of their own reputation and work ethics and not the upfront capital. They leaned on Tony even harder. Told him he'd better figure out a way to get the nano fuel cell patent into their hands."

"So, he killed Stephen."

"Yes. Patent agreements usually contain a clause which speaks to patent ownership in the event of the patent holder's death. Tony knew Stephen planned to leave him his share."

"To think, Tony nearly got away with it."

"Yes. But after Stephen was killed, StarTu made Tony an

offer for the patent that was significantly lower than even the first offer they had made Stephen."

"Oh my god. They had him over a barrel."

"At that point Tony knew he was done. He turned all his attention to covering his tracks, not wanting to add to his misery by being tied to Stephen's death. I don't know if he always intended to frame Joey, but when I came around asking about Joey and Ajeet, the idea solidified in his mind. Stephen was dead, Ajeet was missing, he decided to tie the two together. Give Joey a real motive for wanting to kill Stephen. Up until then, his plan had been to make Joey sound unbalanced."

"Nice guy."

"He asked Conner to fly out to Sparwood with the drone and leave it where it would implicate Joey."

"Why would he ask Conner if he was double crossing him?"

"Tony didn't know Conner was double crossing him. He just knew StarTu was lowballing him, that they knew he was in financial trouble and desperate for a deal."

"I understand the police have the drone."

"Yeah, it was at a remote hunter's cabin. Joey's fingerprints were everywhere of course but they also found Conner's prints. The day after I gave Detective McGuire my recorded conversation with Rob the police swooped in and recovered it. Joey guessed right. The drone had specks of blood that matched Stephen's."

As far as I knew, the gun had not yet been found. A friend of Joey's, who works at the car rental place in Sparwood, said the police had come by to check the rental agreements. They had been interested in the mileage on the vehicle Conner rented to see if it matched his story about being in Elkford for a fishing trip on March 18. Apparently, it did not.

"How did Conner know about the cabin?" Laura asked, nodding to the waitress who arrived to refill our coffee.

"I had mentioned to Tony that Joey's sister had gone there to leave him a message about the trust fund Stephen left him. He contacted Antonia the day before the big storm hit and asked her for the directions. She figured Tony wanted to talk to Joey about maybe settling with Chloe, when she challenged the will."

Laura looked up. "I heard they arrested the guys who shot Chloe."

"Yeah, same guys Conner hired to mug Stephen and later blow up my car. They may have also killed Bernie and lit his house on fire. I hear one of them is spilling his guts trying to cut a deal for a lighter sentence."

"But why shoot Chloe?"

"Conner was getting ready to split. Take his money from StarTu and move on. He knew Chloe could tie him to the whole mess if she ever told the police that he planned to plant listening devices in Stephen's house. And as for Bernie and me, it seems Tony paid Conner to cover his own tracks by getting rid of us when we started to get too close to the truth."

"All of this for money. Do none of these people have any scruples at all? I'm glad they arrested Conner. He's way worse than I even imagined. Are the police going to be able to prove his involvement?"

"Oh yeah. The police have located the car that was used

to transport me from Air Espresso, where I was attacked, to Sparwood. The car was discovered at a wrecking yard in Kindersley and traced to a cousin of one of the men Conner hired, who claimed it had been taken without his permission. It matches the description of the car Chloe's boyfriend saw when she was shot, and they found my DNA in the trunk."

"I hope Tony does a lot of time. He didn't end up with the prize he thought he'd be getting, and he killed his friend for nothing. I wonder how his ego is doing now."

Ironically, Stephen's high-tech house had been penetrated by an equally high-tech innovation. The media had gone ape over it. Apparently, there have already been three other drone offences, although none resulted in death. Police had charged one man in Canada and two teenagers in the United States with rigging up and firing a gun-toting drone. The news was creating a great deal of buzz and controversy. While companies were still working on converting the drone's capability to deliver mail and small packages quickly and cheaply, there were already people out there experimenting with more nefarious uses.

"So, how is Chloe doing? Have you heard from her?"

"She's going to be okay. She told me what Conner wanted her to do and she's told Detective McGuire everything. She didn't commit a crime, but it helped police when they had their conversation with Conner. I got a postcard from her. She and that guy with the dreadlocks she'd been living with are in Vancouver."

"I'm glad to hear she came clean with Detective McGuire herself. Every bit helps. Conner's still claiming he is innocent of everything he's been charged with."

"Of course."

"So, what's happening with the patent for the fuel cell?" I asked.

"Oh, it's going to be tied up in legalities for months. Still too early to tell, but we might end up with Stephen's share."

Laura and I both sat in quiet contemplation for a few minutes. Several geese flew past, their wings spread out, skimming the water until they touched down. I turned back to Laura. She looked tired. Spent. But oddly at peace.

"And how are you doing? You seem better."

Laura smiled "Thank you, I am. I won't ever get over losing Stephen, but knowing what happened, having someone in custody to pay for what he did does give me some sense of peace. Thank you for forging on. I know it wasn't easy and you came within an inch of getting killed too."

I smiled and shrugged. "Just part of the job. I must admit, at one point I was convinced Joey was the guilty party and that Tony was also in danger. Tony did a great job setting Joey up. I'm sure the trial will be interesting."

We sat contemplating the lake, each lost in our own thoughts. It had been a watershed case, the one that made me feel like a real private investigator, not just someone chasing deadbeat dads for failed child support payments or doing hours of mindless surveillance hoping to catch someone trying to stiff an insurance company with a phony injury claim. I knew I'd still get the cheaters and the wife beaters, but also some bigger more complex problems to solve. The idea both excited and terrified me.

CHAPTER SIXTY-THREE

It was Friday night and later than I thought. The evening was already bathed in muted light, where objects became shapes and worried faces melted away in alcohol-inspired laughter. My favourite time of day.

The building had quieted hours ago, people leaving, anxious to start their weekend. I didn't mind being alone at the office—in a strange way, I found it comforting. If I wanted company, all I had to do was head downstairs and join the revellers heading off to various venues. I finished up the last of my paperwork on the Wallis file, and cross-checked that all my invoices had been issued and paid.

I sat back and picked up the remainder of my scotch and took a final sip. The last couple of weeks had flown by. Tony D'Silva had been charged with Stephen's and Bernie's murders and several counts of attempted murder. Conner had also been charged in Bernie's murder and several accounts of attempted murder, including mine and Chloe's.

Joey called to thank me for believing in him. I really hadn't been a hundred percent sure of his innocence until the police arrested Tony, but I didn't admit that to him. The media were having a heyday with the murder weapon. Conversations were springing up all over the country regarding drones and their potential use to kill.

I'd been interviewed by a local TV station and several newspapers ran a story on how my investigation helped lead to Tony D'Silva's arrest. For the first time in two years, I had a bit of money in the bank and people were calling me instead of me chasing potential work. I even got an invite to give a talk at MRU Career Days.

I closed my eyes and smiled. *Watch what you wish for, Jorjie.* My mother always said that to me. I could still see her face, her eyes troubled, pleading caution, yet a faint smile playing on her lips, encouraging me. Would she be proud of the woman I had become? I was getting what I wished for. I was independent, finding my spot in the community, paying my own way.

I'd only seen Luis twice since my abduction. Twice in two months. Not much of a relationship brewing there. Mostly my doing though. The last time we had gotten together, I had told Luis that I needed to step back, give this whole thing, whatever it was, some thought. Luis had readily agreed. *Watch what you wish for, Jorjie.*

At first, I had been miffed at his response. Then I had a good long talk with myself. I was sending him mixed messages. Did I want sex? Of course. But beyond that? I was conflicted. I had taken every opportunity to not meet him halfway. The conclusion I had come to was that I was either afraid we'd get into a relationship and then he'd end it, leaving me to nurse my wounds or I'd lose my independence.

Luis was used to giving orders, taking control. But I had sworn I would never let a man rule my life. Fallout, from my relationship with dear old dad. Intellectually, I knew there were other choices, choices with words in them like mutual respect, partner and compromise. Was that a choice I was ready to make? Sounded like a lot of work. I finally justified it to myself, saying I had already taken on a lot of change in my life. Maybe this wasn't the best time to tackle a new relationship as well.

This morning, I had followed a forensic crew out to Forest Lawn. They had used ground penetrating radar to see if Ajeet Jayaraman's remains could be detected at the location three lots down from where his parents' house had stood. Ajeet's uncle was there and one of Ajeet's brothers. Radar didn't come up with anything; there had been too much ground disturbance from the building activity back then and in subsequent years for the radar to be effective.

As nice as it would have been to let the Jayaraman family find closure, I was relieved. There have been several documented cases where people disappeared for decades and showed up twenty or thirty years later, living a different life and using a different name. It's what I wished for Ajeet, but I could tell Ajeet's family no longer believed it.

Tony of course denied the whole story about Stephen burying Ajeet and went back to declaring they had driven him home that night and left him standing at his parents' doorway, like they had always claimed.

I sat up. The sound of approaching footsteps in the hall grew louder. *Heading my way.* The hairs on the back of my neck prickled. The comforting silence I was sitting in shifted.

A cold spike of fear shot down my spine, sending shivers to all my extremities.

My phone pinged. I jumped, glanced down at the screen then back up at the outer door. The handle turned and Luis walked in.

"Hope I didn't scare you. I should have called. I tried your place and one of your neighbours said you'd gone down to your office."

"The little troll from down the hall?" I stood up and moved toward him.

"What? You mean that sweet little grandma?"

"Sweet grandma my ass. What are you doing here?" He stood there, barely illuminated in the dim light. "It's late."

"I…of course. Just had a rough day. Don't know why, but I had to see you." He ran his hand over the back of his head. "I couldn't face going home, although god knows I could use the sleep."

We now faced each other, like two strangers. I took two more steps. He couldn't say why he needed to see me, yet he was here. I couldn't tell him what I feared, yet here I stood.

His eyes searched mine. My skin began to tingle, like I was about to get a static electricity shock. I cringed inwardly in anticipation. My eyes met his and answered the message written there. The silence was broken by my heart thundering in my chest, the blood pounding in my ears. Our lips met. He smelled like no one I ever knew before, shower soap mixed with leather and moss or the best peaty scotch ever.

His hands slid down my body to the small of my back and he pulled me closer to him. I pulled my lips away from his and kissed his neck and my body surged forward. I found his mouth again and felt his hands, lower now. He whispered something, and I pulled back just far enough so I could look into his eyes. He looked at me, mesmerized, and groaned. We were both breathing hard now.

"I thought we decided we wouldn't do this."

"Worst decision of my life," he answered.

I stared into his eyes, warm and fascinatingly dark. I tipped my head back. "Oh. You're saying you're wrong sometimes?"

His eyes met mine, as he reached for my hand.

"Come on," he tilted his head and smiled. "Let's go find out how wrong I can be."

ACKNOWLEDGEMENTS

WRITING MAY BE a solitary event, but creating a book takes a whole team. I'd to thank all those who read early versions of my book, offered helpful comments, wrote reviews, and cheered me on. A big thank you to my dear friends, Brenda Lissel and Sue Matsalla, for their perceptive input on my early drafts and for being such a huge support throughout my life and my writing journey.

A special thank you to Taija Morgan, brilliant editor and friend, for believing in me right from the start and for providing much appreciated guidance and support.

I have learned so much since I began writing seven years ago, and there is still much to learn. The writing community is a very welcoming and generous one. I'd especially like to acknowledge the learning opportunities and friends I've made through the Calgary Crime Writers, Sisters in Crime – Canada West, and Crime Writers of Canada. I also want to thank and acknowledge all the interviewers, bloggers, podcasters and booksellers, who are working hard to support indie authors like myself, and especially Brian

Richmond—Blue Devil Books, and Joanna Vander Vlugt—JCVArtStudio, for their incredibly generous support.

I'm blessed to have the most amazing family and friends. Thank you to my beautiful family, Kevin, Sean, Katherine, Leanne, Tyler, Malcolm, and Paige, for your constant love and support.

Finally, a huge thank you to my readers. Thank you for reaching out to me on social media, joining my Readers Bulletin newsletter, and for all the messages you send me, telling me you love my books and are eagerly awaiting more. I hope you enjoyed reading *Three Dog Knight* as much as I enjoyed writing it!

THANKS FOR READING

I hope you enjoyed reading *Three Dog Knight*! Authors largely rely on word of mouth to gain exposure. Please let other readers know how much you enjoyed *Three Dog Knight* by leaving a review at your favourite online bookstore.

Read on for an excerpt from the next
JORJA KNIGHT MYSTERY

KNIGHT VISION

AVAILABLE WINTER 2022

KNIGHT VISION - CHAPTER ONE

ALL WINTER I'D been telling myself something big was going to happen, and today was going to be that day. Don't ask me how I knew. I didn't believe in luck. Maybe, I subconsciously worked out the odds of being stuck in starve mode forever, in a business typified by feast or famine cycles, and figured the tide had to change.

As sole proprietor of Knight Investigations, I'd spent the last three weeks doing the new client hustle. This week, I was perfecting my Candy Crush score and working to keep my thoughts in the positive lane.

"Holy Jeez." I jumped up, hand on my chest.

A woman stood in the doorway. The hairs on my neck prickled as dark eyes assessed me from behind emerald-green framed glasses.

"Sorry. I didn't hear you come in."

"I'm looking for Ms. Knight."

"You found her." I held out my hand. "I'm Jorja Knight."

Her grip sent a tingling sensation up my arm. My heart settled into a nice steady pound.

THREE DOG KNIGHT | 385

"My name is Misty Lane. I read about you in the paper. You solved that murder a few months back. The Houdini Killer."

Shaun Allen, a young reporter, had been sent by Postmedia News to do a story on me and my part in capturing the Houdini Killer, a *nom de plume* given to the killer for his vanishing act after murdering a prominent businessman in his highly secured home.

"So, you read Shaun's article. I'm still trying to smooth over some ruffled police feathers." I waved my hand at the beat-up wooden chair in front of my equally beat-up wooden desk. "What can I do for you?"

She sat, crossed her legs, and gazed around the room. My eyes followed hers. The place was a rat hole, but the rent was right, and the décor and musty odour discouraged my innate desire to use it as a hideout from the world.

She was taking her time, and I started to wonder if she was some sort of voyeur, interested in the morbid details of Stephen Bradford's death, the case she referred to.

Her eyes drifted back to mine. "I need your help to prevent a murder."

"Prevent a murder? Whose murder are we talking about?"

"I'm afraid it might be mine."

Her eyes were like frozen ponds, reflecting back nothing. A tiny muscle jumped below her right eye. I admired her ability to deliver the line with so little emotion.

"Why do you think you might be murdered?"

"Someone is watching me, leaving me messages." She pulled her cell phone from her purse and swiped the screen several times. "Here." She held it out to me.

Die bitch die was scrawled in red block letters across the windshield of a white Subaru Forester.

"This is your car?"

"Yes. I phoned the district police office. As far as they're concerned it's just another act of senseless vandalism."

"But you're convinced otherwise."

"There have been other incidents. I'm getting phone calls, several a day, just dead air but I can tell someone is on the line. Yesterday, I found a bird on the back step of my shop—one of those magpies. Its head was missing...sliced right off."

I winced.

"There's more." She took a deep breath. "I'm a psychic medium and clairvoyant. I can see the past and the future."

I managed not to recoil in disbelief. As a former forensic lab analyst, I had spent most of my life putting my faith into science, that which was measurable, observable, repeatable. Then again, when it comes to death, consciousness, and quantum physics, I'll be the first to admit there is a shitload of stuff I don't understand.

"Interesting. Go on."

She exhaled and gave me one of those nods that said she was impressed I even entertained having this conversation.

"I first sensed something wrong about a month ago, at a group reading. At first, the feeling was fleeting, vague. Over the weeks the vision has become clearer, stronger."

"What do you see?"

"A dark-haired woman, about my age and height. She's walking down a dark path. She's in danger." Her hands painted a story only her mind saw. "I feel cold, very cold. The woman falls, tumbles into a dark void. The ground comes up to meet her. It's a dark, desolate place, filled with broken things, all rusted—decayed. Suddenly, I can't breathe—in or out. In that second, I know I'm going to die." She lowered her hands, now clasped below her neck, and sat back. "Now, this vision, this premonition, occurs almost daily."

"In your vision, you describe a dark-haired woman falling and someone observing. Are you the observer, the one who feels cold, or are you the woman who is falling?"

She pursed her lips thoughtfully for a minute. "Impossible to say if we are one and the same."

"What about the place this woman dies. Some sort of junkyard?"

She looked at me steadily. "The images are in my mind's eye. You have to understand that *seeing* can be literal or steeped in symbolism and somewhat open to interpretation."

"Okay. What do you think your vision is telling you?"

"Falling can signify abandonment, by a caregiver, like a parent. Junk often means rejection, being tossed aside, like junk in real life."

"I see. Are you saying the woman in your vision was abandoned? That she's been rejected? If so, does that apply to you?"

A flicker of something crossed her face.

"I suppose it could apply to any number of people. Me, the woman in my vision, possibly the killer. Even you."

Her green eyes pierced mine, and a cold chill ran down my arms. I tore my eyes away from hers and cleared my throat.

"You said this premonition started about a month ago.

Anything happen back then to trigger this vision or cause someone to want to harm you?"

"Nothing I can recall."

"And the dark-haired woman you see. You think it's you?"

Her brow furrowed as she gave it a moment of consideration. "I'm certain I'm foretelling a woman's death. I, or a woman who resembles me, will be strangled to death. Given the disturbing messages and phone calls I'm receiving, I believe that woman is me."

"Okay, so tell me, who wants you dead?"

"I don't know. Otherwise, I'd be telling my story to the police." She smiled, a small, apologetic smile that didn't linger.

I sat back, taking note of her worried eyes, yet confident demeanour. This woman was asking me to prevent a murder, based largely on a psychic forewarning. Of course, the dead-air calls and a guillotined bird meant something. Still, it was an unusual request. My fingers see-sawed the pen they held nervously. Were premonitions really that different than a strong hunch or gut feeling? Could something logical, reasonable, be driving her belief that she would be killed? Or could there be something to her belief in spirits, the afterworld?

Curiosity overrode trepidation. I took the case.

MISTY STOOD IN the middle of the circle, her arms raised shoulder height, her palms facing upward. A soft breeze materialized from nowhere, gently blew back her hair and played with the edges of her bell-sleeved tunic. The soft background music stopped. The room fell silent, save for the occasional muffled sniff of a young woman standing across from me.

I surveyed the circle. A mishmash of paying hopefuls, their rapt faces turned expectantly toward Misty. The demeanour of the older couple to my left made me think they were here for a thrill, a new experience to share with their bridge friends, rather than a desire to connect with the dearly departed. Next to them stood a middle-aged woman who occasionally patted the arm of the young, emotional woman standing to her left. Rounding out the circle, an older man of Mediterranean heritage, a twitchy young man who repeatedly pushed up the frames of his glasses, and two middle-aged men who held hands.

"I'm sensing a woman. A mother figure. Has anyone lost their mother unexpectedly? Perhaps at a young age?"

Misty turned toward me, her eyes on mine. My gut clenched.

The young woman across from me let out a sob. "Oh my god. I did."

Misty tilted her head ever so slightly in my direction, gave me a knowing look, then turned to the woman who spoke.

Somehow, Misty knew the young woman's mother died of cancer two years earlier. That the mother's favourite colour was yellow, that she had collected ornaments—penguins.

Misty addressed the sobbing woman. "She wants you to know she's at peace. She says thank you for always thinking of me, for being a wonderful daughter. She knows you bought her a penguin when you were in San Cabo. You did, didn't you?"

The woman glanced up through tears and nodded.

Misty laughed. "Not an easy feat. A burro from Mexico, yes, but a penguin! She knows she's in your thoughts every day. She's so proud of you. She wants you to live your life, live it fully, and know that she's always with you."

I blinked rapidly. Several people dabbed their eyes. Next Misty had a message for the Mediterranean-looking man, from his recently departed wife. The reading ended shortly afterward. Misty's face was pale. A thin layer of moisture shone on her forehead.

While waiting for the last of Misty's clients to depart, I wandered around the shop. The front was devoted to healing stones, incense, sage. I stopped at a poster offering her

Past-Life Healing service. For a mere two-hundred and eight-five dollars, her guided meditation, with help from spirit, would help one overcome the emotional obstacles from past lives—obstacles hindering present success. And to think I'd spent thousands on my therapist trying to clear the emotional blocks from this lifetime alone and still hadn't moved past them.

"I want you to know your mother's spirit started to come forward before the young woman's mother made herself known."

I startled. Engrossed in reading, I hadn't heard Misty approach.

"Your mother's spirit is like her, timid, somewhat reserved. When the other, brasher spirit rushed forward, she stepped aside."

I swallowed the familiar lump forming in my throat and told myself she could have researched me on the internet. It would have taken some digging but a few articles about my mother's death twenty years ago still lingered in various archives.

"Was today's reading typical?"

"Pretty much. Sometimes spirit comes forth so vividly I can see the expression on their face. Today, I felt the first woman's spirit tap at my chest—that signals they died of something like cancer, or a heart condition." She pushed a strand of hair off her forehead. Her upper lip glistened with moisture.

"You look exhausted. Is everything okay?"

"After the second spirit showed herself to me, a darkness started to form. It's hard to explain. I felt panicky."

"A darkness? Related to that poor man's wife?"

"No, no. It was someone or something else."

"The feeling's gone now?"

"Yes, although I'm still a bit shaky."

"The people at the reading, have you met any of them before today?"

"The older couple have been in the store before. Oh, and that man, the fidgety one with the thick-rimmed glasses. I've seen him at one of my other readings but haven't had a chance to talk to him. He must really want to connect with a loved one but unfortunately no one's stepped forward yet."

"So, spirits don't always come forward to connect with their loved ones?"

"No. I'm merely a conduit for them to speak to their loved ones. I never know who will come forward or when."

"Thanks for inviting me to sit in. It was fascinating. Do you have time for some questions now?"

"Of course."

I had googled Misty after she left my office yesterday. She was starting to garner attention. She was a frequent speaker at a national wellness conference and had even worked with law enforcement agencies on occasion.

"You said you don't know anyone who'd want to kill you. Can you think of anyone who might have an issue with you or you with them?"

Misty bit her lower lip and shook her head. "No, not really."

"I need to start somewhere—even if it's to eliminate people in your life as possibilities."

Misty's forehead crinkled in thought. "Well, there's

Peoria Benson. She owns Healing Waters, at the end of the block. She's got a real hate on for me."

"Why is that?"

"I don't know. I dropped by her store to introduce myself the day I opened shop. She glared at me the whole time. Wouldn't shake my hand. It was so uncomfortable. I said hello, wished her well and left."

"When was that?"

"A little over a year ago. Before this, I had a smaller shop in Marda Loop."

"Is it possible you met this woman, Peoria, before? Any chance you have a mutual friend or acquaintance?"

"No—never laid eyes on her until the day I moved in. I've barely spoken to her since. She bad-mouths me to her customers. I go out of my way to avoid her."

"What about other tenants in the building?"

"There's just me and Healing Waters now. We're not tenants, we're owners. We pay a maintenance fee, like a condo fee, to keep the common areas of the building in good repair. Or we used to. The building's been sold recently. I don't know what the new owners have planned."

"Only two shops in this whole building?"

"Mr. Sherbaz owned the space between us, but the new building owners bought him out. The second floor used to hold small apartments. They've been empty for years."

"Anyone else? Boyfriend? Ex-boyfriend?"

"I haven't dated anyone in nearly a year."

"What about your last boyfriend? What was he like?"

"Doug? He was a total ass. It wasn't obvious at first, but

as time went on, I noticed whenever he didn't get his way, he'd make me pay for it with his bad mood. So, I ended it."

"How did he take it?"

"Not well." She snorted. "I kept bumping into him for months afterwards. At one point, I thought he might be stalking me. I haven't seen him in four or five months now. I heard he's dating someone else. Frankly, I'm relieved to hear he's moved on."

"What's Doug's last name?"

"Liederbach. Please don't go there. I don't need any more drama with that guy."

"Don't worry. I go to great lengths to avoid putting my clients in harm's way. Anyone else? Disgruntled suppliers, business partners, customers?"

"No."

"What about friends, family?"

She turned away, hugging crossed arms against her chest. She took a few steps then turned back. "I don't have much in the way of family. My father died when I was a child, my mother's in a nursing home—dementia. I've moved around a lot, lost track of friends." She shrugged. "Other than the occasional guy I let into my life, there's no one. I'm focused on building my business, my career."

"Is it possible you revealed something in one of your readings, something someone wanted to remain a secret?"

"I suppose it's possible. If I did, it obviously didn't mean anything to me, because I didn't pick up on it."

"You didn't notice anyone becoming upset or agitated?"

"No. I don't recall anything like that. Most people are

grateful to receive a message from loved ones who have passed."

"Mind if I go out back? I want to see where you park, maybe have a chat with this Peoria Benson."

Misty led me through a small office, a tiny kitchenette, and a packed storage area, to the back of the shop. She unlatched and pushed open the back door.

"This is where I found the bird." She nodded at the lone crumbling concrete step leading to the parking area.

Once outside I surveyed the building, a block-long, red-brick structure, punctuated by several doors and a few windows. The brick walls were covered in graffiti, or perhaps in this neighbourhood it was called street art.

I walked the length of the alley. Each store had several reserved parking spaces, for the owner and customers. Across the alley was a row of smaller brick buildings, and two wooden houses converted into stores. Overhead, power lines sagged between wooden poles. Plenty of places to install a surveillance camera if I needed to later.

I stopped at the end of the alley and glanced back. Misty's fear and growing panic during the reading had been clear. The million-dollar question was, who or what was threatening her?

"Hey, you!"

I turned and almost passed out. A shirtless man, hair matted and unkept, lunged at me.

"Are you threaten' me? Dopin' up my coffee?" He grabbled hold of my sleeve, his face now inches from mine, his eyes black, his breath hot and noxious. "You can't shut me up. They tried. Shot me full of drugs. Burned holes in my brain. It didn't work. Know why?"

I wrenched my arm free and staggered back, heart pounding. Keeping eyes on him, I stepped past.

He took a step after me. His voice rose to a crescendo. "I've been saved by the Lord Jesus seven times. Seven times."

His bark followed me as I made my way to the front of the building.

"For true and righteous are his judgments. For he has judged the great whore, which did corrupt the earth with her fornication."

I reached the corner and turned. *Please don't let this be who we're dealing with.*

FREE NOVELLA–KNIGHT SHIFT

Join my Readers Bulletin and let me send you a
free digital copy of Knight Shift, the prequel to the
Jorja Knight Series, along with occasional updates
on new releases, giveaways, and other news!
Download your free copy at *www.alicebienia.com*

ABOUT THE AUTHOR

Alice Bienia is a Canadian Crime Writer and author of the Jorja Knight mystery series. Her debut novel, Knight Blind, was a 2016 Unhanged Arthur Ellis Award finalist. She is a member of Sisters in Crime, Crime Writers of Canada, and the Writers' Guild of Alberta.

With a Bachelor of Science degree in geology, Alice spent her early career conducting field exploration programs in remote regions of Canada, where she honed her passion for reading, storytelling, coffee, and adventure. After riding the energy industry rollercoaster for thirty years, Alice has found a way to put her inherent introversion to use and now writes full time.

When not plotting a murder, Alice amuses herself watching foreign flicks and exploring Calgary's urban parks and pathways. Visit her at www.alicebienia.com

Manufactured by Amazon.ca
Acheson, AB

15907036R00236